Inherent Chaos

Terry Lloyd Vinson

Published by Rogue Phoenix Press, LLP
Copyright © 2022

ISBN: 978-1-62420-686-3

Editor: Sherry Derr-Wille
Cover Art: Designs by Ms G

Dedication

To my wife, Liza, for her eternal patience and understanding

Prologue I

August 1982
Chandler, Arizona

The interior of the payphone booth reeked of rat excrement and stale BO, the outside temperature still hovering around the mid-eighties despite the late-evening's descending cloak of darkness. The man held the phone's handle, greasy at the touch and smelling of booze-smeared spittle, several inches from his parted lips as to avoid potential disease. At the moment the only requirement was to listen, as even if he had attempted to interrupt, finding the appropriate response had thus far eluded him, the party on the opposite end was on a roll that had yet to reach its ranting, raving peak. The payphone sat at the corner of unnamed streets bookended by equally identity-less warehouse buildings, the shadows each cast like the colossal skeletal remains of some ancient, fossilized dinosaur.

As matters stood, the man had little choice except to endure the fiery sermon and, in the aftermath, reach a decision and seal it via a verbal contract. Drenched in sweat, temples pounding, heart racing, his thoughts as scattered as the blowing trash outside the booth, he caught himself drifting in and out of what passed as reality but felt anything but, thus inadvertently redacting portions of the verbal barrage assaulting his senses.

"...course this one denies any knowledge of his kin's past shenanigans, much less carrying on the tradition. Hey, I can be open-minded enough to buy that second part but not so much the first, 'cause you know, said shenanigans are admittedly passé in this day and age. All that said, he stinks of deception, father. Reeks of it, in fact. Just like all the others. They have their skills, we have ours, right? We can peel away that first layer and sniff the corruption beneath, yes? You might not admit it, but you know I'm preachin' the gospel. Anyhow, what I'm offering is a one-time, blue-light special, you dig? After tonight, you can trail me from here to the dark side of Juniper and will find nothin' but a stone-cold print and you know it."

A wild, cackling giggle escaped from between the man's badly chapped lips at the comical misuse of '*Jupiter*' and he was forced to briefly hoist the phone above his head to avoid spewing forth additional, unintentional mockery. *Amazing*, he mused while using a clenched fist to jab his own thigh, how correct the use of the French word for outdated while simultaneously committing the spectacular butchery of a well-known planetary phrase, all in the same blessed sentence. What kind of horrid public school infused such inconsistency? He should know, but sadly had no clue. Upon resetting the receiver against a bare ear, he'd make sure to take a rubbing alcohol-soaked Q-Tip to it later, he found he'd missed little of consequence in terms of the prattling tirade squawking from the opposite end. For the most part, the bulk was nauseatingly familiar.

"…always be several steps ahead, especially considering the tracker really doesn't have the guts to follow-through, right daddy-oh? I know your heart ain't in this. Still, I felt a tugging. A pull, an *obligation*, to clue you in on tonight's proceedings. As obsessions go…"

The man snickered under his breath, so that's why the note was left tacked to his apartment door, requesting his presence to answer some random phone call in the crappiest part of town. All this time, he'd figured it some crank pimp advertising his whorish wares to some lonely, pale sad-sack he'd deemed down-on-his luck and looking for action.

"…overwhelming it was, kept me up countless nights, and you know I'm usually one to sleep like a boulder even if live fire was passing overhead. Maybe there is a higher power behind it. A merciful deity with a soft spot for our clan and the suffering we've endured," There was a lengthy pause, shattered by a piercing, maniacal laugh. Psyche. "More likely some warped puppet-master bored with the whole shebang. I mean, how long has this gone on, right? Kinda like one of those Broadway shows that's long since outlasted it's welcome."

"Regardless father, whether it ends at all depends entirely on you."

A full thirty seconds of silence cued the man that it was finally, mercifully, his time at bat. His throat and lips equally parched, he closed his eyes against the Nuclear-strength migraine that felt as if a twenty-penny nail was being slowly hammered into the base of his skull and croaked out what he prayed would be the beginning of a successful rebuttal.

"You know, deep down to the core, what you're doing is insanity defined. Think about it. I mean, really concentrate. This isn't about them. It's about you. Your urges. Your wants. Your needs. You enjoy it. Revel in it. The innocent have no voice, no defense. Not to a deranged force of chaos who refuses to listen. Do me a favor. Remove all the supernatural…hooey and tell me how this…unending spree isn't just cold-blooded eradication for eradication's sake. A bad seed doing what bad seeds do, staining the soil red. Please elaborate. I'm listening."

The man winced at what might've been a mistake of colossal proportions, that of tossing the mic away so recklessly. Unbelievably, the expected volley never came, only the mild static of a mediocre connection. To this, the man jumped back on the speech train with an overzealousness that was overtly comical.

"Exactly. No magical ending to be had, no matter how many you eliminate. Terminating the innocent is straight out homicide, perpetrated by someone that, in the end, can only be described by any logical mind as criminally psychotic. There is no…justifying this, no matter how you spin it, and there isn't a court on the planet that'll buy what you think passes as an acceptable agenda for murder. Now…" he concluded after a lengthy sigh, falling to one knee with his back pressed against the booth's smudged and slightly cracked glass, "…for god's sake, just cut them loose. That is, if there truly *is* anyone there to be freed."

Instantly regretting speaking aloud, a final, frustration-fueled accusation he realized should've remained parked in the mental hanger, the man's lips parted for an emergency reversal but was cut off by a growling yelp that effectively ended all hopes of a miracle save.

"Say what, daddy-oh? Ohhh, I got it. A classic fake-out, you surmise? Nothing more than a rehearsed ruse to get you here? Hell's belle's, old man, if all we wanted was a little forced facetime, we'd be there already. It ain't like you could ever be resourceful or clever enough to avoid such a meeting."

In that moment, regrets be damned, the man lost all semblance of hope, as deep down he knew this was no bluff, no fraudulent net of deceit being weaved in his honor.

"Fine. If you truly do promote practicing what you preach," he spewed angrily through gnashed teeth, his free hand curled into a shaking, groping claw, "What say we just leave this between the two of us, as it *should* be, and leave the rest of the clan be? Pretty obvious you know where to find me and after all, wouldn't I *alone* be considered the deal breaker, the ultimate catch?"

The mild static dominated yet again, but for only a scant few seconds, wherein the man collapsed onto the other knee with the forefinger and thumb of his free hand digging into the area of his left temple like a desperate prospector for that elusive gold nugget.

"I'm more than happy to meet you halfway on this thing, but contrary to popular opinion, I'm clever enough *not* to walk blindly anywhere near your vicinity," he said wearily, while resembling a pleading, hopelessly broken man offering up a final prayer.

"Listen, for god's sake, can't you understand that this has to st…"

"M-my k-kids are…they're…ti-tied up in t-the b-basement. Pl-please, if y-you don't c-come, the-they're n-next."

The stuttering intrusion sent an icy chill up the man's sweat-soaked spine. The voice of a young man, late twenties, early thirties, and in great, unwholly unmanufactured distress.

"Gene J-Junior is j-just turned si-six and little C-Connie is o-only f-f-four, for C-Christ's sake. P-Please, f-for the love of g-god, do wha-wha…e-e-ever…"

They broke off in a choking sob, following by a piercing, banshee shriek that mere mental anguish alone could never alone birth. No, this level of agony required assistance of a more physical nature, as in exposed flesh being flayed apart by the deep, slashing motion of a razor's edge or perhaps a faint, barely audible puncture between one's ribs by an icepick or maybe even the excruciating aftermath of a syringe's piercing tip penetrating soft cornea. All these images and more flickered and flashed through the man's fevered mind. Understanding oh so very well the sadistic capabilities on display, he knew that these were but a trio of similarly gruesome possibilities.

As the screeching bray was abruptly and mercifully muted, the voice that followed was frighteningly void of all previous good humor or baiting sarcasm. It was, in fact, as cold and inhuman as the proclamation provided.

"You're eight minutes ride from the address I provided. If you're not here in fifteen, well, then you're as guilty as I. Try walking away and living with that one, old man."

The line went dead, the man's planned rebuttal never to be.

Allowing the handle to slip from his sweaty grip, to swing like a swaying noose on a severely twisted cord, he hugged his knees to his chest in a desperate attempt to quell a full-body shiver.

"D-damn you! Damn you!" he screamed, head thrown back like a baying wolf, unsure if the target of said tirade was the threatening presence previously on the other end or himself, as there was little doubt of his choice between the pitifully limited options of stay or go. There could not be, as always, any form of law enforcement intervention. Too many mysteries laid out for solving. Far too many hidden skeletons packed into a very small closet space.

As if to directly contradict this initial decision and thus disprove his very own theory of cowardly self-loathing, he leapt up and shot from the booth like a man afire, only to collapse in a heap with his right hand curled around the driver's side door handle of his Chevy Nova.

"I-I'm so...sorry. So very, very sorry," he whimpered softly, his gut curdling with a heady dose of self-loathing and cowardice. For every pathetic excuse his tattered mind manufactured, the cold, bitter truth revealed self-preservation as the lone justification for allowing yet another family to die.

He briefly considered that strictly taboo third option, but dismissed it just as quickly, as there could never be, under any circumstance, *any* form of police involvement. At the very least, he'd most likely be hauled in and tried as an accomplice of sorts, the mere thought of spending countless decades behind bars providing the most effective of vaccines for reckless, false bravado.

Practically crawling into the Nova's driver seat, the man checked

5

his wristwatch and noted nearly five minutes had already passed since the call ended.

Too late now even if I tried, he surmised gravely, using a bare arm to wipe away a buildup of mucus from both nostrils and his upper lip.

He sat unmoving for another ten-plus minutes, as if timing the horrific events taking place approximately ten miles away in real time. Maybe, he prayed, pleaded and appealed, this time that the outcome would be different, that some form of mercy would be afforded. If not for the father, at least the children.

At five-thirty AM, he picked up a copy of the morning addition and discovered yet again the utter folly of such outlandish pipe dreams.

The tears he shed were as much for himself as the victims.

Next time, he swore, next time I'll stop it. *Next time.*

As always, the hollowness of the promise echoed within his subconscious like the faded memories of a father's frantic cries.

Prologue II

Present Day
Turtle Bend, North Dakota

Boone Lee Harrison, his left eye watering beneath a slightly sagging lid, discovered he was unable to maintain eye contact with the individual standing before him, instead forcing his gaze downward into his own lap, where intertwined fingers grew purple from the constant pressure being applied. It was taking great effort not to flash a wide, toothy grin, clap the aforementioned hands enthusiastically or, heaven forbid, giggle hysterically. As motivations went, perhaps the stoutest was the possibility, however miniscule, of being declared mentally incompetent and held for observation. The mere thought instantly doused the building flames of euphoria into a pile of wet, smoldering ashes.

Palms growing increasingly moist as a fresh wave of inner heat bathed his worn insides, Boone succumbed to a brief fugue state, wherein he alone occupied a dark bubble of solitary confinement. Strange, he ruminated, how such a potentially double-edged sword felt so one-sided in the reveal's aftermath. Fourth time *was* indeed the charm, he noted with great irony.

"Of course, we will run additional tests to confirm the diagnosis, from which we will establish the proper timetable for treatment. I would suggest we begin this immediately. To be blunt, there appears to be little time to waste, additional testing aside."

"Yeah, sure doc. Got'cha," he babbled in reply, snapping from the self-imposed daze with a tight-lipped grin of utter insincerity.

The physician, a fortyish, grim-faced woman with close-set eyes that reflected through reading glasses which were perched atop a massive, pointy-tipped snout that any Jewish grandmother would be proud to claim, retrained all focus on the iPad balanced on her right palm, the forefinger of the left dancing a spastic jig atop its slick surface.

"I understand these findings do appear to confirm previous diagnosis from your primary caregiver," she continued, squinty eyes darting in time with the rapid movements of the continually probing digit.

Boone, thoughts racing far from the cramped, atypically bland confines of the exam room, nodded silently, having instantly and effortlessly shifted into auto-depression mode, complete with labored sigh, forced swallow and slight nod of utter resignation.

"Affirmative, doc. Gotta say, not exactly the update I was hoping for. Can't say I'm overly surprised, mind you, but sometimes a faint portion of hope is all a man has left."

Reaching over, she applied a light, shamelessly perfunctory tap to his left shoulder, her squinty gaze never departing the iPad.

"A natural response, Mister Harrison, under the circumstances, but let us not lose hope. Number one, in terms of overall health, you are without a doubt the healthiest person I've seen at this stage of the disease. Your vitals are uncharacteristically strong. You've lost almost no weight in the past month. Number two, I'm no quitter, no matter the diagnosis, and I expect my patients to follow suit. I hate to lose, Mister Harrison. That in mind, I'm planning a merciless, all-out assault on this disease, with as aggressive a strategy as modern medicine allows."

Harrison, having disconnected yet again, merely nodded amiably as she preached on, something about relocating to a hospital in Bismarck with the necessary equipment and staff to bravely stave off a final outcome so obviously set in stone, as in a grave.

Approximately fifteen minutes of plotting, planning and scheduling later, to which itineraries were handed out and appointments made, Boone was allowed to depart amid a series of gracious nods and apathetic glances from the staff on hand, a few of which appeared at least partially earnest. Of course, he'd lied about having someone nearby to chauffer him off the hospital grounds. Rapidly failing eyesight and shaky reflexes aside, he flat refused to believe he was no longer capable of steering the Big Chief the three miles necessary to reacquaint its hulking fame back into the squared space of his condo's reserved parking space.

As was normally the case, early Fall at the tip of Turtle Bend,

North Dakota, less than fifteen miles from the Canadian border, was akin to the dead of winter in the majority of the Midwest. A gusty, frigid breeze nearly freed Boone's ballcap from his noggin as he zig-zagged painstakingly across the pothole ravaged, semi-paved lot. Early afternoon was rapidly mutating to dusk, wherein a sizeable snowfall was predicated, along with temperatures hovering near the single digits. The first of many cold-storage nights to come, he knew, but also one of the last he would ever endure.

Upon securing himself into the driver's seat of the Jeep Cherokee he had so lovingly referred to as '*Heap Big Chief*', since its cash-only purchase nearly a decade previously from a used lot in Laramie, he inserted the key into the ignition with a badly shaking hand and leaned back to pause before turning the ignition. Staring unblinkingly into a relatively light band of snowflakes sailing horizontally past, a faint hitch shook his chest in a sudden burst, only to be trapped like dried bread at the base of his throat. *Finally.* The single word with twin meanings so dramatically different depending on how it was uttered and the situation at hand. Finally, blurted with resounding relief, as in *at long last*. Finally, mumbled with great duress or worse, numbing dread, as in *this cannot be real.* Like bone-deep cuts executed with expert precision from the sharpest of cutlery, Boone Harrison understood both meanings simultaneously and with surprising clarity. With a labored sigh inhaled and subsequently exhaled through tightly gritted teeth, he gripped the wheel with white-knuckled intensity in an attempt to divert the coming tide. In the end, it was akin to blocking a runaway freight with upraised palms. Once it hit, a schizophrenic's template of mixed emotions the driving force, there was no holding back or controlling the severity. A paralyzing spasm and full-body shimmy wherein all use of limbs was lost, breathing relegated to choking, raspy croaks, clear mucus pouring from both nostrils in the spasmodic, hitching aftermath.

Roughly six minutes from the time it began and having executed a half-hearted cleanup of the sinus leakage, he first used splayed fingers to comb through a still-surprisingly thick mane of graying brown hair before staring into the rearview through swollen, bloodshot eyes. The pencil-thin mustache and matching goatee, each as white as the falling snow, he'd cultivated since the most recent relocation still held remnants of dried snot.

Still, all things considered, he studied his own reflection with comical curiosity, as if truly seeing himself for the first time in ages. Not bad, all things considered, he decided, not bad at all.

"A real shame," surely someone will comment. "Still relatively young considering such distinguished, chiseled looks and trim, healthy physique; an older man but with the vitality of one decade's younger."

The tight smile that formed at the corners of spittle-smeared lips was as full of contradiction as the meltdown that had proceeded it.

The short drive home, less than three miles in length but a somewhat protracted eleven minutes in duration, this despite relatively light traffic, cemented the fact that it would most likely be his last in the captain's chair, as he'd barely avoided clipping a UPS truck head-on and sideswiping a trio of mailboxes. The snow fell heavier as he'd entered the modest, two-story condo, by morning it would collect to the tune of eight inches with foot-deep drifts. No matter, for Boone Harrison had duties to perform that being temporarily shut-in would not alter. Duties he'd stubbornly put off until a second opinion had been confirmed. A trio of duties that he'd managed to procrastinate around for too many years to contemplate, at least without being suffocated beneath a black cloud of guilt. The first was, without a doubt, the easiest of the three, but not without its challenges, especially considering his rapidly deteriorating state.

Through eyes which blinked far too often in a futile attempt to clear the incessant blurring, he powered up the aged PC atop his kitchen table, found home-roll beneath visibly tremoring digits, and commenced to seek the assistance needed to complete tasks two and three. Swallowing a trio of prescription meds with the aid of one of two remaining vices, that being a cool bottle of Old Milwaukee, and a lit Maverick smoke, vice number two, smoldering nearby, he struggled with bouts of blurred vision so severe it limited screen time to five-to-ten-minute increments.

As was becoming routine, a sporadic coughing fit would soon birth a fist-sized wad of bloody tissue, the occasional belch similarly shaded spittle. Desired ad duly typed out and posted via such sites as LetGo, Backpage and Gumtree, he settled in with a heaping serving of well-nuked

Tyson chicken nuggets, fresh brew and a randomly chosen flick on one of the few cable movie channels his antennae provided. Fittingly, the early nineties offering '*My Life*' dealt with a terminally ill man videotaping his last few months of life in order to provide a legacy for those he was leaving behind. Though for the most part he found the content shamelessly maudlin and sappy, Boone couldn't help but appreciate the irony.

Hours later, laying under multiple layers of warmth in the dark confines of the upstairs bedroom, sleep was found to be predictably evasive due to a single, sobering thought. A thought and associated theory that was far from new and, ironically, more like a returning ailment without permanent cure. As with its previous incarnations, the general theme remained intact. Logically and within the framework of a sane mind, what could be more mentally traumatic than being handed a death sentence in the form of a medical diagnosis?

In the case of Boone Lee Harrison, the horrific but not-all-together improbable possibility of said sentence being allowed a stay of execution.

Chapter One

If the initial interview, conducted four days after posting the ad, was any indication, successful completion of task one was not going to be nearly as easy as originally thought.

The first of three who'd answered his query, the heavy-set, bushy-bearded man reeked of recently ingested alcohol, not exactly a positive at nine AM, and appeared to have donned the clothes of someone at least sixty pounds smaller, the buttons of his wool jacket appearing on the verge of imminent blast-off from the slightest of pressure.

"Appreciate your time, Mister, um, ugh…"

"Baker. Maxwell Baker Junior."

"Mister Baker, yes. Well, if you don't mind sharing your cell number, I'll give you a ring wh…"

"So, what say ya? I got the gig or what?"

"Well, I do have a few others to interview."

"No it is then. Mind paying for my coffee? Least you can do for wasting my time."

With that, one Maxwell Baker exited the Turtle Bend McDonalds stage-left to parts unknown, albeit in a drunken stumble ripe with unintentional humor, the rancid scent of stale booze and unwiped rear end in his bulky wake.

Unfazed but not nearly as optimistic as when the day began, Boone returned to the same booth a few hours later for interview two, nibbling a second helping of fries and hoping the bouts of near complete blindness that plagued his day would remain at bay for the duration. The trek back and forth from condo to Micky Dee's had, miraculously, remained uneventful with nary a close call, though he had been forced to endure the blaring horns of those few cars tailgating Heap Big Chief's snail-like pace. Of late, since the vision issues worsened, he rarely drove the speed limit in fear of not being able to brake in time if a sudden attack of the blurs reared up. In addition, he strategically parked at the rear of the lot and thus distanced from the majority of through traffic.

The rail thin, thirty-something woman introduced herself simply as Diana, in a whisper so soft and disinterested as to be near inaudible despite the near empty restaurant. Decked out in blue jeans that were far too baggy for her beanpole frame, and a windbreaker-style jacket far too light for daytime temperatures struggling to reach double-digits, her timid responses were clipped to the extreme, usually of the yes or no variety and little else. When asked why she responded to his offer of temporary employment, she'd offered a pained sneer, as if somehow offended. By the time she'd spat something about 'needing the cash to offset a deadbeat husband's desertion', Boone had all but checked out, the thought of sharing a confined space for days on end with a grumbling, mumbling sourpuss with the personality of a tree-stump sealing the non-deal.

Hopes fading fast as no new candidates surfaced overnight, it wasn't until the following afternoon, snow still piled ankle high despite cloudless skies, a blazing sun and slightly warmer temperatures, that Boone was struck by a vibe the equivalent of striking gold in a dry lakebed. The initial wave of elation born from a single glance building gradually as the conversation had commenced. Greeted by a firm handshake, warm smile and a slight bow of respect, a gesture Boone found as refreshingly retro as the young man's neat, cleanshaven appearance and 'high and tight' hairstyle, the elder statesman found himself struck temporarily speechless, and not nearly due to his interviewee's overt politeness. Neatly dressed in light brown khakis, button-up cotton Oxford and slightly worn black leather jacket, he identified as Bradley Kane. Guesstimated age perhaps thirty, solid build and featuring an odd accent Boone struggled to place. All these factors defined the stereotypical good first impression, though this had little to do with Boone's shell-shocked reaction.

"My apologies, Mister…"

"Kane. Bradly Kane, sir. Brad."

"Of course. It's just that you remind me of someone. Someone I haven't thought of in ages. Again, my apologies."

"No problem, sir. Hope he was a friend."

Boone nodded, forcing his slack-jawed expression into submission with great effort. No small feat that, considering if Brad Kane had appeared sporting a pencil-thin mustache, the older man's lifelong skepticism of all things reincarnation-related would've surely rated a serious rethink.

"I'd say so, short-lived as our relation was. So, about the assignment, I'm sure you have questions. Before we get started, would you like to order something?"

"Thanks, I'm good."

Sipping his own coffee, the rising steam from the cup seemed to sooth his frequently watering eyes, Boone cleared his throat and tasted the coppery buildup, a taste he'd grown sickeningly accustomed to in recent weeks.

"So, what's your calling, son?"

"Pardon, sir?"

"That is to say, what do you do for a living when not volunteering to drive some old codger cross-country?"

"I've worn a few different caps through the years, the most recent as a delivery driver for a local auto parts store. Before that I had a welding gig just outside Fargo that lasted a few years. Been taking some on-line courses in criminal justice."

Boone nodded approvingly.

"Did some law enforcement work in my time. Wise choice. I'd rate it a close second to mortuary services or tax expert in terms of job security."

"Forensic science has always been an interest. I've been freelancing since high school and it hasn't amounted to much," the younger man explained with a shrug, "Figure I'd better get serious, at least once I get settled."

"Time is a sly thief, all right," Boone stated sincerely enough, though with a barely concealed tint of sarcasm and while seemingly fighting off a potential grin. A quick sip of coffee and the mysterious veil of deviousness vanished.

"Well, I do appreciate the quick response to my ad. Being that I barely qualify as a novice in such on-line forays, I couldn't even begin to calculate a potential waiting period."

"Timing is perfect for me, as well," Brad nodded, "Almost as if it were meant to be. That is, if I'm lucky enough to gain your confidence."

A final sip of lukewarm coffee and Boone pushed the nearly empty cup aside, placing both elbows atop the table, intertwining his fingers as if to pray and balancing his chin on upturned thumbs. He simply could not shake the uncanny resemblance, to the point of doubting his own somewhat fragmented memory of Toby McGrew's mug.

After all, wasn't it just a few weeks ago he swore he'd spotted one of his ex-wives in the detergent isle of Hornbachers? Followed her out into the parking lot and nearly got sideswiped by a passing snowplow.

"So then, Brad Kane, as comically cliché as it sounds, please tell me a little more about yourself, to include *why* the interest in pursuing this opportunity."

The younger man's tone, so calm and relaxed as to be slightly unnerving, was that of someone endowed with either extreme confidence or, God forbid, the traits of a natural sociopath.

"Well, as things stand, I was lining up a drive eastward within the next week or so when I ran across your offer. The parts store cut my hours to less than twenty-five a week, so this gives me the chance to pocket some extra cash along the way, not to mention saving me from covering all those many miles by my lonesome."

"Oh, really? What's your final destination?"

"Panama City."

"Hmm. Great this time of year, I'd imagine, especially when compared to what Old Man Winter has in store for this part of the country. If you don't mind my asking, what or who awaits you in the sunshine state?"

For the first time since intros, Boone noted a slight alteration in both the young man's expression and tone. A barely noticeable darker tint that only years, nay, *decades* of human interaction could detect. As if somehow fearing his mask of cool slipped an iota, the young man flashed a toothy smile to possibly deflect the accidental breach, though his eyes remained coolly distant. Windows to the soul indeed, Boone mused.

"All about the better-half," the younger man, beaming as if announcing a recent windfall, hands gesturing wildly, and eyes pulled wide as if suddenly wired from effects of a triple-expresso. "Gina started a new job there a few months back and I stayed behind to tie up the remaining loose ends. You know how it is. Moving is such a royal pain. Harder still when one person is left to do most of the heavy lifting."

"Agreed. Been there, done that more times than I care to recall. Well, then, it seems this trek serves as the one-way variety for us both. You mind divulging your age, Brad?"

"Turned thirty-three this last August."

"Ah, spring chicken status intact," Boone grinned, "Can't even remember being your age."

"Honestly, Mister Harrison, you don't strike me as qualifying for fossilization just yet."

Having briefly broken eye contact, the younger man fell seamlessly back into character, hands tucked back into his lap, exaggerated smile fading into a more natural state and demeanor as unruffled and unflappable as ever.

Meanwhile, Boone was becoming increasingly aware of a faint burning at the corners of each eye, a sure sign a bout with what he referred to as the 'blurries' was a matter of when, not if. In addition, his lower gut was in the midst of a gradual but consistent churn, no doubt the result of the bacon, egg and cheese biscuit he'd so greedily consumed just minutes before the meeting. Over the previous month or so, it was becoming painfully obvious that fatty foods and dairy were no longer his friend.

Silent suffering aside, and as much as he was sincerely enjoying the young man's company, he was going to have to cut the interview much shorter than planned. Besides, since he had obviously found his candidate, they would have ample time to get acquainted.

"Appreciate the kind words, but let's just say I'm older than I look and…" Boone paused, winking playfully with his right eye, from which the burning sting had subsided a tad, "… well, leave it at *that* for the time being, and you can call me Boone."

"Fair enough, Boone. Funny," Brad shrugged, "high school seems like months ago, but where my twenties went is anyone's guess. I guess gaining maturity and the responsibility that accompanies it adds extra turbo fuel to the ol' time machine."

"Perhaps it does at that. Never quite thought of it that way."

The two men of vastly different eras, backgrounds and agendas enjoyed a moment of comfortable silence, Boone having temporarily forgotten his building physical ills, at least until a low grumbling at his midsection served as a reminder to speed up the process.

"I know that a potential employer usually inquires of the applicant of their job history, but in this case, I don't feel it that vital, at least not at this juncture. That little beauty yours?" he inquired, nodding toward the sleek, black Dodge Charger he'd seen the young man dismount upon arrival.

"Yes sir."

"Nice ride. Roomier than it looks, I presume?"

"Plenty of passenger leg room. Trunk is sizeable enough, but we can rent one of those small U-Haul trailers if need be."

Boone waived him off, hoping the periodic tick at his left eye wasn't too noticeable.

"No worries on my end. Just a night bag with the essentials and a regulation briefcase."

"Same here, just a pair of American Touristers marked for the trunk. I've taken the liberty of mapping out the route and estimating a time of arrival to the requested destination."

"Thinking ahead. I like it," Boone replied, forcing a smile that felt as off-kilter as his increasingly agitated gut and the creepy-crawling sensation tracing along his left cheekbone and forehead, the latter like a marching army of claw-footed insects digging a trench into the flesh near his spastically-blinking eye. He estimated five, maybe ten minutes at the outset until he would be depositing the aforementioned biscuit and fixings onto the nearest toilet bowl, not to mention the distinct possibility of being stranded within the Golden Arches from near total-blindness.

"Tell you what though, if you don't mind just hanging onto those facts until the morning of departure. Got to confess I'm not exactly…feeling my best," he managed a weak grin he knew must look hideous. "Could be the less-than-nutritious diet I've consumed of late," he concluded, motioning to the nearby menu board. As if cued by some inner, final failsafe alarm blaring at full bore, his eyes rolled briefly skyward and his head lulled dramatically to the left before righting itself.

The younger man reached out from over the table as if to catch whatever might fly loose, wide-eyed concern in both his expression and tone.

"You okay, Mis…ugh, Boone? You do look a little pale, sir."

Eyeballs no longer playing slots within their respective sockets, Boone steadied himself with a sturdy grip on the underside of the table and sighed deeply before rendering a shaky-voiced response.

"Oh, I'll be…good as gold after a little…sabbatical."

"I can drive you wherever you ne…"

"No, but thank you. I've got…your cell. I'll give you a ring later this afternoon."

The younger man regarded him with a cocked brow, as if pondering the possibility of never receiving said call, save perhaps from the grave.

"So, does this mean I'm hired?"

Boone offered an outstretched hand nearly as unsteady as his wavering voice.

"Yes indeed, if you don't mind chauffeuring a sick old man halfway across the country."

Bradley Kane clasped his new employer's hand as gently as possible in order to qualify as the obligatory deal-sealer, equally elated and apprehensive at the prospect.

"Currently, I'd like to target the day after tomorrow as a departure date, unless you need an extra day to tighten up those loose ends you spoke of."

"Day after tomorrow it is."

"Shall we say seven AM?"

"Sounds good. Where do you need me?"

Fishing a small notepad from his coat's inner pocket, Boone ripped out a page and, folding it with fingers so pale to appear almost translucent, handed it across the table.

"The address to my condo."

Brad allowed himself a quick glance at the scribbled writings before tucking it deep inside his jacket's side pocket.

"Just a few miles from my, well, soon-to-be-former digs."

The older man shrugged, apparently no longer able to muster even the tiniest of smiles.

"Small towns. You've got to love 'em."

"Yes sir. They do have their advantages."

With that, Boone pushed himself away from the table and stood with surprising steadiness, though Brad noted the stiffness of the older man's gait and legs-spread-wide stance, as if balancing atop an invisible high-wire.

"Well then, Brad, I guess that phone call is unnecessary, unless something unforeseen arises. You have my number."

"Yes, sir. Get some rest."

Boone nodded but did not move away, instead using the tabletop as an impromptu podium while waiting for this younger charge to initiate departure.

"I'll do it, and don't sweat it. As downright crappy as I must appear at the moment, I'll be good to go by Thursday morning."

"Yes, sir and thanks for the opportunity."

As if sensing the older man's discomfort in walking away first, Brad sidestepped away with a final nod and half-salute.

It would be an additional half-hour before Boone would depart, this after a wobbling shuffle into a mercifully empty bathroom, where a violent projectile vomit session left the stall walls spattered in dark crimson and the toilet bowl swirling a similarly foreboding shade.

The drive home, quite possibly his last while serving as both active pilot and navigator, would prove to be equally precarious, though he managed to dodge the few vehicles unfortunate enough to share roadway, several trash cans and at least one yield sign had not been so lucky, the latter ripping a deep gash into *Heap Big Chief's* right front fender.

Having reached his assigned spot and by some miracle parking directly between the narrow white lines, Boone switched off the ignition and sat motionless while waiting for the twin nets of blurriness to at least subside enough for him to find the front door to the condo.

With no small amount of palpable dread, he realized that the accumulative totality of his recent ills, both physical and mental, were but a faint blip on the radar compared with what was to come. Going out like a lamb had never been an option. There was always going to be a heady price to pay before that final curtain fell. The miseries of his youth, protracted adulthood and even lengthier title as elder statesman weren't going to hold a candle to the final act.

This he had long understood.

This he had long accepted.

Still, this he *dreaded* with a bone-deep ache that reached his very core.

Chapter Two

The morning of departure, thought predictably chilly, proved mercifully void of any new frozen precipitation, allowing a relatively clear path of travel.

Leather travel duffel and briefcase in hand, Boone locked the condo door, pocketed the keys and stepped cautiously down the snow-slickened drive toward the parking lot, where Brad Kane's Charger sat idling a few spaces down from *Heap Big Chief.* Stopping to face his ride, as dependable a form of transport as he'd ever owned, he ran a gloved hand across the front of its dark blue hood, fading a bit from oxidation in spots, with obvious fondness, a gentle, loving gesture usually reserved for a loyal family pet.

"Good morning," he greeted upon pulling the passenger door ajar. He was forced to place the duffel and briefcase in the back floorboard as the seat held little in the way of available room due to a pair of oversized suitcases.

"Morning sir," Brad nodded, wearing an apologetic expression, thin vapors rising from his lap, where a steaming Styrofoam cup of coffee sat nestled, "Sorry for the lack of available space. I packed 'em in like sardines but quickly ran out of square footage regardless. Think this is bad, you ought to see the trunk. Couldn't fit a toothpick into that bad-boy."

Boone shrugged after officially taking the position of co-pilot, instantly impressed with the ample leg room. As was routine of late, he'd slept only fitfully and dreaded the possibility of being unduly cramped for the duration of the trek.

"No problem. Like I said, I'm traveling as light as possible."

"You weren't kidding. Wish I could say the same. Guess it's true that you never know how much crap you own until you move. Sad part is..." he gestured with a thumb into the back seat, "...all this is what I deemed *only* the necessities."

21

Checking the side mirror, Brad backed slowly before steering them from the condo parking lot and onto a mostly deserted roadway. At not quite seven AM and with dawn's early light still in the process of shaking away the dusk, it appeared the early birds had flown the coup already and the late risers were just that.

"You need some java for the road? I'm on my second serving already," Brad continued, holding up the medium-sized cup before taking a noisy sip from its semi-sealed lid.

"No thanks," Boone said, never bothering to give the condo grounds a second glance, "Already had my morning cup. Wrote off excess caffeine a few years ago."

"Understood. Breakfast?"

"Had some toast and OJ as the sun rose. Afraid it's about all I can handle these days until around midday."

"Just let me know and we'll make a stop on the road. I-29 has no shortage of choices between here and Sioux Falls."

Boone turned towards his newly hired chauffer with a cocked brow.

"So Sioux Falls is the first day goal, is it?"

Reaching into his jean jacket's inner pocket, Brad removed a small four-by-six-inch notepad and laid it in the older man's waiting palm.

"Yes sir. Just over four-hundred and thirty miles. Approximately six hours, give or take a half hour. Sound reasonable?"

As Boone thumbed through the tiny pages, forced to plant his nose so deep within its miniscule folds as to leave a nostril outline, Brad turned left onto a narrow two-lane just past a sign promising interstate twenty-nine was a mere seven miles in the distance.

"Day one destination; Sioux Falls. Day two; Sioux Falls to Kansas City. Day three; Kansas City to Memphis. Day four; arrive at final destination. Um, Mister Harrison?"

"Please, *Boone*."

"Boone, am I off base by asking what's awaits you in Northern Mississippi?"

"Family business. Long delayed. Said business I've sadly put off 'til   now."

"So, since you and I part in Memphis, is someone else meeting you there?"

"I'll be utilizing a long-distance cab via Uber."

"Well, since I'm headed your way, why not allow me to con…"

The older man waved him off politely.

"I appreciate the offer, but I have it mapped out to a tee."

Having donned a pair of aviator shades, Brad nodded and stole a quick sip before resuming.

"Understood. Well, from here to Sioux Falls is the longest stretch. Obviously, a lot depends on the cooperation of the weather and other drivers, neither of which is guaranteed, right?"

Boone returned the notepad, which Brad tucked beneath the overhead visor.

"Sounds like a plan. Just to be clear, all expenditures are solely my responsibility. That includes fuel, food and lodging."

"No arguments here," Brad replied, winking playfully, slowing dramatically as they had run up on a T-Rex-sized garbage truck traveling roughly twenty miles under the forty-five MPH limit.

"Fueled up for now. Should get us at least halfway to the Falls."

Shrugging his shoulders as if to escape tightened bonds, Brad reached over to adjust the heater to its lowest setting.

"You mind taking the wheel for a sec? I'm roasting in this jacket. It isn't as if we're in any danger of spinning out of control with the S.S. Sloth up there blocking the passage."

Boone did so without replying, his thoughts distant and his expression suitably slack, a development not lost on his hired man, who reached back to lay the jacket atop the pyramid of cardboard boxes. Though the older man looked robust enough, he appeared perpetually pale and at times openly winced as if from some mysterious ailment, making Brad ponder his stamina and stability in the face of such a lengthy trek.

"How about you, Boone?"

Having relinquished the wheel, the older man's slack daze remained fully intact.

"Boone? Sir?"

Blinking rapidly, Boone snapped to just as the garbage truck exited stage left, allowing a clear path through a mostly flat, snowclad valley, void of all but the occasional homestead.

"Oh, s-sorry about that. Drifted off in my own little universe there for a second. You were saying?"

"Just wondering if you wanted to peel off that outer layer? Growing kinda toasty in here."

"Yeah, now that you mention it, especially considering we're headed for warmer climes."

Before resting the folded jacket across his bony knees, Boone removed an object from one of the pockets that Brad didn't recognize at first as a stack of CD's rubber-banded together.

"What ya got there, tunes?"

The older man stared down at the discs as if only then discovering their existence.

"A few choice selections, you might say. Just to help pass the time during the longer stretches."

"Anything I'd know?" Brad inquired in a not-really-interested-but-politeness-dictates-I-ask tone while peering out the driver's window at a gathering of Holstein cattle atop a nearby knoll.

"I'd wager not. My musical tastes are what the layman might consider, well, eccentric."

"Nothing wrong with that. I'm a retro country rock man myself. Grew up listening to my pop's preferred selections: Johnny Cash, Ronnie Millsap, Eddie Rabbit, Kenny Rogers. Kind of stuck with me. Drives the wife nuts, as she's all modern jazz and bubblegum pop."

"Well, it could be worse," Boone grinned, "At least you didn't mention hop-hip."

Brad rolled his eyes, not bothering to correct his employer's gaffe, "Touché. Not sure we'd have made it to the alter. Anyhow, feel free to pop one in anytime the mood hits. Unless it's the aforementioned plague of non-sensical garbage, I'm game."

Tucking the CDs inside the folds of the jacket, Boone closed his eyes and leaned back against the headrest.

"Appreciate the open-mindedness, though you might live to regret it."

Soon after, Brad steered the Charger onto a mostly deserted interstate twenty-nine, the narrow shoulders of which still held knee-high snowdrifts. They rode in relative silence for another fifteen minutes with the low hum of the heater and dull drone of tires against pavement as the lone diversion. It was Brad who finally intervened, nervously clearing his throat as a prologue, as if slightly hesitant to broach the subject he'd chosen to rebreak the ice.

"You a married man, Boone?"

The older man's droopy, solemn expression seemed to instantly transform, the many fine lines that punctuated the corners of his lips and eyes vanishing by half.

"Not currently."

"Divorced or, um, widower?"

"Both, at one time or another, depending on the timeline. More recently the latter, nearly six years back."

"Sorry. Hope I'm not off-base asking."

"Not at all. Cynthia was a fine, classy and loyal lady. One of the good ones, if not the best."

"How long you two together?"

"She passed one month short of our twelfth anniversary."

Sitting the cruise-control just under the seventy MPH limit, Brad adjusted the seat as far as it would lean considering the backseat blockade.

"That's tough. Hey," he paused with a deep frown, shooting the older man a quick glance, "by all means, don't hesitate to tell me to put a cork in it if you don't want to discuss this."

"Not a problem, son. It's been a while, a *long* while, since I covered this particular ground. Might be refreshing at that."

"Great. Besides, it's not like we can talk about the weather for another three days, right?"

"Affirmative. So, what would you like to know?"

"You mentioned having experienced divorce as well."

Wincing, Boone sighed heavily, as if physically pained at the mere mention.

"More than once, unfortunately."

"Boone, if you don't mind my asking, how many exe's, that is,

25

how many wi…"

"Six all told."

The younger man's eyes widened even as his jaw dropped, as if surgically unhinged.

"*Six* marriages? *Whoa.* I'm only guessing here, but was Cynthia the longest of the unions, I mean, in duration?"

"Not even close. Sad but it was like we barely got started. Jenny, my third, holds that mark. Twenty-four and a half winters. Perhaps the sweetest, most levelheaded of the lot. Still, they were all special in their own unique way. Loyal to a fault, well, that is…" he concluded, smiling mischievously, "…'cept maybe for Barbara Jean. A loaded pistol without a safety, that one. Had some great times but I just couldn't get past her one glaring fault."

"What was that?"

"Well, kind of like Walmart, she never closed, 'specially her legs."

After a short, cautious pause, Brad laughed aloud and resumed the conversation only after moving over to the fast lane to steer them past a lumbering trio of tractor-trailers then resetting the cruise.

"Mister Harrison sir," he began, regarding his passenger with a pained scowl, "was your first marriage while attending middle school? Honestly, are we talking resurrection, past lives, what?"

Leaning up, the older man laughed into a cupped palm while removing a handkerchief from a back pocket. Covering his mouth, he coughed into the folded cloth and, upon checking it for possible leakage in the aftermath, tucked it back away.

"Like I said yesterday, I'm older than I look."

The younger man shook his head in sincere awe.

"*Incredible.* You need to share whatever template you follow. Not that I'm planning on five more marriages mind you, but there are days I feel a decade *older* than I am."

To that, Boone did not verbally respond but offered instead a slight nod, as if tempted but not quite prepared to delve further into the subject of longevity.

They rode in silence for several minutes, now traveling atop a mostly flat terrain with only sporadic traffic, before Brad reached up to power up the radio, the station of choice playing a mix of classic folk and country, mostly from the sixties and seventies, with the occasional retro-pop tune through in for good measure. He left the volume setting relatively low in case the older man might initiate a new conversation.

"This okay?" Brad asked, Olivia Newton John's '*Let Me Be There*' the current offering from his XM Radio playlist.

"Fine," Boone answered with a slight tilt of his head, "A tad too early for anything but soothingly mellow."

A full hour passed, during which time the passing landscape lost its ivory hue as snow-coated grounds gave way to mostly dead grass, cracked clay and comically bent shrubbery.

"Need a bathroom break?" Brad inquired after silencing the radio.

Boone seemed to contemplate this with great intensity, chin resting atop a clenched fist. Upon leaning up at the sound of his young charge's voice, a large, half-moon-shaped cowlick appeared from where his thick, wavy hair had been pinned against the headrest. Brad, warped smile on display at the sight, barely fought off an audible giggle.

"Think I can hold out a while yet, if you're game," he continued, reaching for the radio's volume knob only to have his hand blocked by the flat of the older man's left hand.

"Brad, I haven't been completely honest. Time to come clean."

The tone utilized was equally stern and grim, catching Brad utterly off guard as he drew back his hand, gripping the wheel in the classic ten and two.

"Yes sir?"

"I sincerely hope this doesn't change all that has come before. It's just that, I wasn't sure you'd take the job, and I simply couldn't afford any more delay in getting to my destination."

Brad swallowed but said nothing, instead keeping his eyes peeled on the road and sliding the charger over into the slow lane.

"I've recently been diagnosed with lung cancer, advanced stage. Due diligence dictated I acquire a second opinion following the initial diagnosis. As it stands, both physicians advised immediate treatment to include surgery, an extended hospital stay and aggressive chemotherapy. All due respect to both and their medical expertise, but I've obviously chosen not to heed their advice. My remaining time is very precious now and I can't, *won't* spend it wasting away on what is certainly a lost cause. When I referred to this as a one-way trip in the ad, well, in my case, I afraid I meant that in the literal sense."

"Mist…Boone, that's certainly your choice," Brad replied softly, unable to yet muster the courage to meet the older man's gaze, "I mean, we hardly know each other so I'm in no position to questi…"

"There's more. The payment we agreed upon isn't near accurate."

Brad felt his gut tighten. Oh, here it comes, he mused dourly, he's either broke as a stone or worse, drowning in some knee-high debt he hopes I'll chip in to pay.

"I know I quoted fifteen-hundred dollars plus expenses. The actual offer is ten thousand to get me there and an additional ten for a final favor."

As his lips prematurely parted in preparation to curse the older man's blatant attempt to defraud, Brad instead mumbled something incoherent, his face frozen in a comically exaggerated, perpetual grimace.

"Also, all the possessions I left behind at the condo, including my Jeep, are yours to do what you please, and fear not, the majority of the former isn't just dirty clothes, chipped dishes and moldy stacks of archaic paper-goods. There are many first-print classic novels and retro vinyl albums probably worth a mint, not to mention baseball card and book collections set to fetch you a nice price. The cards include rookies of Hammering Hank, the Say-Hey Kid and Mantle tucked in among the thousands of commons, but it's the novels that probably hold the most value, what with a dozen or more first editions. You might want to engage an expert in such matters before selling, just to avoid being taken."

"Boone, I don't under…" Brad managed, braking hard as to avoid rear-ending the car in front of him; a tiny Mazda sports car driven by a man whose enormous bulk made one wonder if the use of a crowbar had been instrumental in his presence behind the wheel, and thus potentially initiating a domino-effect crash.

"I have a grandson in Arizona. I'll be entrusting you to contact and wire him the remainder of my vast fortune," Boone continued straight-faced enough, though breaking character long enough to flash a weak, obviously forced smile with that last proclamation.

"Fifty thousand, give or take a few hundred. Enough to pay off some debt and maybe even start a college fund for my great grandson."

Taking a right onto the first available off-ramp, Brad spotted a Flying J truck-stop on the left and carefully navigated them into its vast, mostly deserted lot.

"Boone, Mister Harrison," he huffed, removing his aviators, releasing his seatbelt and turning toward his passenger with a look that defined the word befuddlement, "if you don't mind, I'll need a detailed replay in case I...misheard you."

The older man sighed, inhaled deeply, and did just that.

At the conclusion, Brad still wasn't sure full clarity had been reached.

"It's not that I don't appreciate your kind generosity, but are you sure twenty thousand dollars for basically three and a half days work isn't, well, overkill?"

Instantly regretting his choice of words, Brad resumed when the older man's lone response was a mild shrug.

"Not to mention the Jeep and those other valuables you mentioned. Really, wouldn't your grandson or some other family member be a better choice for personal belongings?"

"The Jeep, lord love the Big Chief, is way past his prime," Boone replied softly, fingers tapping nervously atop his thighs, "Not sure you'll pocket much from that trade. As for mementos, I tucked away all they'll need in the briefcase. The quoted fee is...will be well-deserved, believe you me."

It was soon after, once respective restroom visits had concluded and chosen refreshments purchased, that Boone removed the small duffel from the back floorboard and added still another chapter to the growing mystery.

A cassette tape recorder, Jensen by brand, was held snugly to his chest like some ancient, protective talisman.

"Sorry, Brad. Truly I am."

"For what?" the younger man asked, his gaze darting from Boone's

29

doe-eyed expression to the recorder and back again.

"I'm afraid you're going to grow nauseating sick of hearing my voice drone on and on."

Chapter Three

As the charger sped back onto the interstate and settled into a suitable grove amid the scattered morning traffic, Boone explained in great detail the reasoning behind the recorder's presence and why it represented an element of the trip even more vital than the bundles of earmarked cash tucked neatly inside his briefcase.

"Sure, I get it," Brad reverberated repeatedly, almost apologetically.

"It's just that…" Boone said, having plugged in the recorder's attached adaptor and ensuring, for at least the fifth time, that a blank cassette was properly secured, "…even with all the recent resurgence in searching out family histories and such, many of the younger generation have neglected to seek out the stories *behind* the legacies. I'm fairly positive that Brent, that's my grandson, hasn't a clue such tales even exist. I just want to make sure he's educated in not only *who* came before, but some of their individual histories. You'll understand better in a few decades when looking back becomes more a necessity than luxury. Admittedly I didn't keep in touch with family like I should've, but I had my reasons. Honestly, it was better for them I didn't. I'm hoping these chronicles along with the monetary gift will serve to sweeten up some of the sour feelings."

He cleared his throat noisily, the prep work on the recorder apparently complete.

"Originally I'd planned on delivering the goods myself. That is, hiring someone to drive me west instead of south. That changed only recently, due to unforeseen circumstances I'll divulge at a later time. Anyhow, I'm about as ready as I'll ever be. Best kick off this party before my engine light comes on."

The two men shared a sly glance, the younger of the two gesturing toward the recorder atop his elder's lap with a playful wink.

"Hey, you just knock yourself out, Boone. Gotta confess I'm kind of stoked to hear 'em. Stoked and honored to be the first."

Forehead creased in thought, Boone raised a forefinger and counted off while adding a final note of exposition. In that moment, his profile trapped in the bright rays of the morning sun, the older man's paid chauffer thought his employer, if only for that scant few seconds, appeared to age several decades. No doubt the effects of the terminal disease slowly eating away at his very core.

"I'll be breaking them down into segments, the first two covering relatives of note, the third and last with yours truly in the starring role," Boone resumed with a weak smile, "Invested in a four-pack of ninety-minute cassettes. Here's hoping I don't get too long-winded, but that should be more than enough."

Navigating the charger past a lumbering RV, Brad slid back into the slow lane, set the cruise control on sixty-eight and leaned back against the headrest holding an enormous cup of Dr. Pepper in his free hand.

"Looks as if we've got clear sailing. Fire when ready."

"Okay then. Just as a preview of sorts, part one is a story that was passed onto me by my father and his father before him and deals with my great uncle Dalton Harrison, by all accounts a gypsy type fella who rarely settled in one place for very long. Newly married, Uncle D was barely thirty years of age, living in Wyoming and working as a telegrapher at a remote railroad post during the winter of eighteen ninety-six."

"So then," Boone paused, a shaky forefinger reaching down towards the recorder to gently press record, "Away we go…"

Flashback Part I

The Telegrapher
Dead of Winter, 1896
Four miles east of Rawkins, Carbon County, Wyoming

Dalton Harrison squinted through the shack's lone, dust and condensation-streaked window as the sun took a final day's bow behind a jagged, majestic mountain range, the orange-hue of the sky instantly darkening to a foreboding shade of grayish/brown. Stroking his thick beard and stifling a yawn, he pushed away from a scarred oak desk with intentions of a coffee refill when the register sounded off with its familiar clicking, clacking concerto.

A scant sixteen by eighteen feet, a twenty-plus-foot platform leading to the tracks notwithstanding, the squared timber shack held little in the way of conveniences save a cast iron stove, cot, shaving mirror and single cabinet to hold a select few pots, pans and utensils. The outhouse, a three by four-footer of the 'bucket variety' was located a hundred or so feet east, while a pump-handle a few dozen feet to the west identified the lone nearby water-source. Man's final contribution to the grounds was, by all definitions, no more than a glorified lean-to, a rickety eight-by-eight overhang with a single hitching rail of equal length. As far as job amenities, it was obvious that Union Pacific's higher-ups favored those stations with a less remote setting.

Shuffling toward the cast iron stove like a man suffering from severe rheumatism, though an honest diagnosis of such stiff, awkward movements would involve an overabundance of spirits the night previous, on this day he would've gladly offered a week's pay to the inventor of a muted version of the very same machine.

Tin cup sufficiently filled with the remainder of that evening's brew, as black as tar and nearly as thick, he relocated the shack's lone chair from the miniscule dining table to the even smaller one dedicated to the telegraph, a stack of notepads and handful of cedar pencils.

Collapsing onto the hard pine seat with a resounding huff, he sipped timidly and, scowling at the bitterness of the brew, regarded the machine with open disdain as it continued to tap and bang with the cruel efficiency of a Gatling gun, dots and dashes replacing bullet holes.

He could only surmise some sort of issue to be fretted upon, as the previous eight days of a fourteen-day shift as station sentinel went so smoothly as to be labeled as unnaturally so. Union Pacific paid decent enough, at least he'd been told, though as a complete novice to the railroad industry, this was taken at face value at the time of his hiring. Then again, he conceded without debate, it was preferable to stacking crates or loading untold bags of feed onto wagons for ten hours a day for pennies then spending the night-hours fully awake from back, neck and shoulder aches. He had found the solitude of the job a mixed bag, equal parts curse and blessing. Being naturally introverted, the latter was a comfortable-enough fit on most days, though the former found its footing whenever thoughts of his significant other dominated, especially on the most frigid of nights. This being only his third work shift, all at the same desolate station, '*gotta pay them dues*' he was reminded numerous times at the hiring, the days and nights seemed to meld together as one colossal non-event, at least thus far, though he'd been regaled many a tale of track shenanigans both knee-slapping comical and blood-curdling scary.

Shooting a weary glance at the posted schedule tacked halfway up the opposite wall, he confirmed the night's approximate stopover time. The Bighorn Express was a four-car passenger with usually two or three additional supply cars that, during the winter season, was usually packed with mail and assorted mail goods from Chicago, Kansas City or St Louis. As for the passenger haul, February usually meant nary an empty seat for those escaping the frozen climes of the Northeast for the sun and warmth of the west coast.

Once the clicking mercifully ceased, he laid his cup aside and leaned up with a pained groan and gut-feeling of palpable dread, such long messages were rarely a good sign, scanning and translating the Morse with great care as to not misread or misconstrue the content, as he was apt to do when hungover and rushing the process.

"Ah, hell. I *knew* it. Just knew it," he grumbled, throwing up his hands in comical exasperation, "Lord knows there just had to be a knot twisted somewhere in the strand. It just had to be."

The message, originating from west of Lincoln, was simple and concise enough in context:

MESSAGE BEGINS

-Blizzard Warning—Blizzard Warning—

-Heavy snowfall headed west toward Sierra Madre—

-Two to three feet total possible by AM sunrise for south-central Wyoming to include Casper-Cheyenne to Twin Falls and Salem—

-High wind alert—

-Bighorn Express currently experiencing two-to-three hour delays out of Omaha—

-Current rescheduled arrive time at Rawkins Station East is between ten PM and Midnight—

-Current rescheduled arrive time at Salt Lake City is between nine and ten AM—

-Return message requested upon arrival—

- Return message requested if not arrived by two AM—

-Request forward to Salt Lake City—

MESSAGE ENDS

"Sure, Claude, sure. Ten to midnight my chapped behind," Dalton spat, falling back with arms crossed while glancing at the aged mantelpiece clock propped just to the right of the telegraph, the current reading at seven-oh-eight PM.

"Be lucky to roll in here by that two AM deadline. More 'n likely bury itself up to the crankshaft halfway through Bridger Pass."

As the sender remained conspicuously anonymous, the receiver had little doubt in their identity, that being the Lincoln station's main telegrapher, Claude Akers, he of few words and the personality of a tree stump.

He and Claude swapped messages fairly regularly since the man's initial shift nearly two months past, but other than that initial intro, ol' Claude the Clod gradually regressed in terms of hospitality from signing with full name to his initials to not signing at all. Though they'd never met face-to-face and most likely never would, Dalton painted the picture in his mind of a balding grump toting a substantial gut and equally plump ego. A cocky, snooty, self-proclaimed *'King of Morse'* who thought himself too good to mince words with peers, especially those fairly new to the job.

With this in mind, the mandatory response Dalton offered was as limited as his patience with the news Claude had no doubt so eagerly tapped out.

-*MESSAGE RECEIVED* covered the entirety.

"Take that, ya snooty bastard," he announced with great self-satisfaction, though in the aftermath briefly forced to ponder his own mental wellbeing from the act of despising a total stranger a half-state away over their lack of autographing their work.

Moving with all the enthusiasm and purpose of a heavily sedated codger in search of an empty cot, he arose, fast-cooling coffee in hand, to pose crookedly and peer grimly out toward the distant range.

As darkness had already begun to cloak the jagged range and sloping valley below, he took little solace in the current state of the massive grounds, that being predominately free of snow save a few select patches from a mild event three days' previous. As if to provide a foreboding precursor for things to come, a sudden, stout gust rattled the shack's outer walls like the clutching, squeezing hands of some unseen giant while also bending back a passel of nearby scrubs.

"Well, so much for hitting the sack early," he whispered, following a series of noisy sips, his free hand reaching back to scratch between a narrow space in the seat of the worn, booze-spattered long-john underwear he'd sported for nigh-on two full days.

Back-peddling, he placed the mostly emptied tin-cup on the dining table between a pair of oil lamps and regarded it with a look of utter disgust, as if it held a particularly nasty smell.

"Too late to catch a nap, 'specially with my gut filled with the likes of you."

With the very real possibility of seven to eight hours to kill before the Bighorn's arrival, or non-arrival, if the weather report was to be trusted, he resigned himself to prepping the shack as best he could for the impending blizzard.

By quarter past nine, the first flakes descended, at first no more than flittering specs barely visible through the shroud of night, though soon substantial enough to coat the landscape in the first of what promised to be multiple layers.

Ten-fifteen saw ankle-deep totals on the flat platform, meaning drifts twice that depth beyond it, with winds alternating from slight, nearly nonexistent breezes to wall-rattlers so intense it was as if the shack was being battered by tumbling boulders.

With a fresh load of firewood packed into the stove and two more stacked nearby, Dalton sat at the dining table over a serving of hard rolls, beans and black coffee, the latter two giving off competitive waves of steam amid a dramatic temperature drop inside the shack's cramped confines. He lit both lanterns at his disposal and placed one atop each tabletop, though careful to utilize the lowest settings for each to preserve oil.

In addition to the kindling and firesticks, he'd also paid the outhouse what he hoped would be limited visits on such a bone-chilling night, the mere thought of trudging through three-foot drifts at regular intervals less than comforting, as well as pumping two buckets and three canteens-worth from the well.

Blowing onto a scalding forkful while fingering a paperback book, one of three he'd purchased to pass the time on shift, the act of fiction reading new to him until undertaking such a hermit-friendly position, Dalton paused with mouth agape at the intrusion of an alien sound among the gusty winds. Gently placing H.G. Wells' *'The Time Machine'* atop a trio that included Mary Shelley's *'Frankenstein'* and Mark Twain's *'The Adventures of Huckleberry Finn'*, wooden spoon levitating just below his bushy beard, he cocked his head slightly toward the window side and held his breath to await a possible follow-up.

When it repeated, there was no mistaking the source. A horse whinny, the distance from which was impossible to gauge in the face of winds that could carry for untold miles.

Regardless, there was but one destination for a distant mount in such a storm. Dalton cringed at the thought. Of course, there was the outside chance, however improbable, that the beast was without master.

"Fat chance. Face it, boy. Company's coming," he grumbled, spooning in a heaping helping of beans and following up with the last of his roll, "be damned if I'm sharing that cot with anybody, that is unless the lost party in question is a dancin' gal from Laramie needing a good warming up."

While Union didn't instruct its telegraphers to arm themselves, most did, especially at the remote stations. Dalton had inherited his father's Colt revolver in his late teens and despite some obvious wear and tear, hadn't found a viable reason to replace it. To ensure the weapon's continued effectiveness, he had even got into the habit of executing some on-sight target practice at the beginning of each shift, setting up homemade targets on the opposite side of the tracks. He took special pride in the fact he'd never drawn on another man but saw no reason in being ill-prepared if such an occasion did arise. Checking the cylinder and satisfied of the content, he tucked the Colt into his belt to be concealed by the flap of a thick wool coat while silently praying this streak remained securely intact.

A quarter-hour passed without further hints of a mystery rider, that is until the shack's lone entrance was rattled with a pounding so urgent and with such force it was as if the source used not only both fists but double bootheels as well.

"Hello?" a voice bellowed over gusts so vicious Dalton feared a repeat might well tear the door hinges askew.

Without verbal reply, Dalton figured any croaking attempt would most likely be lost considering the thundering severity of the winds, he shuffled over and unlatched the door's flimsy latch, instantly backing away with a hand resting uneasily on the Colt's walnut grip.

The door flung inward in a blur, a shadowy, statuesque figure filling the blackened void as old man winter's wares blew in all around it, as if it were attempting to block a descending avalanche with its immovable bulk.

"Oh, for Jake's sake, just get in here already," Dalton screeched angrily, aware that not only was precious heat being lost but every loose paper in the shack was joining the intruding flakes in a blistery swirl of debris-soup.

The figure, tall and solid of physique, strode forward and with a single fluid movement—utilizing a reach that appeared supernaturally long, snatched the shack door by its outer edge, whipping it closed and securing the latch. Decked out in an ankle-length black duster, matching Stetson and what appeared to be calvary boots with spurs, the figure slowly peered up from beneath a slightly drooping brim, using gloved hands to wipe away an impressive buildup of winter's fury from each shoulder.

"Appreciate the hospitality," a voice offered, surprisingly refined and unintimidating considering the stranger's imposing stature.

"Tied my buckskin beneath your shed if that's acceptable. Hoping she's not buried to the neck by the time the downpour subsides."

Stepping forward, the single stride placing him literally boot-tip to boot-tip with his host, the stranger tipped the Stetson with his left hand while offering the right in formal greeting.

"Daniel Bain, at your service good sir, and on this hellish night in the middle of nowhere, your mercy as well."

Applying as firm a handshake as he could manage, considering the level of apprehension involved, Dalton cleared his throat and introduced himself with an equal amount of false bravado.

"Dalton Harrison. What brings you out this way on such a night, Mister Bain?"

Removing the Stetson to reveal shoulder-length blonde locks and similarly shaded, crescent shaped sideburns, the otherwise cleanshaven man's response was of the non-verbal variety, unbuttoning the top few buttons of the duster to briefly reveal a silver badge of unknown title or jurisdiction.

"Oh, I see," Dalton half-whispered through a tight squint that spoke otherwise.

"US Marshal out of Kansas City."

"So, you tracking way out here for somebody in particular?"

"That I am, Mister Harrison, that somebody being a scoundrel of the lowest order."

"Got'cha," Dalton nodded, as not to pry despite an inner curiosity that itched like a fresh mosquito bite, instead gesturing with a tilt of the head towards the stove, where the coffee pot spewed thin tendrils of steam flowing gently in their direction via a constant draft of frigid air.

"Coffee? You must need some defrosting."

Sweeping the Stetson in a dramatic arc, the large man bowed like a well-trained stage thespian receiving approving applause.

"That would be most appropriate, yes sir. Much appreciated."

Soon after they sat across from one another, Dalton having offered up his spare tin-cup to the visiting lawman, whose oversized mitt created the allusion of its non-existence save the rising steam from his clenching fist. The chair he'd been provided, by mere inches the roomiest in the seat of the shack's two options, was comically small for a man of his size, his knees even with the table's edge and thus unable to fit beneath. For comfort's sake, Dalton presumed, the lawman unholstered twin Remington-Rider revolvers and positioned them on either side of where his elbows rested. Viewed up-close and directly beneath the lantern light, Bain appeared the stereotypical lawman, adequately square-jawed and steely-eyed, sans the flowing blonde locks, at least in appearance, though Dalton couldn't get past not only the *way* he spoke but the overly dramatic, almost flowery dialogue on display, as if the man were playing a character role in a stage play with an audience of exactly one.

"So, Marshal, are you at liberty to tell me about the scoundrel you seek?"

Lowering the cup, Bain's gaze seemed to lock everywhere save directly upon his inquirer, darting around as if pondering the legality of an impending response.

The two quickly exhausted talk of weather conditions, Dalton no longer willing or able to skirt the subject.

"Don't see why not. The target of my ire…" he paused, a wide grin that the man found less amiable than flat-out predatory, "…is wanted in several states, to include my beloved Missouri, for multiple embezzlements. His specialty is to bilk extremely wealthy, older ladies of their fortune via mimicking a freelancing Lothario."

Dalton's creased forehead and cocked brow screamed befuddlement, to which the marshal quickly identified and responded in kind, the broad smile now resembling a pained grimace.

"A rogue scoundrel."

"Woos 'em and fleece's 'em in equal measure," Dalton shot back knowingly, the act of stroking his beard, a nervous tic since it grew long enough to serve the purpose.

"Exactly, good sir," the marshal replied. "A most depraved, despicable type that I will take great pleasure in hauling back for trial."

The two sipped silently for several minutes, the battering winds providing ample background noise to offset any potential awkwardness.

"That's a hell of a trek," Dalton finally said, leaning back with splayed fingers digging into and vigorously scratching through a thoroughly unkept, absurdly disheveled coif.

"Sir?"

"From Kansas City, I mean, but…" he paused, hands relocated to his beard, where the scratching continued, "…how'd you manage to get ahead of 'im?"

"Had info he'd moved his game to Salt Lake so I caught a freight a few weeks ago and have been forced to backtrack ever since. Got it from a good source he was headed to Rock Springs, then on to Green River."

"Salt Lake? That's still a mighty stretch through some ragged territory."

"Indeed," the marshal said with a tip of his cup, "Got the saddle sores to prove it."

"Why not just telegraph ahead to Rock Springs or Evanston? Have 'im scooped up there?"

Leaning forward, the marshal winked playfully enough, though the vibe created was anything but light-hearted.

"Because, simply put, Mister Carlton Bradshaw's thieving, deceitful, four-flushing ass is mine and mine alone."

"A man on a mission," Dalton replied, swallowing hard, his cheeks instantly reddening, "Guess you law enforcers have to possess some inbred stubbornness to be able to do such a job and do it well."

The marshal leaned back, the miniscule chair creaking its disapproval.

"Perhaps. In Bradshaw's case, it's more about his *methods* of gaining monetary gain than the victim's left behind. Like you folks are apt to say in these parts, lower than a snake's belly in a wagon rut."

"Seems a personal grudge, if you don't mind my saying," Dalton replied with a droll grin, an assumption the marshal's steely gaze all but confirmed.

"Mister Harrison, they're *all* personal."

To this, Dalton tipped his own cup, a final itch of curiosity refusing to subside despite a twinge of apprehension in the pursuit.

"Marshal, and don't take this wrong, but you come off as mighty educated for someone chasing bad guys in a blizzard."

"No offense taken, my good man. Illinois State Normal Class of '81."

"Thought so. So, why lawman work?"

"Simple really. While my degree of learning involved the medical field, I just turned twenty-two when my father was shot down in cold blood over what amounted to the loose change in his pockets. A feedstore manager by trade, what passed for the local sheriff gave the same amount of interest in finding his murderer as wiping away a squashed cockroach from his bootheel. This...travesty of injustice occurred in Hannibal, Missouri. I swore I'd not only seek out the party responsible, but in time, replace that piece of walking excrement passing as the city constable. Roughly two years removed from my father's killing, I managed to satisfy at least one of those listed goals."

After a moment's pause, such theatrics keeping perfectly in tune with the night's building dramatics, Dalton's exasperated follow-up appeared right on cue.

"Well, hell marshal, which goal was that?"

"His identity is unimportant as how I came to find him, but rest assured, I never intended on bringing him in alive."

"How about that sheriff whose badge you so badly desired?"

"Alas, relieved of his duties before I could ever attempt a proper coup. All for the best really," he shrugged, rising from the obvious restrictions of the tiny chair like a gangly Daddy Long-Legs freed from a mini-matchbox and strapping on his gun belt, "Hannibal is a real shithole."

Pleasantly surprised at his guest's comical crudeness, Dalton cackled aloud, barely avoiding a spit-take of warm coffee across the table toward the source, whose response came in the form of a roguish wink before leaning back to stare down the mantel clock.

"So, according to the latest telegraph from your peers to the east, we're looking at another two hours?"

"Sometime around two AM was the approximate," Dalton answered, wiping the fresh spillage from his beard with a coat-sleeve, "but it appears to me the buildup out there is more than predicted, so I'm thinking around three or later if they manage to bull through the passage at all."

"Passage?"

"Bridger's Pass can be a bear, blizzard notwithstanding. They'll have to stoke those coals like the devil spooning out a pitchfork's triple-helping of hellfire. If they do stall, we're probably looking at delays 'til maybe midday depending on whether or not the sun makes an appearance to melt some of the buildup."

With a somber glance out the window, a three-plus inch accumulation already stacked upon the narrow seal, the marshal's tone grew noticeably bleak but also layered with a palpable edge of stubborn grit. Striking a statuesque pose with his left boot propped on the chair and clenched fists parked at each hip of the duster, he appeared no less than some form of regal giant to the still-seated telegrapher.

"I'll wait it out 'til dawn then, and if that delay scenario becomes a reality, do some backtracking."

"Wouldn't advise it, at least not too close to the tracks or your steed is likely to shatter a leg."

"Oh, Daring Daisy and I have covered our share of dicey grounds, believe you me."

"Daring...Daisy?"

"Raised her from a bony-legged filly. Most devoted of the female race I've yet to encounter."

Pushing his empty cup aside, Dalton leaned back with arms crossed and openly shivered.

"A single man, I take it?"

"Lifelong bachelor, confirmed."

Rising with a grimace, the telegrapher shuffled over to toss a few fresh cords into the stove.

"Good for you, Marshal. Hang onto that title long as you can manage."

"The happily-hitched type, I take it?" the marshal asked, gaze still fixed on the web-like net of white descending beyond the window's grungy glass.

"Can't honestly claim that first part of late, but a definite guilty-as-charged to the second."

"Let me guess. Your choice of employment isn't exactly her cup-of-tea."

"Hammer to nail," Dalton confirmed with the click of his tongue.

Meanwhile, the marshal's self-imposed hypnosis had been broken upon spotting the stack of paperbacks, which he studied curiously.

"Yes well, the one time I've treaded closest to the alter of matrimony, it was my career that soured the affair. Sweet Lois simply would not accept playing second fiddle to a silver badge."

"No compromising duty for love, huh?"

"Not in this line of work, no sir."

As if to purposely shift gears, the marshal studied the book spines before returning them to their previous spot atop the rickety tabletop, "Shelley, Wells and Twain. Impressive trio I must say, though I would think such an…isolated locale might not be the best place for reading of vampires, Morlocks and such."

"Maybe, sure beats the hell out of Dickinson, Emerson or Longfellow."

The marshal laughed aloud. A booming retort that almost but not quite drowned out the blustery, battering winds that were presently blowing snow in an almost perfectly horizontal track.

"Touché my good man. I do not, however, recommend anything from Poe, that is if you value a good night's sleep."

"Duly noted," Dalton replied with the tip of a nonexistent cap, relocating his chair to face the window before squatting back down onto its scarred seat and propping equally disfigured bootheels onto the seal.

"Got an extra bucket of water for your steed and a half-bag of feed in the corner there if you're so inclined."

Openly shivering at the very thought, the marshal checked the buttons on the duster before removing a pipe and tin of tobacco from a side pocket.

"Just a spell more of thawing and I will be, thanks. She's going to need some rest and rejuvenation. Got an extra set of blankets in my saddlebag to prevent the old girl from becoming just another frozen lump of tundra."

The shack soon reeked of pipe tobacco, a heady, stout scent that wafted overhead like a pregnant cloud of smooth Irish Whiskey.

"Oh, my apologies, do you mind? I've been craving a taste all day."

"Not at all," Dalton said with a dismissive wave before gesturing out the window with the same hand, "Got a jug of Apple Jack stored away if it needs a companion."

"Mighty kind. I'll keep that in mind for later."

Stroking his beard, the man stifled a yawn.

"From what I can tell and mind you it isn't more than a few feet past the glass, this mess isn't letting up even a tad. No bum steer from the weather boys this time out."

"Well, as much as I despise slogging about in Old Man Winter's droppings, it could be this storm is just what I needed to corner and nab my quarry."

The marshal paced the tiny room, a maximum of two and a half steps in one direction before a forced about-face, a thin tendril of pipe smoke following in his wake.

"Question, since this type of situation is more your expertise."

With a mild shrug, Dalton silently indicated for his guest to resume.

"A hypothetical query, to be precise. That being, could the locomotive conductor decide to barrel on through without stopping if he decides that a sudden decrease in momentum might cause further delay?"

"Not likely, Marshal," Dalton replied sheepishly, "fairly flat terrain once it clears the pass in both directions. If they stall, it'll most likely be a far distance to the east."

"No chance of the locomotive maintaining the set schedule then?"

the marshal continued, extracting a final billow of smoke before laying the still smoldering pipe atop the dining table.

Dalton regarded the marshal with a cocked brow and squinty eyes gleaming with mischief.

"I'd say about as much as Poe penning a nursery rhyme."

With that, the marshal nodded solemnly and, inhaling as if to high dive into the deep, sauntered over to retrieve the waiting bucket and feed. Duster collar tucked tight and Stetson placed as snugly as his thick mane would allow, he paused at the shack door with filled hands, crouching slightly in preparation for a sprinting exit.

"If you ain't back in a reasonable spell, I'll break out the pick-axe and dig ya both out," Dalton quipped, face twisted in comical dread, "After all, the place could always use a quality carving of man and horse as a conversation piece."

"My good man…" the large man shot back with a mocking sneer, "…you obviously spend *far* too much time alone."

~ * ~

Mischief on The Bighorn Express

It was just past one AM, Dalton having allocated the shack's lone cot to the marshal, and thus forced to nod off in one chair with his boots propped atop the other, when a dull yet somehow distinctive noise pierced the night with just enough volume to shake both men from their respective dozes.

"Wha-whazzat?" the marshal stuttered, only an extended arm and flat of a palm preventing a headfirst tumble onto the planked floor.

Dalton's head shot up, ears perked with his head tilted slightly to the left, his cowlick infested do as warped as his disheveled beard.

"I don't, d-didn't he…"

Crouched onto his hunches, the marshal shushed his host with a raised hand.

"Wait for it."

Exactly five ticks later, it repeated, again muffled by the ever-present winds but clear enough for proper identification.

"Whistle," Dalton verified before struggling to remove his bulk from the chair's restrictive binds, "sounded fairly distant."

"How distant?"

"Hang on. Lemme hear a third."

Leaping up with renewed vigor, the marshal moved toward the window and peeked out through cupped hands as Dalton busied himself lighting the lone globe lantern available.

"Damn it. Couldn't see a grizzly if it had its hindquarters stuck to the glass."

This time, in the form of a hard slap of bare palm against tabletop, it was Dalton requesting silence.

The third shriek sounded off a split-second later, a bit lengthier in duration.

"Mile, maybe a mile and a half down the track."

"Stalled?" the marshal inquired, pulling on the duster he'd discarded before turning in for what had turned about to be a solid hour and a half snooze and checking for a revolver's presence at each hip.

"Sounded prone enough to me. Hard to tell. Last one was drawn out, couldn't tell with the other two."

"So?"

"Three long means danger."

"Stalled for sure, I'd wager. Hold down the fort then. I'll need you to telegraph ahead once I have Bradshaw in custo…" the marshal paused, regarding the telegrapher with a cocked brow, "Now where do you think you're go…"

In the time it took the lawman to back from the window to trek toward the shack exit, Dalton tossed on his own cover, to include wool headgear, matching gloves and a pair of fur-lined mukluks.

"Those folks are as much my responsibility as the conductors once they clear the pass. I'll be asking you make room on your steed, Marshal."

The lawman's lips parted in apparent disapproval but clamped shut abruptly upon watching the smaller man snap on a gun belt and snatch up the lantern, a resounding sigh in its place.

"Your decision but know *this*; I can't be protecting you if

Bradshaw takes aim, which he is apt to do if cornered."

"Don't expect you to," Dalton replied dourly, standing up and executing a short jog in place to test the mukluks fit, "Tell ya what," he grinned while joining the taller man at the exit, "I'll do my best to duck whatever slug flies my way."

Marshal Dan Bain laughed despite himself and the pair then stepped out into the frigid, ivory void.

~ * ~

Following alongside the tracks, or at least where the tracks were supposedly located, Daisy moved forward at a cautiously measured pace, at times buried up to the flank and never less than cannon deep.

Propped precariously atop the filly's sloped croup, Dalton's grip across the marshal's midsection constricted with increased tautness with each unsteady motion. The gusting winds disallowed any attempt at communication between the two men, although the marshal would occasionally squirm and flex his torso in an attempt to loosen his passengers near death-grip. They heard but one additional whistle since departing the shack and none since putting notable distance from the same.

Squinting around the marshal's left shoulder, Dalton was far too short in comparison to peek over it, and roughly a half-hour into the trek, he spotted a dim light through the blinding deluge. Having apparently spotted it also, the marshal lifted a gloved hand and pointed in the glow's general direction, yelling something unintelligible before steering Daisy forward with a gentle spurring.

As they grew steadily closer, all illumination vanished into the swirling gloom, as if literally swallowed into its ravenous, all-enveloping maw.

The fall, when it came, did not include a severe lean, slow-motion tumble nor a gradual rollover. Instead, a teeth-rattling, bone-jarring descent so instantaneous it was as if the filly stepped directly into an open well.

All traces of oxygen bludgeoned from his lungs upon landing on his left shoulder, side and leg, Dalton was briefly immobilized until an immense weight, no doubt Daisy's writhing form, lifted, allowing him to roll over onto his back. Mouth agape while struggling to inhale the frigid air, he could taste the snow landing on his exposed tongue while also caking his flaring nostrils. It wasn't until he'd rolled back over onto his right side, reaching down for a quick inventory of both legs, that the power of hearing partially returned to the strangely distant sound of Marshal Bain's impassioned screams. Hauled roughly up to his feet by the armpits and subsequently dragged, a portion of the marshal's dialogue broke through the combination of ringing and squall filling both ears:

"...to the cab...freeze to...ground...see Daisy in all the...this...darted away like...gunshot..."

Soon after Dalton blacked out, he came to splayed on his stomach, with the marshal crouched just to his left, his prone form outlined by a building stream of melting snow as, comparatively, the train cab's interior was a tropical rainforest, the incessant burning at his ears, cheeks and the tips of his fingers symptomatic with the effects of early frostbite.

"Mis...Dalton, you still with me?"

Dalton heard the marshal inquire from what sounded like a great distance, his ears seemingly stuffed with cotton. Upon speaking, there was no gauging the volume of his own words. Whether he'd whispered or screamed was a complete mystery.

"Y-yeah, in w-what ca-capacity I c-can't say."

The Marshal stood, tilting his head slightly downward to avoid rubbing the Stetson on the angled roof, to peer out one side of the cab for several moments before stepping over to the other side and doing the same.

"Seems we're both no worse for wear, nothing short of a miracle considering. Of poor Daisy's fate, I haven't a clue."

"W-what ha-happened?"

"I can only surmise the old girl stepped into a rather deep ravine hidden by the drift that so cleverly disguised it. We were fortunate not to shatter limbs or be rendered unconscious by the sudden jolt. Luckier still that the train was only a few hundred feet from where we were so unceremoniously dumped."

Pulling himself up on all fours, Dalton felt a plethora of aches and pains shoot up his left side before recalling the less than graceful landing he'd previously executed. Removing the glove from his left hand, he attempted to rub the bleariness from his eyes. The cab interior was a dimly lit alien landscape of fogged-over dials, protruding handles and coiled hoses, a sporadic but very welcome wave of steam spewing forth from parts unknown.

"So, we have our health but little else at this juncture," the marshal continued, leaning down to study the boiler, "Lanterns would sure come in handy about now."

Scanning the cramped confines to seek out the cab's source of illumination, the lawman spotted a brass lantern mounted just above a series of circular dials.

"Bizarre. Appears to be the conductor's lantern. Can't imagine leaving the cab without it. Then again, they must've had more than one aboard."

"But...wh-where's th-the conductor, the e-engineer or b-brakeman?" Dalton croaked, his throat growing rawer by the word.

He also took grim note via reaching up to run splayed fingers through a partially frozen coif, that his wool cap had been misplaced in the fall.

"Yet another mystery wrapped within an enigma, it appears. Cab was suitably warm and cozy upon our unannounced arrival, but also completely deserted. I can only figure they're away checking out the rather dire situation they've steered this metal beast into. On the way inside, I noted the snowplow was conspicuously hidden from a thigh-high drift and otherwise buried to its cylinders."

"Wh-what about the whistle an-and light we s-saw?"

"The train's headlamp, I surmise, in the process of being swallowed by that monstrous drift. We saw what little was left of it but enough to announce its location before it was completely snuffed out. As for the whistle, well, fairly safe to assume it don't blow itself. Floor is one big puddle from melted snow."

Locating the pull-down cord, the marshal casually reached up but quickly pulled his hand away as if fearing a sudden burn. Standing eye-level with the bottom-half of the cord, he leaned in until it sat mere inches from the tip of his nose.

"Well now, what do we have here?"

Dalton shifted cautiously until he sat balanced atop both knees, swallowing hard before coughing into a curled palm.

"Wh-what's that?"

"Appears to be blood, recently applied at that."

Scanning the cab floor, he briefly dipped onto one knee to better examine a series of pea-sized, dark maroon spatters that led back to the cab entrance/exit.

"Someone sprung a leak. Perhaps the stall had little to do with that danger signal after all."

"W-wounded?"

"Apparently. Question is, why would they signal then leave the warmth of the cab?"

Removing the glove from the same groping hand, the marshal stood and turned, reaching out with an extended forefinger to poke the upper edge of a nearby coal shovel.

"Still mighty warm to the touch. They must've been loading the firebox when she stalled."

"So, do we w-wait on 'em or search 'em out?" Dalton asked, standing unsteadily and instantly leaning against the cab door.

"Strange, but it was dark as a mine out there," the lawman whispered, barely audible and with his head turned as if unintentionally speaking aloud.

"Marshal?"

"While I was dragging you inside, that is. Why wasn't there a lamp light visible, that is, if an inspection of the track was underway?"

"Damn murk is thick as mulligan stew," Dalton offered weakly, the follow-up infinitely more logical though hardly more comforting, "or maybe they were on the other side when we rode up."

The marshal sighed, slapping the holster at his right hip and again dropping to one knee, no doubt to allow his strained neck a rest from the constant tilt.

"Perhaps on both counts. I'm of the belief they've walked down to the passenger cars to brief the paying customers on the predicament."

Following a full minute of silence, Dalton pushed away from the door. Confident he regained a semblance of balance, he regarded the fidgeting lawman with a slight tilt of the head and a mild shrug.

"Soooo, we going or staying? Your call, of course. I'm just a volunteer deputy."

"We'll go. But we stay together, no separation and no heroics. Best tuck that collar to your ears or you're liable to have one of 'em freeze up and crack off along the way. Oh, and before I forget," he paused, reaching into the duster to remove and unfold a yellow-tinted paper and holding it up to display.

Though it was similar to a standard wanted poster, the difference was there was no civilian reward listed but instead a federal government header, the individual featured a rather plain, partially balding, bespeckled man perhaps in his mid-forties, not nearly the handsome rogue one would naturally associate with such crimes of passion.

"That Bradshaw?"

"Indeed. Once we climb into those passenger cars, you may identify but otherwise steer clear, understand?"

Dalton snickered.

"Appears about as dangerous as the postmaster back home."

"Looks can be deceiving. It's well known he stashes Derringers up both sleeves and isn't shy in using them."

Dalton nodded without reply before reaching to free the Colt from its worn holster, giving it a brief onceover, and holstering it with a satisfied grunt, his slightly shaking hand not lost on the lawman.

"Not to fret," the marshal said with as much faux cheer as he could muster, "You won't be needing it."

"Well, pray that we don't marshal, as my aim is just rusty enough to be a danger to anyone *but* the intended target."

Standing, the marshal chuckled, albeit nervously, while applying a playful slap to the smaller man's left shoulder.

"If the need arises, just showcase that hog-leg and hold her as steady as Wild Bill Hickok. Bradshaw won't know the difference."

Pulling the conductor's lantern free from its base, he stepped to the door and led them back into the storm.

~ * ~

Wading through calf-to-knee-high buildups, careful not to tumble into a sudden drop-off, the marshal's cautiously shuffling pace led them past a pair of supply cars separating the cab and passenger cars, the lantern levitating as far ahead as his ample reach would allow.

"There," he bellowed against the thrashing gusts, pointing with his free hand toward the first of what appeared to be a trio of passenger cars, each lightened somewhat by the faintest of glows, "When we get to that first one, wait until I've given you the okay to enter! Clear?"

In lieu of a verbal response, he'd latched onto the marshal's shoulder upon exiting the cab and utilized the lawman's towering frame for cover, ducking his head to avoid the never-ending onslaught, Dalton delivered a firm double-tap to the taller man's left shoulder.

Upon his boot-tip striking the car's lower entrance step, the marshal unholstered the Remington from his right hip, leaning up with the lantern poised as his talisman. Twisting around, his cheeks inflamed in certain areas and chapped to pasty-white in others, he nodded as to remind the other man of his previous command.

Peering through a constantly shifting ashen wall with only the occasional open space with which to visualize one's surroundings, Dalton maintained a guarded pose at the base of the steps, the Colt held out at his left side and shaking uncontrollably with each savage gust.

Time stood still as he watched the lawman vanish into the gloom, the otherwise impressive combination of long-johns, thick wool shirt, substantially padded winter coat, fur-lined gloves and mukluks hardly a match for a squall threatening to add his shivering frame to the surrounding tundra.

By the time the marshal, or at least the conductor's lantern, swinging like a pendulum blade, reappeared from the interior, Dalton momentarily thought himself paralyzed until what little energy he'd held in reserve allowed a free moment.

He practically collapsed inside. The sudden lack of battering winds was like the release of a great weight as he nearly tripped over a rolling tray that centered the car's middle aisle, from which assorted drinking glasses and ceramic bowls toppled and shattered.

"Wh-what th…" Dalton babbled through chapped-raw, quivering lips not yet ready for normal speech while reaching for a stabilizing force with his non-gun hand and finding nothing more solid than a cloth curtain. The lone lamplight, positioned at the rear of the car, was no more powerful than a lit match.

"Sleeping car," he heard the marshal whisper from the far end of the car. Brushing a fresh coating from his hair and beard, Dalton shook and shimmied his upper torso while blinking rapidly to clear away the rogue flakes glued to each eyelid and attached lash.

"I see only one lamp left out of four possible slots," Bain continued, squinting the length of the car and into the next, where illumination was similarly limited, "Same murkiness rules the day, it appears."

The marshal turned briefly to Dalton, who'd righted the tray, clumsily kicking away several remnants of broken glass, before removing it from the aisle.

"Odd happenstance piled upon odd happenstance," the marshal continued, speech so muffled as to be nearly inaudible, "Hmm, sleeping car indeed. Six curtained off beds for those able to pay for such comforts. Empty on this side. Can you check those three? I'm going to move on up to the ne…"

Equally surprised and angered at the marshal's woeful lack of common sense, the man was just about to question, or should that be, scold, the lawman on just how he was supposed to check anything without the aid of the conductor's lantern when something leapt out from behind curtain one.

~ * ~

"Oh g-god, oh-oh god, thank g-god," the mysterious stranger babbled, spittle flying onto Dalton's face as he struggled to wrestle the squirming figure from his chest.

Twisting hard to the left, he managed to roll them off amid an almost overwhelming stench usually associated with assorted body leakage.

"Y-you...I t-thought y-you were...th-them," the stranger continued to babble, desperately gasping for breath while down on all fours and posed like a baying wolf, "Th-thank god y-you heard...th-the whistle. We t-thought they'd...tr-tracked us back here to the car. W-we t-thought...considered...making a run f-from the cab until Miss...Miss Ruth spotted your lamplight and f-figured those cra-crazy som' bitches...h-had...tr-trialed us. No place to...hide in these damn tin cans!"

Decked out in a four-piece ensemble, dark blue or possibly black, specifics impossible to pin down in limited light, that included an absurdly baggy, double-breasted jacket opened to reveal a satin vest within and gold-banded hat, the stranger's identity was easily deduced upon standing erect.

"Say, you g-got an extra shooting iron I could borrow?"

"You the conductor?" Dalton asked, having tumbled back through the curtain to fall onto the cot beyond it.

Chest pumped out and head thrown back, the stranger snapped to as if called to attention in a calvary formation, the oversized jacket flapping like a windblown tent-flap. Stocky of build and short of stature, he wore a bushy gray mustache that was comically warped at the edges.

"Y-yes, sir, Gorman's the name. Y-you boy's lawmen?"

"Um, my partner there is. Marshal, think I found the conduc..." Dalton began, the remainder of his intended dialogue stuck in his throat like dry toast upon taking note of an additional figure being questioned by the marshal at the rear of the car.

Statuesque with a flowing red mane that rested between trim shoulder blades, she wore a light-colored, perhaps beige, ankle-length bowknot lace dress of the formal variety and had apparently ducked behind the curtain closest to the car's exit. As if studying her shapely frame for wounds, the marshal moved the lantern in close, gradually raising it toward her face. The man thought it strange that in the aftermath, though bathed in shadow, the marshal's expression briefly defined repulsion.

While the conductor appeared weirdly uninterested in their very existence, Dalton stood from the cot and sidestepped down the aisle, hoping to overhear their whispered conversation.

"...yes, ma'am, just calm down and tell me again what hap..."

Much like the conductor, her tone, despite a surprisingly controlled volume, and gestures tittered on the edge of shock. Also similarly, the formal dress that had looked so elegant from a distance held a slack, rumbled appearance, its lace edges brushing the carpet and thus cloaking her feet.

"Th-they just barged in brandishing that cutlery and, well, I declare no one knew how to...react or what to do. It was like...a bad dream. A walking nightmare. Mister Gorman tried to...save a few of the first wounded but in the end he just...grabbed ahold of me and we...we ran. G-got to the cab and h-he proceeded to sound the alarm. Knew we...weren't safe to stay so we just ambled on b-back here. We were about to try for the train cab again when we saw ya'll comin'."

Dalton had spent enough time around southerners to recognize the accent; hers a deep, sultry drawl with the power to entrance those unfamiliar to its exotic charms.

"I...I see. But, *cutlery*, ma'am? Are you suggesting peo...some of the passengers have been injured or even killed?" Bain inquired calmly enough, the lantern, and no doubt his gaze, focused on the front of the woman's dress.

"Sheriff, it ain't no *suggestion*," she retorted, incessant but oddly without passion, as if speaking not of a horrific tragedy but something infinitely more trivial, like perhaps a tear in her dress, "It's fact. I...we saw the...poor souls perish right in front of us. The female had procured a long sword from one of the guards and the other had...what looked like carving knives in both hands, probably procured from tha...the caboose. There's a...a kitchenette. You can question the conductor."

"Marshal, ma'am, Marshal Dan Bain. Are *you* wounded in any way?"

As if debating the question, she hesitated only long enough to execute a mild shrug.

"N-no, I don't...think so, 'cept for my faith in humanity. I never heard-tell of anything like this back in Georgia. I declare I wish I'd listened to my dear mama and stayed where I belonged."

Having holstered his revolver, the marshal tipped his Stetson with the free hand. Dalton found himself both dumbfounded and impressed with the man's cucumber-cool demeanor in the light of such dire revelations.

"Well, just relax. You're safe now," Bain said softly, reaching over to tap her lightly on the shoulder, "Please sit while I speak to him."

Her reply was weirdly stoic, as if she were reading from a printed text.

"Sir, you don't understand. You didn't…see what I…what *we* saw. We're not safe. Any of us. Those…your guns," she pointed a gloved finger at Bain's holster, "…make no mind to *them*. Death seems trivial, even their very own. I'm not at all certain mere lead can kill such demons in human guise."

"Oh, I assure you they can and *will*, ugh, what is your name, ma'am?"

"B-Beverly. Beverly Ruth, and I must fervently disagree, for you see…" she implored, revealing her full facial features to Dalton for the first time, and what he saw there chilled him deeper than any blizzard wind, "…we both saw them each shot at a, well, shockingly close range and it didn't stop what…came next. Please, sir, we have to depart this car before it's too late."

Her delicate features looked to have been whitewashed by a passing paint brush, though the color applied was anything but pallid, but a deep, almost blackish maroon. The marshal gestured Dalton over to sit or at least stand nearby her motionless frame as he sought confirmation with the conductor, thus he'd stood just up the aisle from her, eyes darting nervously from her almost catatonic features toward the entrance to the next car. Upon nearing, he quickly understood the origin of the marshal's obsession with the front of her dress, drenched from neck to lap in the same coppery-scented spillage as her cheeks and forehead.

"It'll be fine and dandy, ma'am. No need to fret now. The marshal there is a skilled shooter and brave as they come."

Peering up through eyes so clear and hazel Dalton momentarily lost his bearings, Miss Beverly Ruth replied with a voice as flat as a Kansas prairie. In the aftermath, and for the second time in a matter of moments, the telegrapher felt himself shudder.

"But what of you, sir? You willing and ready as *he* to perish this night?"

"Gorman, is it?" he heard the marshal ask, turning his attention toward the two men and suddenly grateful for the distraction.

"Yes sir," the conductor nodded with almost childlike enthusiasm, his pose stiffening as if a military salute was imminent, "Gorman Hicks."

"Marshal Bain, Kansas City," Bain replied, the lantern light revealing a similar drenching of the conductor's jacket and vest; the exposed flesh of his neck also stained bloodred, "Are you hurt, sir? Miss Ruth stated there had been an assaul…"

Formal deportment abruptly abandoned, the conductor's entire frame shook and shimmied, arms waving madly, booted feet sliding from side to side as if their possessor needed desperately to urinate.

"Just a scratch here and there. I'll live for now, but that can certainly change now, can't it? All due respect, Cain, this is *not* the time for interviews. As sweet Miss Beverly stated, we need…we *all* need to relocate as soon as possible. From what I saw, those two aren't about either taking prisoners or surrendering. Th-they're about wholesale slaughter. Bad as it was, it could've been a hell of a lot worse."

"It's Bain, Daniel Bain, and how so?"

"Cars were mostly deserted as we dropped off the majority of the booked passengers in Cheyenne and a few more in Laramie. Only five, no, six, counting lovely Miss Beverly, still occupying space with Salt Lake as their destination. That doesn't count the pair escorting those two maniacs, so with my…" he paused, voice cracking with emotion, "…late trainman Jacob, the

Bighorn was hauling a grand total of a dozen souls, though I'm of the opinion that at least two of 'em are of the *lost* variety, as in soulless."

"They had the bloodlust," Beverly Ruth bellowed, so unexpectedly that Dalton openly flinched. "Like a pack of hounds to a wounded coon. Their eyes shone with unnatural joy at taking another's life in the cruelest, shocking of ways. God save us, t-they was…they were grinning, the both of 'em, grinning from ear to ear with such pleasure. Such satisfaction. There was an elderly couple sitting next to me. Lord help us all. I think

I'm drenched in the old woman's brains."

"Husband and wife out of Texas, riding out to California to visit grandkids. Never had a blessed chance," the conductor added somberly, quickly switching tones upon regarding the marshal with a clenched, shaking fist.

"Honestly, Marshal Bain, if you moseyed in here with a ten-man posse loaded for bear, my wager still wouldn't change on who I'd favor in a scrap. Miss Ruth, if asked, would surely agree."

Shooting a worrisome glance toward Beverly Ruth, the marshal's jaw muscles grew taunt then flexed with obvious frustration.

"Mister Hicks, you must understand I do not collect a salary for avoiding such trouble. I ensure you that the safely of yourself and Miss Ruth is a priority, but I must know what I'm dealing with before moving forward. Besides, there's a good chance they've left the train for a safer clime with which to hide away from searching eyes."

"On foot?" the conductor mocked, face contorted in severe disbelief, "and in *that*? Marshal, they're cold-blooded killers, not soft-brained imbeciles."

"Disagreement noted," Bain fired back coldly. "Now back to the two...killers you speak of."

"Oh, I see," Hicks blurted with an animated snap of the fingers, "You seek...descriptions of the...now how is it you lawman-types refer to them?"

"Perpetrators."

"No, that's not..."

"Conductor Hicks, the clock ticks, remember?"

"Oh, yes, s-sorry, it's just that, we...we've seen so much that's not...natural on this night."

"I understand. Now, just a general description will suffice," Bain explained, briefly holstering the revolver to retrieve the same folded flyer he'd earlier displayed to Dalton and holding it directly beneath the lantern light. "Before you begin, and just to state my own curiosity, does this man appear familiar?"

The conductor leaned down until his bulbous nose almost touched the paper, the left side of his otherwise gray mustache blotted dark maroon.

"As a passenger, yes."

"Though not a suspect in the attack."

"*Suspect.* Yes, that's the word I was…"

"Mister Hicks, please…"

As if unaware of the potential scolding, the conductor resumed while pacing back and forth in what little space the narrow aisle allowed, chin tucked in one hand while the other reached up to scratch just beneath his cap's bill.

"No, not a suspect. In fact, I…I'm fairly certain the man in the poster there was one of the first to fall. Yes, he surely was. I remember now. He had one those tiny revolvers, you know, the type that fits in the palm and slides comfortably up the sleeve."

"A Derringer?"

"If that's what it's called. Peashooter at best when facing down such maniacs as that pair. Still, credit due in full, he didn't hesitate to fire 'em off."

"From what you said, the pea…Derringer had no effect?"

"Oh, he got off a shot with each of 'em, had 'em in tucked in both fists, might have even connected. Flat lot of good it did him."

With that, the conductor removed his cap and bowed his head as if preparing to deliver a eulogy.

"Flat lot of good it did any of 'em."

"Mister Hicks, about the perpe…suspects, how would you descr…"

As the conductor commenced, Dalton became aware of a mild tug at the left sleeve of his coat and, having barely refrained from screaming aloud, looked down to see Beverly Ruth regarding him with an expression as blank and emotionless as a store mannequin.

"Cackling devils in the flesh, they was…" she whispered, a slight tick visible at the corner of her right eye, "…collecting souls and riding this here train straight into the mouth of hell."

To this, Dalton could only stroke his beard nervously and reply with a gentle squeeze of her gloved hand, the chill beneath its red-streaked cloth evident despite the slick, satin cloak, and squint with great intensity into the gloomy interior of the next car.

"Jail clothing, you say?" the marshal was asking, the conductor now sitting on the same cot he'd sprang from just moments earlier.

"Black and white striped, yes sir. Both were boarded into the caboose wearing restraints."

"Prison guard escorts, I presume?"

The conductor nodded, the oversized jacket looking baggier than ever with its lower edges rolled into his lap.

"Two tough-looking gents with the charm of a stepped-on rattler. Reckon it goes with the job. Anyhow, they resembled calvary except for the badges and caps. Paperwork read California penal institute, Folsom state prison. Didn't spit more than two words between 'em other than handing me the transport order and claiming the caboose as their own personal cage."

"Perhaps if they are still aboard, that's where we'll find them holed up."

"Pray that you don't, Marshal," the conductor said flatly, holding up both hands palms-out in mock surrender. "No offense, you understand, but I can bear witness to…what they did to those guards. God help me, I wish I hadn't, and poor Miss Ruth, that young lass might never recover."

The marshal turned to give Beverly Ruth a quick once-over and couldn't help but silently agree. Within the gray dimness, she appeared gaunt, ghost-like, haunted. Refocusing on the conductor, the marshal placed the lantern into the man's open hand before removing the extra revolver from its holster.

"Just stay with her, Mister Hicks, and in case of the worst and the need arises, do all that you can to make sure both of you greet the dawn, yes?"

He laid the revolver in the palm of the conductor's free hand.

"A word of advice, Mister Hicks. Aim for the torso. You're apt to be far too nervous for an accurate headshot."

Upon first regarding the pearl-handled Remington as if it were some alien artifact, the conductor tucked it into his belt and removed a silver pocket watch from his vest pocket.

"Ten minutes, Marshal. If you and your gun-hand aren't back in this car wearing the grin of the victorious, the lass and I will take our chances with the storm."

"Your choice, of course," Bain replied with obvious exasperation, "Rest assured I'll do all I can to prevent said risk."

Side-stepping up the narrow aisle to a low crunching as boot-heels met shattered glass, the marshal gestured for Dalton to let him pass in order to take point.

"So here it is, Mister Harrison," he proclaimed dourly with a prolonged glare into the next car. "As a citizen, I cannot ask you to join me into the next phase of whatever skirmish might lay ahead."

Dalton grinned despite every nerve ending he possessed lighting up like a blacksmith's anvil.

"Bain, anyone ever advise you to put away the peacemakers and pick up a grading manual?"

"All horse excrement aside," the marshal replied sternly, "I'd rather have you at my back than do this alone."

For a split-second, a single tick of the conductor's pocket watch, Dalton felt a tidal wave of relief wash over those coal-hot nerves, that is until his badly bloodshot eyes fell upon Miss Ruth and the madness, somehow unholy, reflected there.

"Oh, I'm with you, Marshal," he replied somewhat timidly and feeling as if he'd been gut-punched. "Just don't over-expect." The Colt hanging at his side suddenly felt as heavy as the blunt end of a forty-pound sledge.

"Just follow my lead but at least a full three steps behind. If an ambush is in their plans, I want us separated at least enough to not catch the same slug."

"Slug? You think they've armed themse…"

"Logic dictates they've graduated from knives to guns, what with disabling the two guards."

"Gradua…see that?" Dalton smiled, possibly the most forced gesture of his relatively brief lifespan. "Handing diplomas out already."

Flashing a playful wink as to officially end the rapport, the marshal planted a firm pat to the shorter man's before turning gracefully on a bootheel and stepping toward the exit.

Before following the lawman's lead, careful to maintain the afore-discussed three step distance, Dalton allowed himself a final glance at the pair left behind.

The conductor, stone-faced and slumped of shoulders, remained seated on the cot with the marshal's revolver laying casually across bent knees.

As for Miss Beverly Ruth, she of the south of the Mason-Dixon accent so pronounced it practically oozed honey, she stared straight ahead from her own cot, an unblinking daze accompanied by a frozen, tight-lipped smile, or grimace, that defined insanity.

In retrospect, Dalton deduced, he definitely made the right decision to accompany Bain, potentially fatal dangers be damned. Anything to put space between himself and the creepy Southern Belle's biblically dark, gloomy pronouncements and haunting eyes, as if her very soul had been extracted until only a hollow shell remained.

Just as the cab door secured behind him, the marshal having broken the threshold of the next car, he could have sworn he detected a maniacal giggle echo from over his left shoulder.

Heart pounding, palms slick with sweat despite the obvious chill, professional telegrapher turned emergency deputy Dalton Harrison moved forward on knees of rubber, silently praying that in whatever epilogue was written upon dawn's merciful arrival, he might avoid spewing forth a similarly abnormal cackle.

~ * ~

The Tombs

"Nary a sign of life or death," the Marshal whispered, reaching up to confiscate the car's lone source of illumination and, with one sweeping motion, able to verify said remark. Twenty rows of well-padded vinyl-covered seats, ten on each side, sat empty with no evidence left behind that anyone occupied them.

"I'd have appreciated a better choice of words, professor," Dalton cracked from a few steps behind, somewhat embarrassed but powerless to halt the shaking of his gun-hand. "Especially that last reference. Death's acquaintance is one I'd rather skip if you don't mind, as I highly doubt, we've stumbled onto *Paradise Lost*."

"A Milton reference? Well, color me *impressed,* Dalton. It seems your reading choices hint very little of your literary intellect."

The two men shared a knowing smile.

"Nary a hat, handbag or holster to be had," Bain continued, nearing the rear of the car with the Remington squarely on point. "We can assume this car was empty before any assault took place. Standard coach car, yes?"

The deputized telegrapher stood temporarily hypnotized; weirdly soothed by the whitish torrent descending from the dozen or so small, squared windows, the yellowed curtains pinned back to allow full visibility.

"Economy," Dalton verified, snapping to with a start and in the process nearly toppling into the nearest seat.

"So next up is?"

"Coach. Wider seats, increased leg room."

"After coach is presidential, yes?"

"Yep, First Class and then the caboose."

Sensing the other man's unease, Bain reached back with his free hand and flashed the okay sigh with thumb and forefinger.

"Steady as she goes, Dalton. Deep breaths and remember, not too close. Let's move on."

~ * ~

As with the previous cars, Coach was found deserted, dimly lit and deathly silent. Unlike economy, the seats were wide, built for two or possibly three depending on individual girth, and spaced for comfort. The car housed only five passengers on each side of the aisle with a single, spacious bay window on either side from which to sightsee. Posted near each seat was a flyer that offered assorted libations and snacks, for a nominal fee of course. At face value, it appeared that, like economy, the car had been unoccupied. It wasn't until Bain neared the final set of seats, lantern levitated gradually from one to another, that evidence arose to the contrary.

"Got a satchel here, overturned with some of the contents spilled," he announced, the hoarse whisper almost drowned out by the battering winds. "Handkerchiefs, hair pins, dainty gloves, the like. A female passenger, no doubt."

"Anything else? What about the opposite seat?" Dalton asked, just loud enough to be heard while mindful of keeping the three to four-foot distance between them.

Swinging the light from left to right, but not before giving the exit to the next car a brief but intense glance, the Marshal studied this newest find with a slight tilt of the head before dropping to one knee and allowing the lantern to hover directly over it.

Though a large part of him didn't *want* to know, Dalton understood he'd come too far not to see the mystery to its inevitable conclusion. As tugging on his beard had emerged as the newest nervous tick of choice, he gave it a stout tug. He'd momentarily considered commandeering the car's surviving lantern before imaging the ordeal of stumbling around in the dark on his way back.

"What is it, Marshal?"

"At first I thought it was someone's teeth. Upon closer inspection, what we're looking at is an upper plate of false teeth, male by the size of the choppers."

"False tee…how can you be sure they're not real?"

"Well, the gold wire protruding from each end was my first and most decisive clue. Also present are one pair of spectacles, one arm severely bent back with the right lens badly cracked."

"What does it mean, you think?"

"I'd say while its hardly proof of a scuffle, why would someone leave their chewers lying randomly about?"

"No blood stains? No splatters?"

"Bone dry."

The Marshal stood and faced the exit, jutting his head forward with the lantern held head high.

"Presidential car appears gloomy as a gopher hole as well. Pitch black."

Peering over his left shoulder for at least the tenth time since entering the coach, Dalton felt both palpable relief and stark dread at the tranquil murk found there, the former as retreat might become a definite possibility, the latter for the two cars still yet to peruse.

"Marshal, you think the conductor and Miss Ruth are really apt to chance the…this blizzard?"

Bain paused before pushing through the exit with the flat of a size twelve boot-heel.

"Dalton, if I were the type to wager, I'd bet the farm that they already have."

"Couldn't blame 'em really. I'm one more empty tomb away from hopping off myself."

Half-stepping past the last set of seats, Dalton gave the random objects laying atop each only a perfunctory glance, his fear, however irrational, being that the satchel and false teeth would have somehow switched places or worse, wouldn't be there at all. It wasn't going to take much to fully shatter his already hairline-fractured nerves.

Upon entry to the presidential suite and the initial impression of same, the hairline crack widened to a fully realized chasm.

~ * ~

Since putting up stakes in the great Northwest a decade past, Dalton often heard some of the elder natives speak of *snow-blindness* but had yet to experience the condition despite witnessing untold blizzards much like the one presently battering the Bighorn without mercy.

He'd paid little attention to the curtains that hung lengthwise from the inner car entrance, in retrospect an undeniably clever chess-move instigated to greater enhance the shock value waiting inside, stumbling in and almost instantly forced to bury his face in the crook of a raised elbow. Regardless, a split-second of wide-eyed exposure was found to be the equivalent of staring into a blazing noonday sun, especially when compared to the murk they'd grown accustomed to since departing the telegraph shack.

"Sorry I didn't have time to warn you," he heard the Marshal say in full deep-bass baritone, "Fortunately it's just temporary. When you do reopen them, do it very, very slowly."

"Wh-what the h-hell, Marshal?" Dalton stammered, gradually dropping the arm and squinting through tight slits, all the while groping for a handhold.

"Well, the mystery of the missing lanterns is solved, if nothing else."

Bain stood at the center of the car with arms outspread like a carnival barker posed at center ring. As the presidential suite offered everything in pairs, from spacious recliners to overhead sleeping bins and connecting dining tables for in-service, it seemed only fitting that each was adorned with two lanterns, one a regulation brass and copper type and the other the infinitely more powerful signal light. Just one of the latter blazing away in such a confined space would've sufficed to burn the orbs, much less a trio. Floor-length red lace curtains had been secured to enhance the effect as well as a dark blue blanket draped over the exit door for similar impact. A faint, heady scent lingered, though impossible to define, though Dalton was instantly reminded of a recently gutted deer.

"It appears we've ambled into a trap of sorts, set to blind us and thus gain a strategic advantage. Queer thing is…" Bain paused to turn on a bootheel, a graceful spin that belied the man's size and left him facing his deputized ally with a wide, toothsome and wholly unstable grin "…the enemy has yet to take benefit and thus flittered away a prime opportunity."

Staggering forth and almost directly into his confederate, Dalton's eyes had only begun to adjust, his gun-hand whipping back and forth as to ward off evil spirits.

"Empty?"

"If not, our mystery enemy has gained the power of invisibility in the tradition of H.G. blasted Wells.

"Y-you okay, Mar…" Dalton began, the flat of Bain's gloved hand halting his forward progress.

"Stay back, Dalton," he commanded sternly, leaning in until Dalton could feel his chilled breath, Bain's boisterous bellowing dropping several octaves nearly to mumble status, "At this point I'm as vexed as I am frustrated with this damnable game. I thought perhaps if we'd grown impatient as well, they'd define this as weakness and show themselves. Bear with me on this. Keep on high guard and know that as a young man, I did fancy the dramatic stage, so as unstable as I may sound, its merely an act to draw them out."

Shrugging, Dalton backed away a full two steps.

"Um, y-yeah well, you could've fooled me."

With that, Bain spun around and, blinking madly, resumed a gradual inspection of the car with his own lantern hanging loosely at one side, obviously having lost its usefulness in the surrounding luster and the Remington's sweeping motion following the track of his eyes.

"Cowards lurking in the dark, Deputy Harrison, unwilling to face a threat they cannot take by surprise with pallor tricks. This is our prey, easily recognized by their bright, yellow-streaked spines. I'd wager a white flag will soon wave and tears of surren…"

Upon peeking into the first of the sleeping bins, Bain executed a comical doubletake, visibly stiffened and stepped back, the tip of his Stetson narrowly avoiding impact with the bin directly opposite.

"What's is…what's wrong?" Dalton inquired, freezing in his tracks with the Colt filling his right palm growing heavier by the second.

Twisting around as if expecting impending assault, Bain stood sideways and dead center within the narrow aisle, the newest discovery as unpleasant as the first from the pained expression creasing his normally apathetic mug.

"Well, so much for lack of crime scene evidence," he said flatly, the Remington dropping limply to his side, his shoulders plainly slumping. "Upon face value, this certainly validates our two witnesses' version of events."

While Dalton's statuesque stance remained unchanged, save allowing his own revolver to dip from shoulder level to waist, Bain returned focus on the first bin, reaching into its interior as if to retrieve some unseen object to verify his previous statement. It wasn't until he withdrew the same gloved hand, a dark red stain marking each fingertip, that the lawman turned to his volunteer deputy and spoke as if addressing a small, frightened child.

"You might as well step up for an eyeful, Dalton. The danger, at least for these specific sources, has most certainly passed."

Legs as heavy as anvils and feet forged of hardened clay, Dalton did just that, the Marshal alternating somber glances from one bin to the other.

"It was required I reposition the note for reading purposes, and even then, combining the chicken-scratch handwriting and thick streaking..." Bain expounded, pausing to sidestep several feet down the aisle to allow his charge full visual access, "...it's obvious the author is in desperate need of additional schooling."

Peering cautiously up and into the sleeping bin to his left—also the Marshal's initial pick—there came a split-second where the communication lines from Dalton's eyes to his brain disconnected, thus disallowing a proper definition of the horrors on display. Once that faithful, and undeniably soothing moment passed, he felt his leaden legs transform to the most pliable of rubber.

"I-is tha...isn't that...th-they the ones...the two that the conductor and Miss Beth...Beverly..."

"Not my first suicide note, by any means," Bain interrupted, mercifully halting any further babbling from his wide-eyed partner, "but certainly the most bizarre."

Dalton's voice cracked as if on the verge of an uncontrollable giggling jag while unable to pull his bloodshot, rapidly blinking orbs from the body.

"Sui...you seriously think she did *t-that* to herself?"

"Of course not," the lawman replied, calmly and without offense at the assumption, nodding towards the opposite bin, "From the obvious clues, I'd say those jagged scribbles belong to that one."

Still reeling from the shock of the first corpse on display, Dalton's already battered senses endured yet another gut-punch with the reveal of the second.

"Classic murder-suicide," he heard Bain resume, unaware that his mouth hung askew like a shutter with a shattered hinge, his knees threatening to buckle.

"Those cots must be sewn from sponge from all they've soaked in.

I'd truly hate to be the porter tasked to syphon that unholy me..."

Though the Marshal's shockingly tedious rant continued, Dalton found he was no longer willing or able to decipher the meaning, eyes bouncing spasmodically from one carnage-filled painting to the next and back again.

The woman, perhaps not yet out of her twenties, lay on her right side, a carving knife with the words *'Old Hickory'* burned into the walnut handle buried nearly to the hilt through gapped lips, the edges of the unseen blade having sliced through flayed flesh on its way to penetrating the back of her throat. Petite in size with short brunette locks, her arms remained folded in place across her bosom despite the awkward positioning of the torso.

Amid a lengthy checklist of horrid details, he would never be able to unsee, the slender neck and chest predictably drenched in her own leakage, the butchered mouth and nose unnaturally upturned from the blade handle's intrusion, it was her left eye, frozen agape and somehow aware, that collected the top prize without serious competition.

As for the equally dead male on display, salt-and-pepper facial stubble and graying locks placing his age at approximately several decades older than his supposedly partner-in-crime turned willing victim, lay flat on his back, knees bent in order to accommodate his considerable height. The pillow and cot underneath propping his head was saturated blackish/red from the grotesquely wide vertical smile he'd apparently carved into the center of his own neck, flayed with such surgical precision to clearly display the gleaming white of the thyroid cartilage. While the man's left arm remained tucked from sight, his right rested atop his upper abdomen, fingers of the accompanying hand wrapped loosely around the handle of a straight razor with the bloodstained blade pointing directly towards the wound site it had so effectively inflicted.

As for the note, flyer-sized and vastly similar to the wanted posters Dalton often perused at postmaster stations, it hung just beneath the gaping wound of the woman's fileted lower lip, having been stuck there like a tack nailed to a post. Despite the vast discharge spattered onto its bent edges, the message conveyed there was clear and concise. Much like the body it utilized as a human message board, Dalton knew the words would forever be branded into his mind, no matter how long or hard he prayed to forget:

We done so wrong here
So very wrong
Forgive us these rash actions
We could not resist
Take us back into that darkest of places
Bind us and seal us away
Where we see no one to harm

"Gawd alm-mighty, what does that even mean?" Dalton managed, stumbling down the aisle and swallowing hard in the aftermath as if on the cusp of gagging, his complexion noticeably pasty even in the hard lighting.

Bain continued to study each corpse while holstering the Remington before turning to his shell-shocked deputy, now leaning against the back of one of the recliners for support.

"Only a hopelessly insane mind might correctly speculate. Listen Dalton, if you want to return to coach, I'll understand. I can take it from here. I just want to check the caboose in case the remaining passengers were stashed there for safekeeping. I...hope I'm wrong, but any discoveries made there might well involve more of the same type of atrocities."

"No, no, just give me minute. I...I'm with you. It's just that, well, it isn't every day I lay eyes on..." he paused, blinking rapidly while stroking his beard, "...the recently expired. Especially when said expiration is of the extreme trauma type."

"Completely natural, I can assure you. Take a short sabbatical then. With the potential hazard to our own mortality no longer a factor, there's really no hurry other than tally up the collateral damage."

The Marshal kneeled to study the space between each bunk, using a gloved hand to shield his eyes from the overabundance of surrounding illumination.

"Anyway, I highly doubt we'll find anything of relevance in the caboose. However, those two initiated their escape and subsequent assault on their guards, the conductor and his crew and finally the passengers, the goal, at least initially, was to leave the least amount of evidence possible onboard. More than likely forced the guards and passengers off the train, either before or after inflicting near-fatal wounds."

Following a final, deep inhale and succeeding exhale—executed with great stealth—Dalton pushed himself away from the recliner and, retrieving his holstered Colt, strode purposely back up the aisle, pausing a few short steps from where Bain crouched.

"Ready when you are. Find something down there?" he asked as nonchalantly as possible considering his nerves were so severely frazzled that he felt one minor shock away from collapsing in a squirming heap. To this effect, he avoided even a passing glance at the butchered bodies to his left and right, instead locking his gaze straight down the narrow aisle is if peering into a narrow, albeit brightly lit, tunnel.

"Just pondering."

"Ponder…"

"Bizarre seems to be the byword for this entire situation, Dalton. Why is it, you think, there are only a few, pea-sized droplets of blood beneath the female's bunk and nary a one under her male counterparts?"

Pale lips quivering, Dalton had no answer but was secretly on the verge of screeching aloud just to be able to move from the vicinity of the sleeping bins and most notably the cargo stashed within.

"Logically speaking, it would mean she willingly entered the bin and allowed her own murder and brutal placement of the suicide note, followed by the man entering his own bunk to end the proceedings. No signs of any struggle on her part and as for him, I've never seen such, well, proficiency with a self-inflicted wound."

Adam's apple bobbing wildly, Dalton's mukluks danced a jittery jig born of severe anxiety, his voice cracking with adolescent eagerness no matter the effort to reel it in.

"Y-yeah, well, yeah, she was…felt just as guilty and saw…viewed death as a…her punishment. I've read stories like th…to that effect. Ma-maybe he was a sawbones by profession. That would explain the, well, neatness, right?"

"Indeed. Either a surgeon or professional butcher. Nothing else makes sense," Bain resumed stoically. "If he had killed her elsewhere and dragged her here, there would be a veritable slug-trail of leakage."

Bain arose with a resounding groan and having refilled each hand with lantern and revolver, respectively, strode with painstaking ease toward the car's exit. The lone entry/exit point that was windowless and thus allowed no preview of the caboose.

"Allow me ample space, Dalton, if you please. Remain inside the gangway until you hear me call out," he instructed calmly, head slightly bowed as if studying the thickly carpeted aisle.

"Will do," Dalton replied only after a loud throat-clearing, struggling to minimize an inexplicable, almost overwhelming sense of apprehension, one that should've logically waned in the wake of finding their potential attackers permanently removed as a viable threat.

"Carpet holds no obvious blood stains," Bain concluded while reaching for the door handle, "I'll venture that's a positive."

"Marsh…" Dalton began, stopping short from finishing the request in lieu of being considered more worthless than he'd felt at that very moment, the idea of telling a seasoned lawman to '*be cautious*' idiotic enough, but especially ludicrous considering the source of said advice.

He watched Bain vanish into the relative darkness, a title easily earned considering the blinding radiance of the previous space, and soon found himself standing at the center of the gangway, the winds pounding either side of the contracted space with equal fierceness.

The caboose entrance, void of casements, but instead a solid wood entryway, served as a suitably dark, cold, impersonal blockade; One that fit Dalton's increasingly paranoid state of mind to a tee.

At the sudden screaming of his name, Bain's deep baritone like the piercing blast of a foghorn, Dalton nearly toppled back as if physically shoved and was forced to wildly windmill both arms to regain balance.

Yanking the caboose entrance open with his free hand, he practically dived inside with the Colt holding point.

~ * ~

End of the Line

As the caboose interior was roughly a tenth as lit as the previous car and only a shade brighter than the gangway, it took Dalton's eyes a full five ticks to adjust once he'd righted his stance somewhat from the shambling entrance.

"B-Bain, wha-what?" he stuttered as shock and revulsion gradually transformed to a begrudging acceptance.

A man hung from separate strands of coiled rope that wound so tightly around each ankle his naked feet held a dark purple tint.

"Quick Dalton, give me your belt, the Marshal was saying, gloved hand extended toward him palms up, a glove he recalled as once a shade of light brown transformed to a red so dark it hinted black.

"Your belt man, *NOW*,"

Even as he did so, his movements mechanical, instinctual, Dalton's focus never shifted. Much like the murder-suicide just a car back, there was no looking away no matter how loud the inner voice of reason begged and pleaded for him to do so.

Bain was in the process of cutting through the second of two binds holding the figure airborne via a single strand of steel rebar, sawing away with such frenzy that the blade of his Bowie was but a shiny, silver blur.

The final bind snapped like the cracking of a whipcord, the freed subject collapsing limply into the Marshal's waiting grip. It wasn't until Bain laid the mystery man flat on his back that Dalton spied a second body tucked into a far corner, naked legs splayed out from a slouched torso, the head cocked dramatically to the right.

"Wh-who are they? Is he breathing?"

Bain, having jerked the leather belt from Dalton's open palm, began coiling its length around the man's left forearm, tying it off at the edge of a bloody stump where a hand once occupied.

"Bain, is he alive?"

"Would I be…wasting my time corking his wounds if he…were not?" the Marshal growled, utilizing a jagged section of plank to complete the homemade tourniquet.

Shuffling past the crouched lawman, Dalton felt he no longer commanded his own limbs but levitated under the command of some unseen puppet-master.

"Is he one of the guards?" he inquired of Bain's patient while strolling over to get a better look at mystery guest number two. He halted in mid-step while still a half-dozen feet away, gag reflex on red alert from a putrid, coppery stench emanating from the source, who sat in a wide, circular pool of his own fluids. Though the man's face, perhaps mercifully, remained cloaked in shadow, he'd been stripped of all but his boxer shorts, his ample midsection gutted horizontally from breastbone to bellybutton. Backing with his face tucked tightly into the crock of an elbow, Dalton's took grim mental note not only of the wound itself, but the curled, footlong portion of intestine hanging from its center like a giant, birthing maggot.

"Forget that one," the marshal spat gruffly. "I could use some help here. See if you can find something we can use for bandages."

Housing a lengthy hardwood pew that ran the length of the car, from which cardboard boxes and burlap sacks were haphazardly piled, a pair of built-in wooden cabinets, a desk overflowing with manuals, folders, assorted forms and invoices, it appeared the car was primarily used as a makeshift office of sorts.

Limiting his search to the right side of the car, strategically distancing himself from the discarded corpse on the left, Dalton located a pair of slightly ragged but otherwise unsoiled long johns hanging from an upturned broom handle.

By the time he scrambled back over and handed them to Bain, who immediately began using the Bowie to carve them into lengthy strips, Dalton discontinued the attempt at stifling the smell, which wafted through the car like a rotted carcass roasting on a spit.

The Marshal's patient, this one peeled down to his birthday suit, was gasping desperately for breath, like a catfish tossed onto a creekbank. Short in stature and porky of build, the man's age was impossible to gauge considering the distorted facial features, though if pushed Dalton would've guessed late-thirties to mid-forties. His left cheek looked to have been flayed open in the same manner as the dead man's abdomen, his left hand sliced cleanly at the wrist and among the missing, all of which left little to the imagination in terms of a suspect or suspects, the obvious answer currently occupying matching sleeping bins in the presidential car.

Bain worked with admirable quickness and precision in tying off and bandaging the stump and had just begun to coil a lengthy portion about the slumping man's head and chin in an attempt to at least cover the deep slash at his cheek when the man managed to spit out a brief and mostly comprehensible line of dialogue.

"W-wh-where's B-Bax…Baxter? H-help…B-Baxter f-first…ya h-hear? He-help B-Ba-Baxter."

"Just take it easy now. It's gonna be alright," Bain managed to reply while struggling to still the man's suddenly vigorous movements. "Dalton, help me hold him down so I can finish tying this off."

Dropping to a knee, Dalton gripped the man's pudgy, blood-slickened shoulders, all the while forced to turn his head away from the vile scent spewing forth.

"Wa-was my f-fault…a-all mine. B-Baxter told me s-so many times…not t-to fall for th-their va-veggie a-act. She…t-that de-demon b-bitch is…she's triple j-jointed or s-some sh-shit…to sl-slip those r-restraints."

As Bain tied off the makeshift bandage at the tip of the man's scalp, both he and Dalton glanced briefly over at the dead man in the corner with the same conclusion: Baxter.

"Hey, it's okay. Baxter's fine. We're going to get you both some help," Bain said as convincingly as was possible amid the aura of certain death.

Unable to contain his curiosity, Dalton forced himself to turn and meet the mutilated stranger's wild, bug-eyed gaze.

"You and Baxter, you were guarding the prisoners? The man and woman?"

Instead of scolding the telegrapher, Bain remained neutral, awaiting the answer with equal interest.

"Y-yeah, b-but Jake…t-that's Ja-Jake…Baxter, h-he's the senior…officer. Knows…his onions, oh-oh-old Jake. M-my fault. Th-they don't c-call me Dumb-b-bell Dra-Drake for…n-nothing. N-not ready for transport…duty. J-Jake tried to ta-tell 'em. Ne-never saw…anybody s-slip that re-restraint like she…d-done."

In sudden, horrific realization, the man reached up to grip Bain's left wrist with surprising vigor, eyes bugging and frothy lips quivering.

"W-wh-where is she…are th-they? Damn it, ha-have d-did

you…s-see the…"

"Relax, Drake, they're down for good. No more worries," Bain consoled while gently removing the man's ghost-pale, coiled fingers from his arm.

As the man visually slumped from the news, Dalton scooted strategically over to block any potential glances toward his deceased cohort.

"Bo-both of 'em?"

"Yes sir, got 'em both."

The man visibly deflated.

"Thank god."

"Drake, where are the rest of the passengers?" Bain inquired softly while adding an extra strip to the stump, the crude tourniquet effective only to a certain degree.

Breathing a bit easier, the man lay back with his eyes closed but, forebodingly, spoke through constantly chattering teeth, as if under the throngs of some great inner chill that had little to do with the interior temperature.

"Manifest o-only showed f-five or six when we…left…Cheyanne. All b-but one…y-yeah, all but t-the lass…got off in…La-Laramie d-due to…the incoming Bli-Blizzard."

"I see," Bain replied, issuing with a simple nod a silent order for Dalton to take over close watch of the injured man, before standing and stepping over to the aged desk and pawing through the spattering of paperwork piled there.

"So just one paying customer, your partner and yourself, the conductor and a trainman, I presume?"

"Y-yeah, and t-the Eagle-eye, um, engineer. Rollins I th-think…was his name. Gr-grumpy…old codger b-but k-knew h-his onions about…this here Iron h-horse. Neither h-he nor the grab-grabber…were too thrilled to h-have us…aboard, much l-less taking up space here in h-his…doghouse. Rollins had this…longsword h-he saved…since his calvary d-days. Devil bitch…had sn-snatched it off t-the wall in a b-blink."

Dalton and Bain shared a knowing glance, the conductor's earlier mention of the sword duly verified.

"H-have you…seen h-him? The…conductor, I m-mean?"

As Bain had apparently become lost in his search and failed to reply, Dalton reluctantly took the reins.

"Yes. Yes, we did, in fact. Both he and the female passenger are on board. Spoke to them just moments ago. The conductor is steering us to Rock Springs to find a sawbones to fix you up."

A smile, made somewhat hideous by the red-stained teeth it revealed, flashed over the man's ashen features.

"Guess he m-must be…talking w-with a la-lisp."

"Sir?"

"Without his…fa-falsies, I mean. M-maybe he was…able to retrieve 'em, but th-they'd yanked 'em ri-right outta his maw 'fore he ma-managed to give 'em…th-the slip. Fu-funny as hell under…different circumstances."

Dalton's own grin froze in mid-beam, his left eye cocking inquisitively.

"Fal…you mean the conductor wore dent…"

His frazzled thoughts had only begun to piece together a vaguely patterned puzzle when the Marshal's croaking baritone effectively obliterated all coherent train of thought.

Gripping a brown-tinted flyer with one hand as the other slowly tilted back the bill of his Stetson, Bain's squint was so severe that it appeared he was attempting to read the content through his eyelids. As with two of the three previous cars, a single lantern supplied illumination, ease of interpretation depending heavily on paper-color and size and tint of lettering.

"Come here please. I require confirmation."

"But, Drake…" Dalton replied, gesturing towards their prone patient.

"He seems to be sedate enough now. Please, Dalton."

They soon stood side-by-side, Dalton a half-head shorter than the lofty lawman, who displayed the crinkled flyer without surrendering it.

"Humor me please, by reading from top to bottom, beginning at the header."

Dalton did so, though cautious to keep the volume low as not to reignite panic in their patient.

Upon completion, the two men locked eyes, the Marshal's expression as stony and grim as Dalton's was comically perplexed.

"Richard Harmon, Verta Bueley. Each considered extremely unstable and dangerous. Transport to Napa Mental Hospital, Napa Valley, California. So, they weren't prisoners but...patients?"

"Order seems plain enough. Signed and stamped all officially," Bain answered, leaning forward to peek past Dalton towards Drake, "Speaking of official, let's see if we can get some official confirmation from someone in the know."

They crouched on opposite sides next to Drake, who looked to have dozed off in their absence.

"Drake? Mis...Deputy Drake, is that the correct title?"

Startlingly, Drake's response was instantaneous, though his eyes remained shut, his breathing appeared steady.

"Ac-actually it'd be De-Detention Offcifer...Of-Officer. Tho-though we're oft...re-referred to onsite...as ta-turnkeys."

"Fine. So, Drake, you and Officer Baxter were tasked to transport those two to a California mental hospital?"

"Y-yeah, th-that's right. A-all the way from Je-Jefferson City."

"A mental hospital in Jefferson City?"

Drake shook his head in mild defiance, eyelids parting just slightly.

"N-no sir. Missouri St-State Prison. Th-those two...peaches of inhu-humanity were...deemed to b-be crim-criminals of...insanity. Th-that means not only...cra-crazy as bedbugs but w-with an unnatural...yearning to k-kill. I'll be...the first to say..." he paused, a random giggle soon mutating into a choking sob and back again, "...th-the pen d-doc's sure n-nailed that particular...d-diagnosis. Ain't that...r-right, Jake? J-Jake?"

"Um, he's fast asleep," Dalton managed to adlib, again taking up a blocking position between the live man and the dead one, "I'm sure he'd agree wholeheartedly."

Bain, seemingly ignoring the exchange, sidestepped over and, leaning down, whispered into Dalton's right ear while handing him the lantern, the flyer clenched in his left as he filled his right with the

Remington.

"Listen, I've got an itch that simply cannot go unscratched. Stay here and guard Drake and do it with that Colt cocked and ready, just in case the hunch pans out."

"Hunch?" Dalton barked, instantly lowering his tone upon proceeding, "Hang on just a damn minute, you're leaving me *alone* with…with," he jerked a thumb in Drake's direction, "…this?"

Undaunted, the marshal fired a final salvo before stepping around his peeved deputy and towards the exit leading back into the Presidential suite.

"Well, we can't very well leave him alone now, can we?"

"Damn it, Bain, how long you gonna be?"

Dalton's agitated query, bleated at full volume, was fated to go unanswered, the lawman vanishing into the gangway with his duster flowing like a showman's cape.

"H-hey, mister, I forgot to ask, you the la-law?"

"Um, yeah, yes sir. Marshal Bain and his trusty gun-hand, Deputy Harrison, at your service. You just lay back and rest as best you can, hear? There's a doctor waiting for you in Rock Springs."

"B-but, we ain't moving, are we?"

It struck Dalton as queer that the severely injured man was coherent enough to notice this, though through ample practice he was becoming quite apt at thinking on his feet.

"Oh, it's just a quick stop at the telegrapher's shack to drop off the patients to the proper authorities. We'll be back on schedule in no time."

"G-got'cha. Yeah, I'm a-assuming I probably could use a st-stich or two at that."

Dropping down to a low crouch, the Colt resting across bent knees, Dalton peered down at Drake's stump and was pleasantly surprised at the lack of blood smearing Bain's emergency bandage, a testament to the makeshift tourniquet's effectiveness.

"Just a couple. You're gonna be fine, officer. Good as new in no time."

"Ya he-hear…that Jake?" the man warbled, eyes flittering wildly as he drifted in and out of consciousness, "Weee g-gon…gonna b-be g-goo…as…g-god…gold."

It was while quietly studying the brutalized prison officer drifting in and out of coherence, that Dalton first noticed the relative silence, or moreover the lack of battering of the car walls. Lifting the lantern eye-level and gazing up and out the nearest window, one of only two the car provided other than the Cupola, it became obvious that the ferocious winds subsided to no more than a stiff breeze, though the snowfall continued at a fairly consistent clip.

Within what was almost a deafening silence when compared to the constant ruckus of earlier, the echo of distant gunfire was crisp and clear. Two distinct shots fired, one directly after the other, and though Dalton Harrison was far from claiming expert status in terms of ballistics, he'd witnessed enough pistol shooting to recognize the origin.

"Oh s-shit," he murmured, standing stiffly and oblivious to the fact he'd pointed the Colt directly at his slumbering patient's forehead.

Unaware he was holding his breath until a burning at his chest sounded the alarm, he awaited succeeding shots that never materialized. His mind scrambling for a clear path of action, a hopeful thought briefly shattered the barricade of pessimism, in that the Marshal, a fine lawman and thus most likely a deadeye shot—hadn't required more than two bullets to settle whatever conflict had arisen.

"Yeah, that's right. Man knows his craft."

He'd taken a single step toward the exit before halting, an already tattered brainpan assaulted by a Mulligan's Stew of questions with one leading the pack by a mountain mile.

Who specifically had been the target of Bain's federally approved gunfire? Was there *something* or someone they missed on that arduous trek from conductor's car to Caboose? Had someone new hopped aboard behind them? What of Hicks or Ruth? Had the conductor fired the fateful shots from the borrowed Remington and if so, what part had Bains played? What if each fired but once? What exactly did this entail within the narrative?

"Depu…d-deputy?" he heard Drake stutter, mercifully breaking his self-trance.

Stepping back toward the prone man and kneeling yet again, he noticed Drake's position had changed subtly, with his torso and neck repositioned slightly to the right.

"Yes sir? I'm here."

"Looks l-like…they but-butchered….J-Jake like a…prize h-hog…at the c-co-county f-fair."

Unable to respond with anything remotely comforting in the wake of being caught in such a blatant fib, Dalton instead reached down and applied a gentle squeeze to the man's blood-smeared shoulder.

In return, Drake, first name unknown, laid his remaining hand atop Dalton's, his tone spookily rational for just long enough to complete the sentence.

"I…it's o-okay. R-really. I 'ppreciate th-the…effort. L-listen, I'll…be all ri-right here. You just…go check o-on the sheri…the Marshal. He…might need s-some backup 'bout now or…is running out of time for backup to matter. Just…go."

Until that moment in his relatively brief lifespan, thirty-three winters and counting, Dalton had never witnessed such purely defined heroism up close and personal.

Again, he found no reply worthy but instead executed a firm nod and light tap to the man's bared chest before rising and turning back to the exit with the Colt clenched in a veritable death grip. Moments later, he stood in the gangway with lantern in hand, the Colt temporarily holstered as fingers clenched the entrance back into the Presidential suite, a space he'd hoped to skip revisiting for obvious reasons. The blinding glow, the cold, stiffening bodies, the suicide note and perhaps most terrifying of all, an overwhelming sense that all was not what it appeared.

With knees as wobbly as his present deportment, he jerked open the door and lunged inside in one surprisingly fluid motion, only to find the oppressing light of earlier doused in favor of a murk so thick it was like walking directly into a thundercloud.

~ * ~

"Bain? Marshal?" he whispered, feeling as foolish in the aftermath as the duckwalk he'd initiated upon entry, both knees popping like splintered kindling with each sprawling advance.

It wasn't until he'd felt something moist strike his left cheek that he lifted the lantern airborne to see the sleeping bin previously containing the dead woman directly overhead.

"Awww, ssssheeeet," he groaned, leaning into the center of the aisle upon feeling an additional drop strike his forehead.

Wiping both areas with the back of one gloved hand, he avoided glancing at the smear left there, most likely a sickly shade of dark maroon, and instead squinted the remaining length of the car via severely limited illumination provided by two lamps, one at the front of the car and the other at the opposite end and both apparently set on their lowest possible setting.

"Marshal? Conductor Hicks?" he bellowed at full volume, with the Colt aimed dead-center at the darkened entrance from Coach.

Silence was soon followed by the sound of muffled footsteps, though maddeningly impossible to determine from which direction they originated.

"Marshal?" he repeated, gradually rising to a crouch, the Colt once more gaining untold pounds in his suddenly shaky grip.

The figure darted from the gloom, shambling forth like a wounded animal on the verge of collapse.

Holding the lantern out in front like a coalminer wandering the blackest of tunnels, Dalton's pummeled psyche was introduced to the next, much-dreaded shock to the system.

"C-c-con…duc….t—t-tor…" the lumbering horror stuttered, stumbling to a clumsy halt mere steps away from chest-bumping Dalton, who had neither the energy nor sharpness of mind to elude a possible impact.

"Ba-Bain? Wh-what th…m-my god…" he finally managed, dropping the lantern to land with a stifled thump next to his left mukluk, groping out towards the marshal with the freed hand.

His head lolling about like a ball-bearing with a loose fitting, Marshal Daniel Bain stood on wobbly, bended knees, sporting a dual handicap that it took Dalton a full ten seconds to first identify and then begrudgingly accept.

The man no longer possessed his arms.

"D-da…ta…b-be…i-in…c-c-ch…b-be…d-dah," he continued to babble, lower lip coated in frothy spittle, the sawed-off stump of his left arm wriggling as if the missing limb still existed, and the detached hand was attempting to point.

Dalton lunged forward as to provide support just as the marshal collapsed onto his back like a toppled oak.

Dragging the lantern along as he crawled toward the fallen lawman, Dalton's nostrils were struck by the now familiar scent of freshly spilled blood.

"J-just lay st-still, Daniel," he whispered softly, oblivious of the warm tears building at the corners of each eye, gun-hand tremoring so badly the firearm nearly flipped from his grip, the other groping helplessly to find a purpose.

"G-g-ga….slee…slee….b-b-be…." Bain spat incoherently, eyes having spun upward to reveal only the whites, the bloody stumps spasming like the flapping fins of a beached fish.

It was mere seconds before the next mystery guest's dramatic arrival, that Dalton was able to view the marshal's wounds beneath the lantern's weaving glow.

Each appendage had been sliced off with shocking preciseness, a double amputee executed with surgical expertise and by the sharpest of carving instruments. *A mad doctor*, Dalton thought crazily just as a shadowy figure dashed forth, gesturing and shouting as if being pursued by a similarly unstable and potentially deadly villain.

"Deputy! Gain cover! He…th-they're s r-right behind me!" Conductor Hicks shouted, pointing the borrowed Remington behind him as he ran forward, the gun's incessant clicking of empty chambers barely audible over his shrill ranting.

Lunging back and nearly toppling over, Dalton did as he was instructed; duckwalking behind one of the leather recliners just as the conductor leapt the marshal's spasming frame and slid behind the couch on the opposite side.

"Damn it," Hicks growled, pointing and clicking several more times before flipping the revolver over and checking its cylinder, then regarding it as if it were somehow to blame, "Wh-why in the hell would someone even bother to only load a single blessed bullet?"

Dalton held his own peacemaker in both hands, the left serving to quell the constant tremors of the right, the query he finally managed to spit between labored gasps no more comprehensible than an infant's random babbling.

"Wh-who? Wha-whe-the-they?"

Through the hazy gloom he alternated glances from the squirming, bellowing Hicks and Dan Bain, whose crumpled form had ceased all visible movement.

"Hot damn, a Colt," he heard Hicks exclaim excitedly across the aisle, though unwilling to peel his gaze from the darkened entranceway. "Fired a peacekeeper just like that one at many a redskin during my calvary days."

As the peripheral of his left eye caught the man scoot across the aisle toward him, Dalton also caught a stout whiff of the conductor's scent. A heady aroma that included cordite, recent blood spillage and various body odors.

"Say deputy, nothing personal but I'd, well, feel a whole better about our chances of survival if you let me handle that six-shooter."

Before he could drudge up even the feeblest of protests, Dalton felt the weapon being pulled from his grip with a gentle firmness.

"Nothing to be ashamed of, deputy. I may appear less than fierce in my present state, but in my prime I was a certified dead-dye Dick."

Allowing the conductor to take point at the edge of the recliner, Dalton slouched into the near wall. Utterly drained, he nonetheless determined that the feeling of utter uselessness he felt wasn't nearly as severe as the icy spear of stark fear digging a crater into his gut.

"T-the mar-marshal...wh-who did...that to...?"

"Oh my, the poor *poor* sheriff," Hicks replied, at first somber of tone with head bowed but increasingly wide-eyed, like an excited schoolboy reciting his first visit to a county fair's target shoot. "Never saw it coming, at least not that first sweeping blow. *Amazing* he was able to fire off a shot, and with his left hand no less. Imagine..." he continued, no longer spying the entrance but staring directly at Dalton and practically salivating, "…having your gun-hand sliced off as clean as a pig's snout 'neath a butcher's cleaver but still possessing the internal grit to bend down and not just pull that thumb-buster from your own detached hand but then get off a clear shot to boot. Hoo-boy, but if a man's about to breathe his last, he might as well go out firing, right?"

Pushing himself up, the conductor stood stiffly and inexplicably fired off a rapid series of exaggerated military salutes in the direction of Daniel Bain's motionless frame.

"I hereby salute ya, Sheriff Bart. Ya might've fallen, but ya fell like a man," he groaned, shoulders visibly slumping and head bowing, the remainder of his dialogue peppered with wet, child-like giggles. "An armless, circus *freak* of a man, waddling about like a headless goose, but a man nonetheless."

"C-conductor, Hicks, get down," Dalton spat while reaching with his free hand, the other still clutching the lantern, its dim glow barely a glimmer, toward the other man, whose baggy blue uniform pants appeared to be falling away.

To this, the other man turned on a heel, arms spread as wide as a carnival barker wooing a crowd of potential pigeons.

"For what reason, deputy? You jumpin' at shadows, boy. It's downright embarrassing. Try to show at least an ounce of the grit your partner there possessed, will ya?"

Gripping the man by his jacket-sleeve, this too overly flappy as it hung well past his knuckles, Dalton's tone flowed with equal measures of desperation and anger.

"Duck down, y-you idiot! For cripes sake, I'm *not* a deputy!"

"Not a lawman?" Hicks bit, jerking his free hand away and dropping into a semi-crouch.

Reeling back upon losing his grip, Dalton backed to the wall while keeping close watch on the entrance.

"Telegrapher by trade, recruited by Bai…by the Marshal in his search for a man named Bradley, um, *Bradshaw*, a conman supposedly riding this locomotive."

"Bradshaw? Bradshaw…Brad…shaw…" the conductor repeated, staring blankly upward while using the Colt's barrel to scratch just beneath the bill of his cap.

In wake of the man's bizarre behavior and jaw-dropping lack of either urgency or fear, especially considering the state of total panic in which he'd entered the car, Dalton knew he needed to retrieve the revolver if they were to have any chance of survival.

"Mister Hicks, I'm gonna need my colt ba..." he began, taking a half step forward with an extended hand, only to jump back once the conductor swung toward him with the colt barrel leading the way.

"Bradshaw. Yeah, that's right," Hicks practically shrieked with an animated snap of the fingers from his free hand, "Balding, little mustache, sharp duds. I remember labeling him a dandy of sorts, right? Am I right, deputy? Ya know, I rarely forget a face. It's my business, ya know. The *people* business."

Discarding the lantern, Dalton raised both arms in mock surrender, eyes slightly crossed in the wake of staring down the revolver parked mere inches from the center of his face.

"Um, Hicks, y-you mind pointing that somewhere else? Like, maybe *that* way," he gestured with a slight nod toward the car entrance, "Better yet. maybe you ought to give it back t..."

Instead, the conductor slid to the wall at his back, presumably to obtain maximum space between the two men, while lowering the gun pointed at Dalton to chest level.

"Mister Telegrapher, if you don't mind my saying, you ain't the sharpest nail in the bag."

"Wh-what?"

The conductor's expanded, weirdly warped smile held a slight tic at the right corner of his mouth.

"Dumb as a stump. *Not* the brightest candle in the window."

Mouth hanging agape, head tilted slightly to the left, Dalton instantly forced his gaze from the barrel to its possessor. Lower lip atremble, the upper twitching in time, the power of speech was suddenly as elusive as his backbone.

"The sheriff there, rest his badge-totin' soul, could've used a brainier sidekick, though I take it options were limited to Deputy Dense," he paused, leaning in and winking playfully, "Um, that be *you*, pilgrim."

"Hicks, listen, J-just gi-give me the revolver. I don't think you're in any frame of mind to prote..." Dalton said, raised hands with palms displayed directly across from the gun barrel.

"Oh, I'm in no state of mind, am I? Hell's belles, if it's a mental evaluation you're hinting at, you're gonna have to stand in line, sport. Telegrapher turned deputy turned doctor of psychoanalysis. For a man without a shred of common sense, you are one skilled son-of-a-bitch."

"Hicks, I know you're scar..."

Dalton's words halted with jarring abruptness with the intrusion of the colt's cold muzzle shoved forcefully to his breastbone. Though the space between them remained a full arm's reach, plus the barrel, Dalton could smell the rancidity of the man's breath. A sickly-warm waft that reeked of rotted vegetables and raw pork on the cusp of turning.

"It's not *Hicks*, you thick bastard, don't you get that yet?"

"I...I d-don't...don't...u-under st-stand."

With his free hand, the man swiped away the conductor's hat before using the same hand to grip the saggy lapels of the jacket.

"Son, I could cut a better fit of clothes from a revival tent. In a similar vein, sweet Verta or Miss Ruth to you, since I'm tasked to spell this out so even retards might follow along," he hesitated, hanging his head briefly to reveal a circular space shaved bare to his scalp, "Sweet, misunderstood Verta's dress was hanging off her like a sagging bedsheet. I was surprised and a little disappointed at the good Marshal's lack of suspicion and hell, even your own. Seasoned lawman he appeared to be, how was it neither of you noted the lack of wetness or fresh tracking of snow when I'd claimed we'd just left the railway car and set off the whistle? We were both dry as bone with nary a flake of snow as evidence, but you two just accepted us and our story on good faith. Marshal must've figured it out soon enough, but I'm of the sad belief you never would've, since its only taken me a few short minutes in your company to sense the amazing dullness behind that blank stare."

"Harmon," Dalton croaked, his lower extremities falling victim to a slow, agonizing paralysis,

"*Now* he gets it," came the sarcastic reply, complete with animated eyeroll.

"So, the conductor w-was....is..."

"Oh, you've been introduced. The Marshal sneaked a return peek on the way back as well. Verta snaked beneath the bench, I swear sometimes that woman was birthed boneless, and spied his every cautious step through the car. Watched him re-check the sleeping bins and spend additional time on one in particular."

The man pointed the Colt's barrel downward toward the lantern while nodding in the general direction of the dreaded bins.

"Go ahead, telegrapher, take a quick gander and it'll all fall in place for ya. Well, maybe not all, but a good size piece of the puzzle."

"I don't see any re-reason..."

The Colt's muzzle swung rapidly upward, halting once it lined up directly across from Dalton's bare forehead.

"I said, take a look."

Sidestepping into the aisle, the temptation of taking a wild swipe at the man's gun-hand passing as quickly as it came, Dalton backed toward the sleeping bins with the lantern at eyelevel.

The lantern shook and swayed in his wavering grip, levitating first near the mystery lady, now easily assumed to be the train's lone paying customer who hadn't disembarked to avoid the blizzard. Thin but sufficiently statured, the female victim possessed the perfect build for the dress that had so loosely hung from the woman calling herself Beverly Ruth. Opposite, the bland duds chosen for a mental patient in transit were noticeably snug and shortened, a detail he'd easily missed due to purposely avoiding a close inspection the first time around.

"Other side, genius," he heard the man grumble, "Damn if you ain't dense as Mississippi mud."

Swinging the lantern around, its brightness level just a notch above a lit match, its lower edge brushed the edge of the dead man's chin, his lower jaw frozen agape to reveal purplish gums where a set of dentures once occupied. Miraculously, Dalton avoided yelping aloud or, more amazingly, even the slightest flinch at the sudden, horrid sight, and he secretly wondered if his frayed senses were now beyond such base reactions.

"Ya see? The Marshal had an inkling, otherwise he wouldn't have been playing dentist on his way through the car. We figured he'd run across the missing chewers the first time through but didn't put it together to check 'til later on."

For what little good it did him now, Dalton recalled Drake's off-kilter remark about how the conductor would be 'talking with a lisp' without his false teeth.

Lowering the lantern to his side, the effect transforming the man who'd hoodwinked him into an unarmed state into a still, shadowy wraith posed barely a dozen feet away, Dalton's mind raced to form a plan, however farfetched, of survival. Before a single coherent option could spring forth, the faux conductor inadvertently presented yet another unneeded distraction.

"I take it you made the acquaintance of Mister's Baxter and Drake?"

Dalton merely nodded, initially unsure of a proper response. He doubted Drake was going to make it back to the civilized world without bleeding out but informing Harmon of the poor guard's present state would surely seal his fate.

"Baxter was a sadistic bastard. Never passed on an opportunity to belt me around or knee my privates when nobody was looking. It was just a matter of time before he had his way with Verta. I saw 'im drooling over her, rubbing his personals," he paused as to mentally rewind that last memory, his wide, toothy smile the picture of gleeful derangement. "Too bad Verta didn't get a shot at 'im. Wouldn't have been the first potential rapist she'd skinned, no sir. Anyhow, it was a genuine pleasure gutting that one. Drake was a dunce who didn't have any business guarding anybody, much less transporting 'em. Boy couldn't secure a restraint for shit, obviously. Almost felt a twinge of guilt carving 'im up. *Almost.*"

Figuring a change of subject was in order, Dalton veered slightly off subject.

"Wh-where then is Miss Ru...um, Miss Verta?" he asked offhandedly, figuring any moment he wasn't being either stabbed or shot a positive one.

"Verta's her given name, dummy," Harmon snapped, "Maiden name is Bueley, pronounced B E W L E, got it? Miss Bueley is in the next car. C'mon, I'll formally introduce you."

Dalton didn't budge other than crouching down for strategic placement of the lantern, already dimmed to candlelight status but practically blinked out upon his tucking it behind a portion of blanket hanging loose from the deceased conductor's sleeping bin.

"I won't ask again, mister. Truth be told, you don't even rate a meeting. You got two seconds to move your ass down that aisle before I open up a third eye right between the two ya got."

"Oh-okay, I'm coming, I'm coming," Dalton replied cravenly, briefly tripping forward and almost headfirst into the dead woman's bin. Upon straightening, he reached back and retrieved the lantern, its feeble light nearly extinguished.

Shuffling past his leering captor, he thought again, briefly, as before, of attempting a lurching blow but quickly relented in the face of staring down the colt's unwavering muzzle.

"That's it, boy. We'll resume questions and answers in better lighting."

Dalton felt his gag-reflex activate upon stepping over Bain's mutilated frame, the Marshal's eyes reflected in the lantern's dim glow as he passed over. A dead, blank stare the telegrapher could only compare to dulled marbles.

"Oh, don't *fret* the sheriff," he heard Harmon remark at his back just as he yanked ajar the door leading onto the gangway, "Died like a man. We'll soon see if his volunteer deputy can claim similar glory on *his* way to the promised land."

~ * ~

Upon first view, one would've naturally assumed the lady had simply taken a much-deserved sabbatical while patiently awaiting their arrival. Sitting upright in the third seat on the right from the rear of the car, the baggy lace dress tucked into her lap and held in place by dainty gloved hands, the lone hint something was amiss being a dime-sized hole at the center of a forehead so pasty it appeared dipped in corn flour.

The car itself wasn't quite as lit as the presidential had been on their first trek through, though comparable, as at least two dozen lanterns had obviously been relocated in the short time Bain and Dalton spent in the caboose. It was as if the cars had purposely been swapped as to showcase whatever horrors rated the most recent.

Stumbling forward, Dalton discarded his own, practically flameless light on the seat opposite Verta Bueley's propped corpse, her lifeless eyes, much like Daniel Bain's, frozen agape in that terrifying moment when the soul behind them had permanently flown the coop.

It wasn't until he strolled past, having seen his fill of similarly extinguished husks for one night, that Dalton took grisly note of the true damage of the surprisingly neat bullet wound. The seat to her rear coated in a wide, wet smear of blood, brain matter and lengthy strings of hair, the back of her skull resembled a dark maroon pumpkin having given violent birth to a cannonball, the matted hair standing nearly straight out from the gaping chasm.

Dalton halted at Harmon's harsh command to do so, though at least initially refusing to turn around and face him, mostly to allow at least a few moments tranquility before what might possibly be his own personal end-of-the-line scenario. Weirdly, as he spun around on a heel, his level of apprehension wasn't nearly as crippling as expected. Instead, he focused solely on his captor's movements, expression and overall demeanor in search of an element of weakness or even better, complacency. Dalton instantly noted a despicable alternation of Harmon's wardrobe, the conductor hat replaced by Dan Bain's Stetson, blood-spattered and as ill-fitting as the uniform he'd also absconded from the dead. In addition, hitched within his belt hung a long saber, the type usually associated with the calvary and without a doubt, the weapon of butchery utilized to so cruelly end Bain's life.

"Verta Bueley, tigress extraordinaire, meet Digby Higgins, part-time telegrapher and full-time coot without a badge," Harmon announced with a slight bow, though careful to maintain the Colt's steady aim.

Part one of Dalton's plan was pure, adrenaline-fueled adlib, birthed by not only a slowly percolating rage from the constant berating and perhaps more so by the theft and subsequent donning of the dead Marshal's hair-case.

"More like a low-rent Calico Queen, I'm guessing."

His face a comical mask of disbelief, Harmon took a single step forward, the distance between the two men cut to near reaching distance from either party, his usually steady gun-head visibly wavering.

"Say again, telegrapher. Not sure I heard you right."

Despite the thundering of his heart and palms coated in fresh sweat, Dalton's tone remained adequately flat and with nary a hint of nervousness. What had been a tiny sliver of hope blossomed greatly in knowing the key to getting the man's dander up and hopefully his guard down.

"Typical wag-tail. Seen plenty of her kind in Abilene," he replied, staring down at the blown-out crater wound and somehow able to manufacture a small but lethally wicked grin, "Painted cats own a certain stink. I thought I recognized it when she and I jawed earlier."

A lunge, sudden and executed with shocking quickness, concluded with the barrel of the Colt planted firmly against Dalton's chin, the muzzle buried deep within his bushy whiskers.

"So, just a skunky old whore, was she?" Harmon replied, each word punctuated by a stout jab of the barrel against bone, Dalton openly wincing with east thrust.

"I...call 'em as I smell 'em," he managed, head forced slightly upward from the constant battering beneath his chin and praying that at such close range his sneaking a gloved hand inside his coat would go unnoticed just long enough to prevent swallowing a bullet.

A guttural growl, more animal than human, was barely audible but in terms of the fear it instilled, equal to a tiger's predatory roar.

"Not even close, shitter. Miss Bueley was, before being forcibly committed by an evil, heartless stepfather she'd openly accused of forced buggery when she was but an innocent child, an up-and-coming high-wire and trapeze artist for Downy Brothers Circus. She longed to relive past glories, that is until that bastard partner of yours struck her down. How? *How* in the devil's name? I'd already sliced away his shooting arm and...damned if he didn't use the *other* and...and...*damn* him to hell. Bless her triple-jointed soul, she never...saw the bullet coming."

Sensing the man's vulnerability, Dalton didn't hesitate.

"Please allow me to turn my head away before you start spewing tears for a dead, crazy whore."

The muzzle dug ever deeper, digging a small grove into his chin.

"You know, in poor Verta's absence, I *was* counting on you to assist in steering this iron horse back to the civilized world and in return I'd only cripple you, maybe take an eye or that smart-assed tongue but still leave you breathing."

Pausing his rant only briefly in the wake of a slight shift in position, Harmon resumed as the origin of said modification was revealed in the arrival of the long-sword's sharp-tipped blade snaking its way inside Dalton's coat to lightly jab his ribcage. Tensing in anticipation of excruciating pain, he felt the pressure reposition to his left kneecap, followed by a light tap there for emphasis.

"Maybe, just *maybe*, I'll carve away those clodhopper legs just below the knee, so you'll spend the rest of your days belly-crawling. Best believe me, telegrapher, I can cut away a big slab and still leave you breathing, unlike the admittedly crude results doled out to the Mars..."

Despite the negatives outweighing the positives by roughly the weight of the car beneath their boots. Despite self-doubts that nearly caused what would've surely been a fatal hesitation, Dalton simply *acted*. In the end, it simply came down to a matter of opportunity, as suffering such close quarters to the murdering lunatic might never again surface, nor would the same lunatic's blatant self-confidence. In the end, Dalton discovered the power to control the shakes, to avoid clumsy, sluggish movements, despite every nerve ending he possessed supercharged with a level of fear never before experienced. In the end, the knife he'd pulled from the lining of his lone winter coat, a carving blade so skillfully yanked from the bloodied forehead of Miss Beverly Ruth with the words *Old Hickory* carved into the handle, seemed to seek out and find its intended target as if magically or perhaps even supernaturally guided.

In the aftermath, Richard Harmon's expression of wide-eyed disbelief at the wooden knife handle protruding from just underneath his right collarbone, the seven-inch blade buried to the hilt, struck Dalton as equal parts tragic and comical, the conductor's saggy pants providing the final insult to his stained dignity by collapsing around his ankles as he'd stumbled back. Dalton, meanwhile, briefly gazed downward at what his victim had left behind, his own recollection of procuring said object not merely hazy but non-existent.

Snapping from his daze, Dalton heard instead of visualized the conclusion of Harmon's tumble, a resounding thump and subsequent moan providing audible evidence; the decision to escape back into the caboose made without hesitation. A decision he would live, undetermined for how long, to regret.

For, reaching for the exit door's shiny silver handle, his extended hand never made contact, the attached arm instead collapsing to his side at precisely the same moment the presidential suite exploded with a single, ear-splitting retort he knew so well from many a target shoot. It wasn't until he'd managed to crawl into one of the car's rear seats, dragging his dead arm along like some paralyzed conjoined twin, that the potentially fatal severity of the wound hit home. The back portion of his coat sleeve instantly drenched in a sickening warmth.

"Well, well, well, if you ain't one sneaky, fiendishly clever telegrapher," Harmon's voice boomed out from the front of the car with a terrifying level of vim and vigor, "Damn slick using one of my own weapons against me. Never...saw that coming, no sir. Congratulations are...in order. Then again, even dunderheads get lucky from time to time."

Lying flat on his back across the poorly padded seat, Dalton was unable to determine the exact location of the slug's entry, though the lack of any exit from his frontside was less than comforting. From the increasingly fierce burning sensation at his upper right shoulder, he could only assume somewhere either just above or below the blade. Meanwhile, he could hear Harmon squirming and struggling to get upright, certain words emphasized to coincide with the level of strain. A momentary panic of epic proportions was barely avoided once he felt the procured object pinned against the seatback, its slim frame pinching his outer left thigh while digging a permanent grove into the outer pant leg.

"You've left me in quite the quandary, I must say," Harmon continued with the blatant cockiness of a veteran predator void even of a trace of natural concern for his own mortality.

A second blast reverberated, sounding strangely muffled compared to the first, removing a half-dollar-sized chunk of seat no more than half a foot above Dalton's scalp and coating his chest and beard in splinters and dust.

"This here pork-carver you've so rudely planted in my person is kinda like a woman. Can't live with it and sure as hell can't properly remove it if I wanna live."

Though doing his best to block out the man's almost supernatural feat of survival, Dalton could clearly envision the knife's slightly splintered handle sticking from his neck like a protruding bone, he feared time was a dwindling commodity. Planting the heels of his mukluks firmly into the thick carpeting, Dalton prepped for a second mad dash, only this time in the opposite direction and only when and if Harmon closed ranks to near reaching distance.

It was apparent he had foolishly underestimated the madman's resolve. Then again, it wasn't as if he'd ever had reason to study the most effective way to permanently disable the hopelessly insane. Perhaps those ravaged by madness and thus soulless were simply *harder* to put down, much like a rampaging, rapid dog set loose upon a crowded henhouse.

Fortunately, there seemed to be an equal tradeoff in that in their unbridled tenacity to terminate, there was also a noted lack of concentration, of recklessness, of detailed memory. If this were not so, Harmon would've surely inspected him closer following that choreographed 'stumble' into the dead woman's sleeping bin, not to mention this latest gaffe, wherein such a vital cog in his murder machine had gone so mysteriously missing.

A third shot punched a hole in the car's back wall, a few inches above the seat.

"Don't...blame me for the...back shot," Harmon resumed, his vocal delivery not only noticeably slower but vaguely slurred in places, "This wooden-handled cutter sticking from...my neck like some...third arm...plays hell with one's...aim."

Dalton sucked in a fresh lungful and held it in order to remain as quiet and still as possible, no small feat considering the whole of his back throbbed like a rotted tooth jabbed with an icepick, and to better feign unconsciousness. He could only hope and pray that Harmon's natural overconfidence hadn't completely abated despite a potentially fatal wound, such brass recklessness perhaps due to such a sick, twisted, sadistic mind being unable to properly calculate fear.

"Nothing personal, you…u-understand. You seem a…nice enough c-chap, despite…the gullibility and…slow t-thinking. Fate is a…fickle bitch. She demands…proper closure."

A second passed, two, and then a third in relative silence other than the occasional gust of wind rattling the car walls as a stark reminder of who was really in charge to those few who remained.

His face a molded, motionless mask of anguish, Dalton's lungs screamed for release, said burgeoning shriek birthed from the rapidly spreading misery trailing up his blood-soaked spine.

It wasn't until his seat vibrated from a light thump at its metal base—most likely impacted by Harmon's boot-tip, that Dalton tensed his thighs and midsection to their maximum torque, his injured, paralyzed arm flopping uselessly over the side even as the other whipped across his torso from left to right in a looping blur.

The long-held breath whooshed free in a wailing moan just as his arm and attached hand recoiled back as if ricocheting off a brick wall. Shoved onto his back with Harmon's grinning mug looming overhead, a thick stream of dark red drool cascaded onto Dalton's upturned face. The saber handle hung near Harmon's belt with the cutting edge of its blade imbedded in a horizontal line from his upper right shoulder to the lower abdomen.

As both men had lost the use of their right arms, Dalton's left hand coiled around the wrist of Harmon's left, the latter attempting to twist the grasped revolver into close-range firing position.

"Haaaaa ha…ahhhh hahaaaa…" Harmon giggled maniacally, using his full-body weight but unable to get past Dalton's upturned knees, the Colt's aim swaying wildly from east to west to straight up and back again, "B-battle…o-of…t-t-the…crip…cri…crip-ples…"

The Colt recoiled wildly, the slug striking a far window dead-center and shattering the foot-wide, foot-high pane, a spattering of ivory flakes immediately blowing in through the fresh void like invading moths.

Feeling his grip gradually slipping, unbelievably, Harmon seemed to be growing stronger despite potentially mortal wounds, Dalton's squinting, darting eyes fixed on the carving knife handle, standing erect and in virtually the same position since its original insertion. Remarkably, the wound appeared to have hardly bled, as if the handle's base had somehow corked the parted flesh. In stark contrast, the sword's torso-length laceration had sprung a massive spill that had begun to pool at their booted foot, transforming beige carpet to the deepest shade of red.

Harmon, bloody lunatic's grin firmly in place but obviously frustrated by the futility of being unable to gain an upper hand, temporarily eased his body weight off Dalton's knees by backing a single step and attempting to yank the gun-hand free.

"S-stubborn s-son...b-b-bitch..." he growled, yanking and jerking from left to right but unable to break free, his dead arm failing about like a hollow shirtsleeve on a clothesline, the conductor's jacket and inner shirt soggy with his own spillage. Amazingly, he seemed to pay little attention to the imbedding saber, from which sprung a veritable river of leakage.

His grip growing weaker with each jerk or tug, Dalton drew back his right foot while simultaneously releasing Harmon's wrist. As he'd been pulling exclusively to the right and not back on the snared hand, Harmon's stiff-kneed stance remained mostly intact save a slight tilt in that direction.

Just as Harmon swung the freed revolver down and around, his toothy, malevolent grin having manifested into the warped, frozen grimace of a severe stroke victim, the flat heel of a mukluk boot shot forth with such speed and force Harmon had no time but to openly flinch in the aftermath.

Momentarily distracted by the attempted kick, the lunatic-in-conductor's guise hesitated in following through with his intended aim and instead cackled aloud at what he'd thought was a close miss.

By the time Dalton delivered a second kick with the opposite heel, impacting just to the left of the saber's suspended handle near the lower abdomen, Harmon realized the first hadn't missed it's intended target at all, but struck it as effectively as hammer to nail-head.

Staggering back and falling into the opposite seat, the Colt jarred from his hand to destinations unknown, Harmon gazed doe-eyed downward and to the right, where the carving knife's handle position had been dramatically altered. The initial kick had, in effect, opened the floodgates, forcing the handle in an upward trajectory and thus driving the blade directly into the neck, while Harmon's upturned knee inadvertently pried the saber free for additional outflow.

Sitting upright with his back to the wall and knees upright, Harmon's eyes locked with the individual across the aisle and executed a slight nod of what might've been begrudging respect, that single miniscule movement triggering the full release of his jugular; a single jutting fountain that sailed over two sets of seats to splatter the front of Verta Bueley's confiscated dress and coat her ghostly visage in a mask of darkest maroon.

Amazingly, as Dalton was in the process of tumbling into the narrow space between seats, Harmon somehow managed to pull himself upright. Head bowed and soaked from chest to boots in his own runway life-source, he appeared to be reaching for the dropped saber before slumping face-first into the aisle, his head striking the seat nearest Dalton with his face turned toward his intended victim. Eyes only half shut and mouth hanging ajar, Harmon's last gasp escaped as a labored sigh that spat a fresh glut of gore onto the back of Dalton's already bloodstained coat. As if expecting the man to magically resuscitate, Dalton lay motionless for a full minute before rolling into the aisle to retrieve both the saber and Colt as potential weapons in the outside chance Harmon was somehow able to rise from the dead in his absence.

Staggering weakly toward the car exit and pausing briefly as if to turn for a final glance, having already decided to depart the train via the caboose, he vehemently declined adding yet another nightmarish image to the plethora of terrors already present and instead stumbled into the gangway without regret.

~ * ~

Not surprisingly, Officer Drake had passed since his departure. Just how the man had survived such shock and trauma to be conscious and at least partially coherent upon intros had been nothing short of miraculous. Remaining hand resting on his upper chest and a peaceful smile creasing blood-smeared lips, it appeared to Dalton that the man had at least made peace with his maker.

He'd thought of at least covering the bodies of Drake and Baxter as well as that of Marshal Bain but decided against it for two distinct reasons. *One:* Whatever lawmen were the first on the scene would surely not appreciate the alteration and *Two:* The sad truth was, he simply wasn't up to the physical assertion. The bleeding of his back wound had abated somewhat, if not he would've already passed from blood loss, and he was going to need to keep additional leakage to a minimum if he was going to make it back to the shack alive.

Exiting the caboose, having donned both guard's uniform jackets and a thick toboggan belonging to one, all of which he'd found stashed in a gunny sack, Dalton could only guess dawn was still three to four hours away. The skies spit only the occasional flake, and the winds had all but died down save a sporadic gust.

Traversing gingerly from the caboose steps onto the tracks with borrowed lantern in hand, a two-to-three-foot snowdrift on either side, he took note of a length of chain running from the car's undercarriage to perhaps a hundred down the line.

As the frigid cold provided both a natural numbing to the wound and substantial recharging of the senses, Dalton allowed curiosity to rule the moment, following the linked chain to its conclusion a few hundred feet later, just a few yards from the right of the tracks.

From the deep drift protruded a boot, roper style with fancy-stitch design, the chain so tightly wound around the possessor's ankle it had pulled flesh, muscle and strips of the boot-leather away to reveal the ivory bone beneath.

Having seen, smelled and witnessed enough bloodletting for a lifetime, Dalton turned away without further inspection and, to both his utter surprise and delight, there stood Dixie just to the left of the caboose. Making his way painstakingly back toward the caboose, barely avoiding tripping numerous times, he thought the rag-tail's presence just a cruel hallucination until he'd reached gingerly out to stroke her all-too-real muzzle. Climbing into the saddle had been a struggle, she'd nearly dragged him by a single stirrup at one terrifying juncture, but once aboard he guided her past the still-foreboding husk of the Big Horn Express, snow up to the filly's forearms. Dalton knew all too well another tumble like that first, it seemed to have occurred literally days ago, would surely spell his doom.

Attempting to follow the well-covered train tracks leading back to the shack, memory was obviously useless as not only had the marshal steered but he'd ridden the majority of the trek with his head bowed from the blizzard's rage, Dalton pulled back on the reins only once, that with the discovery of yet another casualty.

The dead man he could only guess to be either the train's engineer or brakeman, as, even in his frozen state, he didn't fit the description Bain gave of the fugitive rake, Bradshaw.

Face down in a mound of snow, the corpse's tracks had been covered on the last stretch before his collapse, meaning he fell just as the blizzard subsided. Tall and lanky and wearing only a light jacket, he'd more than likely escaped the train with only minor wounds, there was a heavy matting to the back of his head notably darker than the sandy shade that dominated, but he hadn't made it more than a half mile before succumbing to the elements. As for Mister Carlton Bradshaw, Dalton could only assume via process of elimination he had been the unfortunate bastard on the other end of that chain trailing the caboose.

It took just over an hour more to reach the shed, Dixie doing yeoman's work to avoid untold dangers beneath the snow as Dalton guided her at roughly half the speed of Bain's earlier trek. High tension aside, Dalton still caught himself nodding off numerous times, such innate drowsiness no doubt due to a heady mix of complete exhaustion and blood loss. Though his back wound numbed considerably, a sporadic and intense throbbing served to wake him from the occasional nods, thus preventing a potentially fatal tumble from the saddle.

The telegraph was short and simple and riddled with uncharacteristic spelling errors. Days later, he would recall nary a detail of sending it.

Big Horn Express stalled.

Prisoners escaped
Many dead inside.
Come as soon as possible

As fate would have it, 'as soon as possible' came just in time to save Dalton Harrison's life, making him the lone survivor of the night soon to be infamously known for all of American western lore as The Big Horn Massacre.

~ * ~

"By the time the nearest authority reached him, Uncle Dalton had been comatose for nearly two full days. The loss of blood, teamed with severe dehydration wasn't quite enough to kill 'im, but it was close. They told 'im he'd been fortunate the Colt slug ricocheted off his scapula bone. In and out almost the same hole. All told, he spent ten days in a Laramie hospital, all expenses paid by the railroad company, which I have to say is the very least they could do."

Steering the Charger over a steep grade while cruising by a trio of semi's clogging the slow lane, Brad noted Boone ending the recording before beginning this latest portion of the story's epilogue, thus openly inviting his driver's feedback.

"I'll say. Damn, but what an ordeal," he offered, shocked via a glance at the dash's digital clock that well over an hour passed since Boone's tale commenced. "In today's world, your uncle would be choosing between book and movie offers. Was there any coverage, I mean at least locally?"

Pale and pastier than he'd appeared at the story's inception, Boone's voice was still strong; eyes glistening and hands lively and animated.

"Oh yes indeed. Newspaper reporters from Cheyenne, Laramie and even Casper arrived in Rock Springs before Uncle Dalton even came to, each of 'em itching for the exclusive. 'Course by then the lurid details came to light. Lawmen from three states, including a Texas Ranger and even a Pinkerton man all converged on the Big Horn, the latter all too willing to share all he'd seen, for a substantial price, of course. He said the saddest of all was meeting with several of Daniel Bain's deputies at the Marshal's funeral service."

"So, your uncle made a trip all the way to Missouri?"

Boone nodded, the tone of his reply ripe with pride, a renewed gleam in his eyes.

"Yes sir. Said he wouldn't have missed it, no matter the lack of healing to his own wounds. My uncle was said to have claimed Dan Bain as the bravest man he'd ever met, and from what I've heard of Dalton's subsequent travels, that was no small feat. Anyhow, Uncle Dalton gave the papers the scoop, but only after clearing himself as a suspect. Got a grainy old photo from the Natrona County Times tucked away in my scrapbook. That was Casper's main rag at that time. Uncle Dalton appears mighty ragged, all right."

Hitting a lengthy straight, flat stretch of road with little in the way of accompanying traffic, Brad set the Charger on cruise as to better focus.

"So, you're telling me your uncle was actually a *suspect*? I get there was no CSI in those days, but how blind could they be?"

"Just a formality," Boone replied, smiling and waving off the younger man. "You have to understand, trains filled with mutilated bodies wasn't exactly the norm in those days. Not that such horrors would be considered routine even now, but nobody saw anything like that outside an Apache raid. Once they'd confirmed Harmon and Bueley's official presence on the Big Horn, all was, how do they say these days? Copasetic."

Brad nodded eagerly, lips already forming the next query.

"Speaking of bodies, who were the two found outside the train?"

"As my uncle had suspected, what remained of Carlton Bradshaw had been dragged countless miles across that frozen track, though, what was never clear was why he alone suffered such a cruel fate. Speculation was his mouth wrote checks his ass couldn't cash, so to speak, and he paid dearly for it. Maybe he even made the fatal mistake of flirting with Verta. The other body had been that of Luther Colins, the train engineer. Unknown to my uncle at the time, Collins suffered a substantial gut wound, no doubt administered at Verta's hands with that damned saber.

Honestly, her and Harmon couldn't scrape up a shred of humanity between 'em."

Steering them past yet another lumbering semi, Brad's voice crackled with adolescent excitement.

"Yeah, about *those* two. What was their story? I mean, why the transfer from state prison to the nuthouse? Must've been some seriously sick acts."

Squinting out the window, clear blue skies had resulted in a particularly bright day considering all the gray days preceding it, Boone appeared to phase out as if temporarily hypnotized by the passing landscape. Still a good three hours from Sioux Falls, there was little in the way of landmarks since passing Fargo, just mile after mile of rocky hills, concave valleys and distant mountain ranges. Brad gave it a full two minutes before restarting the conversation, his curiosity overpowering any normal good manners or politeness.

"Boone?"

"Yes, yes, I heard you," Boone replied, breaking contact with the great outdoors and instead peering down into his lap to check the recorder, "I was just...I can't recall the last time I regaled to anyone that particular chapter of dark family history. Didn't expect it to...take so much out of me."

Brad, checking the rearview, cleared his throat noisily.

"Well, hey, if you'd like to continue a bit later or just drop the sub..."

"No, no, it's fine. I think I owe the proper conclusion to both you and my loved ones. Plus, which, it just might be the therapy I need in order to face the music before crossing that Mississippi line."

"Tape still holding out?"

"Should be enough to fill in the blanks. Now, you asked about the two mass murderers."

"Yeah, what was their names? Harvey and Bule? I wanna be able to Google 'em later."

The older man laughed, a welcome sight and sound to his transporter.

"Harmon, Richard and Bueley, first name Verta. Those two put the insane in *criminally* insane before such a term became the norm. At age twelve while living in his third orphanage, Harmon somehow got access to cans of turpentine and set the place ablaze in the middle of the night. If I recall correctly, they pulled the charred bodies of more than a dozen children from the ruins. At seventeen, he raped and strangled an eleven-year-old retarded girl, then murdered a rookie orderly who'd made the mistake of leaving him unattended in the institute's tool room. Dismembered the poor bastard with a bone saw. All told he'd tallied twenty-two murders, counting the six both he and Verta shared credit for on the Big Horn."

Brad practically hooted.

"What about Miss Congeniality?"

"If possible, an even higher level of sadistic derangement. She was just eight when she murdered her younger sister by drowning her in a creek beside their house, their very own parent's the star witnesses. Soon after she was treated with the drugs of the day; opium, morphine, assorted mood breakers, before being placed with stepparents.

"As I recall, the new folks were deeply Christian and took in troubled kids as a habit."

The comical double-take Brad executed birthed the tiniest grin from his host, who shrugged weakly.

"You're kidding? They just doped up the little psycho before handing her over to another set of potential victims?"

"Brad, remember this was still the 19th century. Obviously, treatments and methods have progressed substantially."

Mouth hanging open, Brad just shook his head in stunned disbelief.

"So, I'm guessing this new family unit didn't exactly bond either?"

"Tragically, no. As a teen, Verta developed a penchant for cutlery, stealing every sharp-edged instrument she could get her hands on. Used a Bowie to slash her stepmother's throat and a scythe to decapitate a younger stepbrother. Dumped his head in a well out back for his stepfather to discover days after the fact. So, after a series of chemical treatments and years of supervision in a small-town monastery, she came of age and was released.

"Verta was nineteen when she met a carny worker and joined a traveling side show, as it was found she was unusually, almost supernaturally flexible, what folks used to refer to as triple-jointed, but we know now as hypermobile. Sure explained a lot to me about how she was able to slip that restraint on the Big Horn, plus cram herself in such tight quarters while hiding from my uncle and the Marshal. Anyhow, she was considered quite the multitalented lass in the show, both as a knife thrower and trapeze artist."

"Uh-huh, so how long did she make it before cracking up?"

"A couple of years, believe it or not, though there was speculation that she left a few scattered body's behind, what with all the different towns the show passed through. If you think on it, it was the perfect profession for those who came to be labeled serial killers. It was just a year, maybe two before the Big Horn killings that she was nabbed after knifing a co-worker, some young lass who'd dared outperform her on the high wire.

"Once jailed, I think the hoosegow was just outside Wichita, she'd allegedly bitten the ear off one guard and beaten another damn near to death with his own Billy-club. That was how she ended up on the Big Horn, and well, the rest is history, though I noticed the Wikerpedia version leaves out the grisly details. Probably for the best. I kinda wish I wasn't privy to 'em."

Several moments of silence passed, Boone having pressed the recorder's rewind button before Brad turned towards him, face scrunched in utter befuddlement.

"*Two* things, Boone. Number one, what the hell is a hoosegow and two: I think you meant Wikipedia."

For the second time since story-time's conclusion, Boone laughed long and well, his complexion briefly gaining a sudden rush of color.

Approximately a half hour later and still over one-hundred miles away from the first day's planned stop, Boone politely asked his personal chauffer to pull over at the next service station that might offer an old man a chilled brew and a pack of cigarettes.

Chapter Four

"Mmm, just hits the spot. Appreciate the introduction to this new version of my favorite brew."

Boone tipped the frosty can in Brad's direction, the latter pulling back onto an almost deserted stretch of interstate.

"Can't honesty take the credit. Old Milwaukee *Ice* was the only version in the cooler."

"Mother's milk. Sure, you don't mind the cancer-stick?" the older man inquired, thin tendrils of smoke pouring from each nostril.

Securing the Charger's regular place in the slow lane after setting the cruise for a just-under-the-limit sixty-eight MPH, Brad cleared his throat as if delaying a response.

"Oh, yes, excuse the careless phrasing," Boone resumed, delivering a light tap to the younger man's shoulder. "Then again considering the diagnosis, I can't find a logical reason to re-kick what was once a treasured habit."

"I'm fine," Brad replied, though red-eyed and teary beneath the dark shades, "I understand where you're coming from."

The brew parked at his lap, Boone held the half-smoked Maverick eye-level, staring at it with gleeful admiration.

"Think it was around eighty-seven or eighty-eight a buddy of mine introduced me to Harley-Davidson brand smokes, the precursor to these little beauties. Considering I started out rolling my own before graduating to Marlboro, these bad-boys were like trading in an Edsel for a DeLorean."

Brad snorted, sipping from a bottled Dr. Pepper.

"Sounds like true love."

"Well, as far as relationships go, it *has* outlasted several of my marriages."

The older man scooped up the beer can and, lowering the smoldering fag, lifted it airborne for a similar gaze of unbridled admiration.

"As for this heavenly can of midwestern prime hops and barley, it replaced Hubor Bock, Miller High Life and eventually even Bud and PBR as the favorite to please this old man's picky palate."

Yet again, Brad's warped expression defined befuddlement.

"A connoisseur of aged obscurity, a mystic for the misled and misinformed, *Rip Van Relic*, that's me."

If anything, the younger man's mask of utter perplexity stretched to comical proportions.

"Boss, there are times I wonder if we're speaking the same language or maybe it's just your wiseman's dialect that's tossing me into a continual loop of miscommunication."

The two shared yet another sincere moment of jocularity, both spit-taking their respective libations in the process.

"So, not to backtrack to the point of exhausting, but whatever happened to Dalt…your great uncle? I mean, was he able to cash in on the celebrity in any way or did he even pursue such a thing?"

"Not at all. I guess in what passes for entertainment these days, he would at least be hosting his own reality show or be drawing quite the crowd on *YouTube*. Got his picture taken with a grouping of lawmen that got shared to most of the northwestern papers but that was about all they wrote as far as recognition. From what I gathered, he did his best to avoid any and all mention of it. To that point, he and the wife packed up and relocated several states away, to Arkansas of all places. According to my elders, he never worked the telegraph again but instead tried his hand at various labor-type jobs such as lumberman, painter and even farm laborer. Pretty much anything to keep the family fed and by age forty he had sired both a son and daughter. It wasn't until after WW-one that he finally found his niche. Have to say I thought my pop was selling me a bill of goods when I heard exactly what that niche was.

By that time Dalton was in his late forties and scuffling a bit and had moved the family to the west coast since jobs were supposedly springing up out there like oil strikes in Texas. Still, hard to believe even today, considering what he'd been through in Wyoming. I guess time does have a way of building a protective shell over the past."

"Don't tell me...movie actor?" Brad offered, though visibly flinching at the possibility.

"Act..." Boone howled, "Well you know, that's probably the one profession my great uncle Dalton didn't take a stab at. No, believe it or not, he opened up his own private security company, and in Southern California of all places. Seems he worked a few gigs for Brinks just to get a toe in the door and after a few summers, decided he could run it better and for a slightly lower price. The rest is history, at least for four or five more decades' worth. H&B Security it was called, the 'B' for his partner in the venture, a co-worker and buddy from Brinks named Teddy Brooks. Uncle Dalton passed at the ripe old age of seventy-nine with a substantial nest-egg to share with the surviving kin."

Brad took a long swig and belched loudly before responding.

"Good for him and his. But geez, *security?* This of course involving guns, self-defense and dealing with potential violence. Wow. Yep, I can surely understand your disbelief. Maybe it was one of those *face your fear* situations. If so, your uncle did just that, kicking it squarely in the ass."

Staring down his half-emptied brew with a gunfighter's squint, Boone pursed his lips and exhaled a perfectly formed, quarter-sized smoke ring.

"Bingo, young man. We've discussed this at family gatherings and that did seem to be the popular opinion."

In the aftermath, both sipped and/or toked in comfortable silence until Boone, retrieving the duffel, replaced the recorder with a handful of unmarked CDs he shuffled slowly through.

"Hey, in the mood for some music?" he finally asked, having settled on a specific disc.

"Sure. Actually, I've been kind of curious since you mentioned the eccentric nature of the collection," Brad said, careful to grip the offered disc at its smooth, smudge-free center and pushing it gently into the player.

"Well, all I can say is that, like my literary choices, there is quite a timespan involved, not to mention countless genres. Please, *please* let me know if you start to bleed from the ears."

Adjusting the CD players bass and volume levels, Brad glanced over at the older man and winked playfully.

"My music allergies are limited to rap."

"Oh…" Boone chimed in, waving a forefinger in the air, "…and speaking of literature, I heard-tell my great uncle passed on to me a love of mystery and thriller type fiction, thus the treasured collection I'm passing on to you. My father said he'd donated at least two-hundred novels to a local library upon passing. Collected 'em most of his life. Probably nothing to match that real-life trauma he alone survived."

Brad nodded in agreement before alluding to the previous subject, "So bookworms share the same gene. I can't really think of anyone in my family that's a fiction reader. Not to worry though, I'll make certain those treasures of yours end up in the right hands."

The older man nodded, packing away the remainder of the unchosen CDs.

"I'd appreciate that more than you know. Perhaps a library of *your* choice."

Over the next hour or so, they were regaled with an embarrassment of musical riches from eras long passed, from the big band magic of Glenn Miller to the irrepressible vocalizations of Billie Holiday, Bing Crosby and Perry Como to the bluesy perfection of Robert Johnson, Muddy Waters and BB King and finally to early rock 'n roll pioneers Little Richard, Jerry Lee Lewis, The Everly Brothers, Elvis and the Beatles. Through it all, Brad's fingers constantly tapped the wheel, occasionally nodding in apparent approval of whatever offering flowed from the Charger's multitude of speakers.

"You weren't kidding," Brad bellowed over Alice Cooper's early seventies staple '*No More Mister Nice Guy.*"

"About what?" Boone roared back, fingers tapping along atop bony knees.

"You are one genre-hopping musical wizard."

The older man flashed the international 'okay' gesture with the thumb and forefinger of his left hand.

"Just wait. You ain't heard nothing yet."

They'd spotted the road sign announcing Sioux Falls city limits at one-thirty PM. A half hour later, Brad steered the Charger onto an exit just past an additional posted logo claiming *'Lowest Seasonal Rates'* for a nearby Holiday Inn Express.

Double-bed duly booked, Brad carried their sparse luggage; a small American Tourister for himself and an even more compact Samsonite briefcase for Boone, to the second-floor corner room, taking mental note of a Chinese restaurant located within walking distance.

An hour later, while curled into a fetal position on one of two twin beds, Boone tried, in between low, pained moans, to convince Brad to head over to the restaurant without him.

Brad reluctantly agreed, only after failing to convince his patron and employer that a trip to the nearest ER seemed a more logical choice than Asian-American take-out.

"Just need some rest," the older man repeated ad nauseum, this after spending the better part of a half-hour vomiting into the room's ultra-sanitized toilet and blaming the consumption of two full cans of beer for the sudden need to upchuck. The fact that what had been so fiercely evacuated was a bloodred mucus did little to back the said claim.

"Maybe, must *maybe* some moo goo gai pan is just what the old gizzard needs," Boone grinned miserably, cupping his abdomen with the splayed fingers of both, visibly shaking hands.

Brad filled two Styrofoam food plates before returning to the room as quickly as possible, the skies spitting a light snow and sleet mix as temperatures began a rapid descent from gauges already reading just below freezing. Predictably, local weather reports mentioned potentially icy road conditions for the next morning. As it was just past three PM, he wished they could've driven a few hundred more miles to the south before nightfall to avoid the coming storm but realized this would've been far too taxing on Boone.

Fast-walking back to the hotel, Brad's many concerns ping-ponged from Boone's swiftly declining health to whether or not the progress of their trip might be hindered by unpassable roadways. It was obvious that any delay was too much, and though Brad felt a growing fondness for the older man, the quicker he got him to Memphis the better.

Keying the hotel room door with great trepidation, he was pleasantly surprised to find Boone sitting up on the bed, shoes off and clicker in hand while perusing the local cable channel offerings.

Later that evening, as Brad stared from a second-story window onto the nearby interstate, where the light snow/sleet mix had yet to impede traffic, Boone peered drowsy-eyed at the wide flatscreen, a '*Rifleman*' marathon playing on one of the many nostalgia channels. While Brad wolfed down the main dishes, the older man had wisely stuck to a heaping pile of sliced fruit with no immediate consequences. He had, however, stood on the balcony soon after to ingest not one but two Maverick smokes, commenting in the aftermath that 'nothing capped off a meal quite like a double lungful of tar and nicotine.' Meanwhile, Brad alternated glances at Chuck Connors punching out or outgunning whatever baddies crossed his path in the fictional town of North Fork and cruising the internet highway via his Samsung smart phone.

The two spoke only sparingly as the night passed, Boone drifting off just after nine and Brad following suit no more than an hour later. Brad attempted a good-natured grilling of what to expect on day two of 'story-time', but Boone refused to relent other than simply stating that 'it would make the Big Horn tale seem tame by comparison.'

They planned on a six AM departure, immediately following coffee and a continental breakfast.

The preset alarm sounded off at precisely five, prompting Brad to immediately roll from the bed and peer out into pre-dawn darkness to check the extent of Mother Nature's predicted damage. Fortunately, though there did appear to be accumulation, it was far less than the prognosticated six to seven inches by at least half. As for any sleet/ice buildup, it didn't seem to be an issue if judged by the sporadic passing of vehicles on the nearby interstate, all of which appeared to be cruising by at the posted limit. There had been a moment of concern as Brad initially saw no evidence of life in the older man, rolled into a funnel-cloud shaped cocoon of sheets and blankets, that is until a long, squeaky fart announced his employer's arrival into a new day. Additionally, the old man's cheeks held a rosy hue so desperately lacking the night before. His deportment as a whole, lively and chipper, spoke volumes to the positive dividends reaped by a long, deep slumber.

Keying the door at five-forty-five, Brad showered the night before in order to allow Boone a free reign in the morning, the continental chow consisting of coffee with a honey biscuit for Brad and orange juice with buttered toast for Boone, the Charger pulled from the snowy lot at precisely six-fifteen.

"Well then, Kansas City here we come," Brad announced cheerily, steering them onto the entrance ramp to the interstate, to which a smiling Boone Harrison reached over to deliver a light tap to his right shoulder.

Brad scanned the local radio stations for the day's weather before loading in yet another mixed CD from the dozen or more stashed away in the older man's duffel. Soon they were tooling down a mostly snow-free interstate at just under the speed limit to sounds as diversified as Pat Boone, Earth, Wind and Fire, Bad Company and the Bee Gees.

By seven-thirty, duly gassed up and sharing the two-lane roadway with sparse at best company, Brad glanced over to see Boone loading a fresh cassette into his recorder. As they'd spoken little since waking, Brad figured the older man had been saving both his voice and newfound vigor for the road.

"How long to KC by your estimate?" Boone inquired, the recorder sufficiently locked and loaded.

"Oh, another four, maybe four and a half hours. One of our shorter treks. KC to Memphis is the marathon. Looks like the weathers on our side all the way past the Mason Dixon, or so my smart phone claims via Forecast dot com."

"Fine. That ought to do it, restroom and eatery stops included."

Brad gestured with the quick nod towards the recorder.

"So do I get a preamble on this one or you just gonna dive right in?"

The older man's left eye cocked dramatically, as if Brad just spoke in tongue.

"You know, a prologue. If my wife were here, she'd tell you I'm a movie trailer junkie. As a general rule I've found that if the trailer sucks, so sucks the movie."

When Boone didn't respond right away, Brad cleared his throat, cheeks instantly reddening.

"Um, no offense, I...hey, if this one is even half the nail-biter of that first chapter, and I'm sure it will be, we're good to g…"

"No offense taken," Boone cut in, his forehead creased as if by deep concentration or struck by a sudden migraine, staring unblinkingly straight ahead, "I'm just…it's just that while it *is* vital to present the proper intro, I want to get the facts down in my mind before the lips commence to flap. I know once my motor revs up to head on down the road, well, there's no reverse gear. Not to mention editing one of these baby's once taped is dang near impossible."

Breathing a silent sigh of relief in that he hadn't offended after all, Brad squinted hard as the sun broke through a distant cloud line, reaching up to the visor to snatch his shades.

"Oh yeah, got it. Well, just take your time. I know you want to get it just right for the relatives."

"True," Boone nodded, playfully jabbing an extended elbow lightly into his driver's side, "Plus I'd rather my chauffer not drift off behind the wheel."

"Fat chance. I've gotta confess that as much as I dig all those vintage tunes, this family history thing is fascinating. I get the feeling that once we settle in the sunshine state, I'm apt to pay a visit to Ancestry dot com, if for no other reason than to see if *anyone* in my clan is half as interesting."

Donning his own pair of glare-dimmers, the lens so comically oversized he'd once overheard a stranger inquire how he rated one of Elton John's concert props, Boone ran jittery fingers atop the recorder's buttons.

"Interesting is a unique way to put it. I'd venture to say you might change that to *cursed* once all is said and done. Anyway, on to the Harrison chronicles, part two. This time it involves my very own father, Drake Jerome Harrison, or simply DJ to those closest to him in later years.

A man of many talents, pop inadvertently followed Uncle Dalton's footsteps in that he started his own security company after returning from the great war to end all wars. I'll save any further backstory, though sufficed to say Dad saw his share of strife in his time, what with surviving the great depression *and* faraway battlefields. Still, nothing could hold a candle to what he bore witness to over twenty years after coming home from war-torn Europe.

Mama…my mother flat refused to ever broach the subject and I'd only heard whispers 'til I was past draft age myself, when I overheard my older brother tell a buddy of his who'd claimed his own father was the toughest, meanest SOB on the planet. Gotta give my older bro credit, he one-upped this jughead without breaking a sweat. It was the dawn of the seventies and the height of the peace, drugs and love era. Vietnam split the country. Folks were screaming from every street corner.

Meanwhile, in the southern US, there was another war taking place with civil rights at the core. Over a ten-year span, Dad moved the brood from Santa Fe to Oklahoma City and finally to central Florida, yours truly recalling only flashes of that final move being that I was barely six at the time. Now, even though we were only a backstroke from Tampa, you'd have thought we were safely distanced from the hippie culture's psychedelic, doped-up trappings. Truth is, we probably would've been, save one little detail. A visitor to our fair state who unintentionally brought hell with 'im."

Flashback Part II

The Guardsman
Late Spring 1969
Jet Sands, Florida
Four miles south of Tampa

So, the deal was this. This bigshot record spinner from the west coast was touring the Midwest and deep south, thirty-some cities all told, famously preaching, screeching and lecturing on the evils of the hippie counterculture. WZTX out of Tampa, the bay area's King of Top Forty Pop and Rock, had, somewhat reluctantly I'd later discover, hopped aboard the '*nip that subversive crap squarely in the bud*' train. Word had it that the tour and its fearless leader came with considerable baggage from those opposed to his radical ideals. Being that the majority of the stops on the tour were of the heavily conservative variety, from Dallas/Fort Worth to Nashville to Birmingham to Atlanta, Trevor '*TNT*' Nichols, he of the Elvis the Pelvis sideburns, blue-swede shoes, Johnny Cash black suits and Jerry Lee Lewis shrieks, was all about traveling the safe route with that left-coast entourage of his. Leastways, that was the plan. As it was, what they so recklessly presumed would be just another groovy evening of 'preaching to the choir' took a severe turn for the worst. What's that old saying? Sometimes the best laid plans? As the kids say, *dig it*, they stepped into a world of hurt and pulled anyone within reach straight down into that deep, dark pit with 'em. I digress….

Anyhow, less than forty-eight hours before his turn at the mike at WZTX, the station manager gave us a ring and asked if we'd provide security for the evening. Not exactly our usual gig, warehouse, campus or special events more our regular bag. Thing is, I'd been offered what amounted to triple our regular rate for a six hour, two-man shift. Being that I had already booked three of our guys at other locales for that

116

particular Thursday, I had no choice. Peel my lazy carcass from behind the bosses' chair, strap on the old gun belt and join the party. Hey, there was no way I was turning my back on that kinda bread. I'd only recently moved the whole kit and kaboodle from Lawton to Jet Sands and was barely keeping my nostrils above the waterline, if you can dig that.

At that time, *The Guardsman Inc.* consisted of five full-time and four part-time slots, including yours truly. I hoped to add another two, possibly three warm bodies by the coming Fall, depending on how many long-term contracts I could secure in the bay area. For that moment anyway, beggars could hardly be choosers. Seven-hundred clams for six hours work, slapped into my palm in the form of cold, hard cash. I would happily miss one dinner with the family. As long as I'm spouting chestnuts of old, hindsight is definitely twenty-twenty. I digress…

As for the gig itself, the station director called me direct, no doubt because I'd made it a point to undersell every damn security outfit in the area. Apparently 'TNT' and his anti-flowerchild stance pissed off the local hipster community to the point of some very vocal demonstrations in Saint Louis, Atlanta and even Memphis. Hippies in Memphis? Who knew?

Anyhow, a few of 'em even involved some rock tossing and assorted trash fires in and around the participating stations. With that in mind, Miss Tanner, Judith as I came to know her, wasn't about to take any chances with, worse-case scenario, her baby going up in flames or even at the very least losing the majority of their windows courtesy of a good, old-fashioned stoning. Makes one wonder why they agreed to sponsor the guy's sideshow to begin with, then again it was the south and any strike against the left-coast is a strike worth landing. Can't count how many times I've heard California in particular referred to as 'the land of fruits and nuts.'

As a confessed Midwesterner, I didn't have a dog in that fight, but I will admit over time to developing quite the begrudging admiration for the locals' bulldog-stubborn, old-fashioned as home-squeezed lemonade attitudes towards anything resembling cultural change. Now, that's not saying I agreed with all or even the *majority* of it, but damned if they didn't stick to their conservative guns, right or wrong.

As for TNT Nichols and his traveling circus of tongue-flappers—

we found out upon arrival at the station he'd brought along a former road-groupie of several of the targeted bands and even a reformed LSD dealer who'd supposedly helped keep a few of the bigger names nice and juiced before and after live gigs.

Now, as far as I'd known at the time, the Tampa-St Pete area wasn't exactly a hotbed of flowerchildren. Come to think of it, since I was working twelve to fourteen hours a day, six days a week while attempting, halfheartedly if I'm honest, to maintain a marriage and family, there was probably a whole *hell* of a lot I didn't know that was transpiring right before my eyes. Thing was, I surely wasn't the only one, not by a long shot. Plenty of folks walked into that evening festivities mole blind. There was a hard lesson to learn. That is as demonstrations go, sometimes it ain't about quantity, but quality. Not only that, but sometimes it's what you *don't see* that can hurt you or even prove potentially fatal. Slight-of-hand, the nearly translucent distraction. Learned this the hard way in the security biz through the years.

The date of this specific learned lesson was fourteen May in the year of our lord nineteen sixty-nine. Late spring humidity was just cranking toward its early summer prime, but still oppressive enough to sufficiently moisten the pits. In true seasonal tradition, the skies cried a trio of times since dawn. The most recent of downpours just a half-hour before our arrival at the station, the air thick, dewy and stinking of recently toked weed. I digress…

My partner on this night was my first hire, a walking stick of a dude named Deke Carpenter. He of the Barney Fife physique and a cookie-duster so bushy it was more a matter of a mustache wearing a man than the other way around. Comical appearance issues aside, Deke was no pantywaist. Far from it. Slim but sturdy, he was a forty-something former Miami patrolman and Army infantryman who knew the difference between flakes, freedom riders, bad-asses or doves. Deke wasn't much for conversation, which was a big plus in my book. Just signed in, worked his shift and booked without causing a ripple. My kinda subordinate. Never turned down a shift and, recently divorced, wasn't hogtied by family obligations.

As for the '*Cancel Counter-Culture Tour*' delegates, besides the main mouthpiece, the former groupie and the dope-dealer, there was TNT's personal bodyguard. Known as *'The Spleen Smasher'* or simply *'Thick'*. Leroy Shoates was a former nose-guard for the Chargers, Giants and Chiefs who'd retired a few years back with scarred knees from what I'd heard was a dozen separate surgeries. With his shiny bald head, permanent squint and perpetual scowl, nobody was dog-stupid enough to test the rep of a six-five, two-hundred-eighty-pound dude whose appetite hadn't yet got the memo about scarfing less once you've hung up the cleats. Still, the man's arms were bigger than both my thighs shoved together and the second I saw 'im hop from their ride to run interference, stompin' around like a Tyrannosaurus with smoke pumpin' from both nostrils, apparently, he'd just flicked away a spent Winston-Salem upon exiting, I felt pretty damn confident myself and Deke had it made in the shade in terms of any substantial issues arising. Ah man, the dangers of complacency. I digress…

I hadn't broken out the Barracuda for a nightshift since the first few weeks of opening for business. Had the air and tunes cranked on high as we'd cruised the coastal parkway toward WZTX, *The Bay's Rockin' Rascals*. The station HQ, nicknamed the 'Silver Octagon' for its eight-sided appearance, was a thirty to forty-minute ride from the office, so I'd been careful to make tracks at half-past three to allow for unseen delays to make the five PM shift time. Sure enough, that afternoon's downpour birthed the usual number of fender-benders coming into downtown, but we just managed to dodge the predictable backup.

After passing through a wrought-iron entrance gate, where we were required to enter a keypad code provided by the station, I steered us through what seemed like several miles of a narrow, winding, twisted two-lane, walled in on both sides with sabal palmettos and bald cypress. Negotiating a final curve, the pavement gave way to a dirt/sand mix for another hundred yards before dead-ending at the outer edge of what appeared to be a recently paved lot. At the moment of our arrival, it was damn obvious we were late to the party.

For one, it appeared a large grouping of vehicles, everything from Roadrunners to VW bugs to microbuses, were packed into maybe a dozen available spaces, while another dozen were splayed across a narrow field of Bermuda grass like crooked, jagged teeth toward the rear of the building. Nary a clue how such a motley collection bypassed the entrance gate. So much for a secure perimeter. As for that ragtag grouping of wheels, nearly all sported Dade County tags and the cultural accessories of the day, from painted on peace or flower-power signs to pot-shaped stick-on's. Safe to say the word of TNT's arrival made it to Miami and a road-trip duly organized.

Standing out like a sore thumb was a white panel Ford van announcing '*Wired for Sound*' stereo and electrical repair, parked at an angle at the rear of the building. Thus, blocking off the one-lane path leading back there.

As for the famed octagon itself, its shape being pretty self-explanatory, the 'silver' portion of its moniker derived from the shiny silver dome from which its antennae stood. As she stood, a fairly compact structure, though I had the feeling it was one of those 'bigger on the inside than it looks on the outside' propositions.

Now, the unexpected car-lot was one thing, but it was more the gathering of those transported by the former that birthed immediate concern. Deke and I exchanged both a knowing glance and telepathic message that, roughly translated, might've been verbalized as 'exactly what kind of freakshow exhibit have we agreed to babysit?'

Zigzagging around the lot, I was forced to park my beloved Barracuda in knee-high cordgrass just to the left of a faded blue Ford T-bird with a rusted-out hood, cracked windshield with what appeared to be a pot bong in the shape of bare female breasts propped on the dash.

Normally I would've pasted one of my own handy stick-on signs announcing our presence to each of its doors via the company name and crest, being that the company's only official vehicle had been on assignment at a downtown warehouse in Clearwater, but wisely decided a little anonymity was in order.

I remember asking Deke to guess a headcount from the squirming, screeching masses. He'd shouted somewhere in the ballpark of fifty or so. I nodded in lieu of a verbal reply, thinking he'd undershot it by a dozen or more. Though an accurate count was impossible considering the majority donned the familiar hippie threads, baggy, flowy shirts, sun or micro dresses and above-the-knee boots, and were swaying, gyrating, even boogying in mass, creating a sort of hippie stew. I figured closer to seventy-five or eighty.

Deke and I made our way toward the station entrance via a lengthy stone walkway with little choice but to take note of a few of the signs being waved around as the usual counterpoint to TNT and the conservative voice he represented. From the relatively tame and oft-repeated, *'Make Love-Not War'*, *'Power to the People'*, to those solely Vietnam-war related, *'Drop acid, not bombs'*, *'Get the HELL out of Vietnam'*, to a select few relating closer to the demonstration at hand, *'DICKols-Respect my existence or expect resistance'*, *'Just spin the records and shut the F&^K up,'* and finally to the downright threatening, *'Play the music or get a real stick of TNT rammed straight up your ass."*

The first group to notice our advance did so with great relish, damn near salivating at the prospect of an up-close-and-personal with anyone representing the establishment of law and order. Be they commissioned or merely of the rental variety. At first glance, it appeared more than half were female, though I gotta admit if long hair alone was the lone characteristic on display, at least a dozen could've gone either way.

If I had a nickel for each and every insult tossed our way as we'd wound our way to the double-door entrance, colorful terms such as *'rent-a-swine'*, "*stormtrooper*', *'Nazi-for-hire'*, or *'Johnny one-bullet'*, that next day could've been spent making retirement plans in the Bahamas. As it was, Deke and I reached our destination without a physical scratch, though we both agreed in the aftermath that our nostrils hadn't been nearly as lucky. To put it mildly, those folks reeked like unwashed rear-end. Not to say all of 'em stunk, but the majority definitely held the stench of stale BO, rotting choppers and neglected ass-cracks. It was as if they'd made it a point to uphold the west coast hippie-stereotype we'd all heard about.

A line of 'em, sneering and growling like we'd pocketed their stashes, stood in a blocking pose at the bottom of some stone steps leading in, but they backed away quick enough once we made it obvious we weren't about to slow our pace.

By the time the station manager's assistant keyed the door, we'd practically dived inside just for a whiff of semi-fresh air. Surprisingly, not a single demonstrator tried to weasel their way in, content to step back, chant, curse and sway.

I did feel a light misting on the back of my neck, cleanly shaven just that morning courtesy of Bub's Barber Shop in Jet Sands. At one point Deke later confessed he'd felt a similar spit shower tickle his jawline as well, flat refusing, much like myself, to acknowledge it in fear of an impending tidal wave.

Shutting and relocking the door behind us, the assistant to Miss Tanner introduced herself as Patti Webb, a squirrely little chick of maybe twenty-five with coke-bottle-thick glasses, buckteeth and a bouffant doo thick enough to provide air cover. The lobby was fairly bland as such spaces went, just a couple of small leather couches, a single recliner bookended by lamp tables and centered by an entertainment center holding a small tv and stereo system; the entire setup as blue-light bargain-basement as the cut-rate framed, Kmart-rate pastoral pics adorning each wall.

Music echoed from all directions from assorted wall-speakers courtesy of the live broadcast, Otis Redding's 'Sittin' on the dock of the bay' the current selection. We followed Miss Webb, she of the baggy purple pantsuit, spindly frame and stiff, upright gait, down a narrow hall, its paneled-wood walls littered with photos of past DJ's.

I glanced at my wristwatch as we veered right and directly into a well-lit conference room, where at least two of the three folks present greeted us with varying degrees of disinterest. It was just past seventeen hours, five-oh-eight PM to be exact. TNT Nichols and his entourage were inbound within the half-hour and tensions were predictably high. Miss Judy Tanner, a snappily dressed, brunette beauty of perhaps forty with piercing brown eyes and the graceful agility of a professional dancer, breezed past her two colleagues to provide a warm smile, gentle handshake and prerequisite howdy. Meanwhile her assistant secured the door behind us with one hand while nervously gnawing the pinky finger of the other. I swear if someone popped a balloon in her vicinity that girl would've surely blown an artery and soiled herself, not necessarily in that order.

"Welcome to the octagon, gentleman," Miss Tanner announced

matter-of-factly, a gleaming twinkle in those gorgeous orbs. "For this particular evening however, we'll simply refer to it as our little corner of hades. The mission that you have chosen to accept, is to help us survive the next three hours with our collective skins intact. I have the feeling that whatever payment we agreed upon for your services will prove to be one of the great bargains in private security history."

I liked that lady from minute one. I would also grow to *respect* her greatly. I just wish she hadn't proven to be so damned prophetic.

~ * ~

Inmates of The Octagon

"So once Nichols and his crew arrive, you want us to form a cordon at least wide enough for them to make it inside, basically to prevent one of his many admirers from snatchin' his toupee?"

Drake Harrison stood stiffly behind the podium as if preaching a Sunday sermon or chairing an executive meeting.

"Precisely that, Officer Harrison," Miss Tanner confirmed, flawless dimples briefly on full display from the flash of a smile that evaporated all too quickly.

"All due respect, ma'am'," Deke said, twirling the right corner of his enormous mustache like a classic villain from a black and white serial, "The two of us don't make much of a cordon, considering the mob of thoroughly perturbed longhairs out there."

"Well, truth be told, we didn't expect such an…impressive turnout. Just do the best you can to help protect our guests."

"As for those perturbed longhairs, by all means, feel free to shoot 'em if you feel the need," a balding, bespeckled man wearing a perpetual frown first introduced as Trent Daniels, station sales manager, spat sourly. Wearing a blue suit that appeared at least two sizes too small for his pudgy build, he appeared on the verge of taking a header into the nearest wall "Well, maybe even if you *don't*. Do society a favor."

"Please, Trent," Tanner injected, shooting the man a stern glance that strongly suggested he cease and desist. To which Daniels stared down at his Buster Browns and did just that. A second male representative, who's blonde, shoulder-length locks matched any of those outside, Jody Gilliam by name and program director by trade, sat motionless and expressionless at the conference table with heavily tattooed arms crossed, staring into a far wall as if daydreaming of when the entire mess was just an unpleasant memory.

"It goes without saying that the least publicity we need is active gunplay," Tanner continued, pacing the narrow space between the conference table and back wall. "Channels two and four are on their way, probably to arrive either just at or near the time Nichols and his crew pull up. As for any probable riots, we're hoping your presence alone will provide ample deterrent."

"Not to worry, boys," Gilliam spoke up, his ragged, gravelly voice that of a lifetime smoker. "You got *The Spleen Smasher* himself backing you up. I'd bet he's more than willing to crack some hippie-skull if push comes to shove. I saw the guy play in his prime and I'd confidently lay my money on him against forty or fifty doped-out draft-dodgers."

"Good to know," Deke mumbled drolly, shooting Drake a somber glance.

Noticing Tanner's deep frown at his associate's reckless statement, Drake quickly intervened.

"Well then, Officer Carpenter and I will do our best to keep space between Mister Shoates and the crowd."

In the aftermath, he and Miss Tanner locked eyes and nodded in unison.

Meanwhile, Patti Webb began desperately tugging at her bosses' jacket sleeve as if to ask for permission to use the head.

"They should be, um, pulling up within the next five to ten minutes, Miss Tanner. Perhaps these men, um, the guards should take up position at the edge of the walkway."

"Calm yourself, Patti," Tanner consoled with a gentle tap to her assistant's shoulder, "I think Officers Harrison and Carpenter deserve the ten-cent tour. Join me, gentlemen?"

"Yes, ma'am," Drake answered, stepping away from the podium and joining his partner at the door as Tanner calmly doled out instructions to her staff in-between random grumblings and complaints.

"...bad idea all along, Judith...not exactly doing my ulcer any favors..." Daniels moaned between labored sighs.

"...we got with the program. The tunes his kind are targeting are headed straight up the charts no matter the amount of bitchin'..." Gilliam said, pointing upturned thumbs into the air.

"Listen people, I don't completely agree with the decision either, but Stevenson okayed it and that is that. Now, just do your jobs and in a few hours it'll all be over but the crying."

Bernard Stevenson, it was to be learned, owned the octagon along with two additional Tampa area stations. As a decorated World War II vet, he was a harsh critic of hippie culture and all it stood for.

Daniels continued his rant even as Drake pulled the conference room door ajar and held it there for Tanner to take point.

"Hey, I understand the PR aspect of it, but like everything else, there's bad and good public relations and this has bad with a capital B written all ov..."

An overheard speaker suddenly chopped short both the man's incessant whine *and* Simon and Garfunkel's '*Mrs. Robinson*', a downtrodden male voice announcing that a pair of media vans had been spotted exiting off the highway toward the station, obviously an in-house announcement since one of the previous year's biggest hits instantly cut back in.

"That's Rockin' Rick Ross, our senior DJ," Tanner said, leading them back out into the hallway and briefly pointing out a specific wall-pic featuring a grinning, long-bearded, silver-haired gentleman sporting a fringe jacket straight out of the Vegas Elvis catalog of flamboyance, "C'mon, I'll introduce you."

They took a sharp left and into a spacious breakroom, home to two large fridges, a trio of dining tables and assorted snack machines. In one corner sat, not one, but two retro jukeboxes and a cleared, circular space that could only be a dance floor.

"Nice," Drake commented, "You know you've got it made in the shade as an employee when the prime room in your workplace is the break room."

Tanner nodded as they continued through. "Mister Stevenson's vision. His blueprint for the building came partially from a fifties diner."

As a dead-end loomed, all slowed to sidestep a man half-submerged into the ceiling, and removing false tiles being propped nearby, while another peered upward from under the bill of a multi-stained baseball cap into the same darkened space without ever acknowledging the passerby's presence, the back of his faded blue uniform shirt declaring *'Wired for Sound Inc. – Where clarity is next to godliness'*.

"Some issue with the output or input. It shouldn't affect the broadcast," Tanner said flatly, all but drowning out the muffled echoes of the half-hidden worker mumbling something to the effect of 'diced 'em and spliced 'em without a hitch.'

As the hall veered right, the faint but unmistakable sound of Tommy James and The Shondells *'Crimson and Clover'* echoing through the narrow corridor, the trio passed a grouping of assorted office spaces, the last of which featured Judith Tanner's name and title stenciled in bold lettering.

The Disc Jockey's *'Jam Cave'*, as it was labeled in poster board across the entry door was surprisingly cramped, with enough room for the on-air DJ and perhaps one other guest, depending on the collective bulk of each. Tanner, having entered first to greet the man she referred to as *'Triple R'*, then backed out to allow the officer's room to enter, though to do so they were forced to turn sideways.

Upon side-stepping inside, both scanned the surrounding walls, where full-blown posters had been created from recent album covers; Drake's wandering eye fixating on the Beatle's rainbow-colored *'Hey Jude, Revolution'* offering while Deke's intrusive stare found and studied, head slightly tilted, Creedence Clearwater Revival's 3D-like *'Bayou Country'*.

"Well, if it isn't the rent-a-fuzz boys. What's up, fellas?" Rockin' Rick bellowed, deep-set blue eyes gleaming and surprisingly toned arms outspread as if to receive a group hug. Decked out in a sleeveless T displaying Jim Hendrix's profile, cut-off blue jeans and beach sandals, his silver hair was wound into a tight ponytail that slung over his right shoulder like a reptile's tail-end. His thick, gray-tinted beard was braided as well, its pointy end reaching his breastbone. If first impressions meant anything, it wasn't hard to guess which side of the counter-culture fence Ross favored.

"Mister Ross," Drake replied with a slight nod, obviously still distracted, this time by the alphabetized stacks of LP's lining the wall to his right.

"Triple...R, is it?" Deke inquired, reaching out to take the man's hand and instantly forced to participate in the intricate three-step *'Dignity and Pride'* shake of the times.

"R...R...R. *Rockin' Rick Ross?*" the older man ribbed with a dramatic arch of a brow. "It ain't calculus, dude."

Deke shot him a wink that was anything but playful.

"Nope, I'd imagine it isn't."

"So, we've gauged your co-workers. How do you feel about Nichols' stepping onto your turf?" Drake asked, regretting the question but hapless to refrain.

"I think he's a rightwing jackass whose pockets are well-padded with the tinted bread of those pulling his strings. He probably doesn't even believe in half the manure he's spreading, but hey, scuttlebutt is that brand-spankin' new condos in Beverly Hills, fresh-off-the-assembly-line sportscars and top-of-the-line mistresses don't come cheap. Slick-talkin' turkey will say whatever they suggest. Guess it's obvious even to a couple of radio rubes like yourself why the once-revered Triple-R has been relegated to the day shift. I flat refuse to smooch the cheeks of anyone I don't respect."

"Not exactly one of your DJ heroes, I take it?"

Ross regarded Drake as if octopi tentacles were sprouting from both ears.

"He...dude, I was spinning records in Motown when this guy was knee-high to a beetle, and I *don't* mean John Lennon."

Leaning over until his face was practically flush with a row of LP's, Drake's inquiry was more a sly shot than actual concern.

"Noted. You gonna be able to maintain professionalism for the interview?"

The veteran DJ openly cringed, his pinched expression that of someone assaulted by a sudden, rank odor.

"Not *me*, man. Judy's pegged Gilliam for the question-and-answer segment. The less time I spend in the same space with that egomaniacal media-whore, the better."

With the timing and expertise expected of a veteran disc jockey, Ross spun around, pulled a fresh LP from one of a dozen album sleeves stacked to his right and tossed it onto the only one of three not currently occupied.

Seconds later, the opening cords of the Grass Roots' *'Midnight Confessions'* flowed faintly, just loud enough to be heard, from a trio of overhead speakers.

"I mean, sincere or not, and I highly doubt the former, the dude and all like 'im are fighting a losing battle. Those songs they're condemning speak to the new generation like no other form of music ever has to those older. Like Dylan says, the times they are a'changin'. Either change with 'em or hop off the track. Don't get me wrong. I still groove on Elvis and Wilson Pickett as much as the next guy, but before them it was Pat Boone and old Blue Eyes. The landscape changes with the times, so should the tunes. Dig it," he gestured in the general direction of the building's entrance, "I realize I'm old enough to have sired most of those children of peace and love standing out there chantin', but I get it. I get *them*. History will show they were right on."

Patti Webb, eyes bulging behind comically thick lenses, poked her head inside just as Deke's open smirk might've lit the fuse on yet another speech from Rockin' Rick, his lips parted in a frozen sneer.

"News media is on site, currently being mobbed by, well, that mob. Nichols and company's ETA presently stands at between five and eight minutes, plus another ten allowed for brief media contact, building entry and staff introductions. Rick, you might want to prep the next four songs, just as discussed."

Leaning back while lighting up a fresh smoke, displeased frown firmly in place, Rick sighed disgustedly before flashing her the 'okay' sign.

"Yeah, yeah. I can count, Pat. Go pop yourself a valium and wind down, will ya?"

Flipping through a fresh stack of LP's, he turned briefly to address the departing guards, lit cigarette bobbing freely from his lower lip, while freeing them from their respective sleeves.

"The plan is that I shag ass before Mister High 'n Mighty contaminates the booth with his pompous aroma."

As the two men exited, they heard Rockin' Rick mumble, between maniacal giggles, "If I had any balls, I'd toss away stale Frankie Valli for some prime Jefferson Airplane."

"So, what's the difference?" Deke inquired as they made their way back to the building lobby.

"Country fan, I take it?" Drake shot back with a smile.

The slender man shrugged rounded shoulders, his broomlike 'stache twitching.

"Nope. Dolphins."

In reaching the station entrance and receiving a sneak preview of the chaos beyond, Drake was beginning to seriously wonder if they hadn't been *underpaid* after all.

~ * ~

Petals of War

The doors flung inward just as Deke reached for one of the handles, followed by a mini stampede that both men were hapless to do anything but witness by backing away from a line of incoming bodies.

For a fleeting moment, Drake considered the possibility someone gassed them using something akin to 'acid gas' or perhaps the air conditioning was laced with LSD particles. As for his subordinate, Deke's wide-eyed stare and unhinged lower jaw expressed a similar belief. It wasn't until all ceased their frantic movements, a few dancing wild jigs as if an army of ants trespassed within their respective underpants and stood somewhat still, that all possibilities of hallucinogen-use were solidly debunked.

All but two who rushed in, six in total, by Drake's count, were coated in flower petals. From tulips to daisies to pansies to daffodils, they stuck to their targets in clumps and bunches that no amount of shaking, juking or random swipes could hope to clear away.

"Close 'em, damn it!" someone shouted angrily, "Close 'em and lock 'em!"

"Not just yet. Just hang on. Got me some trash to throw out!" another chimed in with equal ire, only much less shrilly but more a guttural growl as much animal as human. The source a massive black male in a cut-off muscle tee that accentuated his ample bulk. Baring teeth layered in gold, he dragged two squirming forms by the collars of their overly baggy shirts toward the entrance, their flowing locks making it virtually impossible to successfully gauge a definitive sex. Despite the quite impressive physical feat of slinging them one at a time through the space provided like so much bagged laundry, there was a marked loss of machismo in that a wad of yellow buttercups stuck to his forehead like a mutating fungus.

"*Now* you can bolt that mother," the man Drake assumed simply had to be Leroy Shoates blared, strutting from the doors while extending a barrel chest roughly the width of a Mac truck grill.

The remainder of the new arrivals stood in a semi-circle, tearing at the mass of assorted petal's attached to their person. Trevor 'TNT' Nichols, perhaps the easiest to ID other than The Spleen Smasher, appeared the least perturbed at the flower-shower, peeking beneath the lens of his dark tinted shades to gently pinch off groupings of white magnolias from his black suit jacket and sleeves and shaking several more from his trademark blue suede shoes. Drake couldn't help but think that with his tall, lanky build, signature sideburns and granite jaw, Nichols was better suited to pose in front of a camera, maybe a news anchor or weather prognosticator, instead of parked anonymously behind a radio mic.

As for the former roadie to the rock stars or '*The Divine Miss G*' as she was infamous known, Jennifer Greene was dressed relatively conservative in dress slacks, red pumps and a light brown blouse, a spattering of purple violet's sprouting from the tightly wound bun atop her noggin. Once petal-free, she came off surprisingly soft-spoken and well-mannered and one could hardly picture the petite, only moderately attractive young woman as the backstage and tour-bus slut of legend.

Unlike Miss Greene, the physical appearance of once noted but recently retired pot and LSU dealer for several as-yet-to-be-named bands known as Casey McCormick did little to alter the stereotypical look of his past profession. Decked out in a fringed hippie waistcoat, bubble-sleeved shirt, laced moccasins and frayed bellbottom jeans, the lone component separating him from the chanting enemy outside the station doors was a relatively short, conventional haircut.

Also, unlike the others, McCormick seemed less enraged but amused by the flowery assault, to the point where he showed no inclination to remove the many pink carnations hitching a ride on the back of the waistcoat, nor the bright yellow daisy petals perched on each shoulder and layering his coif.

Despite the flurry of sudden activity and a viable sense of danger, however temporarily stifled, Drake simply could not get over the fact that all four had been doused with different petals, as if each held a specific meaning for the victim.

"Is everyone okay?" he heard Miss Tanner ask, a bug-eyed Patti Webb standing directly behind her and peeking around a shoulder as if using her employer as a human shield.

"We're fine," Trevor Nichols stated firmly, having extracted all but one petal, currently balanced atop his left ear, "I had a feeling they were up to something. Once we'd hopped out of the van, they parted like the red sea to allow us a clear path to the doors. Why, they even remained downright cordial while I spoke to the reporters, but once we cleared those steps…bombs away."

Jennifer Greene, having unclipped the hair bun, was stretching out several lengthy strands with one hand while pinching off random petals with the other.

"Well, drat, they must've poured molasses or honey on some of the flowers."

"Better hope it was *just* syrup, sweetie," McCormick quipped, hands on hips with squinting eyes scanning the lobby.

"Oh yuck," she replied, scowling, either oblivious or indifferent to McCormick's girlish giggle in the aftermath. With his overplayed flamboyance, feminine gestures and pooched-out lips, the famed dealer to the stars appeared to mimic both Liberace and Mick Jagger simultaneously.

"Miss Tanner, shouldn't we contact the proper authorities?" Patti Webb inquired nervously while peering over at Drake and Deke, both of whom were scanning the gathering crowd outside the double doors.

"Oh, I don't think so, Patti. I highly doubt that flower petals, even when thrown in bulk, are considered deadly weapons. I'm sure the officers on hand can handle things from here."

"Yes, ma'am," Drake responded without turning around, "If we see anything that concerns us to the point of needing the Bay's finest, we'll give 'em a ring."

Slapping away the last of the buttercups from his massive right shoulder, Shoates fronted the station manager and executed a slight bow, golden grill gleaming.

"Rest assured, madame, that if the officers require assistance in tamin', shooin' away or even restrainin', I'll be more than happy to assist."

"I don't think that'll be necessary, Mister Shoates, but thank you for offering. So, are we ready to relocate to the booth?"

"Indeed, we are. While the naysayers toss insults and vegetation in the name of hate, I shall retaliate with honesty and a much deadlier weapon; cold, hard *facts*," Nichols bellowed in his best radio-ready voice, reaching up with groping fingers to reset what was obviously, top of the line or not, a hairpiece.

With a smile as obviously forced as Nichols' wig, Tanner waved them toward the hallway.

"Um, very well then. This way please."

Halting in mid-stride, she instructed Patti to take point before striding back over toward the station entrance.

"Officer Harrison, don't hesitate to call for police assistance if needed. I mean it," she gestured toward a deserted welcoming desk and a black phone taking up space on one corner.

"Will do. Just FYI. Officer Carpenter will be manning the lobby while I make my way towards the back entrance, just in case, heaven forbid, someone attempts a breech during the broadcast. I have a feeling that if trouble arises, that will be the time and place."

"Understood. I'll brief the wiring guys on my way to the booth to just stay in place for now. We don't need to be opening that door for any reason until Nichols and his crew finish up."

"Agreed. Well," he said with a tip of the cap, "Good luck with the broadcast. Who knows? Maybe Nichols isn't the pompous jackass he appears."

She laughed into a curled palm, nodded, and strode quickly away, her shapely rear not lost on Harrison's wandering gaze.

"Ten bucks says he *is,* boss," Deke jibed, straight-faced once she'd vanished down the hall.

"No bet," Drake with a roll of the eyes, "Hey, keep that radio clutched and if anything resembling shit starts to descend, give me a buzz, hear?"

Pulling the handheld walkie-talkie from his utility belt, from which also hung a two-foot in length, hard-hickory truncheon and a Smith & Wesson thirty-eight, Deke held it airborne in apparent compliance.

"Yes, mother. You do the same."

Securing his own radio, Drake powered it up and executed a quick operational check by punching the talk button three times, to which Deke responded in kind.

"Will do, though potheads aren't generally known to tote battering rams around in their togas, much less have the energy to use 'em."

To acknowledge this, Deke poked the send button one final time.

As Drake walked purposely down the hall to the faint sound of Van Morrison's *'Brown-eyed Girl'* reverberating overhead, he briefly second-guessed his casual dismissal of the station manager's advice to contact the bay area PD for additional backup. Although there was the vague sense that something was amiss, totally unconnected to the collective chemically altered masses out front, he quickly dismissed this natural apprehension as being a product of the job itself. A company used to checking ID's or strolling around empty warehouses simply wasn't used to crowd-control. Still, a series of deep breaths as he negotiated the twisting hall did little to sooth the foreboding vibe. A vibe he had felt only one other time in his life in a time and circumstance best forgotten least a full-blown meltdown was in order.

By the time he reached the station's trio of offices and noticed the door slightly ajar to one labeled 'J. Gilliam-Programming', pausing in mid-step for a brief glimpse inside, slight regret swiftly transformed to full-blown remorse.

A set of splayed, bare legs.

A sneaker dislodged from a socked foot and flipped upside down just inside the door frame.

A muffled series of thuds, as if someone were repeatedly striking a well-padded couch with a blunt object.

Slowly retrieving the Colt thirty-eight from its holster, the handheld walkie held mere inches from pursed lips, Drake used a highly polished boot-tip to ease the door fully ajar.

Gasping aloud, he had only begun to process the indescribable terrors reflected in each of his own suddenly dilated eyes when darkness fell.

~ * ~

The Sounds of Violence

Noise: Intrusive, invasive, blaring. *Light:* Penetrating, all-encompassing, blinding. *Smells:* Unrecognizable, overwhelming, putrid. A light tap to the right shoulder. Another. Still another but this one noticeably firmer. Someone whispers, the words hopelessly garbled. The next blow is more a solid jab to the bicep region, accompanied not by a whisper but a scream. A banshee-shriek that feels as if it entered one ear, drilled straight through bone and brain-matter to blow out the other side.

When he comes to, it isn't the gentle, gradual revival one might associate from the faint singing of songbirds and morning sunshine through opened blinds. No, more a sudden, brutal shock to the senses akin to a pointy icicle rammed into the groin.

Though he has little hope that what his bugging, bloodshot eyes take in with that initial visual is anything but real and not some insane fever-dream, he executes a silent, sputtering prayer for it to be so.

Someone is screaming and cannot stop. A non-stop scream/cackle hybrid that doesn't require a replenished oxygen supply to resume. It isn't until someone slaps him hard enough to loosen several teeth and the anguished wail abruptly ceases that the source hits home.

Loosened teeth and stinging flesh aside, he screams with newfound vigor.

~ * ~

Mucus and blood, thick and gummy, poured from Drake Harrison's nostrils in glutinous globs as a hand squeezed his cheeks with such force no air could possibly enter or exit via the usual routes.

"Wakey-wakey little piggy-wannabe," a shrill voice, presumably male, brayed near his left ear. "Wakey-wakey or you're gonna miss out on all the party favors. Gonna be a gas for sure, fuzzy-wuzzy."

As his lungs burned with increased need, the failed attempt at reaching up to free the constriction birthed still another mystery until the realization that both arms were bound in some yet-unknown fashion.

"Oh, for the love of…Huck, cease and desist poundin' 'im and maybe he will," Another voice weighs in, this one unmistakably female and originating from behind him as well, but from a greater distance than his assailant.

With the hasty release of his jaws, his chin immediately collapsed onto his upper chest before bouncing back up just as rapidly. A single inhale of precious oxygen was executed before being cut off yet again, courtesy of a gummy, rough-edge wrap wound so snugly it forced his jaws apart, leaving mucus-packed nostrils as the sole breathing option.

"You've already missed some far-out damage, Officer Rent-a-Piglet," the male cackled again at his back, this time near his right ear. A feeble attempt at a headbutt struck only air, followed by a sharp smack to the back of his head, where an existing wound, throbbing and stinging like a reopened gash, was instantly awakened.

"Would you stop clubbing him? I swear, Magnus is gonna peel your noggin if you end up croaking him premature!" the female voice scolded, though with no real venom.

As the assorted horrors all around slowly extracted their festering bowels, like warm pus from a long-disregarded infection, onto an already thoroughly pummeled psyche, Drake's natural defenses attempted to build a wall to protect what few cells of sanity remained intact. Unfortunately, retreating in this case, meant returning to the most recent, similarly tragic event before the present one. This being the natural assumption that whatever came before simply had to be better. In this case, the visuals that flooded back were of little consolation:

The station manager's office door parted to reveal two figures standing over a third, the latter sitting on a section of thick shag carpeting previously shaded light beige now layered in wet splotches of darkest maroon.

Initially both figures had their back to him, their '*Wired for Sound*' shirts on full display, though the baseball caps were conspicuously missing, revealing shoulder length coifs what swayed and wavered like flowing seaweed with each jerky movement.

Raising and dropping their arms, one his right and the other his left, with an almost timed efficiency, like gold miners from another era smashing rock for buried treasure. For those few moments, Drake was unable to visualize the seated man due to the other men filling the space. He was, however, witness to the office ceiling, the tile dotted and spattered, respectively, with both single red droplets and lengthier smears. With each lift of an arm, an additional spatter appeared, along with the sporadic blob of red/grayish goo that Drake could only compare with thickened globs of cooked oatmeal.

It wasn't until the men paused, as if finally feeling his presence, that the blurry movement of their arms ceased, revealing the thick metal pipes each clutched at one rounded end. As each twisted gradually around, metal clubs suspended overhead, a space was created between them. A space which allowed Drake his first glimpse of the third figure present.

The cloaked figure with the spaced legs and splayed feet.

The figure wearing the sandaled feet of a beatnik, pale, bony legs bared beneath a pair of blue shorts, the shirt above revealing a famous black guitarist whose name Drake was unable to drudge up, at least what little portion of the rocker's visage wasn't obscured by what appeared to a bucket's worth of spilled red paint.

Propped in a sitting position with its neck propped on the edge of an ottoman, the face and head had been pulped beyond any recognition, to the point where it was impossible to ID as a human head at all, more a glob of discarded goulash from which patches of matted hair had sprouted.

No matter, Drake realized with an inner shudder. Faceless state and scrambled egg-skull aside, Drake had little doubt that *Rockin' Rick Ross* had definitely spun his last disc.

Hot bile burning the back of his throat, Drake shot another quick gaze upward, where chunks of gore hung from random tiles like bloody stalagmites. Instinctively backing away a step, he tossed the walkie-talkie onto the hallway carpet and gripped the Colt in both hands just as the pair completed their turn. Their faces had just begun to come into full focus, his aim swaying smoothly from one to the other, when a muffled thump ensued, followed by an explosion of sparks and sharp pain at the back of his skull. A cloudy swill of darkness, anything but soothing, washed over his fevered senses with an arctic chill.

His reintroduction to the terrors of the present was no less terrifying, if only for the horror of not knowing if there was to be a future to be found beyond it.

"Hey pig, snap to! Pay attention now or I'm liable to let Huck have his jollies," the female voice shrieked, ever closer, accompanied by a solid slap to the back of his noggin and lighting up the previous wound yet again. Regardless, there were questions that required immediate answers. Only then could the situation be accurately assessed, and a possible solution mapped out and executed.

He was seated and obviously bound. He was in the breakroom, that much was clear, though it had been dramatically redecorated since that initial walkthrough.

To his left sat Judith Tanner and to his right the guy introduced as the former dope dealer to the stars, McCloud or McCartney, something similar, strapped to breakroom chairs by what looked like several rolls of duct tape apiece. Arms pulled back, ankles crossed, mouth wrapped tight with the jaws agape. A quick self-inventory proved he bore similar handicaps, the searing pain at the back of his skull and groin, apparently 'Huck' or another of the gang had mistaken his testicles for soccer balls and kicked the stew out of them, having provided ample distraction from a checklist of additional injuries.

Tanner cried so heavily her black mascara ran down each jawline until she resembled an Indian squaw donning war paint. He saw her eyes skip over him then reel back to relock upon realizing he was conscious and at least semi-aware. The desperation behind those tear-filled orbs was palpable.

As for the former dealer to the stars, it appeared someone had used his face for a speedbag, his lower lip split and oozing bloody drool, his nose crooked and swollen, his blackened eyes so grotesquely bloated only narrow slits remained. His waistcoat and puffy shirt had been ripped away with the word 'queer' carved into his upper chest so neatly it appeared the wound had been repeatedly cleaned and finally coated with some sort of healing salve.

Several burning questions immediately shot to the forefront of Drake's frayed mind. Just how long had he been out? Where were Trevor Nichols or the female roadie whose name escaped him and the perpetually nervous Miss Webb? Most importantly, where the hell was Deke?

From the wall speakers blared Jefferson Airplane's '*White Rabbit*', an ode to casual drug use that was being cranked so loudly it nearly drowned out the surrounding clamor.

His vision nearly clear of the previous blurriness, Drake noticed Tanner gaping wild-eyed toward the breakroom dance floor and immediately followed her unblinking gaze.

Leroy Shoates staggered drunkenly in a circle, head bowed, eyes closed with his massive arms swinging loosely at his sides. As he stumbled around, miraculously able to stand upright, he briefly posed with his back to them, where at least a dozen syringes, buried to the hilt, protruded from his lower back like porcupine quills.

"Righteous. You came to just in time, Fuzzy-Wuzzy," the figure identified as Huck hooted, darting out from behind Drake towards a clearly dazed Shoates, who legs had parted in a semi-split and was swaying dramatically from front to back, his bowed head rolling like a marble atop a thick stump of a neck.

As for Huck, the man was colossal both in height and width,

standing at least a half-a-foot taller than Shoates, no height-challenged man himself by any means, with a bulk that at least matched the former pro d-lineman. Like the faux electricians, Huck's hair dipped well past his massive shoulders though he was cleanshaven and dressed fairly conservative in blue jeans, sneakers and a light blue casual shirt opened at the chest.

Dashing over with surprising grace, the giant hippie gripped the shorter man's shoulders and righted his balance before backing away with a howl.

"C'mon now, boy, don't flake out on us now. There are folks here that paid some serious bread to watch you boogie like a good native spear-chucker should. You seeing this, Ophelia? Mister badass spleen-crusher was thinking of crashing. Talk about a lightweight."

Executed what sounded like mere inches from his left ear, Drake could picture a wart-nosed witch stirring a boiling cauldron of bat parts at the piercing wail that was the female's inane braying.

"Now, now, Huck. Cut him some slack. To be fair, he's absorbed enough to croak a bull elephant."

Frowning, the big man danced a spastic jig around Shoates as if to provide a human crutch if he did begin to topple.

"No shit. I still don't get why we gotta waste such prime skag on this waste of space when an iron pipe would've done the job a hell of a lot faster."

"Big picture, Huck, remember the big picture," she scolded, having moved to Drake's immediate right but not yet far enough over to allow a clear visual.

"Yeah, yeah, I get it," he bellowed loudly due to competing with the Beatles' '*Lucy in the sky with Diamonds*' for audible airspace, rolling his eyes while reaching out with an open palm to steady Shoates' forward momentum, "But it's still a bummer."

The female seemed to be pacing behind him, as Drake noted the location of her voice at his back rotated from left to right then back again.

"Dude, Magnus knows what he's doing. Sacrifices had to be made. We all understood that. The message has got to be clear. For that to happen, certain things have to be spelled out, spoon-fed."

The giant hippie, still frowning, gripped Shoates by the back of his shirt collar to prevent yet another potential tumble forward.

"I said I *get* it, chickie-pie. Don't mean I gotta like it."

The two continued their bizarre two-step as if dancing to the current song blaring over the speakers, Shoates periodically slumping downward only to be hauled back up for what appeared to be nothing more than humiliation's sake.

As The Beatle's smash hit from the previous year faded to dead air, so too did the two men slow their collective movements, the overhead speakers soon showcasing the man so many had come to scoff and chastise and others to possibly exterminate with extreme prejudice.

'Trent Nichols here folks, proud to be live at WZTX, The Bay's Rockin' Rascals, and honored to have been…invited to share my message to all you, well, rocking rascals out there.'

"Well, well, well, finally!" Huck bellowed, by now forced to hold Shoates upright by the armpits.

"Sssshhh," the female reprimanded yet again, "Let the skuzz-bucket make the scene."

'…tour the southern states with a message to jam-lovers of all ages, that is of the many tangible dangers what these so-called psychedelic songs are creating, first and foremost being the rampant illegal drug experimentation…'

"Damn, there ain't even a trace of nervousness in that slicker's tone. Incredible."

"Huck, would you clam up already?"

Wearing a mad grin, the big man showed no hint of remorse while hauling Shoates' bulky form from side to side with little effort, as if two-hundred-seventy-plus pounds of dead weight were no more than an empty husk.

'…been on the front lines, boys and girls. Spinning records in and around San Francisco for the past decade, let me tell you, TNT has seen it first-hand. The addiction, the overdoses, the lives permanently snuffed out and countless others forever altered. While rock 'n roll is not solely to blame for this tragic shift in culture, neither is that so-called police action in southeast Asia. More it's a combination of many elements, to

include a slowly eroding family unit birthed by a nationwide epidemic of divorce. Hey, we all agree that popular music speaks to youth as nothing else quite does and the younger generation will in many cases emulate their rock and roll heroes for no other reason, quite frankly, than to give the finger to their parents and those in authori..."

Drake caught himself dozing, as much from Nichols' unexpectedly robotic monotone as the beating he'd endured, only the constant strain of obtaining sufficient oxygen keeping him conscious. To his right he could hear Judith Tanner's muffled sobs and from his left the occasional wet garbling noise escaping the comatose former dealer.

He had little doubt that both himself, Deke and the entire staff, whomever was unfortunate enough to be in the building at the time, weren't meant to survive the terrorist act underway. To this end, he tried desperately to drudge up a workable plan, any plan, though realistically the present scenario did little to breed confidence. He pondered not only Deke's fate, but Patti Webb, Gilliam and Daniels. From the savage brutality he'd witnessed already, Rockin' Rick's grisly death a less-than-welcome flashback, they were here, as the yet-unseen female hinted, to send a message. He had, of course, heard tales of west coast hippie cults, a few of which not only dabbled in black magic but human sacrifice. Until this date, this *very* night, all the stories and urban legends had been just that.

Chin dipping, he stared down at his own thoroughly bound torso, attempting to wriggle his wrists and feeling nothing but a numb paralysis. He decided to concentrate instead on the binds at his ankles, when a new commotion intervened, one that was simply not to be ignored.

"Sooo, what do we think, gang? C'mon now, let's hear it for King Sanctimony himself, Trevor...T...N...T...Nichols and his traveling band of suck-ups on the last leg of their farewell tour."

Despite this being his initial appearance, the man behind the cheerleading intro required little introduction, regardless of outwardly nerdy physical features there was a definitive air of cockiness and authority about him.

As for the male associate accompanying him, Drake recalled him as the wiring guy who'd been staring up into the ceiling as they'd passed by on the station tour. Like an overgrown kid competing in a cart race, the man referred to as Magnus steered the latest bound hostage into the breakroom at breakneck speed via a tilted-back rolling chair.

"Hiya, um, boss," Huck said, allowing Shoates' slumping bulk to collapse onto the hardwood and gesturing first toward Nichols then toward the nearest overhead speaker, "Um, …how is it…how come I can still hear *him* yappin'?"

"It's called a *recording*, Einstein," the mystery female shot back just to Drakes left, her slim outline drifting in and out of his peripheral vision.

"TNT's greatest hits, you might say," the man verified with a wink, the pencil-thin mustache he exhibited so miniscule to mimic drawn on ink-marks. Of stout, porky build and round, plump face, his eyes practically gleamed madness of a higher plain, his accent a bizarre hybrid of deep south dandy and SoCal surfer-dude.

"I do believe this particular segment was from the Nashville stop but hey, it wasn't like he didn't repeat the same stale crap from Phoenix to Shreveport to Mobile. Ad nauseam. Verbatim. Word for stinking word. Nobody would ever be the wiser. Dude was all about the bread. All show and no go. Had some bottomless pockets out there sponsoring his tour. Typical republican hawks stirring up shit back home. I guess sending our boys to the slaughter in some random rice-paddy wasn't enough."

The obviously procured electrician's work-shirt he'd donned appeared at least two sizes too small, as had the pleated pants, the former unbuttoned to the waist and the latter unfastened below his ample gut. Like the two similarly dressed associates, his straight black hair flowed over both round shoulders, though Drake could've sworn he saw the entire hairline shift at the scalp, slipping free until he'd reached up to right its warped trajectory.

The man playfully spun the chair in a wide circle before braking. As he parked the chair facing Drake and the others, one fact was crystal clear amongst all the cloak and dagger; Trevor Nichols had given his final dissertation on the evils of psychedelic rock. Unlike the others, his lifeless form clung to his own personal padded throne by a single strand of tape across the chest, his stocking feet, minus the trademark blue suedes, dragging limply near the wheels. As for the cause of his demise, there was little mystery, as the left side of his face, from forehead to lower jaw, appeared grotesquely warped, as if caved in with great force. Like a balloon being squeezed from one side, the right side appeared severely swollen, the eyeball protruding from its bloated socket like a bloodshot white marble on the cusp of popping free.

Drake instantly recalled all-too-well how a pair of metal pipes had so dramatically altered Rick Ross's personality.

"Shall I?" the female inquired timidly.

Overhead, Trevor Nichols ranted and raved on, albeit mechanically. Drake wondered if any of the gathering masses outside the station had an inkling of what was going on inside, and if so, would they lift a unmanicured nail to assist the victims or the villains?

"Lay it on 'em, Ophelia," Huck shot back with childish enthusiasm, clapping his enormous hands.

"Lady and gentleman," the female then brayed, still standing tantalizingly just out of frame, "I give you this era's newest renaissance man. Our fearless leader, Magnus Orion Skye! Consider yourselves fortunate. A face-to-face with Magnus, no matter how short-lived, is an unreal rarity, especially amongst those willingly serving *the man.*"

Stepping out from behind the lifeless corpse, the target of such godlike praise executed a semi-curtsy as if awaiting a stage curtain to descend.

"Many thanks as always, my feral fox. I must return the complement for the awesome binding job. I'm sure if they could speak, our guests would second the awesomeness!"

Inhaling as deeply as possible through semi-clogged nostrils, Drake forced himself to look away from Nichol's shattered visage while simultaneously drowning out Judith Tanner's increasingly wrenching sobs.

If experience had taught him anything, it was that although brief moments of insanity were expected within such a surreal scenario, too long a dip into those strangely soothing waters could only lead directly into a swirling channel of no return.

"Huck, what the hell?" he heard Magnus inquire, none-too-happy.

"Boss?" Came the befuddled reply.

"Does *that* still possess a working pulse?"

To this, Drake couldn't help but redirect back to the land of the semi-living, peering over to see Magnus looming over Leroy Shoates' massive frame, the big man's arms reaching out in an attempt to pull himself along the slick tile by grasping, clutching fingertips and failing miserably.

"Boss, you can ask Ophelia, I pumped 'im with enough smack to down a herd of buffalo! Weren't easy neither. First off, I hit 'im hard enough to crack a coconut shell and he just stared at me like that axe handle was a fly-swatter. Took three more shots that rock noggin just to put 'im on his knees. Big ass Mandango was as tough as advertised."

The giant hippie flashed a toothy, imbecilic grin. Obviously, Drake deduced, he was useful only as muscle, though there was an underlining ruthlessness that no doubt was an attractive quality to Magnus and his cult. Huck the cuck, Drake figured, had been the type of cruel, sadistic playground bully that wallowed in inflicting pain for pain's sake, usually on those smaller than himself.

"I think you mean *Mandingo*. Dig it, I *do* like all the embedded needles. Nice touch," Magnus grinned back.

The mystery female, as if on cue, tossed in her two cents.

"You would've been proud, Mag. Huck was downright surgical."

"Looks like it. Alright Huck, be a good man-ster and finish it up."

Magnus backed away, performing a textbook about face, ending his spin directly in front of Casey McCormick's motionless frame.

As he kneeled down, leaning in to inspect the man's badly beaten features, Drake was able to peer over the crouched form to watch Huck saunter over, gripping either side of Larry Shoates' bloated face and execute a vicious twist to the left to a concerto of sickening crunches. The head was then unceremoniously dropped to the tile with a resounding thump. Drake heard Tanner's sobs increase in both volume and desperation level.

"Done and *done*. Anything else, boss?" the giant hippie inquired, hands on hips.

"Nothing to be done here, it appears. This one ceased breathing a while back. This your work, Huck?"

"No sir, it was Atticus went to work on that boy with that rusty pipe of his. I wasn't about to intervene, boss. Jackass was a real yapper 'til the first blow removed about six teeth. Hoo-boy, not much to say after that. It was all over but the cry…"

"Speaking of Atticus," Magnus interrupted, standing stiffly and scanning the surroundings, "Has he not come back yet?"

As Huck appeared typically flummoxed, the female answered.

"Not yet. Said he was gonna give the offices and hallways one last check."

Falling to one knee, Magnus knelt directly in front of Drake and the two immediately locked eyes.

"He needs to put it in gear. We've gotta beat feet. If I'm not mistaken, Nichols' sermon is about to hit the final stretch, and we'd only preset a handful of post-interview tunes."

Be it anger-fueled or downright stubbornness, Drake refused to break eye contact. In turn, Magnus tilted his head and pooched his lips as if addressing a misbehaving toddler.

"Now, don't flip your wig, rent-a-badge, just hang tough. It'll all be over soon enough."

At that moment, if allowed a last request, Drake felt no regret in said wish not involving a final embrace with his wife or child, but instead the power to reach over and throttle the smarminess right out of the smug lunatic so casually crouched before him. Choke the pudgy little bastard 'til his head popped like a mashed pimple and then drag him along by that ever-flapping tongue 'til it popped off its rollers.

"I gotta say, I don't like the way you're eyeballing me, boy. Hey Huck, you feel like a little game of Whack-a-mole is in order?"

"Groovy. More like Whack-an-*asshole*." the giant said, howling like a hysterical child hearing his first fart joke.

Death threat and lack of suitable oxygen aside, Drake's intrusive stare never faltered. The colossal hippie took but one purposeful stride forward, presumably for execution purposes, when fate seemingly intervened. If able to sigh in relief, Drake would've been hapless to refrain.

"Well, look what the pussycat dragged in," the female announced,

Magnus instantly turning toward whomever she referred.

"Sir Zephyr, it's about damn time."

"You can officially drop the Zephyr garbage, Lenny. Nary a roving eye or noisy bug in the place," the new arrival replied with a mild shrug, his electrician's uniform shirt now tied snugly around his slender waist. *The guy crawling around in the ceiling*, Drake concluded, *looks like the gangs all here. All, that is, but my partner in peacekeeping.* There was no sugarcoating the fact Deke was probably either dead or wishing he was. Still, Drake faced hopelessness before and wasn't beyond maintaining a shred of optimism despite such rotten odds.

Magnus, chin resting atop clenched fist, appeared less than confident.

"If talking percentages, just how sure are we of this?"

"One-hundred. We are inconclusively free of spying eyes or ears."

"Not ninety-nine point nine?"

"No sir. No audio, no video. Pat was spot-on concerning the woeful lack of security. I mean, look no further than the cut-rate hired guns on display."

Head twisting toward Drake then back to his subordinate. Magnus began to slowly peel off the work shirt, the undershirt beneath a green V-neck tee unable to cloak what appeared as a snake head tattoo on his upper chest and a spattering of similar body art winding up both forearms to the bicep.

"Hmm, can't dispute that. Well then everybody, it seems, mercifully I'm sure we all agree, that the jig…is…o-ffically…up."

Wild applause and even a few random claps ensued, followed by an almost ritualistic removing of outer garments by all present. Drake could only presume the female was executing the same striptease, at least until she ambled casually by, lightly bumping his shoulder on the way past.

Toting a large black suitcase that she placed directly between the men, who stood in a semi-circle as they continued to disrobe to various states of semi-nudity. Kneeling, the station's assistant to the manger removed a small key from her pantsuit's front left pants pocket and calmly unlocked the case. Upon lifting one end, she reached in and removed a sizeable stack of neatly folded clothes before rising and, peering briefly over towards Drake and then Judy Tanner, began to unbutton the pantsuit beginning at the top vest. Without speaking or a hint of even non-verbal communication, the men stepped over in single file to retrieve individual sections of the folded clothing. All save Huck, subsequently undressed down to underwear and tee, discarding the outlandish wigs, now that they'd been officially identified as such, the former removing only his stained tee, his naked torso riddled with assorted body art to include a plethora of ghastly images, to include a large section of his massive back dominated by a levitating grim reaper.

As for the young, outwardly awkward and perpetually nervous Miss Patti Webb, having already substituted the oversized pantsuit with tattered blue jeans and multi-colored Pink Floyd tee, continued her transformation by tossing away the shrub-like bouffant wig and replacing it with one of straight, pitch-black variety, her natural strawberry-blonde doo cut pixie-style.

Though he was finding the power to effectively gauge time virtually impossible, Drake guesstimated it took the five terrorists less than three full minutes to complete their individual amendments, all the while Trevor Nichols' monotone prattling continued overhead, the words of the recently murdered man now akin to a hive of bothersome bees swarming overhead, the message lost and wholly inconsequential.

Tossing their used duds back into the suitcase, all but Magnus posed in single file as if for proper inspection and approval by their leader.

He did so silently, a single stiff nod issued to each as if to confirm a job well done.

Examination complete, they turned as one towards the two lone survivors of the apparent premediated massacre of The Bay's Rockin' Rascals.

"So, what do ya think, boss-lady?" Patti Webb inquired directly to a sniveling Judith Tanner behind a set of pink-framed Ray-bans, spindly arms spread wide as if preaching to an admiring flock.

"Are we ready to do this thing right or what?"

~ * ~

Cult of Personality

When the duct tape had been ripped away with a single, savage pull, Drake momentarily feared his lips had detached in the process, the initial sting quickly replaced by facial paralysis so severe he wondered if a slight stroke was responsible.

Shaking his head weakly from side to side, watery mucus spraying from each flaring nostril, he sucked air greedily through his mouth as Judith Tanner received a similarly painful liberation.

Her mouth bind-free following a small, wistful cry at the moment of release, the station manager regarded her former subordinate no longer through the tear-filled eyes of a hapless hostage, but instead a steely, hate-filled glare.

"I would apologize, Judith, but I have a feeling you'd doubt the sincerity," Patti Webb remarked stoically, standing at the far right of the makeshift formation, her persona altered to resemble the same stereotypical clique the others of the group had just discarded.

Though a ragged, wet coughing fit preceded her strained words, Tanner maintained an icy coldness and surprisingly calm demeanor while never breaking eye contact.

"W-what…is…is this, P-Patti? Who are…th-these p-people?"

Webb turned to the left toward Magnus and shrugged, holding both hands out palms-up.

"Lenny, is there time? I mean, I think an explanation is the *least* we   can   do."

Minus the pencil-thin mustache, his tattooed arms and torso now effectively cloaked by a fresh wardrobe that included a dark brown, striped double-breasted suit, checkered tie and tar-black, slickly waxed penny loafers, Magnus deliberated but a few short ticks before stepping from formation to formally readdress the tattered twosome.

"You'll understand I do have to make this rather quick. Not only do I despise lengthy exposition, but we *really* are fighting the clock."

Drake noted that not only had his mannerisms changed, but also his accent, no longer either west coast or southern in origin, but as midwestern as if he just stepped off a Chi-town bus.

"Obviously, we're not at all the characters you've seen portrayed to his point. We are, in fact, the exact opposite. Quick intros if you may," he paused, backing gracefully until all the players were fully visible, as if each stood on the edge of a massive stage awaiting applause, "The part of Magnus Syke, wanna-be cult god and dastardly, ruthless enemy of the people, was of course played by myself. Leonard is the name, Lenny to my friends. Patti there was, of course, our plant, hired by the station just three weeks ago, and exactly one month following Nichols' booking by your late program manager. She cased the place and the staff, something we weren't able to do with any real efficiency with the other tour cities. Best of all, she gained Miss Tanner here's confidence so quickly and effectively, the hiring of security was placed solely in her charge. The rest of the gang, left to right from your perspective..."

First in line, previously referred to as Zephyr, was Reggie, nicknamed 'the natural' referring to his self-taught expertise in all things electronic, his Wired for Sound duds exchanged for a dark brown plaid suit with yellow tie and matching, flared pants.

Second came Jason, formerly known as Atticus, yet another faux electrician whose actual talents lie in the field of explosives, nearly unrecognizable in a blue sweater vest, dress shirt and gray slacks.

Lastly, the cruel, sadistic giant called Huck, whose stupid grin, man-child observations and simpleton mannerisms gave the impression of slight retardation. Known as Richard or simply Rich, he claimed a bachelor's degree in psychology, his updated duds consisting of a red knit shirt, light brown slacks and black wingtips.

Re-intros complete, Leonard's subtle nod scattered, all save Richard, who took up position a full step behind his illustrious leader as the others sprinted quickly away, the one identified as Jason scooping up the suitcase as he went. While he and Reggie exited the hall leading towards the back exit, Patti had headed in the opposite direction, whistling cheerily as she went.

Overhead, following a full thirty seconds of the always dreaded dead air came the opening cords of Manfred Mann's '*The Mighty Quinn*'.

"Now, I'm sure you have questions. I can empathize, be it if I was in your unfortunate position. I'm afraid it's simply one of those 'wrong place, wrong time' situations. You must understand, to bring about change or in this case, curtail same, there has to be true sacrifice, and in this case that entails martyrs," he paused, head bowed and hands locked at his back while pacing from the left a few steps then back again, resuming the monologue only after a quick, intense study of Leroy Shoates' motionless frame, "I understand it may not be much in the way of consolation at this particular moment, just know that all who are sacrificed here today are vital cogs in a wheel still under construction, the prime colors in a colossal canvas still in the outline stages. Know that so many enlightened souls you will never meet will forever think of you not as victims, but brothers and sisters to the cause."

Retrieving a gold-plated pocket watch from the suit's inner pocket, he stole a quick glance, lips parting for what would presumably be the sermon's epilogue.

"H-hey, can I ask you just one thing?"

Pocketing the watch, Leonard regarded Drake with outward scorn and even a hint of disgust, as if the bound prisoner, heroic martyr rap aside, rated no higher in the big picture than a scuttling cockroach that had yet to be squashed beneath his heel.

"Make it quick, Officer Hammond."

"H-Harrison."

To this, the giant named Richard clearly rolled his eyes and cleared his throat in obvious revolt.

"Yes, yes, what is it then?" Leonard chided with the accompanying hand gesture meaning 'wrap it up already'.

"To...what c-cause e-exactly are we...being...sacrificed for a-again?"

As if frustrated by the denseness of an obtuse child, Leonard bent forward and spoke slowly with exaggerated gestures.

"We are here to stamp out the coming plague, Harrison, a highly contagious plague the majority of this clueless country thinks of as some harmless phase, like hula-hoops or pet rocks. A plague from which they think their local communities are magically immune. A plague that has taken family members from all present, all brain-washed by willing sheep and eventually snuffed out by false prophets preaching of peace, love and eternal tranquility but offering only a reaper's menu of PCP, smack and LSD.

"The horror of today's death and destruction will be laid sorely in the laps of such prophets, the aftershocks felt from coast-to-coast. Not all, but many will be awakened, shocked into the reality of what a vile society these people will make for their children and grandchildren. Clear enough, officer?"

"B-but...why the ru-ruse of dress...dressing like them un...until now?" Tanner inquired, one of her eyelids stuck into place via clumps of dried eyeliner.

"We had to underline, emphasize as dramatically as possible how depraved and merciless these dopers are, ma'am. That in mind, we armed Patti with the photographic means to...capture some of the more wicked moments for the authorities to discover in the wreckage. Filmed evidence of various atrocities implemented by our alter-egos that will eventually be commandeered by the media to share with the masses. That, plus one final coup de grace now mere minutes away," he hesitated yet again to steal a glance at the pocket watch, "Just over seven to be exact, should be all that's needed to plant the seed of national discontent."

Unphased by the man's obviously rehearsed spiel, Tanner fired back through gritted teeth.

"But the...innocents you've murdered today, w-what of their families?"

"Nichols was no innocent, lady. A money-mongering fraud. Save your sympathies. Same for the dealer of Santa Monica boulevard over the..."

"I'm talking about my staff, asshole," she shrieked, voice growing instantly raspy and hoarse from the effort.

"I'm afraid they, you all, fall under the unfortunate heading of collateral damage. If it helps, you are the first but far from the last. Currently, we've got our eyes on a very popular tri-state station on the east coast that's been pushing the agenda a bit too hard for our tastes. Fact is, Patti has an interview for an intern position this coming Tuesday and if all works ou..."

"W-where is m-my…partner?" Drake interrupted, alternating deep breathes and flexing his shoulders and arms beneath the tape as to possibly weaken its grip.

Leonard signed heavily and checked his watch yet again, finally turning to briefly lock eyes with Richard, who in-turn used an extended forefinger to tap the opposite wrist as a reminder of the rapidly evaporating time.

In the brief silence, The Grass Roots could be heard singing of "Temptation Eyes."

"Last answer then, I regret to say, and a protracted one at that. Um, what was the question again?"

The man's blatant pomposity in the wake of cold-blooded, premeditated homicide torched the fuse on Drake's inner pilot light.

"My partner, you cr-crazy son of a bitch. The officer who…blindly followed my…my lead into this…this slaughterhouse. My employee. My…*friend*," he growled, lurching forth and nearly tipping the chair forward as a result, a substantial rip in the duct tape trailing his spine either going unheard or utterly dismissed by his captors.

Lunging past his superior, Richard revealed the blood-smeared iron pipe he'd previously kept hidden at his back, actually rearing back as to strike before being reeled in like an attacking canine via a simple verbal command.

"Richard, no," Leonard blurted, though with surprising aplomb, a tiny smile creasing his worm-like lips, "Calm yourself, big guy. Patience. They're not going anywhere."

The angry giant backed away a single step, albeit reluctantly with wide eyes ablaze with bloodlust, the pipe descending only a fraction.

"Officer Harrison," Leonard resumed, having already turned towards the hall leading to the building's rear exit, "You *should* be proud to know that your subordinate and chum is serving the greatest purpose of all. I regret I don't have time to explain the details. For now, just know he's alive and well and being prepared for a great reawakening the likes few have experienced."

Before stepping away, he directed a single nod Richard's way, to which the giant returned in kind, a simplistic enough gesture of non-verbal communication, the grim meaning of which was not lost on Drake.

"You're no god of ch-change, son. No...renaissance m-man," he raged, openly squirming and straining against the bonds in a final attempt at liberation, "J-just another in a l-long line of wanna-be dictators with a s-serious...Napoleon complex. No-nothing but...a sawed-off, dumpy loser who g-gets his kicks...by pl-playing commandant to...a gang of...socially retarded...psychopaths. History will not...b-be kind, boy."

"Amen," Judith Tanner rasped, eyes squinted, head thrown back, jaw jutted in the facial gesture equivalent of displaying double middle-fingers. Having briefly paused in mid-step as Drake's rant progressed, Leonard refused to meet their collective gaze, instead merely nodding in mock pity before strolling purposefully away. Overhead, Gary Puckett's haunting *'Young Girl'* spoke of the dangers of taboo love.

"When it's done, find Patti and get to the checkpoint," he said in parting, nonchalantly straightening the checkered tie.

"Check," Richard replied, watching the smaller man depart as if purposely avoiding performing the actual deed until his leader was safely distanced. It suddenly struck Drake that for all the talk of his *fearless* leadership, Leonard the Great was more likely Lenny the weak-of-stomach, the type of cowardly chicken shit blowhard whose sole power was limited to ordering others to do his dirty-work.

Apparently satisfied that his little general was both out of sight and audible range, he turned back around and, shifting the head of the iron pipe over a broad shoulder, extracted a heavy sigh.

Lips tightly pursed, grip firmed and torso twisting to form a batter's stance, he fronted Drake while peering over at Judith Tanner, the station manager's fiery gaze searing into his own.

"You might want to look away, ma'am. This isn't apt to be pre..."

Drakes cracked, parched lips parted for what he realized would surely be his dying message, the words he'd randomly chosen abruptly stalled in the mental stage at the intrusion of a faint popping sound, one he immediately dismissed as static from one of the overhead speakers. Meanwhile, the cult's chosen assassin similarly stalled in place, the iron pipe coiled as if awaiting the perfect hanging curve which with to take a cut.

Head tilting and mouth agape, Drake couldn't immediately comprehend what occurred to halt the giant's half-hearted warning while seemingly paralyzing his colossal frame in mid-pose.

A second popping sound, this one sharper than the previous, a crackling snap that Drake noted had not interrupted Johnny Cash's rich baritone tearing through the live rendition of '*Folsom Prison Blues*'.

"Oh, oh god, g-god help u-us," he heard Judith stammer, though the cry wasn't deemed worthy in that moment to pry Drake's stony stare from the bizarre behavior of his potential murderer.

Stumbling back a step, a wide-eyed Richard relinquished his grip on the pipe, which clanked to the tile floor and rolled just to Drake's right, directly between himself and the stiffening corpse of Casey McCormick.

He spasmed, bulky arms flailing wildly, torso shimmying and head jerking from side to side, before collapsing like a felled Sequoia, flopping like a beached fish while within reaching distance of Leroy Shoates' stilled corpse. All the while, nary a sound escaped the man's tightly clamped lips, which had turned first a dark shade of purple and then pale gray before that final backward tumble.

The big man's legs twitched with enough force to jar the wingtip shoe from his left foot, the right arm shooting straight up in a spastic, unspecified 'salute' before descending just as rapidly.

"Officer, can you stand?" Drake heard a voice inquire from afar, or at least what sounded it.

It wasn't until he felt a sudden pressure, random tugs and pulls, at his upper back that the mystery voice, female and vaguely familiar, sounded off at much closer quarters.

"It's got some rips at the top, just hang on. I'm gonna tear you lose, okay?"

"Y-yeah, sure," he blurted, unable to twist his head around enough to catch a glimpse of this would-be savior, instead locking eyes with Judith Tanner, who's mad grin was either a positive sign of great hope or the toothy smile of the hopelessly insane.

"B-but how…did…what did you d-do?" he continued, regarding the fallen hulk with nothing short of awestruck wonder while amazingly, too bashful to come out and ask of the shooter's identity.

"Baby...Browning, twenty-five. Never...leave home on go on tour...without it. Listen, you need...to help me free her..." the voice instructed before labored grunts, "...and fast. Your...the other officer...he's in a...bad way. I'm...talking about...as bad as it gets."

When the tape finally split with a resounding rip, Drake toppled forward onto all fours and immediately began to mildly hyperventilate.

Upon rising to his knees and subsequently peeling away the multi-layers of tape from his uniform shirt, his ribs throbbing from the sudden release of protracted constriction, he looked over toward Tanner, where his rescuer was already tugging and pulling at her bonds.

"Mi-Miss Greene?" he gasped, still struggling to regulate his breathing to something resembling normal.

"In the...battered flesh, officer," she concurred while wrestling with the bottom half of the binds, "I understand if...you're a bit winded, but you...mind giving me a...hand here? We...really need to...vamoose...about two minutes...ago."

Upon standing, Drake briefly tittering forward then back before stabilizing by leaning down and planting a bare palm atop each knee.

"Steady, officer. You've got...one nasty gash at the back of the...old brain-pan."

"D-Deke. Whe-where's De...the other officer?" he managed, a sudden, stout wave of dizziness sending him stumbling forward until he stood almost directly over Richard's immobile form.

Arms spread wide as if to take flight, the behemoth's left eye stuck half-ajar, a dime-sized hole drilled just a half inch or so above it. Similar in size but with considerably more leakage was the wound at the center of his throat, just below the Adam's Apple. In recalling the giant's impromptu spaz-dance-of-death, Drake could only deduce the latter of the bullets penetrated the spine, thus triggering assorted nerves to essentially short-circuit. Regardless, impressive shooting to eliminate such a monumental threat.

"Officer Drake, I get the loyalty thing. You...took an oath. For now, I think we should stick together. Strength in numbers and all that."

Staggering over, forcing Jennifer Greene to lurch back to avoid possible impact, he fell to one knee and dug curled fingers beneath a partially split seam. A half-dozen tugs later and the seam gave way. Judith Tanner's limp form immediately following suit as she tumbled off the chair and onto her right side.

It took an additional thirty-plus seconds to sit her upright and peel the clutching, gummy blanket from her blouse, Drake taking at least half that span to inspect Miss Greene at close range. Sporting a swollen, blackened right eye, split top lip and scraped chin, she'd obviously run afoul of the cult with their brute tactics, managing to not merely survive but replace a former pro football lineman in the role of brawler *slash* rescuer.

Despite losing both pumps, her dress slacks ripped at the knees and her blouse shredded at both shoulders, Drake couldn't help but find this plucky, tough-as-nails chick more attractive now than at introduction. *A groupie that doubles as a bodyguard*, he mused. As for Judith Tanner, she appeared no worse for wear save a swollen left cheek, riddled with lines of streaked mascara, and comically fluffed hair that hinted at electrocution.

"Can you walk, Miss T?" Drake heard Greene inquire as he tested rubber legs by standing upright.

Tanner nodded, in lieu of verbal reply, while being assisted onto shaky feet by the former tour-bus party-girl, the aforementioned Browning pistol, laughably diminutive, tucked at her waist near the beltline.

Confident his own equilibrium had stabilized at least somewhat, Drake stepped over to the opposite side of Greene's position and hooked an arm around the dazed station manager.

"M-my staff, T-Trent and Jody? H-have you s-s-seen," Tanner murmured between weak coughs.

"Before I found the security guard, I checked an office marked Sales Manager."

"Th-that's Trent's office."

Greene instantly broke eye contact with the older woman, instead staring straight ahead.

"Two bodies. Both male. Deceased."

"Are you s-sure? I mean, did you check their pu..."

"Miss Tanner, their faces were...gone."

Bowing her head, Tanner openly sobbed, yet another moistened streak soon added to an already striped visage. Drake meanwhile, resurrected enough to not only stand without tipping, but speak full sentences sans the constant stutter.

"My partner, where is he?"

Greene gestured with an upturned chin towards the hallway leading into the heart of the station.

"DJ booth. Just…be prepared. I have no words to explain, nor would I want to try. Whatever we're doing, let's just do it and bug the hell out."

Greene explained between huffs as, ironically, they wobbled their way down the hall to Del Shannon's '*Runaway*'. On a rare positive note, Tanner's breathing slowly began to steady, her rubbery legs following suit.

"I heard enough of the plan to know they…they've planted some explosives."

"You know where?" Drake asked, forced to walk in a semi-crouch to compensate for Tanner's shorter stature.

"Well, I know *one* for sure, but you're not gonna like it."

Treading deep shag carpet spotted with dark red splotches, the trio hobbled into the DJ booth only after a brief reunion with Miss Patti Webb, sprawled half-in, half-out of what was labeled as a supply closet. The Pink Floyd tee hung askew from her bony frame, the Ray-bans hanging crooked from a bloodied snot.

"She alive?" Drake inquired as they stepped over her painfully thin legs, splayed so dramatically apart it appeared she'd done the splits upon landing.

Jennifer Greene snorted; nose pinched as if suddenly exposed to a nasty scent.

"Possibly. Can't honestly say I'll be losing any sleep if not.

"After the initial ambush and a few solid shots to my kidneys and back of the head for good measure, they tied me to what just might be the

Titanic's old water heater. Paid me…sporadic *visits* afterward, including the Jolly Green Giant."

Eyebrow severely cocked, Drake took the bait.

"The one they called Huck?"

Greene's head briefly dipped.

"Yeah. Didn't even bother to buy me dinner first, if you catch my drift."

There was a faint tinge of regret in the aftermath of his reply, growled through gritted teeth, but *very* faint.

"Asshole. Must've felt damn good pluggin' 'im,"

Her silent response of a mild shrug and hint of a smile told him all he needed.

Donning a mask of unbridled disdain, Tanner glared over at her former co-worker as they passed and spoke aloud words that could've easily been a hushed declaration.

"Oh, Patti. Where did you go so…horribly wrong? You seemed such a nice, conscientious sort."

Nearing the DJ booth, Drake intentionally slowed the pace, gesturing with a stiff nod toward Tanner's former assistant.

"If she comes to, we could have a pro…"

"She won't," Greene replied sternly. "I'm no doctor, but I'm fairly certain I crushed her larynx."

To this, Drake could only manage a raspy '*damn*'.

"I just knew all those Jun Fan Gung Fu classes would pay off someday."

Drake's mystified expression oozed uncertainty.

"Gung fu?"

"Yes sir, taught by Taky Kimura himself."

"Tack-key?"

Greene snorted in lieu of laughing aloud at the veteran security guard's obvious befuddlement.

"One of Bruce Lee's star pupils, no less. A man of few words but at least a thousand moves. Shared both a classroom and dojo with McQueen and Coburn, that being Steve and James."

"Hey, if you ever need a job, feel free to give me a ring," he stated with nary a tint of humor. "Hell, better yet, let me know if *you're* hiring."

A half dozen more steps saw their arrival at the booth's open entrance.

At the shocking reveal of his employee and co-worker, Drake very nearly abandoned all physical support for Tanner in favor of running to his side. Instead, he and Greene helped the station manager into one of three available seats, the latter immediately rolling back to retrieve a nearby wall phone and immediately cursing its lack of a dial tone.

"Tried that already, sister," Greene snapped harshly, instantly wincing with regret. In turn, a distraught Tanner nearly toppled from the chair but was quickly propped upright by the other woman.

"I've got her," Greene assured Drake, both women clearly avoiding locking eyes with Deke Carpenter despite sitting within reaching distance of his seated form.

"Hey man, I'm here," Drake whispered, laying a visibly shaking hand gently atop the other man's damp scalp.

Unlike the full-torso duct-taping Drake and Tanner endured, Deke's binds held at the wrists and ankles only, the former bound at his back but in no way connected to what had been Rockin' Rick's throne, the latter a single strand to hold the ankles snug.

"H-hiya, boss. What took ya...so long?"

With no less than a Herculean effort, Drake's voice did not crack, nor did his expression give away the raw repulsion threatening to trigger his gag reflex.

"Been kinda tied up, you understand. Gotta say, dude, you look like heavily trod-upon excrement."

Though it would seem a virtual impossibility upon surveying the extension damage on graphic display, Deke's light brown eyes were clear, his responses concise, his words only faintly slurred and their meanings sensible.

"Cannot argue the point. Lucky I've built up a helluva tolerance for pain meds through the years. Four car crashes and just as many surgeries."

In truth, Deke Carpenter had no business possessing an operational pulse, much less speaking as casually as if he were nursing a hangnail.

His uniform shirt was laid open to better display the footlong gash between breastbone and bellybutton. The wound itself looked to have been stapled together, approximately a dozen such stabilizers laced perhaps an inch and a half apart. Surprisingly, fresh leakage was at a minimum, though a pencil-thin stream was evident at the wound's lower end, Deke's uniform pants saturated at the groin and thighs. There was little mystery then, of the man's ghastly, pasty-white complexion, considering such a major loss of life source. The burning questions thus remained. What exactly had the cult done to him and more astonishingly, how was he even breathing in the aftermath, much less remaining upright or attentive?

"Drake, we *really* have to go," Jennifer Greene chimed in, her gaze briefly tracing Deke's wounds but unable to lock on to it before darting away to focus on a nearby turntable, where the selection of The Door's *'Light my Fire'* surely served as the forbearer for the evening's final selection. Worse yet, the fading out of Jim Morrison's seductive crooning represented a codeword of sorts, signaling that an already bad situation was about escalate to a full-blown, large-scale disaster.

"Turntable number two is last call, you might say," she continued, nodding towards the LP prepped as the last to fall, "*Hey Jude*, long version."

Drake's face contorted with a combustible mix of rage, confusion and frustration, a far cry from the elation he'd felt upon finding Deke alive.

"How could you possibly know this? Any of it? Do all former groupies develop telekinesis?"

Greene grinned despite or perhaps because of the man's sarcasm.

"Nothing that supernatural, chief. I heard a sizeable chunk of their plan while lying in that closet waiting to be gang groped. They planted explosives in your partner's…" she paused, pointing at his carved torso, "…in his gut. The one they called Atticus used to be an ambulance medic or something similar. At first they tried shoving 'em down his throat via tied-up balloons but he kept gagging them up. From there, they didn't…they didn't hesitate in going to plan B. From what I surmised their mad medic never leaves their compound without his little black bag of butchery. Must've shot 'im," she gazed briefly toward Deke, careful to avoid his mutilated midsection, "…shot you up with enough pain meds to

OD a T-Rex."

As she spoke, Deke, head tilted and ghostly lips parted—studied her with great interest, like a small child listening to a particularly gripping bedtime yarn.

"Anyhow, the crazy chick, Patti, had a detonator. She was going to roll his chair out to the center of the lobby, then invite the hippie protestors in. As they congregated around Deke, wondering what the hell was going on, she'd slip out the front to punch the detonator."

"Where's the detonator now?" Drake nearly shouted, arm resting around his slim partner's rounded shoulders.

Digging into a front pants pocket, Greene displayed a small black square roughly the size of a cigarette pack.

Drake pumped a fist weakly airborne even as Judith Tanner clapped enthusiastically.

"Well then, we're holding the face cards, aren't w...?"

Greene's stern nod and grim, tight-lipped countenance served as the   ultimate   killjoy.

"Leonard has a second one. A back-up. To be used if, for whatever reason, Patti didn't come through. I heard 'em bitching back and forth on the use of walkie-talkies to signal. Lenny was stressing about potential radio frequency piracy or some such big brother paranoia."

"Guess that explains why he didn't bag our radios."

"Um, not really, Officer Carpenter."

"Please ma'am, it's Deke."

"Deke. They shattered yours by accident in that...the initial ambush."

"Oh yeah, one of the phony electricians distracted me with small talk and next thing I knew, lights out."

"Well apparently you landed right on top of that walkie. Pureed it but good,"-

"People, focus please," Drake cut in while leaning over to inspect the small box through squinted dyes and discovering with no small measure of frustration that he might as well be looking at a pet rock for all he knew about the inner working of such gadgets.

"You sure about this?" he snapped toward Greene. "The backup detonator and hidden explosives?"

"She's right, boss," Deke answered instead, "Even doped to the gills, I caught segments, especially the part about 'a big surprise' for the gathered crowd, all of it nitro based, including whatever they…impregnated me with."

At the use of the word '*impregnated*', Judith Tanner inadvertently gasped, to which Deke responded by flashing perhaps the saddest smile on record.

"It's okay, Miss T. I've come to accept it for *what* it is. Honestly, as I've been sittin' here with nothing else in particular to do, I've cooked up a little plan myself."

Deke regarded his taped wrists with bemused indifference before glancing up at a wall clock then back to his employer.

"Like the lady said, boss, no more time to chew the fat or *Hey Jude*'s gonna seque into *Hell Jude*. They left a scalpel on that blank turntable there. Careless, guess they figured the blast would take care of any evidence left behind."

Sure enough, the sharp edge still moist from surgery lay just to Drake's left. Four quick slices, to include freeing Deke's ankles, later, he cupped both hands gingerly beneath his partner's armpits to hoist him from the chair, this after a brief argument that simply rolling the chair would be less of a strain.

"Can you move, partner?" Drake inquired, secretly terrified that the wound might reopen and release a torrent of warm, wet innards for all to witness. At least until the implanted explosives ignited upon impact with the floor.

"Just get me upright, boss, and I got this. 'Sides, I'm gonna need to retain the pegs for what I got in mind. Shake loose the rust, you…might say."

"Deke, you sure about thi…"

"Boss, you just try to keep up," Deke grinned without looking back, "Historically, walkin' timebombs are known for their speed and grace."

Amazingly, Deke not only stood with only token assistance, but took point in departing the DJ booth with shocking vigor. Still, Drake couldn't help shadowing his subordinate's back with outspread arms, in case of a sudden collapse.

They reached the breakroom in less than half the time it had taken to get there, Jennifer Greene serving as a human crutch for Judith Tanner as they brought up the rear, Deke slowing only slightly to survey the foursome of corpses both seated, McCormick, Nichols, and laid out, Shoates and Huck. Dragging Tanner to a far corner, Greene tried another mounted phone with similar results.

"The two big guys cancel each other out?" Deke asked off-handedly before resuming the previous pace.

Drake shrugged, shooting a wry glance in the former groupie's direction.

"Not hardly. We can thank Miss Greene for clearing our path."

Drake, openly gasping and on the cusp of collapse, reached out as to slow the other's man blistering pace while in shocked, silent disbelief that he was struggling to keep up with a man who'd recently been butchered like a side of beef.

"Deke, pump the brakes, pal..."

Gracefully twisting on a heel just as they neared a final stretch of hallway leading to the back exit, his bare midsection bared and bleeding profusely from top to bottom. All previous good humor departed both Deke's tone and demeanor.

"Here it is, boss. I'm gonna lead the charge out that back door 'cause there's a chance the lead nut-bag has a shooter standing by to plug the first body out. Once I clear it, get these good folks the hell out and as far from the Octagon as you can manage."

"Hang on. Who else has a working timepiece?" Drake asked, checking the shattered face of the Timex attached to his right wrist.

Though neither Drake, his own wristwatch removed since being abducted, or Jennifer did, while Judith produced a small pocket-watch that somehow escaped damage.

"So, we know once Hey Jude fades, presumably, to silence, is the zero hour for detonation. Miss Tanner, we'll time it once the times comes."

Frowning, Judith Tanner broke Greene's loose grip and stepped forward on wobbly legs, her voice gaining strength as time progressed.

"What about the...those people out front? Must be fifty or more, counting media."

"Time ain't on your side, ma'am, so I can't really advise it. Thing is, even if I do accomplish my mission, more than likely the detonator will trigger whatever else they planted. Standing out on the front porch like they are, well, those wanna-be hippies and shenanigan-lovin' reporters don't have a clue they're walking the edge of a minefield."

While Tanner, Greene and Drake exchanged guarded looks, the station manager's next suggestion met with agreeable nods.

"We have to at least *try* to warn them."

"Drake, you understand..." Deke turned exclusively to his employer, nervously shuffling his booted feet as if at least a portion of the pain med's kick was wearing off, "...I was given this one shot for a reason, yeah? Don't think I don't wish like hell that there was a better option. I might be numb as a stump but I ain't blind. I...see the wound, understand the long-term ramifications. Deadman walking ain't just for death-row types."

"Listen, as...bad as that looks, there's always a chance..."

"Boss please..." Deke scolded good-naturedly, "...I'm being held together by baling wire and assorted painkillers. You know this. I know this. Appreciate the concern, but it's misplaced. That sick bunch out there has to be stopped and stopped here and now. I'm dive-bombing that van, plain and simple. Instant karma, baby."

Gripping the injured man's wrist with far more force than he'd intended, Drake breathlessly countered this plan. Horrific slash wound aside, it appeared to be on the cusp of parting like a pair of ruby-red, oversized lips with each additional movement, he simply couldn't accept such a dramatic turn of events within what amounted to less than a quarter-hour time span. From a near certain death to miraculous, last-minute rescue to the unexpected elation of finding his friend and co-worker alive only to bear reluctant witness the man's voluntary suicide.

"Deke, you don't have to...what I mean is, there is another option. We can hunker down and call the Bay's finest. We've got the detonator, remember?"

"Boss, from that bloody dap coating your brain-pan, I kinda

figured ya took a helluva belt. The kind that works on short-term memory."

"Oh, oooh shit," Drake cursed with a sudden recall that drained what little color remained from his cheeks, "Leonard."

"Bingo. If I don't, well, *light up* as scheduled, I mean by the very second, he'll do the honors from a distance. Webb and Huck agreed that if things went south inside, for any reason, not to wait on 'em.'"

Growing pastier by the second, Deke's breathing was becoming noticeably strained, his once-stiff posture beginning to sag.

"Now, I heard 'em say they were all to meet once Patti did punch the button. I plan on payin' 'em a surprise visit before Lenny's fat little finger can find that button, get me?"

"I caught part of that," Greene added. "They arrived in two vans, the work one parked out on the front side of the building and another tucked away for the great escape. They were gonna leave the work van behind and take some side exit."

Judith Tanner, chimed in between hacking coughs, eyes darting wildly as not to land on Deke's wound nor the ever-widening blood-smear trailing thinly back to the DJ booth.

"There's a dirt lane just past that wooded area out back, down a grassy knoll. It used to lead to an old tobacco barn. A few miles past that is a backroad leading to the highway."

"Perfect place to lay low until the smoke clears," Drake said, peering over and back to the space dedicated to two very large, very deceased bodies. "Lay back and let the newsies and local badges logically blame the hippies, all the while dressed to the nines and resembling squeaky-clean choir boys in those duds."

To the chagrin of the battered foursome, was heard Paul McCartney's first utterance of the song title serving as their personal stopwatch.

"Cheese and crackers," Tanner muttered, Greene unable to smile broadly in the aftermath.

"All right, Miss Tanner," Drake said, holding the cracked Timex nearly flush with his nose, nostrils flaring wildly, and reading it's barely illuminated screen, "Synchronize seven minutes from right...now."

For a few precious ticks afterward, the four stepped back and stood motionless as if in quiet meditation.

Walking over and leaning down over Richard's massive frame, the dead man's head resting in a wide pool of his own blood, Drake performed a quick frisk before struggling mightily to lift his bulk enough to find the prize he'd sought.

"It's yours, Deke," he said, standing and checking the cylinders, "Still fully loaded. Guess they were big on not leaving behind forensic evidence. No knives or guns, just steel bars and the random scalpel." Remembering how he'd freed Deke with the latter just minutes ago, Drake wondered where he'd left it. "Guess Patti was gonna clean up 'til you clocked her, Miss G."

Deke held out his right hand, palms up.

"Give 'er here, boss. I might just need to self-cover in case they spot me lurchin' down that hill. If we don't beat feet soon, I may end up playing human bowling pin."

Momentarily oblivious that both his holster and belt had been long-misplaced, Drake tucked the revolver into thin air before allowing it to hang freely at his side.

"No way, man. Providing cover is the *least* I can do."

"Boss…Drake…" Deke replied, a brow cocked mischievously with the extended hand unmoved, "…they're likely to plug you long before you fire off the first round."

Steely glare intact and jaw firmly jutted, Drake refused to blink.

"Guess that's a chance *I'll* have to take."

"Here hero," Greene injected, walking up to gently place the tiny Browning into Deke's palm,

"My little contribution to the mission."

His quivering lips so pale they appeared to be coated in chalk, Deke's warped grin wavered only slightly.

"Damn, no way we can lose with this here cannon leading the charge."

Drake smiled despite himself while Tanner stared directly into the tiled floor in front of her, her stockinged feet split on either side of the ever-widening smear the wounded officer left in his wake.

No one spoke as they covered the last forty or so feet to the rear exit door. Upon arrival at this final barricade, they formed a single line with the ladies at the rear and the men striking guarded poses with their respective weapons on point.

With Deke's lurching gait leading the charge, the surprisingly lightweight metal door was shouldered ajar but only wide enough to peek through.

Spotting no obvious dangers, he leaned back and sighed, elbow flush with the door's surface.

"Good luck and god-speed, officers," Judith Tanner whispered, to which the Divine Miss G added, patting each man gently atop the shoulder. "Same here, atheistic beliefs temporarily be hanged."

Drake reached with his free hand and lightly patted the top of her hand, only then noticing the raw, bloodied knuckle.

As if on cue, Judith Tanner sighed wearily upon checking the lone working watch among them and announcing that a little over five minutes remained before the Fab Five faded to a brief burst of faint static, then dead air.

"You two be careful," Drake concluded, "Warn 'em as best you can but don't steer too close to the station."

The lady's nodded in unison, taking each other's hand as if prepping for a group prayer.

"It's been real, folks," Deke concluded, "Happy trails."

They filed out and, a few steps out onto the dirt path, split into separate pairs headed in opposite directions.

~ * ~

A Real Blast

Treading through thigh-high cord and wire grass while utilizing the sporadically spaced Palmetto for bracing, Drake struggled to remain within reaching distance with his subordinate, whose gait varied from graceful and steady to clumsily lumbering while blazing a weaving path down the slope.

They spotted the light blue Chevy van from the top of the hill, pointed north on a narrow gravel path just a stone's toss away. While Deke insisted they circle to the right, in order to better utilize a thick growth of arrowwood viburnum at the bottom of the slope and just off to the back right side of the van, Drake argued the shortage of time.

Crouching less than thirty yards from the van, its dark tinted windows giving no clue to the passenger's position or possible visual in regard to theirs, Deke's breathing was a moist rasp, like an overheating radiator spewing steam from a loosened cap. His chalky flesh gleaming from fresh sweat, he clutched the detonator in his left hand and the revolver in his right, the constant kneeling slowly opening the wound at his chest until Drake feared he might soon eviscerate himself with the next squat. A quick glance of his watch, at least his tenth such peek since they'd departed the station, gave them three minutes and eight seconds.

"Just…cover me, boss, if the lead starts…to fly. If I…can't access…the back door…I'm planning on crawling…underneath."

Momentarily balancing the revolver atop his bent knee, Deke Carpenter offered a pale, shaking hand. Drake took it, squeezing it ever-so-gently, his squinted eyes gleaming with fresh moisture. In that moment, he wished like hell he'd known the man longer and better.

"You can bet your ass everyone will know what you did here today."

Deke, his bushy mustache as warped as the smile creasing his thin face, winked playfully.

"Long as…my ex knows. Lydia always claimed…my coldness and…selfishness would be…my undoing. She…mistook my…aloofness as…uncaring. Well, if only…she could see me now."

With exactly two-minutes and twenty-one seconds remaining until time ran out on proving his ex-spouse wrong, Deke Carpenter sprouted invisible wings and practically flew down that hill.

At exactly the one-minute point, about the same time the Fab Four's lengthy chorus of '*na na-na-na-na…Hey Jude*' led to the song's conclusion, Drake watched Deke break from the overgrowth of shrubbery and fast-walk toward the back of the van in a slight crouch, the Smith & Wesson's blue-steel barrel aimed ahead of outstretched arms.

A sharp crack, at first unidentifiable as a gunshot, was followed two seconds later by another, each sounding strangely distant, as if originating miles away. It was in the aftermath of the second that Drake noticed the dramatic change in Deke's gait, his left leg being dragged along as if suddenly paralyzed. A third retort and Deke, stumbling forward with less than ten yards between himself and the van, began to fire back with one, two, three shots in rapid succession. Either crouched or standing upright, Drake was unable to spot a shooter due to the levitated angle and took off in a shambling sprint just as the sound of tires spitting gravel drowned out all else.

Still ten yards or more from level ground, Drake slid to a stop and, barely avoiding tumbling forward, aimed the baby Browning as best he could while his peripheral could just make out Deke down on his knees firing off his last few rounds.

The van, right front and left back tires flattened, spun off the narrow path and straight into a ravine deep enough to tip the vehicle forward, the back wheels aloft and spinning madly.

He crawled back up the hill with legs pumping and arms extended, the empty Browning tossed aside as grasping fingers clawed grass, roots and embedded rock for climbing leverage. The last thing Drake witnessed was his partner staggering toward the wrecked van and the passenger door opening, a shadowy form scrambling to exit. Legs pumping, Drake braced, at least emotionally, for the blast, his face contorted in a permanent wince.

It was, as he reached the top of the slope amid a building wave of panic, that Deke either dropped the detonator or the many gunshot wounds left him too weak and incoherent to engage the button, that a series of anguished wails, some obviously born in fear but at least one birthed in the cradle of sweet retribution, preceded a deafening, all-engulfing silence, followed by a gust of scorching wind so vicious he felt himself hoisted airborne.

~ * ~

Rolled in blackness, he felt a silent breeze lightly tap the flesh of his face. A sudden movement, heard but unseen, followed by the intrusion, not at all frightening but weirdly soothing, of gentle hands first cupping him beneath each armpit before hauling him upright. Legs and arms previously leaden grew feather-light as the mystery force took flight with him in tow, the exhilaration matched only by an overwhelming unburdening.

Up ahead, a hazy outline grew steadily brighter, and he squinted mightily in search of definition. A familiar shape, a sign. He visualized only a pleasant cube of light, circular in shape like a car's headlight.

The power of hearing returned with such subtleness it was as if it never waned.

The sound he heard was as unmistakable as it was befuddling, that is until he was repositioned, the grip beneath his left arm released.

Now sailing to the left of and even with his mystery courier, he smiled as broadly as was humanly possible as the billowy edges of the other's wing tickled his torso both on descent and ascent.

As they flew toward the comfort of the light, the angel in tattered blue held out and displayed something tucked in the palm of his free hand, a tiny remote device of some kind, and playfully flicked it into the blackened void.

They bathed in the approaching light, which accepted them into its majestic fold.

~ * ~

"Like I said, I was ignorant of this whole ordeal 'til I was well into junior high, and the dream portion was a new wrinkle I wasn't privy to at all until I was well into my forties, when my brother clued me in. He said Mom told him while under the influence of Percocet following gallbladder surgery. Supposedly, Mom just starting randomly rattling off tales of Dad's health woes, both physically and mentally following the Bay incident, saying how if treated these days, he'd have rattled when he walked from all the anti-depressants and pain meds."

Smiling as if in full recall, Boone fell silent while first removing the cassette then packing it along with the recorder into the briefcase, blissfully ignorant of his traveling companion's impatient sighs. Brad was practically bursting while nervously drumming the fingers of both hands atop the steering wheel. A recently spotted road-sign showed them only forty-one miles from the outskirts of Kansas City, having made great time under mostly sunny fall skies and light traffic.

"So, I take it he *did* survive to tell the tale? I mean, he wouldn't be divulging dream details otherwise, right?"

Casually scanning the contents of the case, presumably for a future music choice, Boone remained oblivious to the younger man's edginess.

"Oh, I get it. They used to call this cliffhanger, right? Like, leave 'em hanging by a fingernail on the cliff's edge 'til next week's episode?"

"Oh, I'm so sorry, Brad," Boone exclaimed, nearly closing the case on his own fingers, "Yes, yes, my father did indeed make it out with at least most of his skin intact."

Brad's expression, upon the older man pausing yet again, was like that of a small child denied a cookie.

Inhaling deeply, as if justifiable winded, Boone lightly tapped both knees with bare palms.

"Epilogue time then."

The younger man rolled his eyes for obvious effect.

"Thank god I don't have to wait for the movie. Which, if I'm allowed an opinion, this could definitely qualify, maybe even more than your uncle's story. Hard to believe two members of the same bloodline had such, well, shitty luck, pardon my French."

Removing his colossal shades, Boone rubbed both eyes vigorously and squinted into the glare of the early afternoon sun blazing down from the east.

"Both harrowing to the point of disbelief, I know, but it's all in the history books, or at least the brittle, yellowed pages of ancient newsprint."

Stealing a quick but hard stare at the older man, Brad thought he appeared as haggard and worn as the previous night, if not more.

"Hey boss, seriously, you sound pretty winded. We're less than a half-hour from KC if you want to just lay back and recharge the battery. Just toss in some retro-tunes and doze away. All kidding aside, I can wait. We've got tonight and tomorrow, if need be."

"It's alright, son," Boone replied while redonning the shades and reopening the case, "It's better I fill in the blanks now as later, while they're still semi-fresh in my mind."

The recorder taking its customary space atop his knees, he double-checked the cassette before pressing record.

"I'm definitely slipping. Powered 'er down before the curtain was properly closed."

Brad, steering them past a wide-load trailer pulling a manufactured home, remained politely silent with the occasional nod to acknowledge.

"Now, where were we? Oh yes, father in the aftermath. Well, he'd been blown from the crest of that grassy slope into the station's back lot, found flat down on the pavement with the back of his uniform shirt and seat of his pants singed away. He didn't come too for nearly twenty-four hours, and once he did it was to find out he'd suffered a severe concussion, second degree burns on his back," he paused for effect, forefinger pointed skyward to wave back and forth like the second hand of a grandfather clock, "...for a final consolation prize, they pulled an inch-long piece of shrapnel from his left butt cheek, later identified as a piece of the cult's van."

Though maintaining focus on the road ahead, Brad's lips quivered and squirmed while struggling for the most vital, prioritized query among so many possibilities.

"So, Deke actually did...?"

"Explode? Yes indeed. Now, keeping in mind forensics weren't near as modernized as today, they were still able to eventually ID all the bodies. Pretty impressive considering there wasn't enough left of that van to fill two shovels. The explosives in Carpenter's gut were the equivalent of ten sticks of TNT. Nitro capsules or some such, tucked inside surgical bladders."

"Holy crow. How about the two women and the hippies? Were they able to get 'em back or was that second potential explosion a non-event?"

Boone lowered his head briefly and seemed to contemplate if not the answer itself, the best way to deliver it, his left hand mysteriously levitating at eye-level.

"Oh, a non-event it was definitely *not*."

172

Lowering the hand, Brad noted the tremors, so prevalent until the hand regripped the recorder, Boone's tone shifted to a more mechanical, matter-of-fact delivery, the earlier tinge of emotion stilted in favor of that of a radio newscaster spewing out the morning headlines.

"As for Judith Tanner and Jennifer Greene, they did survive the blast with little more than minor scrapes that had little or nothing to do with the explosion.

"Six others weren't so fortunate, including two local TV reporters and four of the protestors. Another dozen were injured. As I recall reading, a few sustained lifelong disabilities.

"The cult planted enough of the same nitro packs along the station's ceiling to all but disintegrate the north side of the building. Went up the same time as the van, so obviously the whole shebang was tied to the same detonator. What the blast itself didn't kill, maim or cripple, scraps of metal and stone debris surely did."

"So, they weren't able to warn 'em all before it blew?"

"I've read numerous newspaper interviews with both women. Both said that by the time they sprinted from the back of the station to the front, screaming their lungs out for everybody to back away, only a few took 'em seriously and only then because they were able to understand the message over all the random protesting chants.

"Jennifer Greene claimed one of the media types present actually snickered at 'em, turning their back as if the whole thing was some kind of loony attention-grab or rightwing practical gag. The irony was, the casualty count included that same reporter.

"Oh, and just for that extra kick of sadism, the VC gang also booby-trapped the work van. A van, by the way, they intercepted and confiscated on its way to the station that morning. The actual electricians had been sedated and hog-tied in some nearby woods. Always amazed me that they were allowed to live. No hippie ties, I presumed.

"Anyway, the van's nitro-load was tied to the same detonator and definitely added to the carnage, though the bomb squad who investigated the scene said it could've been much worse. They explained that the majority of its load blew vertically, not horizontally. That is, straight up and not out, otherwise the final body count might've doubled if not tripled."

Passing a sign announcing '*Kansas City – Next 11 Exits*', Brad disengaged the Charger's cruise control and steered them into the slow lane, presumably to give Boone ample time to place a fitting bow on the tale's epilogue.

"What's VC stand for?"

"*Vulture Culture*. They defined it as stripping away the flesh of the hippie culture and reshaping the remains to something more in line with their own beliefs.

"It took the feds several months to break 'em down, first individually, then as a group. What they found did make sense in a warped way. All of 'em except Patti Webb, real name Patti Webster, had biker gang ties. Mostly west coast affiliations. Similarly, all of 'em, including Webster, lost family members to the culture, or what they deemed the '*cult mentality*'. Leonard Patterson, alias Magnus and the group's founder, joined the ranks of the Displaced Souls biker gang out of Hawthorne right after dropping out of high school. Lost his old lady and infant son to a hippie cult a few years later. The wife soon overdosed on some bad smack with the baby still AWOL, presumably taken in by the group and shipped off to parts unknown. Supposedly, Patterson was still employing several private dicks to track 'em down even after founding VC and subsequently hatching the whole radio station bombing plot. Patti Webb's younger sister had been raped and killed by a van load of hippies near Portland a few years before she signed on. You get the picture."

Brad scoffed, "So, their road to revenge from losing kin to the cults was to exterminate the culture, to somehow assassinate a whole way of thinking? How exactly does murdering some second-rate DJ and his entourage while blowing an obscure radio station to smithereens accomplish that?"

"The Bay area was just the beginning, chosen solely due to Webster's inside access to the station and what they viewed as a glaring lack of security scheduled for the day of Nichol's visit. The gang planned on at least a half-dozen similar attacks, this from personal notes seized from Patterson's Bakersfield apartment.

"The disguises, video footage and bombings were to lay the blame of the terrorist acts on the hippies and thus mark the drug culture as purely malevolent. Hey, sincere in his disdain for the movement or not, Trevor Nichols made a pretty decent martyr, at least for starters.

"It was rumored they were actively recruiting new blood from those labeled victims of the hippie culture and had a substantial following in what served as the west coast underground. Though it was never substantiated, one theory had 'em working with some high-ranking feds on ways to undermine the movement, essentially nipping it in the bud as it moved eastward."

"So, what became of Misses Tanner and Greene?"

Brad thought he spotted a thin smile briefly crease Boone's chapped lips that just as quickly evaporated.

"Well, Judith Tanner went on to manage stations in Miami and later up the coast in Myrtle Beach. Believe she passed about a decade back from breast cancer.

"I believe we heard Jennifer eventually settled in Montana. A few years later she published a novel on her experiences as both a rock groupie and near victim of what became known as the Hippie Bay Bombing. Don't believe she ever married and is still living somewhere out west, though it's been a while since I checked."

This time, Boone's smile stuck.

"Mom always joked that Dad had a thing for Jenny Greene and when he did speak of the bombing, which was rarely, referred to her as that Left-Coast Firecracker."

As Boone appeared to again drift, visualizing a faint memory unique to his own mind's eye, Brad waited patiently for several minutes before breaking the silence.

"And what of your father?"

Hands crossed and fingers intertwined at his lap, Boone appeared not to hear for another thirty seconds before replying, his tone noticeably softer, just above a whisper.

"Oh, I only have faint memories myself, but Mom later told me he struggled for a few years, not just from the physical wounds but more the psychological. The burns left scars of course, but she hinted the mental scarring was a much bigger hurtle. His security business went belly-up of course, despite a small settlement from the station. They basically paid his medical bills, which were substantial I'm sure, but we basically survived on his unemployment until it ran out. As a kid, I'm sure I sensed the money struggles, but at that age such adult issues just roll off the back like water off a duck. We moved to South Carolina near my tenth birthday. Little town south of Florence. Dad had a buddy there that helped him get a job as a delivery driver. Got his CDL soon after and began steering the big rigs up and down the east coast. After what he'd been through, such a solitary profession was just what the doctor ordered. Far as I know, he never possessed nor held another firearm. Must've covered a few hundred thousand miles of US blacktop by the time he retired. Passed on about a decade back of a massive coronary. As per his wishes, we had him cremated and his ashes spread into the Atlantic."

"Sad he wasn't able to cash in on the whole Hippie Bay Bombing thing. I mean, as not only a survivor but for full-blown hero status. Kinda like your uncle."

Boone's perplexed expression required Brad provide further explanation.

"That is, these days both could've lived off their celebrity. Book and movie deals, maybe even host a reality TV show or YouTube channel showcasing similar feats of heroism."

"Oh, *that*," the older man nodded, stifling a yawn, "Well, can't say for sure about my great uncle, who I obviously never met, but Dad was the private sort, what do they call 'em? Introverted, at least after the bombing."

"What, no magazine or newspaper articles? Nothing?"

"I seem to recall a few random clippings in Mom's scrapbook, but as far as I know, he only granted a single interview on the subject. This was right about the same time the unemployment money dried up and we were prepping for the move to Carolina. In other words, the timing was just what it seemed; financially motivated. Oh, Mom said he'd had numerous offers, and that Jennifer Greene and Judith Tanner, succumbed to interviews early on *and* often."

Rambling down a steep grade while riding the bumper of a semi's wobbly trailer, Brad briefly eyed a road-sign announcing several upcoming hotels, fast food eateries and gas stations.

"So, don't keep me in suspense," he said, passing yet another KC exit sign.

"Newsweek? Time? Rolling Stone? Who was allowed the privilege?"

"I think it was the Miami Herald or whatever served as the rag of choice in those days," Boone shrugged, "Deepest pockets, I can only guess. Hey, I was into The Batman comics at the time, so what did I know of such adult reading?

"The only magazine Mom could remember offering was Life, and this was just weeks after the incident and Dad was just out of the hospital. Not exactly prime time to pick one's traumatized brain. Anyhow, from what Mom said, the assigned reporter awarded the scoop wasn't exactly blown away by Dad's blasé, matter-of-fact attitude, basically just stating facts as he knew 'em. She said the guy was likely counting on Dad to scream 'n shout out his own opinions on the changing culture, possibly even paint the cult as victims of society's downturn toward loose morals, rampant drug use, etcetera, etcetera. Instead, Dad provided a step-by-step, first-person witness account of what he and he alone saw that day. In other words, SOS as far as the reporter was concerned, as Tanner and Greene already covered much of the same terrain.

He did take the time to celebrate the bravery of Judith, Jennifer and especially Deke Carpenter, a series of pointed shoutouts that the interviewer seemed less than thrilled with, to the point of redacting all but a perfunctory mention out of the article. Obnoxious jackass.

Mom said that Dad was so disgusted with the finished spread that he jettisoned any possibility of a proposed book deal."

"Oh, so he'd been offered a publishing contract?" Brad asked, slowing the Charger considerably as the interstate grew increasingly crowded the closer to down-town they got.

"Yeah, supposedly one of the big boys out of New York City no less, but Dad figured no matter what he proposed about the book's theme, the editors would just twist it into some campy, true-crime tripe, and essentially told 'em to pound sand. Years later, around the mid-seventies, there was even talk of one of those TV mini-series, but it just kind of fizzled in the shadow of the Manson murders, the Vietnam war, Nixon and a half-dozen fresher tragedies."

Boone lifted the recorder while leaning down and peeking underneath his shades, presumably to check how much unused tape remained. Seemingly satisfied, he lowered both the device and glasses before resuming.

"Mom told my sister that Dad was more than happy to live in relative obscurity, just another working Joe bringing home the bacon. In retrospect, I guess I was a lucky kid to never have to answer questions from peers, older kids or adults about the incident. By the time I hit my teens, Dad and the bombing were old news or, in our case since the move, *no news*, as Carolina was a long way from FLA. No doubt it's still hot copy in the Tampa area, at least to any of the older residents still kicking around the same patch of sand. I saw a short blurb on some cable crime show a few years back. Listed the Hippie Bay Bombing as one of the top-ten terrorist acts in US history. It was strange hearing my father's name mentioned along with a blurry black and white snapshot they'd dug up from his security days. It was, I dunno, like they were talking about somebody else. Some fictional character maybe. Hearing him labeled a hero was a prideful moment, I'll admit, but it was just downright bizarre as well, probably because I was so young when it all happened. To me, he was just my dad. The truck driver. The quiet, unassuming dude occupying our dinner table three or four nights a week when he wasn't on the road.

"I guess it's that way with all kids whose kinfolk are labeled something they can't connect with personally.

"As a teen, I used to wonder what it would be like to be the son of say, Al Kaline, Lew Alcindor or maybe Johnny Unitas. It would be weird, that's what. Dad never saw himself as anything special, that much I knew from just being around him. I guess, all these years later and being almost as old as he was when he passed, I can appreciate how tough it must've been for 'im to readjust after such trauma. If he hadn't had Mom and us, I wonder if he'd been able to retain enough sanity to live a normal life. Fortunately for all of us, it was never an issue."

"Boone, ask you something?" Brad inquired timidly as they had rolled to what was essentially a complete stop in what served as North

Kansas City rush-hour.

"Shoot."

"Who is Al, um, Lou Alcantor or John…United?"

What started as a light giggle soon erupted into a belly-laugh so severe Boone's shades were jarred off his bowed head and dumped into the floorboard. Upon recomposing himself, both hands still visibly shaking, the older man's laughter instantly transformed into a rasping, hacking cough and finally a series of labored wheezes.

"Sorry, Boone, *really*," Brad said, reaching over to gently pat the man's upper back as if to magically clear his airwaves. "You need me to pull over? Maybe some fresh a…"

Leaning back, Boone waved him off with one hand while pointing over the dash with the other.

"N-no, no need. C-carry on. That last inhale just trailed down the wrong tunnel, I'm afraid."

Removing a fresh hankie from his back pants pocket, Boone planted his face into its willowy center and snorted with such force, a foghorn echoing, that despite his sympathetic offer and sincere concern, Brad was unable to refrain from cracking the tiniest of smiles.

"Those were sports legends from another era. You really never heard of Johnny Unitas?"

"Lemme guess, golfer?"

Checking the hankie, presumably for red smears, before folding it and tucking it away, Boone shrugged weakly, his features ghostly pale even as his breathing normalized.

"Hall of fame quarterback, Baltimore Colts."

"Oh, well, as you can probably guess, I was never too big on sports. Played a little baseball in school but mostly rode the pine even back then. Pro sports were never my thing."

"To each his own. Besides, all those fellas I mentioned are considered relics these days. Fossils from another time. A better time, I'd argue. Things were more innocent back then. More about a love for the game itself and not fame or monetary riches."

Brad simply nodded while navigating through a seemingly infinite sea of SUV's, pickups and hulking tractor-trailers, finally settling in the far-right lane behind a boxy hybrid.

"I guess we've covered everything, then?"

Thoughtfully scratching his stubble-infested chin, Brad simultaneously studied the digital GPS at the center of the dash.

"I'm drawing a blank for the moment. Want to grab some drive-thru and book a room? There's a Quality Inn just two exits down."

"Sounds fine. I am a little drained."

Rescued shades balanced atop his scalp, Boone clicked off the recorder and stashed it carefully away in the briefcase.

"No mystery why. Just over two hours of non-stop regaling. Boss, I have to ask, and take no offense…"

Head back against the rest, arms-crossed and eyes closed, Boone groaned weakly as if to indicate permission to resume.

"…these stories, my god, they…they're jaw-dropping. You've clearly got the documented history to back them up. Have you ever, I mean, even *slightly* considering maybe putting them down on paper for someone other than relatives?"

"Take after my old man, I guess, in that as a clan we prefer privacy. That is to say, there's really nothing to gloat or celebrate about surviving such events. To seek monetary gain or fame, in someone else's misfortune is, at best, self-serving. At worst, it's downright despicable."

His worn, haggard face turned toward the younger man's, Boone's eyes briefly opened and regarded his temporary employee with something akin to empathy.

"I take no offense, and I understand your point completely. Let's just say that, if you live through enough in his life, it's *vital* to focus on the positive that life throws you. Lord knows they can be kibble-sized, but relish 'em we must."

Twisting toward the passenger window, his tone dropping to a barely audible whisper, Brad wondered if Boone even meant to verbalize the final point aloud.

"Be careful not to allow the negative to hog the spotlight for too long a duration, least you find yourself unable to recapture the good, or worse, no longer recognize the difference."

~ * ~

The fast-food purchases consisted of a cheeseburger, fries and Diet Dr Pepper for Brad and an apple harvest salad and water for Boone, the latter entrée mostly left intact at evening's end as only sparingly picked though. Brad insisted on a bottom floor room to spare Boone any unnecessary exertion, as the older man's breathing sounded noticeably strained since that laughing jag at the recording's conclusion.

A light rain commenced as darkness fell, though unlike the previous night, the pleasant temperatures provided no overnight threat to road conditions.

Almost immediately upon their entry into the small but neatly maintained single room, Boone removed his shoes, staked a claim to the TV remote and collapsed onto one of two twin beds. As Brad greedily consumed his burger and fries, belching loudly between sips of iced soda, Boone forked his salad with little of the same enthusiasm, instead silently flipping channels.

Brad dozed off at just past ten, underestimating his own fatigue until he'd showered and laid down, his gut full and his eye-lids leaden. The two men spoke only sporadically, the majority of their dialogue involving the ironic nature of the movie Boone chose to peruse from the seemingly infinite cable channels offered, that being a crime-thriller set in the hippie-culture of late sixty's Hollywood and more specifically, set around the Manson family murders.

"You sure about this, boss?" Brad inquired between stifled yawns. "Hits a little close to home."

"It's always fascinating to see what they get wrong and what they get right," Boone replied wearily as the movie's clueless hero, his car broken down nearby, the tires intentionally flattered by hidden nails planted within the dirt road's many grooves, wanders up to a massive bonfire surrounded by a mixed group of long-haired, loose-clothed, unbathed and barefoot hippies.

"The stereotypes are extreme, but for the most part, sadly on point. That dopey hipster dialogue and the dated threads, not so much."

Brad soon drifted into a deep, dreamless slumber to the sound of the older man's incessant wheezing, blissfully sleeping through the many bathroom trips that followed and even the thunderous vomiting sessions contained within.

Rising at four-forty-five AM, a full fifteen minutes before the clock radio sounded off, Brad was horrified to discover his employer sprawled half-on, half-off the twin bed, pasty legs hanging off the bottom edge with his head buried face-down on a blood-smeared pillow.

Following a moment of terror when Boone didn't respond to his efforts to wake him, a gentle shoulder tap and whisper almost immediately elevated to a fierce shake and shout, the older man groaned and, with some assistance, rolled over onto his back.

Shirtless, Boone's neck and chest were dotted in dark red splotches, his lips chapped a similar shade. Wearing only blue boxers and a single tube sock on his right foot, his left conspicuously bare, he managed to mumble a hoarse request for water, to which Brad quickly supplied via a small plastic cup.

"As you can…probably guess, it wasn't…an easy night," Boone said upon downing a few swallows. His voice instantly improved from a harsh rasp to a more recognizable tone.

Taking a knee next to his upright but wobbly employer, Brad appeared to be prepping for prayer.

"Goes without saying. Boss, you're really, *really* starting to worry me. *That…*" he gestured toward the streaks, dots and smears of leakage, "…is not good. Did I sleep through something as ominous as that appears?"

"I'm fine, *Mother*. Really. Looks worse than it is, if that's…possible," he jabbed playfully between gentle wipes of his face and torso from a damp towel Brad previously offered.

"Son, you could snooze through a train derailment."

Brad apologized again despite understanding the man's lighthearted dig, though a part of him was secretly grateful he had avoided the older man's struggles, since in truth there would've been little he could've offered, save sympathy and a ride to the nearest ER.

Despite Boone's half-hearted objections, the younger man helped him into the bathroom and into the shower, standing guard, actually, sitting on the toilet, until he was sure the older man's equilibrium stabilized.

It was nearly seven AM before they spoke of breakfast and subsequent departure, Brad grilling his employer in three to five-minute increments on the potential dangers of pushing it too soon.

"The ER argument is moot..." Boone grumbled, "...as my condition is no mystery, nor is it treatable. The pills they'd provide offer a form of coma, not a cure."

Finally convinced via Boone's continual, at times surprisingly spirited affirmation, the younger man hoisted their respective overnight bags and led them out into the nearby hall to the heady scent of fried bacon and freshly baked biscuits.

They pulled from the parking lot at half-past seven, Brad having only nibbled at his plateful of breakfast staples, though he did eagerly suck down two cups of extra stout java. As for his employer, Boone struggled to consume half a piece of toast, openly wincing while washing it down with a cup of orange juice he'd managed to finish, though with obvious difficulty. Perhaps to quell his driver's growing apprehension, he pocketed a couple of apple-cinnamon muffins for the trip, promising that by mid-morning his appetite would reappear.

"Let's make one thing crystal clear this fine morning, boss," Brad announced as they'd pulled onto a relatively lively but still manageable interstate, the majority of their company of the delivery van or semi-truck variety. "I know I'm starting to sound like a broken record, but please don't feel any obligation as far as today's recording goes. After all, it's more for your family's legacy. I mean, you could always give me the Reader's Digest version when you're up to it."

Half expecting an argument, Brad was equally pleased and petrified at the older man's uncharacteristically meek response.

"How long to Memphis, you figure?"

"Pretty long haul. Six, maybe six and a half hours."

Balancing the briefcase atop his knees, Boone began shuffling through a stack of CDs.

"Plenty of time, then."

"Precisely. No strain."

They two exchanged a pleasant enough look, though in retrospect Brad would ponder a jarring absence of the usual glint reflected in the older man's eyes, like a blown pilot light.

For the next two hours-plus, they rode beneath mostly cloudy skies with the occasional light drizzle and, accompanied by voices as varied as Dusty Springfield, Simon & Garfunkel, Billy Joel, Robert Palmer and Phil Collins, discovering a psychological sabbatical of sorts that was as welcome as it was apparently needed between the two men. Two men separated by decades and a wide chasm of life experiences, sharing a space in time that for one served as a new beginning and the other a potentially bittersweet conclusion.

Following a quick stop to freshen and gas up on the outskirts of Springfield, Boone even managing to force down a banana and several sips of Sprite, compact discs and the recorder swapped places inside the briefcase with a fresh cassette inserted into the latter.

Unlit Maverick hanging from the left corner of his downturned mouth, Boone shot his driver an obligatory glance and subsequent nod. As a heavier rain began to pelt the Charger's roof, the weightiest droplets providing a drumroll of sorts, the older man set his jaw tight, inhaled deeply and commenced to speak.

Chapter Five

"Pam and I relocated from south Texas to the east coast just after the millennium. We'd met in Corpus Christi and married just a few months later. Long story short, though a diehard Texan through-and-through, she was as ready for a change of scenery as I, so it didn't take much of a nudge on my part and we were off to the races. We'd been hitched for just over a dozen years at that point and had yet to hit the dreaded wall of complacency that sinks a slew of marriages.

"Not to unduly badmouth my two previous hookups, but Pamela was the closest thing to the mythical soulmate I would ever know. Ah, sweet Pammy. I used to call her the ultimate triple-threat: Princess Diana's class, Madam Curie's smarts and Cheryl Ladd's beauty. Lord, but she passed far too young. Breast cancer, stage three by the time they caught it. Might sound corny as one of those Harlequin paperbacks, but when she went, a large chuck of my soul went along for the ride.

"I won't go into the details of my many past employments but suffice to say a new career was sought with equal fervor as the search for greener pastures. Pam served a tour in the Air Force before a year or two of substitute teaching and finally a short turn as a dental office receptionist. Neither of us was tied to anything permanent at the time, so once the decision was agreeable, it was goodbye Brownsville and hello South Carolina coast. As I'd spent my formable teen years trapesing up and down that very strip of coastline, in some ways it was like being reacquainted with an old friend.

"While Pam took a job as an office manager of a local tire shop, I secured what at first, I'd considered stop-gap work, at least 'til I found something permanent. As fate would have it, less than three years in and I found myself promoted to branch manager and stop-gap quickly transformed to concrete-solid.

"The company itself was a proven commodity, opening its doors in the late seventies. This despite some healthy local competition. Jack Waylon Floyd was the founder and owner of all three branches, one in Sumpter and the headquarters located in Myrtle Beach. Shared space with the 'head cheese' just once in those first several years and that was during my initial interview. Big, gregarious son-of-a-gun. You couldn't help but like 'im right away. As luck would have it, the feeling was mutual, and I was put on the payroll almost immediately.

"Now, the company name did garner a few giggles whenever selling to prospective customers, but it was the top-notch service that reeled 'em in and kept 'em on the line. Hey, with a moniker like '*The Pest Patrol*', you had better be good, and the company logo didn't exactly help matters. Lemme think, how to put this. Well, just think the mutated love children of Captain Marvel and the Maytag repair man and you get the picture...*Shazam.*

"Pete Daniels, the branches' lone salesman, landed a whopper of a deal, his words, not mine, for us to treat a site a few miles offshore of the Isle. Some random island approximately the size of a Walmart that had been used for seasonal renting. Story was that a husband-and-wife realty team came over from Vegas in the mid-nineties, searching out just such locales to build exclusive vacation homes. Soon enough what had been an overgrown mound of useless sand was rechristened '*The Shangri la Shacks*', an upscale island paradise consisting of a trio of two-room log cabins, high-end Tiki bar, buffet-style bistro, tennis courts, basketball courts and even an Olympic-sized pool. Not exactly cheap digs, as I'd heard they rented for somewhere in the ballpark of two grand per weekend booking and four G's for the full week package. Pretty high-dollar even for a quarter-century back, but at least for the first five summers, they reportedly had no problems keeping those cabins booked, remarkable considering meals and booze were not inclusive. Basically, just the digs and use of the pool. Pete did some impressive research on the place before hooking up with the new landlords. Said it was going gangbusters before tropical storm Liza rampaged up the coast in the summer of two thousand, flattening the bar and ripping the roof off the bistro and two of the cabins. Did something like a quarter-million in damages and instead of attempting a rebuild, Mister and Misses power-couple wrote it off as a loss and went their merry way back to the left coast.

"According to Pete, it lay deserted in partial ruins until the Spring of two-thousand two, when a resort mogul from Mobile purchased the rights and not only repaired what was already in place but added a few extras to the original blueprint.

"The reopening goal was late Spring two-thousand four, this time not only featuring a fourth cabin and redesigned tiki bar and bistro but also an outdoor amphitheater for the occasional island concert. Various contractor issues and an overly feisty typhoon season led to delays until the following summer, despite the majority of the rebuild complete.

"That's where '*The Pest Patrol*' came in. Super-heroes in dark blue ball caps, matching short-sleeve Dickie shirts, skinny khakis and high-polished black Timberlake boots, the cap and shirt displaying that infamous company logo. Well, infamous for those forced to don it in order to collect a regular paycheck, anyway.

"If nothing else, the company emblem was nothing if not an attention-grabber. The letters 'PP' spelled out in crimson lightning bolts on a dark blue background, the 'bolts oozing comic-book blood splatter in an even darker shade of red with tiny bug corpses littered on the bill of the cap and onto the shirt's oversized patch. Problem was, what was supposed to be roach and spider carcasses were often mistaken for severed human toes and fingers, at least from a fair distance. What started as comical got old pretty damn quick, but Dennis just shrugged it off. Dennis Pratt being the parent company CEO, accepted all the minor misunderstandings and even the harsh criticisms that the logo was too damn violent as a positive for sales, he being of the belief that any PR was *good* PR. Easy for him to say, as his only customer contact was over the talk-box while lounging around in an air-conditioned office sipping iced tea and sucking down grape popsicles.

"As for the mini-resort job, not only had Pete secured a monthly service contract with the new owners, but an initial treatment referred to in the business as 'the works' meaning each structure was to receive a full inspection and subsequent treatment before the grand opening. For this, all-day three-person job, the company was to pocket a mind-boggling five grand, a nice percentage of which would line the pockets of the lucky trio tasked in the form of a one-time bonus check. Thing was, it wasn't like they were being hoodwinked. Such commercial de-critter missions were a company specialty as opposed to residential sprayings and such. Small potatoes, baby. PP was all about square footage covered and payment in kind.

"As far as my co-workers and myself there wasn't a critter we wouldn't bash or a bug we wouldn't stomp for a price, from Norway rats to vampire bats, German roaches to brown recluses, copperheads to crayfish. We were equal opportunity terminators.

"Honestly, as a crew we were a true rarity in the extermination game, a business known for its heavy employee turnover, usually due to a mix of low wages and equally low self-esteem in doing a job not exactly known for its class or glamor. Of the eleven exterminators in my charge, I held seniority over only three. With just over five years of experience, eight of 'em eclipsed me, with two approaching twenty. Though there's no way to ever fact-check such an obscure claim, I'd lay even money it was the most experienced band of pest assassins ever assembled under one small roof.

"As things panned out for what Pete referred to as '*Assignment: Shangri la*', our ranks were somewhat skeletal, what with two away on well-earned vacations, another bedridden with flu symptoms and six others obligated to downtown jobs for the majority of that week. Such happens when a contract is signed, and an agreement made practically overnight.

"Regardless, this left yours truly, Toby McGrew, a ten-year vet of the bug wars who was loyalty defined, and Janet Dwyer, a fiery, hardworking perfectionist and the crew's lone female representative with just over six years in the business as the default trio for that well-paid trip to Shangri la.

"Now, while dependable, amiable ol' Toby was always a welcome addition to any assignment, I was particularly relieved to have Janet on board. She'd earned her nickname *Tropical Thunder* long before my arrival and for good reason. Janet was a barely-thirty-something, straight-taking, ball-busting Amerasian firecracker with a Filipino mom and Irish

American dad and who was, without a doubt, the lynchpin of the entire crew. Copper-haired, slim of build and absolutely striking, at the time she was juggling two other part-time jobs without ever missing a beat on the bug-stomping circuit. Never turned down an assignment that I can recall in the half-decade we shared the same employer, no matter how bone-weary or sleep deprived. You see, while Toby also tinkered with another career—hey, if you're in the extermination business long enough, you discover those who actually admit to pursuing it as career about as common as your basic flying unicorn—Miss Janet's situation didn't have squat to do with any unfulfilled fantasies. Bottom line, baby. As a single mom of a young son, I think he was four or five at the time, it was all about the bread.

"Though she rarely spoke of it, easily the most lucrative of her two moonlighting gigs was as an exotic dancer at a club in Charleston, hence the colorful nick, which she'd adopted as her professional stage name. From what I gathered from our few conversations on the subject, she was neither proud nor ashamed of the *Tropical Thunder* persona, it was simply a way to best support herself and her kid at the time. It goes without saying that Janet was not hard on the eyes, thus the hard-edged, no-nonsense attitude she toted around like a sledgehammer. Only those closest to her understood the Dragon Lady act was nothing more than a protective shield. For the most part, we all saw and understood that she felt it necessary in a business dominated by men, some of which weren't exactly the most polished or polite. There were more than a few clueless new hires over those years that learned the hard way that *Tropical Thunder* was the product of a very fine young actress. Openly flirting or worse, attempting to charm or win her over with some smut-filled opening line was to ask for a verbal dressing down any Marine DI would've been proud to mimic. Janet's private life was just *that*, and the veterans on the crew respected it, that and her unmatched work ethic and dedication to task. No one was ever going to outhustle 'TT', as I so lovingly referred to her when we alone shared the occasional beer after office hours. It was those memories of her I treasure the most, since it was such a rare phenomenon to see her mask of steely, independent toughness slip. Without a doubt, the most gorgeous smile I've ever seen. In another life, I'd have fallen hard for her, but thank

God, I never embarrassed myself by revealing that little secret.

"Toby, he of the pencil-thin 'stache, boxy noggin and buzzcut, on the other hand, thirty-six years young with an ex-wife and three kids to feed, was one of life's incessant dreamers. In the almost six years we were co-workers, not once did Toby refer to his slot as anything *but* temporary. Built like a Sherman tank with long arms, broad shoulders and a face that bore the scars of his secondary profession, those being such standard clichés as a slightly bent nose and squared jaw, Toby's dream, more like an *obsession,* was the sweet science. To be specific, he was a pugilist, or what we used to call a pug. A steel-jawed brawler whose pure punching power made up for a glaring lack of technique.

"Sad thing was the poor guy was constantly in training for some grand event that didn't even exist. The story goes that just a few years past high school graduation, Toby made the mistake of winning a local Tough Guy contest and won it such grand style it caught the eye of none other than George Benton, one of the all-time great boxing trainers who just happened to be on hand as a celebrity judge. Even Toby admits that Benton's glowing review is what fueled his dream of ring fame.

"I attended two of his tough-guy tourneys, one in Columbia and the other in Charleston and watched him reach the semi-finals in both cases, winning his first four fights in each. The Charleston semi match nearly pushed him into retirement. I guess that's only natural when nursing a broken jaw, two cracked ribs and a concussion, all this damage incurred *with* the required headgear in place. When I visited him at the hospital, all he could talk about was putting away the gloves. Well, it took 'im all of three months to get over it and he was back in training again. At six-three and a solid two-twenty, he had the size. Definitely had the heart and tenacity. Punched with Rhino impact and could take a beating as well as give it out. Problem was, he had lead in his heels and his chin caught more punches than his gloves. You see, Toby *knew* these things. Talked about his weaknesses and how he had a new trainer that was gonna cure 'im of all the bad habits. If I were to guess, he went through as many of these 'miracle' trainers as he had years under his belt as an exterminator. Thing is, there was no quitting in Toby McGrew. Hell, it was almost normal to see 'im work a route with taped ribs, swollen lips and a shiner. I had to respect his determination if not his good sense.

"It was just past six AM on a misty Saturday morning, the fourteenth of April, the weather unseasonably warm and humid with the sporadic downpour predicted, that the three of us met up at Dan Mac's Marina. Sufficiently geared up for the job at hand, we sipped coffee in a comfortable silence before hopping aboard a rented Back Cove 340, captained by a grinning, pink-cheeked young man who'd insisted we step aboard right-foot first to ensure a safe and prosperous endeavor.

"Never one for superstition, I recall laughing it off even as I half-heartedly complied. Damned if I recall if either Toby or Janet had done the same. Not that I really believe it would've made any kind of difference if they had. Still, in sad, tragic retrospect, it sure as hell couldn't have hurt.

"So often since I've pondered hopping into some mythical time machine and the myriad of changes I might've inferred to prevent that day from ever happening. If changing fate meant something as simple as toting around the necessary talisman, I would've packed a duffel full enough of four-leaf clovers, silver crosses, shamrocks and rabbits' feet to sink that boat.

"Time-travel fantasies and good-luck charms notwithstanding, the three of us simply fell victim to one of the oldest clichés known to man. An oldie but certainly no goodie.

Wrong place, wrong time.

Cliché or not, there is no better description."

Flashback Part III

Bug Hunt
Spring, 2004

Off the coast of Isle of Palms, South Carolina.

"Talk to me, Tobe."

"Permission to at least finish my coffee, boss? That first cup barely dented the fog, and I don't mean this bowl of soup we're presently passing through."

Extracting thick smoke-streams from each nostril, Boone flicked away what little remained of the Harley-Davidson brand fag over the boat's side, a stout breeze and accompanying mist nearly tossing it back toward his face, boomerang-style.

"Gulp away. Janet?"

Dropping to one knee, she gracefully shimmied the worn backpack from her shoulders and began pilfering through it with gloved hands.

"Termidor SC, twenty ounces. Tempo Ultra, two-four-oh ML. Tomcat Rodenticide, four pounds. Doctor T's snake-away Granules, five-spot."

Though he knew the answer, regulations dictated he inquire.

"Check. Sprayer sufficiently locked and loaded for round one?"

Laying the backpack aside, she reached back and retrieved a dark red tank sprayer, complete with brass nozzle, the former littered with various stickers, mostly of the skull & cross-bone's variety. Meanwhile, Toby first crunched the empty Styrofoam cup in one palm in true beer-can-crushing fashion and casually flipped it overboard, his visage growing ghostlier with each passing tick.

"Double-check."

Standing to re-don the backpack, Janet winced from the effort before shooting her boss a playful wink.

"Little stiff this fine coastal Gamecock morning, are we?" he teased, forced to palm the top of his ballcap to prevent it sailing off and into the passing waves.

"Tough night, Boo. Let a co-worker talk me into a new pole maneuver. Think I strained a quad."

Boo was her nick for Boone, so cutesy a reference that a large majority of the crew were convinced the two were occasionally sharing a bed.

"Just such hazards forced me into early retirement," Boone retorted, shaking his head in mock sympathy. "On the bright side, the pole does make a great clothesline."

She blew a noisy raspberry his way while executing a series of shoulder and tricep stretches.

Despite a thick AM fog and equally girthy swell, their young pilot steered them forward at a faster clip than Boone would've preferred. From Toby's pale mug and the death-grip he applied to the nearby rail, it went without saying he agreed whole-heartedly. As for Janet, she stood statuesque and with no apparent need for extra bracing, peering into the passing waters through a tight squint. Unlike Boone or Toby, she wore no windbreaker but just the required Pest Patrol short sleeve.

"Tobe, you gonna make it, man?"

The big man nodded as if to acknowledge he would indeed survive, though his paleness gained new levels of pallidness with each fresh lurch or sway of the slick Back Cove.

"How's about a quick inventory then?"

"Ugh, you mind if we wait 'til we slap sand, boss?" he replied weakly, peering down at the backpack like it was the narrow edge of a cliff.

Alternating glances from the boat's skipper, the kid was stick-thin to the point of appearing downright fragile, back to his hulking yet currently sickly subordinate, Boone seriously doubted if the latter was going to make landfall before losing his breakfast.

"Sure, no problem. Did you at least pre-mix the sprayer with Paraquat? Remember, you're the weed-assassin this trip."

To this, Toby merely nodded, swallowing hard as if to barely avoid regurgitating a mouthful of warm bile.

"Hope ya'll packed some midday chow as instructed…" Boone resumed, reaching down to lightly pat his duffel, "… 'cause I won't be sharing Mama Harrison's BLT's."

"Good to go, boo," Janet said flatly. "Sliced Gala apples and mango."

Boone nodded, equally impressed and unsurprised by her ultra-healthy menu.

"Tobe?"

The big man swallowed hard, obviously struggling with the mere mention of edibles.

"PBJ's and a couple of energy bars."

"Solid. I brought along a twelve-pack of icy Aquafina. Well, icy for now. Not so much by lunchtime, but at least mildly chilled."

Boone saw Janet eyeing his sprayer, a sarcastic smirk painted on an otherwise flawless mug, and could guess what was coming.

"How 'bout you, boo? What kinda magic stew you got in that overpriced cement mixer?"

"A little of this, a little of that. Guaranteed to send any and all of the pestilence species mandibles-up to either bug or varmint *boot hill.*"

Propped between his knees was a two-gallon tank, top-of-the-line B&G, referred to as the 'Cadillac of sprayers', a sturdy, steely, nearly two-hundred-dollar investment he'd made upon landing the managerial role. Giving his own worn duffel a quick once-over, other than mimicking Janet's stock almost to a tee, a trio of heavy-duty, long-handled Maglite's and extra batteries added both substantial bulk and weight.

"How much further there, Cap?" he shouted toward their youthful navigator, who responded without turning, a shrieking, unmasculine retort, like the crackling voice of a prepubescent teen.

"Two, maybe three nautical miles. Six, seven minutes tops."

Boone gave no effort to block the ear-to-ear grin bloomed in the aftermath.

"So declares Captain Opie Cunningham," he heard Janet quip, reading her full lips as much as hearing the actual words, and nodded in sincere agreement.

Such cutting humor was apparently lost on a slumping, droopy-eyed Toby McGrew, whose lone concern at the time appeared to be holding down his cookies.

Taking a substantial soaking from the passing mist, Boone peered briefly upward at a thick band of rapidly darkening cloud-cover and logically deduced the most effective spraying would be the interiors by default, the use of granules and rodenticide most likely a waste of time and resources if only to be washed away almost immediately after placement. Rainy days were not, needless to say, the exterminator's friend where outdoor treatments were concerned.

"Shangri la, three o'clock," Commodore Opie yelped minutes later, pointing with a toothpick-thin bare arm to the right, where the island floated hazily into view through the slowly spreading murk.

The palpable relief in Tobe's sagging eyes, briefly rolling back as if to emphasize, birthed yet another involuntarily smile from his superior.

As for the island itself, Pete Daniel's vague description that its overall size mimicked that of your basic Super Walmart might've been an exaggeration, as, at least from their initial angle facing its northside, it rated barely half said total circumstance.

"Manmade lagoon is on her western edge," he resumed, gesturing toward the left and steering the vessel in that direction. "I was told the pier was rebuilt and a concrete walkway added."

Minutes later, as the boat approached the lengthy pier through a U-shaped inlet, its squared outer edge levitating at least a half-dozen feet off the water's surface, Boone regarded his charges through a tight squint and flashed each a double thumbs-up.

"Pest Patrol is here to do *what?*" he inquired sternly; jaw comically jutted with a gloved fist raised eye level.

In unison, eyes rolling in time as if synchronized, his subordinates barked out, though in a stale, weary monotone lacking actual enthusiasm.

"Eradicate all things that live to annoy, vex or irritate humankind."

"I…can't…*HEAR YOU!*" Boone screeched through cupped hands before resuming his stoic, militaristic stance, their young pilot twisting about for a brief, befuddled glance at the sudden hullabaloo.

Shoulders similarly slumped, the pair somehow avoided a redux of the eye roll while repeating the earlier refrain with a tad more fervor, or at least enough to prevent a third go-round.

"Damn straight," Boone beamed, "My trained killers, ready to do that voodoo that they do best."

"*Hoo-wah*, coach," Janet replied sourly, the corners of her mouth slightly upturned in a half-smile, half-smirk.

The trio gathered their gear, Toby noticeably sluggish, as the pilot steered the port side to line up with the edge of the pier.

"It's now oh-seven-oh-five, Mister Harrison," the young skipper announced minutes later, peering from beneath the flat of one palm into a light shower as the dismounted trio stood perched several feet above.

"Per your request, I'll reappear at fifteen-hundred hours for the return trip. Again, if you require an earlier pickup for any reason, just activate that pager and I'll shoot on over."

"Sounds good, cap. See ya then," Boone replied with a half-wave, his free hand checking a front pants pocket and, feeling the pager's tiny, squared presence, completing the gesture.

As the sleek, Back Cove sped away, the skipper cranked the boat's previously muted radio to the tune of Daniel Powter's '*Bad Day*'.

"A *pager*, huh? I guess they'll bill us in crayon," Toby cracked as all three kneeled to recheck their individual backpacks.

"Hey, they could use a stone tablet for all Pratt cares," Boone answered, hands submerged in his duffel, the light rain gradually transforming into a substantial downpour, "Cheap maybe, but darn practical as well. It doesn't have to be the latest in technology to get the job done."

Standing and strolling further up the rain-slickened dock, Janet frowned as if detecting a particularly putrid scent.

"Yeah, but that Flintstone-era gadget doesn't even have text capability. It's like the pagers they used to use to tell you your table was ready at Denny's."

Boone shrugged, rising stiffly while adjusting the bill of his ballcap.

"Low-budget on the front end means less expense on the back. Besides, a cell phone is about as useful as breasts on a bull out here.

Hey…" he paused, regarding the increasingly drenched sleeves of his windbreaker, "…anybody clever enough to bring along their rain gear?"

From one knee, Tobe shrugged, "Nope."

"Right here, Boo," Janet said, digging into her backpack and retrieving a meticulously folded garment which she unfurled via a single flick of the wrist.

"Should've known," Boone grinned, securing his own pack while scanning the stone path past the inner edge of the pier.

"Tobe, looks like we've got interiors by default. Let's hit 'em, gang. The faster we finish, the quicker we get home. But first…" he kneeled to dig both hands into his duffel, removing two of the Maglite's and tossing one to each subordinate, "…assist me not adding additional girth to my hernia."

While Janet immediately tucked the light into her backpack with a graceful reverse stab, Toby tossed the hefty light from hand to hand.

"Shit boss, these bad-boys could double as nightsticks. Why the laser bats anyhow?"

Passing by her bulky co-worker, Janet landed a light jab to his broad right shoulder.

"See any powerlines, Einstein?"

"Oh, yeah. There is *that*."

"Place runs on generators the size of your basic Mack truck, which won't be operational 'til there are paying customers to help with the fuel bill."

With Boone on point, they walked single file until reaching the pathway, treading cautiously on the increasingly slickened pine while scanning the approaching forest past the perimeter of the initial sandbar.

"Welcome to *Fan-ta-seee ihh-lend*," Toby croaked, hopping into the damp sand with arms spread dramatically.

Standing to his left, Boone scanned the beach on either side, its otherwise spotless surface dotted with the sporadic scallop, giant cockle, or shark-eye shell.

"Nice enough first impression. Something's missing though."

Janet stood posed to Boone's right, having donned the comically baggy raingear jacket and connecting hood.

"A sign maybe? Hula dancers?"

"I like the way you think," Toby said, grinding and stomping his size thirteen boots into the sand before glancing back at the plaster-cast like prints left behind, "Maybe bring some of your co-workers out for a mud-wrestling tournament."

Hopping past her superior, Janet side-booted a clump of sand that spattered the back of his already damp khakis, the big man yelping playfully while step-stepping away, "Maybe rename it Boner Island?"

"That'll do, kiddies," Boone chided, stepping onto the wide concrete walk, it's sleek, virgin appearance a testament to its newness, and thumping the heels of his boots to free clumps of sand wedged between the treads.

"Let's see where this here yellow-brick road leads."

Almost immediately upon departing the beachhead, the path curved hard to the right before taking a hard left, either side framed by rubber, cecropia and Norfolk Island Pines that enclosed the path as if carved to precise specifications from some giant mold. If nothing else, the crisscrossing limbs overhead provided temporary cover from the precipitation.

Another slight right and the path, now lined on both sides by thick growths of both black and white mangrove and bracken ferns, straightened for an approximate twenty-yard stretch, followed by a slight left up a gradual incline.

"I do believe we've found civilization," Boone announced, pointing up and to the left, where a sloping grass roof swam into view. As if on cue, the rain diminished to a light drizzle.

Minutes later, they stood in a semi-circle facing the first such abode, not so much a cabin in the classic sense of the word but instead a hale, a Hawaiian or Polynesian styled hut. To the left, perhaps fifteen yards in the distance with its bulk blocked by a thick mass of mangold, stood the second of four huts and, its placement obvious as to center the huts, was the outer edges of the swimming pool. Though they each remained out of sight, twin tennis courts and a basketball court stood somewhere even further west. The Tiki bar and restaurant, also as-of-yet-undiscovered, supposedly stood on a slight ridge overlooking the rest. It went without saying that the eatery would require extra focus, as, unlike the other structures, health department certificates were required in order to begin operation.

Boone, removing his ballcap and shaking off the access, backed away a few steps to take in the structure's surprising mass.

"Cool. Thatched roof and Ti leaf walls. Smell that? Sugar cane, baby. Hale Noho style, I do believe."

Head tilted, her otherwise flawless mug scrunched in sincere mystification, Janet studied her superior as if he'd just spoken in some unintelligible, alien tongue.

"How the hell do you *know* these things?"

"It's called reading, oh young bewildered one. Try scanning something other than clothing labels sometime," Boone fired back, taking in the grayish structure's ultra-steep roof and thick grass walls. "Hey, maybe hula dancers wouldn't be so farfetched after all."

Toby frowned, thick arms crossed, "I dunno, boss. Looks kinda bargain basement for, what was the nightly rent again? Two grand? I'd expect more for that amount of scratch than some glorified teepee."

Already priming her sprayer, Janet scoffed.

"I'd withhold judgement 'til I've peeked inside there, punchy Pete."

"Lady has a point. Besides, I like it. A touch of Honolulu on the Carolina coast."

Toby grunted, squirming like a man with an unreachable itch to remove his backpack.

"Well *hell*, Boone, at those prices you can have the real thing."

"Maybe, but a half-hour ride from the coastline is a helluva lot more convenient than eleven hours in a flying tin-can."

Breaking into a hip-grinding, undeniably seductive dance, despite the circus-tent sized raingear, Janet gracefully passed the sprayer from hand to hand while circling Toby, who regarded her with a warped sneer.

"Game, set, *match*. Down goes Punchy, *down* goes Punchy."

"Dad, make her stop," the big man spat through comically pooched lips.

Ignoring these latest hijinks, Boone stepped onto the hut's hard pine porch, so finely waxed that a veritable army of rain droplets bubbled on the gleaming surface and, eyeing a squared metal box to the right of the entrance, flipped its cover and carefully tapped a four-digit code onto a numbered keypad. Retrieving his Maglite, he flicked the on switch and reached for the door's silver lever handle.

"Entre-vous. Flashlights on stun, children, and don't forget to wipe your boots before entering."

Filing in one at a time with Boone on point, the trio were, at least temporarily struck mute. Upon passing a relatively small, thickly carpeted foyer littered with assorted tiki statues and statuettes, they soon stood at the threshold of a classically sunken living room, the floor not the expected laminate or vinyl but strand woven bamboo stained a yellow cream color. Despite all three effectively aiming their lights within the same squared space, the living room nonetheless appeared astonishingly spacious considering such a compact-looking shell, housing twin black couches and matching ottoman, genuine leather from their sleek appearance, a pair of cloth, teal-shaded reclining love seats, all of which were perfectly angled toward the room's clear centerpiece and a big-screen TV that redefined the word 'vast'. Curved inward at its squared edges, Boone could only estimate its overall girth at seventy inches, perhaps even eighty.

"Talk about bigger on the *inside*," Toby marveled, wide-eyed, "Kinda like finding the Titanic shoved inside a Pringles can."

"Ay caramba. Is that a TV or a walk-in closet?" Janet added, the beam of her light frozen on the big screen.

Hands on hips, Boone's darting eyes gleamed, "Hey, I told you, Tobe. No mud floors or bucket-toilets in this pad. Check out the sleeping quarters," he paused, pointing with his light's beam to the opposite side, where a wood staircase, also presumably bamboo, led to an open bedroom elevated ever slightly from the first floor, "That ain't no army cot, brother."

Beneath a massive, mirrored ceiling sat a California King adorned with a pink blanket, its center a heart-shaped crimson, along with at least six pillows of assorted sizes, including a pair of the body-length variety. Two walnut dressers sat nearby, one of which included a diamond-shaped makeup mirror and the other a globe lamp with each embellished with gleaming marble tops.

"Straight from a Playboy mansion blueprint."

"Perhaps, maybe Larry Flynt's," Toby countered, applying a faint jab to Boone's left shoulder, "Five spot says those dresser drawers are stuffed with enough lubes and oils to cause a major coastal spill."

Even as the two men, both grinning like pubescent teens privy to a particularly risqué joke, gravitated to the right, Janet stood her ground, lips pursed as if to whistle in appreciation.

"Well…" she stated, side-stepping over to join the boys but still unable to pry the light's slightly wavering beam from the boudoir, "…I can state with the upmost confidence that neither Kmart or Sears had a hand in these furnishings."

In the far-right corner was a small kitchenette featuring a mini-fridge, microwave and combination coffee maker/expresso machine.

"Kinda skimpy, ain't it?" Toby exclaimed, frowning, kneeling to open and close the door to the mini fridge. "Barely hold a pack of cold-cuts and a six-pack."

"Think about it, Tobe. Every meal is provided at the eatery and every drink the tiki bar. Other than the occasional doggie bag, what're you gonna store?"

"Touché. Well, that's why you rate the big bucks."

"Lavatories on the opposite side," Janet noted, light trained to the left, where an open door revealed a bathroom sink and mirror, a clear reflection from the latter revealing both the toilet and tub/shower contained within.

"Whoa, that is one big-ass sauna. Probably penis shaped," the big man cracked, his warped smile fading quickly upon noticing his co-workers exaggeratingly flummoxed expressions.

Performing a quick walk-through of the kitchenette, Boone bent down to peek into the trio of cabinets before standing and scanning behind the mini-fridge and microwave.

"No hint of roaches, but there are a few rat droppings behind the fridge," he said, turning back to face his charges, both of whom were scanning the grass ceiling and walls, their lights occasionally crossing.

"JD, for now I'd just lay down some granules and rodenticide.

Hopefully the rain stays on the light side."

Boone focused his light on Toby's sprayer.

"What flavor you carrying?"

Toby shook the container from side to side for the desired 'sloshing' effect.

"Paraquat, remember?"

"Oh yeah, weed and grass destroyer. JD…" Boone turned back to Janet, who paused at the door to readjust the baggy raingear, "…leave Toby your sprayer for now. Once you've laid down all the granules and rat-bullets, meet us at cabin four."

The raingear's oversized hood cloaking all but her mouth and chin, she dropped the container just inside the door.

"Try not to drain it dry," she grumbled.

"That's what *he* said," Toby replied, clicking his bootheels as if to gain attention.

Boone smiled despite himself.

" Tobe, you have the door code list?"

"Affirmative, Herr Commandant."

"Alright then. Tromp on over to cabin two and lay down a perimeter spray with the Tempo. Might as well hit the weeds on the outside before switching to the Termidor. Don't forget the cabinets and the john and be on the lookout for snakeskin."

"Check. Meet you outside cabin three."

Boone nodded, watching the pair trudge toward the exit while giving his sprayer a few priming pumps.

"Once the cabins are good and juiced, inside and out, we'll focus on the Tiki bar and around the pool and courts. Do 'em up good. Empty those cans to the last drop."

"Aye-aye, skip. See ya on the other side," Toby shouted over one shoulder while holding the door for his female counterpart, the door shutting silently behind them. Boone had thought about leaving it propped open before reconsidering the considerable mosquito population buzzing about.

Having already laid down a fine bead of roach-killer along the kitchenette and level-floor perimeter, he'd just ascended the wooden staircase leading to the bedroom when an alien sound froze him poised on the top step. Like a muted mix tape of assorted grunts, groans and moans, it was soon accompanied by rapidly approaching footsteps just outside the cabin walls.

"B-Boone! Sh-shit! *BOOOONE!*" the voice roared just as the source snagged the door handle and gave it a colossal tug, to no avail since it had auto-locked upon closing.

In the six years the two traversed the same paths, through the hundreds of jobs, countless shared meals and beers after the fact, Boone never heard anything resembling fear or panic in the big man's tone. The effect of bearing witness to what sounded like an almost complete meltdown from one of the toughest people he'd ever known birthed a temporary paralysis, wherein Boone's lower extremities briefly refused his commands and his vocal cords stuck in neutral.

"Damn it, Boone, o-open the door!"

As if pulling his booted feet from buckets of semi-dried cement, Boone lurched forward and lumbered blindly toward the door, the Maglite's beam thrashing about the dark space like a thousand reflecting lights from some antique disco ball.

"For shits sake, BOONE!" the voice on the other side cracked, the door rattling with renewed fervor.

Boone fumbled blindly, bare hand sliding all around the handle and yelping in sudden shock upon smacking his wrist against its metal base.

It as much collapsed inward as merely opened, Toby and Boone nearly chest bumping, the latter briefly blinded by the sudden infusion of light.

"Toby, wh-what the hell?"

"Y-you gotta come see," the big man huffed. Wide-eyed and slouched over with one hand atop a bent knee with the opposite using the long flashlight to point down the rain-soaked cement path, the light sprinkle of earlier mutating into a torrential downpour. Discarding his sprayer and leaving the cabin door ajar, Boone and his longtime subordinate lurched more than sprinted down the curved walkway beneath increasingly darkening skies. As distance between the two cabins diminished, Boone had taken point by default, his winded subordinate Toby's thick arms hung simian-like at his sides, struggling to keep pace.

A scream, fleeting but shrill, like a klaxon's single blaring retort, its source frighteningly obvious, momentarily froze both in their tracks, Toby barely avoiding sliding headfirst into his superiors crouched frame.

Reaching back, Boone managed to slow his husky companions forward momentum, his impromptu stiff-arm impacting Toby's upper chest as their boots kicked up a veritable tidal wave of standing water, this as they'd neared a slight downslope between a grouping of cecropia trees, its limp palmate leaves hanging like malformed, groping fingers.

A second chorus, this less a piercing shriek than a garbled wail, provided an instant recharge for their shaky legs, Boone taking off as if forcefully shoved, with Toby not far behind, arms no longer hanging but pumping like well-lubricated pistons.

Clearing a U-turn like bend, their ankles and boots forced to kick free of a thick, overlapping entanglement of bracken ferns, the second cabin swam immediately into view to the right, Janet standing just outside its open door, down on one knee and vomiting into a nearby scrub.

"Janet, w-what?" Boone stammered, hopping onto the rain-soaked wooden porch and crouching next to her slumped frame while not daring to turn his back to the opening.

Toby arrived a split-second later, wheezing and snorting as clear mucus dripped from both nostrils, his bowed form to Janet's left allowing the trio to mimic an impromptu football huddle.

"H-h-he…" she babbled and spat, her back tensing and head bowed in preparation for an impending heave while reaching back to point with a visibly shaking hand toward the entrance, "…in…there. O-oh g-god…"

Peering over to Toby in hopes of gaining additional information before barreling blindly into the cabin's dark, suddenly foreboding maw, Boone waited for the big man's strained breathing to normalize somewhat while gently wrapping an arm around Janet's trembling shoulders. As Toby seemed strangely oblivious to this immediate need, this noble attempt at patience failed before a full half-minute passed.

"So, what the hell's in there? Is it, I mean, *safe* to enter?"

Leaning up with hands on hips, Toby's reply came only after a series of machine-gun like respires, his squared chin playing cliff wall to a veritable waterfall of phlegm and rain droplets.

"It's a…it's a man. He's…tied d-down. Strapped down. Bound."

Boone's bug-eyed doubletake would've been comical under different circumstances.

"Alive?"

Between darting glances at the entrance, Toby shook the water from his ballcap with the sporadic headshake.

"Damned if I…took t-the time to…ch-check his pulse, but it's highly doubtful. He's…been t-trashed but good."

Turning to Janet, his vaguely pained, impossibly stoic expression appeared to beg for a more positive perspective that was destined not to be.

"JD?"

Up off one knee, Janet remained crouched, spitting greenish wads of puke between clipped offerings of dialogue.

"No way…he's…breathing. N-not a chance."

Boone stood stiffly, sucking air greedily between pursed lips as if preparing for a deep-sea dive into potentially treacherous waters, pausing only to reach over and procure an additional flashlight from Toby's limp grip.

Stepping cautiously forward, he paused briefly in mid-step at Janet's hoarse proclamation.

"Prepare yourself, Boo. It ain't pretty."

Teeth gritted and shoulders pulled back, Boone sidestepped in, heavy-duty Maglite's clenched in each hand like cocked revolvers.

The twin beams, shifting from side to side as well as up and down within the large space like searchlights at a Hollywood premiere, finally settled as one at the center of the sunken living room.

Boone tip-toed forward as if negotiating a live minefield, neck protruding and eyes squinted floss-thin even as the quivering of both hands caused the beams to similarly quake in and around the still target showcased.

"Oh m-my…ga…" he mumbled, barely audible over a sudden

crash of thunder.

The first realization that he had instinctively backed from the room was the moment his upper back struck the front door's outer edge.

Vocal cords temporarily out-of-order, Boone faced his subordinates with his arms hanging limply, jaw-dangling and mouth agape, the pale reflection in their eyes mimicking the shellshocked daze seen in his own mere minutes earlier.

In that terrible moment, a flood of memories so vivid and darkly visceral bludgeoned Boone with such physical and psychological force that he briefly tittered on the cusp of utter collapse. Even as he fought off, hyperventilating in the process, fainting atop that rain-soaked wooden porch, there was a palpable sense of disappointment, as this only meant he would remain conscious to deal with the horrific reality at hand.

~ * ~

Bound and Gag-Reflexes

"All right then. Message sent. Now all we can do is wait."

The trio stood huddled on the porch of the last of the four cabins, having found the others, mercifully, as deserted as the first. Though the rain subsided, wind gusts increased and the passing clouds appeared a shade darker, such negative signs no doubt a foreshadowing of storms to come. Pocketing the pager and checking his wristwatch, Boone noted it had been less than ten minutes since they'd left the ghastly discovery uncloaked in cabin two. He couldn't help but wonder if they had taken a vital detail concerning said find for granted, their recklessness fueled by both natural revulsion and primal fear.

Hugging herself across the bosom as if chilled, Janet was staring intently at the cell phone laying across the palm of her left hand, as if sheer will might create a useable signal.

"Give it up already," Toby growled, face scrunched as if suffering severe stomach cramps. The big man was pacing the squared porch like an expectant father in a cramped waiting room.

"Unless we can toss you onto the wing of a passing plane, you ain't making contact with the mainland."

"How long you think, Boone?" Janet inquired without looking up, her use of his proper given name a sure sign of sincere concern.

"Took us about thirty, thirty-five minutes from shore. Not knowing the situation, you figure he's not gonna be in any great rush to get started," Boone replied, staring across a relatively clear stretch of sand toward the Tiki restaurant and bar. "I figure forty-five minutes. Maybe even an hour."

Toby's pace slowed considerably. His huge hands cupped at his lower back.

"I dunno, boss. Even that prep-school skipper has to be wondering why you're paging him at quarter past eight, not even an hour-and-a-half since he dropped us off."

"We can hope. 'Course, he might also consider it the equivalent of a butt-call."

Cursed with toting the leadership mantle, a position he secretly reviled though often found himself forced into by circumstances beyond his control, Boone came to two distinct decisions simultaneously though hesitated sharing the details. That is, until a loud crack of thunder jarred the hesitation from his very bones.

"Listen, I'm headed back to the cabin. You two check out the restaurant and surrounding grounds. Meet me back there when you're done. That is, unless you find something worth sharing. In that case, just yell out and I'll come to *you*."

Before he could take a single step to exit the porch for the moistened sand, a fierce grip clamped the inner elbow of his left arm, essentially swinging him back around.

"Why in god's name do you want to walk back into that slaughterhouse?"

Janet's meticulously slanted jade-green eyes glistened with building tears as she nervously chewed her upper lip.

"JD, try to understand. I just...I need to know for sure."

As he'd continued pacing silently behind them at a frantic pace, Toby halted in mid-step at this, regarding his superior as if the older man proclaimed himself the high deity of turnip-land and wore a veggie-based crown to prove it.

"Know *what*, boss? Who or what left 'im that way? He sure as hell ain't in no shape to provide any answers."

"What if he *isn't* dead, Toby?" Boone shot back, jaw jutted defiantly as he alternated stony glances to each of them, to the point of even Janet breaking eye contact.

"Listen, I swear I saw him move. I'm probably wrong and it was just a…a hallucination, my mind playing tricks. Still, if there's even the smallest chance…"

Turning away, Toby hopped into the wet sand with both arms waving madly.

"Well shit, boss. I saw 'im move too. Only it wasn't *his* movements. That is, there was movement, but I think we *both* know the source. Besides, nothing still breathing smells like that."

"He's right, Boo," Janet added, maintaining her death grip on his inner arm even as he half-heartedly attempted to pull away. "There is *zero* chance he's alive, and even if by some miracle he is, what can we do to help him? I really, really think we should stick together here."

Twisting back around, Toby stretched out both arms and pointed in opposite directions.

"I agree. Who's to say whoever is responsible isn't still roaming this burg? Maybe even watching us this very second. There's strength in numbers, boss."

"Can't argue that. Come with me and we'll check 'im together."

Janet winced as if slapped across the face.

"I'm not going back in there. Nowhere *near* it. I don't want to even be near that damn stench again."

Head twisting around as if on a swivel, eyes darting to scan every angle in case of an impending assault, Toby chimed in sternly, leaving no space for a potential rebuttal.

"Ditto, boss. I'd rather go out to the dock and wait for the boat. Hell, maybe even dog paddle to the shore."

As gently as was possible, considering her initial unwillingness to let go, Boone removed Janet's clenching fingers from his arm and stepped off the porch, addressing them only after he'd exited wet sand for the stone walkway a dozen steps or more from the cabin.

"Decide for yourselves then, but the dock is this way."

"Ah *shit*," Toby grumbled, exchanging a 'what now?' look at his petite co-worker, who in turn shrugged, sighed heavily and trudged toward the stone path just as her superior vanished behind a thick wall of head-high mangroves.

~ * ~

"We'll be out here if you need us, boss."

Toby and Janet stood shoulder to elbow a few steps off the porch, having searched out and found a spot downwind from the cabin's partially ajar entrance.

"Can't promise for how long," Janet added, turning her head in the opposite direction.

"I'll just be a few minutes…" Boone announced grimly, clutching dual Maglite's yet again, this time confiscating Janet's. "…and we'll head on down to the dock together."

"Boss?"

Boone halted at the entrance, where he had used the edge of a boot to ease it farther ajar.

"Yeah?"

"Clap those lights together, stomp your feet, scream like a damned banshee if you have to. Anything to drive 'em away."

"Roger that," he nodded, inhaling deeply and holding it before stepping into the murk.

Not surprisingly, the man's position was unchanged. Not merely bound to the leather recliner, he appeared to have merged with it, the blackness effectively cloaking the chair's precise color in lieu of a recently caked-on, blood-spattered surface that if anything, darkened its original shade.

Completely naked, his binds were no mere rope or chain, but barbed wire that had been wound tightly from ankles to neck in at least two dozen evenly placed rows, the majority pinning his arms and torso. No mere barbed wire, Boone recognized it as concertina razor wire, the type routinely used atop chain-link fences at prison sites or historically by the military to set battlefield perimeters.

As Boone inched forward, the stout odor of spilled blood, feces and urine testing his gag reflex, he kept one light on the path ahead and the other frozen, as best he could considering a bad case of the shakes, on the tilted recliner and its grisly cargo.

"Sir? Can you hear me?" he croaked, his throat suddenly as parched and spittle-free as a desert gulch.

"Sir, I'm...here to help. Don't be alarmed. I'm going to come down now and see how I can..." he resumed between hard swallows, the rancid scent caking his tongue and flaring nostrils until he decided it wise to clamp his lips and cease further dialogue.

The gathering of Norway rats were as large as he had ever seen. Many cat-sized, but then again, they had obviously eaten well of late. Feasted without distraction, without haste, in some cases gorging themselves to pot-bellied lethargy.

Boone cautiously negotiated the trio of steps leading down to the sunken area, clapping the ends of the Maglite's together and even tossing in a rather feeble whistle once he'd reached level ground. As with his earlier visit, albeit much shorter in duration, the feeding rats hardly budged. Half-stepping forward, he purposely stomped the heels of each boot with each completed stride. This time several did scuttle away, though the majority remained unintimidated.

"Get off him, damn it, get OFF!" he bellowed, kicking over a nearby table, a glass-domed lamp sailing off and shattering in a dark corner.

Halting less than a dozen feet from the motionless, gruesomely trussed individual, Boone inhaled deeply and held it while training both lights as steadily as he could manage while begrudgingly initiating a head-to-toe inspection.

Despite the considerable carnage to his scalp and facial features, Boone guessed the olive-skinned male's age to be in the late twenties/early thirties range with a thin but well-toned, athletic build.

As for the butchery to said features, it was extensive, as in left ear gnawed almost to non-existence, the right nostril eaten completely away, and the left eye hollowed out like a walnut shell. Still, if rating the worst of the worst in terms of mutilation, Boone knew very well the damage a grouping of feeding Norway's could inflict. He'd seen canine and feline carcasses from which only the skeletal remains survived. In terms of gut-churning grisliness, the man's groin area won the grisly grand prize. Nothing surprising really, as Boone long understood the genitalia as the rodent version of a dessert tray of sweetmeats. Soft, easily shredded, consumed and digested. As for the mysterious corpse on display, Boone came to the sad realization the earlier 'movement' he'd seen was just as Toby and Janet hinted, they had indeed *tied on the old feedbag* and as such, relieved the man of not only his family jewels, but the entire damn reproductive package.

"Jesus mister, who the *hell* did you piss off?" he whispered, the twin beams reflected in the yellowish eyes of several of the feeders, one of which turned to regard Boone in between removing tiny strips of raw, bloodless flesh from around the man's left nipple. In allowing the lights to linger a bit longer on the young man's horribly disfigured visage, imagining him minus the many vermin-initiated tears, rips or complete voids, he could envision the chiseled good looks of one perhaps accustomed to upper-crust living. Either a high-society type with blueblood origins or a fraudulent slickster lying or conning his way into unearned riches, only to be found out and handed the bill for same.

Inching a few steps closer, almost to within reaching distance, Boone kicked out at a pair of bloated vermin that scuttled by, missing them both and using the twin beams to trail their hasty retreat into the kitchenette.

Swinging the lights back around in a chest-high, horizontal arc, he briefly thought he had accidentally leaned in too far as the Maglite's tip nearly brushed what remained of the bound man's nose.

That is, until the man's cracked lips, the bottom missing a sizeable chuck, the top leaking red/yellowish pus, parted and a huff of putrid air escaped to fill Boone's own flaring nostrils like a whiff of raw sewage, a single, croaked word escaped amongst the stench.

"Ma-Maaarrr...ti-na..."

Boone budged nary an inch with the shocking revelation, instead leaning even closer in an attempt to determine if the man's remaining eye

211

would soon follow-suit in the unnatural process of miraculous resuscitation.

"Come on, man, out with it. Who is *Martina*? She the one that did this to you?" he asked in a borderline accusatory tone. He'd tucked one of the Maglite's beneath one arm while using the free arm to mask his mouth and nostrils from further airborne stenches of the gagging variety.

The man's torso jerked and spasmed, his mangled lips pursing and un-pursing like a beached fish, his eye blinking madly before finally sticking ajar, a milky white glow revealed beneath the trapped lid.

Even as the man continued to gyrate, wriggle and squirm until the razor wire dug deeper trenches into his rotting flesh, Boone's rant grew on a sudden surge of adrenalin as he waved the light in a circular swirl like some medieval warlock casting a magical resurrection spell.

"Spit it out, boy. C'mon. I gotta have something to tell the cops, right? Don't let 'em get away with this ghoulish, inhuman shit."

The milky eye darted spastically from side to side, as if trying to gauge the stranger's exact locale, the damaged lips quivering and the tongue within flicking in and out like a serpent's, a low, wet groan sporadically exhumed.

"Hey, maybe just conserve your energy for now," Boone resumed calmly, purposely lowering the decibels while easing back the gung-ho rhetoric and concentrating instead on the feeding masses still hovering around the man's ravaged carcass, "*Shit*. Damn scavengers!"

Kicking at yet another chubby rat, this time connecting with enough force to send it spinning into the murk, Boone then used the handle end of a Maglite to bat another off the man's shredded left shoulder before dropping to one knee and turning his attention to stripping away the razor-wire. As if sensing Boone's intentions, the man ceased his struggles, his head leaning back just slightly, his lower jaw slack and his mouth pulled unnaturally wide, as if the former had been dislocated from some earlier trauma.

"Just stay as still as possible," Boone instructed through gritted teeth, a fine line of sweat running the length of his forehead to form a clear bubble at the tip of his nose as he reached tentatively toward the strand circling, and tearing a frighteningly deep groove into, the man's lower midsection, "This is apt to sting a bit."

Tugging with one hand while focusing the light's beam with the other, Boone first took notice of an unknown substance smeared onto yet undamaged portions of the man's clammy flesh. Greenish in hue, the scent had previously been so effectively cloaked by that of feces, urine and impending rot.

"Peanut butter? Holy…blessed…Moses," he whispered, wholly unaware he'd spoken aloud while trying and mostly failing in budging the wire, a lengthy portion of which embedded itself beneath the skin to an unknown depth.

Boone leaned back onto his haunches and began gnawing his lower lip in frantic contemplation.

"Listen, man. I'm not gonna blow smoke here. It's gonna take a professional, maybe a team of professionals of the medical persuasion, to loosen those…these binds without…terminally bleedingly you out. I'm…we're gonna get you help, all right?"

The man's reaction, blunt and instantaneous, was to resume wriggling and squirming with renewed fervor, his head lolling crazily and his jaw muscles visibly clenching and unclenching.

In equally panicked response, Boone stood and, waving his arms madly despite the man's visionless state, loomed over the terrified captive in a classic pleading pose. Arms extended and palms exposed.

"*No, no, no,* just…*whoa.* Stay still, damn it. Listen, I'm not going anywhere, okay? I'll stay here with you and keep those damn ra…keep you company 'til help arrives. I just have to walk outside for a minute and tell my…the others. They're…they'll go for help, all right? I'll stay. Just hang on while I give 'em the news and for god's sake, stop fighting those bonds."

As quickly as his struggles began, they ceased, a pained, drawn-out sigh announcing his apparent surrender to Boone's terms.

Boone backed away gradually, keeping a light trained on the man's tattered visage, suddenly as still and lifeless as when he had first approached, and he briefly mused if he'd only imagined an almost supernatural resuscitation. That is, until, just as he had whirled around to ascend the steps leading to the level portion of the floor, a single word—

half-gasped but unmistakable—pierced the air at his back. No stuttering, no fractured syllables. A given name, uttered with such clarity it was hard to fathom the source as the broken, dying husk on display.

"*Sebastian,*" was proclaimed with a surreal calm.

Fast walking toward the exit, beams of light bobbing and weaving like glittering disco strobes from another era, two questions tugged fiercely at Boone's mind, potential meltdown of same notwithstanding, those being, in no particular order, as they ran and rewound on a continuous reel: *One*: How the hell was this Sebastian fella still breathing and able to verbalize? *Two,* and easily the more cringe-worthy of the pair: Considering the mutilated condition of certain portions of his former self, and complete *removal* of others, just how much gratitude would he feel in the aftermath of such revelations? Boone wondered if survival in this case might be considered the cruelest of punishments.

Regardless, this didn't change the fact of that, in the here and now, *all* that mattered was the rescue itself. Saving a human life. Just how grateful the subject felt in the aftermath was not the immediate concern.

Lunging through the open door to the porch, Boone first took note that the hard rain had diminished to a light sprinkle once again, before a second detail, so dramatic an alteration in what his mind has expected to see that he nearly executed a doubletake, trumped even the shocking revelation he'd prepared to belt out with Shakespearian flare.

Though the moment felt weirdly frozen in time, a slow-motion reveal where all present appeared to be posing for the same surreal, abstract painting, Boone soon enough realized that the population of the tiny island had indeed recently increased by three.

~ * ~

A Woman Scorned

"So, just so's we're on the same page here, are there any more of you?"

The barrel-chested, olive-skinned man in dark blue slacks, a striped, button-up Oxford, presently unbuttoned to the upper abdomen to reveal a veritable shag carpet's worth of chest hair, and tan Doc Martens, sported arms so long and legs so stubby his knuckles appeared to levitate mere inches from the stone walk. Looking as if he strolled off the set of a Seventy's-era Scorsese mafia flick, his slick-backed black hair, peppered with gray around the ears, his bulbous nose and close-set eyes firmly cemented the stereotype.

As he was being directly addressed, Boone nodded, unaware of the warped sneer he donned like a pullover mask since lumbering outside. Eyes darting first to Toby then Janet, there was little mistaking their grim, fearful expressions and stiff, robotic poses as anything but extremely troubling if not plain terrifying.

"Just the three of us."

The two other new additions stuck out as even an odder pair of castaways. A young, Boone guesstimated mid-to-late twenties, and inexplicably barefooted strawberry-blonde in a slightly disheveled white tee featuring Ann and Nancy Wilson of the band *Heart* and blue jeans, her shoulder-length hair so comically shambolic it was as if she'd just exited a wind tunnel. Hands hidden behind her back, she was cute and petite in a Meg Ryan sort of way, despite a myriad of obvious ills, to include a swollen, blue-shaded shiner over her left eye, a dark bruise across her left cheek and several visible scrapes on both elbows. Intermediately sobbing between strained breaths, it was obvious she'd been on the receiving end of a nasty slapping around. To her left stood a slim, raven-haired woman at least fifteen years her senior, wearing what appeared to be a maroon cocktail dress, her chestnut complexion and dark-eyed squint stereotypical of either South American or Islander descent. Lips pursed in either discomfort or anger, her searing gaze wavered between the blonde woman and the trio of strangers, hands wringing nervously.

"Good to know, Ace," the mafioso stereotype beamed, flashing perfectly squared, oversized teeth so unnaturally white to resemble mutated chicklets. "Now do me a favor and add that light-sabre to the growing pile." Tilting his massive head, he gestured past Janet, who stood posed defiantly with arms crossed and left boot tip tapping nervously, toward where their packs and flashlights lay just off the concrete path.

"Where's your duffel?"

"Left it in the first cabin. Um, just, um, point of order," Boone said, focusing exclusively on the young blonde, who's pleading, bloodshot eyes spoke volumes. "This island is private property for *all* except those contracted."

The thick man's smile stuck, his upper lip squirming atop the upper plate like a slug on a glue-board.

"Not a problem then, Ace, as *contracted* is just what we be, so to speak."

Keeping his beady eyes locked on Boone's own, he spoke from the left side of his mouth, the warped smile finally collapsing into a downturned grimace.

"Ya see, red? Ain't never as cut 'n dry as it appears on paper."

The older woman's lone response was an exasperated roll of the eyes.

Backing away a step, the stout man shot a quick glance to the winding stretch of walkway at their backs, his left hand clearly revealed for only a brief moment before disappearing again behind the blonde's slumping form.

Blue steel, Boone recognized, either a forty-four or forty-five Smith & Wesson. King of the thunder sticks. Make big boom and even bigger hole. A Harry Callahan Special.

"About time, Huggy Bear," the stout man announced, Boone secretly dubbed him '*Magilla Gorilla*' but wouldn't dare share this aloud, as yet another cast member was added to the roll, this being a rail-thin, bald black male with a pointy goatee wearing light brown sweats, the top unzipped to his slim waist, and what appeared to be mostly unlaced combat boots, "We was beginnin' ta ponder your dedication to the task at hand. Ya take the scenic route or what?"

"Hey, that fair-haired boy was a scrapper after all, playing possum 'til I started to bag 'im. Had to choke 'im out with the same rope I used on the drop bag. After that, it was just a matter of drifting out far enough to dump the chum," the man retorted rhythmically as if reciting the first verse in a burgeoning rap song, his right hand vanishing into the fold of his sweats and retrieving a small, silver-barreled handgun.

The trio of exterminators exchanged knowing glances in the grim realization that they had just lost their ride back to the civilization, as it sounded as if young Captain Opie Cunningham took a fatal, involuntary dive down to Davey Jones' locker.

"Well, well, what we got here? Three stranded postmen? Dang, talk about your *rural* delivery."

As the lanky male stepped up to stand shoulder to forehead to his stumpy ally, Boone was forced to place a hand over his mouth to stifle a barely restrained giggle, the stark contrast between the pair instantly bringing to mind *Chester and Spike* of classic Loony-Tunes fame.

Despite the displayed hardware and cocky attitudes, neither seemed particularly intimidating, that is, until one thought of the brutalized man razor-wired and purposely fed to rats in the cabin's darkened interior. With that sudden, stark realization, Boone was able to lower his hand without further fear of random jocularity.

"What can...what are we going...*you* going to do now?" the older woman inquired to her alleged cohorts, hugging herself as if severely chilled. Her accent, slight and barely noticeable at first, grew more pronounced the more upset she became.

"We didn't plan on this. On...*them.*"

"Hey, not my call, lady," the man referred to as Huggy shot back, raising his free hand airborne with the palm out. "I earned my OT with sailor-boy already. You and no-neck Nitti got this one."

Pouting, the woman snorted and stared at the shorter man, her high-heeled left shoe nervously tapping the concrete.

"I warned you of possible complications, red," he said with a firm nod, firing stern glances directed at Boone and his subordinates.

"Never figured we'd have guests, but hey, it ain't like the problem here don't have a simple enough solution."

Following a short pause and eerie silence, the thin black man howled, throwing his head back like a baying wolf.

"Well hell, most such conundrum's *do,* that is if one has the testicular fortitude to solve it."

"You got that right, Hugs," the thicker man agreed, pushing his blonde captive forward several steps until they faced Boone directly, "Ya darted out here fast enough, bug-man. So, what was it you was so all-fired up to announce before clammin' up?"

Before Boone could begin to response, the blonde girl fell to one knee and began to openly sob.

"Oh, doesn't that just clutch one's heart?" the older woman jeered, sauntering casually over and bending down so the two would be on level terms.

"True love knows no higher level of anguish than separation by death."

Reaching over as if to perhaps comfort the other with the gentle stroke of a cheek or pat on the head, the older woman instead tangled splayed fingers within the blonde's scruffy coif. Clenching a handful of same, she roughly yanked and jerked until her victim was toppled forward, gasping and collapsing onto all fours.

As the older woman released what hair she hadn't pulled completely free, flicking her hand back and forth to free the loose strands, her victim muttered a muted response barely audible due to a sudden gust of wind.

"H-he...hated...y-you.   S-said...your   touch   wa-was...cold...repulsive." Despite the many pauses and stutters, the accent was pure dixie-land, Boone deduced, probably a local.

The older woman's reply was hissed through tightly gritted teeth so glowing white they appeared positively fluorescent.

"Sweetie, I'm willing to bet *his* touch is a hell of a lot colder about now."

As the older woman shuffled away, apparently more than satisfied with that final salvo, her stumpy cohort walked up and pulled the younger woman to her feet.

"Bug-man, I'm still waitin'," he grumbled, right eye arched dramatically.

Somewhere in the distance, a rumble of thunder as a steady mist fell.

"The man in there," Boone replied, suddenly bone-weary. "He's still alive. Not sure how or how long. We're here to treat the island for its reopening."

Purposely avoiding the stocky man's intrusive glare, Boone

instead glanced off to his immediate left, where he noticed the older woman's head snap toward him, wide-eyed and mouth ajar. Predictably, the younger one collapsed back onto one knee. The volume of her sobs cranked two-fold. Meanwhile, both Toby and Janet nudged toward him, heads similarly tilted and faces scrunched, the former's voice so hoarse as to be almost unrecognizable.

"Shit boss, you sure? I saw the dude. He was lunch meat."

Boone merely nodded in their direction before turning his gaze back to the older woman, whose narrow shoulders had noticeably slumped.

"Jake," she said, voice cracking with emotion, "He's suffered enough, for god's sake. Go take care of it, *please*."

Using a thick forearm to wipe away the building wetness from his forehead and eyes, the stubby man turned to the black male and gestured just once toward the felled blonde, now laying prone on her left side and crying hysterically.

As the man now known as Jake walked briskly and with a definite purpose past a flinching Boone, his associate took up position directly behind the prone woman, though his gaze centered around the exterminating trio.

"I got 'em, man. Go do your thing," he said, just as Jake hesitated only briefly at the entrance before vanishing past its threshold.

"As for you," he barked, smiling ghoulishly while directing the snub-nosed thirty-eight's sites Boone's way and waving the firearm from left to right, "Stand over there with the other bug stompers."

"N-n-nooooo. D-don't…y-you…d-d-dare. M-mu-murderers!" the blonde shrieked, crawling and pawing her way toward the cabin porch before being pulled back by an ankle, the black man giggling manically while doing so, all the while keeping the handgun trained in the trio's general direction.

"This your party, lady?" a red-faced, obviously incensed Toby asked the older woman, who'd turned her back to the cabin and began to pace slowly away. "You directing this cold-blooded shit?"

"Di-rec-ting, pro-ducing and most importantly, fi-nancing," the black male proclaimed with a devilish grin, having yanked the blonde to her feet by her hair and, upon enduring a series of mostly ineffective slaps and punches, landed a solid right hook that sent her sprawling onto her chest with a resounding huff.

"Best settle down, Katey-baby, or I'll forget I'm a gentleman."

Lunging forth to either assist the fallen woman or assault her assaulter, a scowling Janet stopped short upon staring down the thirty-eight's extended barrel, its possessor waving a forefinger back and forth like the hand of a grandfather clock, having pulled the blonde back upright by her hair.

"Tsk, tsk, tsk. In due time, Floatin' Tiger, in due time. What say you three just sit tight and zip your lips for now? In fact, I *insist* on it."

"Chickenshit bastard," Janet growled as Toby gently pulled her back by the shoulders. Boone meanwhile scanned the surrounding area with darting eyes while purposely keeping his head still as to not look too obvious.

Parked a dozen feet or more from the cabin porch, the three of them had zilch in terms of immediate cover if attempting an abrupt escape and, as least as far as he knew, the same number of options in terms of useable weapons, that is unless one counted Toby's discarded sprayer sitting just to the left of the open cabin door. Being that the big man opted for the cheap hard plastic model, in stark contrast to Boone's own solid steel version, its lightweight, single gallon design was apt to accomplish little more than thoroughly piss-off a perspective victim.

A clap of thunder, this one considerably closer, did little to ease the building tension.

His broad back turned from their captors, Toby addressed the older woman while keeping Janet at bay with a classic two-handed block.

"Let me guess. Your paid orangutan is in there taking care of a little unfinished business?"

Moments passed, a response from the constantly pacing woman obviously not forthcoming. In lieu, the black male replied by default.

"Best put a cork in it, Lurch. She don't owe you an explanation."

As if on cue, the stout man referred to earlier as Jake re-emerged from the cabin entrance, the Magnum hanging loosely at his side, his expression bland and unreadable as to the happenings inside. Taking up position between the quietly sniveling blonde and the older woman, who remained silent while busily gnawing a pinky finger, Jake lifted the revolver and casually fiddled with the tip of its barrel, screwing and unscrewing an attachment Boone recognized as a muzzle or silencer. With a heavy sigh, his cohort broke the silence.

"Soooo, I take it there'll be no more unexpected encores?"

"Safe to say."

"Why the muffler, bro? I mean, who's the wiser if big gun go boom-boom?"

"Force of habit, ya might say."

Jake briefly locked eyes with the older woman, hers brimming with tears, the well-chewed nail yanked from between gritted teeth and quickly replaced by the filter of a Virginia-Slim light, the long-fingered, meticulously manicured hand providing the light, wracked with tremors.

"Hey, hey now, little late in the game for sproutin' a conscience, ya think?" he mocked, pointing the Magnum's barrel toward the entrance. "Gotta say, right now I gotta a hell of lot more respect for pretty boy in there than his former patron. Might'a been nothin' more than a smooth-talkin' gigolo, but he was tough as a twenty-penny nail when it came to his own mortality. Go on, take a peek, Martina. Rats chewed 'im to meatloaf but it didn't finish 'im. Two fuckin' days of playin' human buffet but when I walked in there, he actually had the balls to curse me. Even tried to spit at me. Now that's cast-iron will, lady. So do me a favor an' shut off the waterworks."

The older woman openly wept, clenched fists shaking at her sides.

"Shut up, you a-animal. J-just *SHUT UP!*"

"Red darlin'..." he replied calmly and in the same tone one would use to scold a small child, "...let's be clear of our roles, what say? That said, if I'm the animal, you're the zookeeper. Just going by your instructions: peanut butter, imported Jersey rats. Not my usual MO, for sure."

The black man, still holding the blonde by a thick tangle of hair, though her sobs went mute, her semi-limp frame still trembled with a surprising fierceness, just shook his head as if particularly amused at the pair's verbal sparring and half-whispered into her ear, though loud enough for all to hear.

"Look at 'em, Katie, just look at 'em, arguing over the cruelty of the kill. This kind of shit is exactly why when my boys cap somebody, it's simple and quick. No torture, no drawn-out anguish that might come back to haunt. Bet you wish I'd drawn your boy's contract too, huh?"

The blonde paid no heed, her features gone slack save trembling lips and the occasional hitch of her torso.

As the stocky man and his erstwhile employer continued their verbal spar, Toby and Janet had, as inconspicuously as possible, closed ranks with their own supervisor, the former's harsh whisper executed while attempting a woefully ineffective ventriloquist act.

"Boss, these guys are pros. They're not gonna just let us sail off free and easy. We have to rush 'em and soon. The girl is probably next, then us."

Boone nearly flinched at the big man's unexpected intrusion and in the aftermath was unsure how to safely respond. His uncertainty wasn't just about being seen conversing, but more that he had no immediate answer. Logic was, without a doubt, on Toby's side. These boys were veterans of their trade and leaving behind witnesses was certainly *not* the way to obtain veteran status. Oppositely, to act recklessly and clumsily would surely not end well.

Stern of posture and stoic of expression, Janet's lone reaction to her co-worker's rather grim synopsis of their present scenario was to briefly lock eyes with Boone and the slightest of nods. Both impressed and terrified at the pair's stone-faced bravado in the face of probable death, Boone felt a sadly familiar twinge of icy fear coil his gut in the realization that the only way they were sailing away from that island with a working pulse would require elements of luck, skill or impeccable timing. Sadly, mostly luck.

"Boss, the sprayer," Toby muttered between the older woman's high-pitched shrieks and her stocky hitman's sarcasm-drenched reply's. "Might make a workable mace and it's loaded with almost pure Paraquat. A quick squirt directly to the eyes and they'll be shooting each other."

Not even bothering to mimic the big man's ventriloquist dummy routine while all eyes were trained on the employer-employee sparring match, Boone's mind raced with possibilities, all of which were highly questionable as far as ultimately surviving was concerned.

"Question is, how we gonna get to it without catching a bullet? I'm slow as a drugged sloth on my *best* day."

Before Toby could possibly reply, Janet chimed in, portions of her hushed suggestion lost in the black man's incessant giggling jag, though easily enough comprehended.

"I'll go for sprayer. Just need two seconds. Two measly ticks."

"Two seconds to grab it, but what then?" Boone asked, fighting an urge to roll his eyes in dismay, though deep down he knew hers was the lone logical option.

"Toss it over to you or punchy. I'll take out their employer. Stuff her gullet with rodenticide." Pausing, she lightly patted her left pants pocket, indicating the secret stash of rat poison.

Toby had started to reply, perhaps argue, when Huggy's gaze drifted over to the trio and froze, his broad smile slowly evaporating.

"Ya'll getting itchy feet over there?" he asked with a half-grin, half-sneer, jerking the blonde's head roughly to the left as to acquire a better angle. "I suggest patience, get me?"

"Got'cha," Boone answered, once it was obvious the floor was his by default. Seemingly satisfied, Huggy turned back to the squabbling pair, securing his grip on the blonde with a single, fierce yank that nearly toppled her backward.

Another thunderclap roared overhead, followed by a flash of lightning that briefly lit the skies in a yellowish streak. As if blissfully unaware of Mother Nature's latest intrusion, the stout man ranted on, his gun-free arm waving forcefully enough to trigger its own dust-devil.

"Jeez crow. Enough already. You don't wanna check the corpse and take my word for it, so be it then. My fee's the same. His whore's Huggy's problem, not mine. I'm sure he won't mind a more humane technique to spare your suddenly brittle feelings, right Hugs?"

With a reply as frigid and emotionless as her expression, the older woman regarded the young blonde with a hard, squinty-eyed glare of unbridled disgust.

"Now *she* may be hurt without reservation and repeatedly if time allows."

"Oooooh shit, Katie-girl," Huggy crowed as if on the cusp of breaking out in song, head thrown back in unscripted hilarity. "It seems the lady's lone soft spot was reserved solely for the ex."

In non-response, the blank-faced blonde merely blinked once, her mind obviously having checked out with the news of her lover's grisly demise.

A temporary silence, easily the longest in duration within those present, ensued just as the rain began to fall noticeably harder, all present briefly scanning the blackish storm clouds building overhead.

"How's about we finish this little conference inside the cab..." the stocky man suggested, only to be cut off by a banshee-like squeal.

"*NO! NOT...IN...THERE!*"

Lowering her head, her previously fluffed red locks now matted to her skull in twisted, soggy strands, the older woman's suddenly hoarse voice trailed off dramatically to complete this latest fiery exposition.

"...for god's sake, you sick, heartless idiot."

"Weellll excuse the fuck outta me, red," the stout man conceded, arms upraised in mock surrender. "Shit on whole wheat toast...." he shot Huggy a quick glance while shrugging his massive shoulders. "Women. What can ya do, right? Can't live with 'em, can't kill 'em all."

Turning back to his employer, the Magnum now dripping rain from its glistening barrel and hanging loosely by his side, the man executed a slight bow in her direction.

"Shall we then move to the next available cabin, ma'am? All this wanton wetness is washin' all the color from my coiffure."

Boone noted with what minute measure of humor he could muster that, sure enough, the stout man's jowls were streaked in thin streams of black hair dye.

Hugging herself, the older woman nodded soberly and had just started to turn when Huggy spoke up, all previous good humor void in his suddenly stern tone.

"Listen here, I'm fed up to hell and back well past the bloated village baby stage with you two and the squablin' couple bit. Ya'll can tiptoe all over this sandbox if you want, strip naked and dance around a campfire. Personally, I'm damn tired of leadin' this traitorous whore around, 'specially now that she's gone full zombie."

Either from simple carelessness or perhaps blatant disinterest, the stocky man and his raven-haired patron had temporary neglected the trio of uninvited guests, casually turning their backs to same while facing their annoyed cohort as he continued to pull and wrench his slumping captive's head from side to side like a wigged marionette.

"I vote we do as planned. That is reunite the two lovebirds for one last farewell...." Huggy sermonized through visibly bared teeth, equally oblivious to the newest arrivals, who had instinctively nudged closer together until they stood practically shoulder-to-shoulder, "...then torch the place to a cinder 'til even their molars are ash."

"Now or *never*, Boo," Janet whispered to Boone's left.

"I'm in. Otherwise, we're gonna end up tossed in the fire, boss," Toby chimed in from the right, the flat, calm state of the man's voice one Boone had heard before, that of one who is ready to act but not necessarily expecting to survive the aftermath. Acceptance. Fear evaporates, mutates. Rebirth. Come what may. Perish with dignity or live to die another day. In Boone's admittedly broad view, fickle fate had already written, edited and published the last chapter of this particular tragedy.

Sighing heavily, his shoulders, calves and neck instantly tensed, fingers clenching and unclenching. This simply not being his first rodeo made enduring the process no easier. Acceptance. Release. Act. The plan:

"JD, just spin that bastard airborne between us and go after Red. I'll play receiver. Toby, run interference and jack that no-neck fuck with all you've got. Once I lay Huggy's bony ass out, I'll help you finish 'im off if you haven't already done so."

Meanwhile, though the collective eyes of the captive trio never departed the captor threesome, they essentially muted the latter's dialogue via a magical silencer that allowed for only their own muttered offerings, all other sounds, rain, gusty winds creating rustles of vegetation, became only the bustling movements of a muted television.

Thus, while their captors' parted lips, wide-eyed expressions of dismay, disgust and exaggerated movements continued unabated, Boone, Toby and Janet communicated as freely as if seated around a conference table, sans the usual eye contact.

"Boone, maybe she outta haul ass behind the cabin, then into the jungle after tossing the sprayer," Toby suggested. "I mean, she is the fastest and if we don't make it, maybe she can hide out until help arrives or even find a way off this burg."

"The *hell* with that, Boo," Janet hissed, arms and torso visibly tensing.

"He's got a point," Boone said with a barely noticeable shrug. "Red doesn't seem the dangerous type. We take out her goons, she's no threat."

"We don't know that for sure, do we?"

"No, but in case we don't...make it, you won't be around for 'em to finish off."

"You might just need my help to survive, Boo. Ever think of that?"

Before either man could respond, the shrillness of her tone abruptly departed.

"Hey, don't think I don't appreciate the offer. I *do*. It isn't like I want to claim the role of final girl in this shitstorm, but I'm stronger than I look. They'll underestimate me. Story of my life."

The two men both inhaled deeply through their nostrils and appeared to sigh in perfectly timed synchronization.

"All right. If need be, go for the eyes, throat and groin," Boone offered somewhat reluctantly, lowering his head in the aftermath.

"I do love me a brave, sexy tigress," Toby added, straight-faced, though offering her a quick wink. "*Tropical Thunder* with claws fully extracted."

"You just watch my smoke, Punchy," she countered, playfully returning the gesture.

Feeling every nerve-ending he possessed lit aflame, Boone momentarily pondered with great sadness if fate dictated that this would conclude to be the last conversation they would ever share.

"On three then, kick it into overdrive," he instructed, a clenched fist only visible to his comrades extending a gloved forefinger with two additional digits forthcoming.

As their captors seemed to be calming, all but a still animated

Huggy sporting expressions of beleaguered acceptance, Boone realized the window of opportunity was rapidly closing.

It was then, as both Red and the stocky hitman swung around to possibly check their briefly forgotten guest's status, that the manager of '*The Pest Patrol*' extended, fittingly perhaps, a middle finger and rediscovered his own personal *overdrive*.

~ * ~

Ninety Seconds of Hell-Give or Take

"Boone...boss, you okay?"

Reaching out his right arm, Brad's hand levitated inches from the older man's upper back, the splayed fingers wriggling like worms on a hook and in suspended animation as to exactly what to do next: a gentle pat or firm massage. Eyes darting from the road ahead, traffic along highway 63 just past Jonesboro was pleasantly light with only the occasional semi with which to dance, Brad slowed the Charger to ten MPH under the sixty-five limit to better tend to his employer, currently hacking into a white hanky smeared mostly crimson.

"I'm gonna take the next exit, all right? It's just a half-mile up, maybe get you some fresh air and water and let you stretch the legs."

The older man appeared to shrug, shoulders tense and head thrown slightly back as if to fight off a building sneeze.

Veering right on the rain-slickened offramp announcing the township of Trumann a mere two miles in the distance, Brad harbored serious doubts they would make Memphis, less than an hour away, without a lengthy sabbatical or ER visit. Spotting a truck-stop to their left, he wheeled into a mostly deserted side lot, already making plans to google the nearest hospital once Boone was out of sight while cursing the fates for allowing them to pass the decently populous Jonesboro for the Arkansas boonies.

Parked, with the engine running and heater turned to its lowest setting, the windshield instantly fogging, Brad turned to the older man even as his gaze drifted to a spattering of signs to the left of the frontage road, all of which displayed either fast-food or gas station ads further up the highway.

"Boone, what can I do?" he blurted out, a sudden burst of fear for the man's mortality trumping any preplanned subterfuge. "Listen, I'm gonna run over to the truck-stop and find out where the closest emergen…"

Just then, the older man raised a quivering hand to interrupt, the forefinger and thumb clearly blood-spattered. When he spoke, the words were muffled and nasal due to the hanky's blockage, though audible enough for comprehension.

"I…I'll be…with y-you in a…minute or t-two, Brad. S-sorry for the…interruption. Felt this…coming on about a…an hour b-back but thought I…could soldier my…way through it."

"I dunno, boss, that looks like a pretty heavy bleed."

"It's…dwindling…" Boone croaked, pausing to blow his nose before leaning back with a resounding sigh, "…from…Old Faithful to a…drippin' faucet. Kinda like…my bladder these last few years."

"You need anything? I'm sure we can find a Walgreen's around he…"

The same hand arose yet again, palms out and not quite as shaky.

"Brad, I…don't want…mean to sound rude, but we…I really need to reach the destination as soon…as poss….as we can."

"You mean all the way into Mississippi?"

The older man, finally allowing the bloody handkerchief to fall away, peered over sheepishly, his thin mustache and goatee spotted a dark crimson.

"It's…just past Corinth, maybe…an hour south of…Memphis. Little place called Baymont. Barely a town really. More of the…one horse variety."

"You know it? I mean, you've been there?"

"Not in person. Let's just say I've heard it described quite…vividly. I know I…we planned on another stop in-between…but at this point I'm afraid I don't dare."

Breaking eye contact, Brad instead stared out the Charger's rain-specked windshield into an open field.

"Boone, sir, you are officially scaring the hell out of me. Please, let me find you a hospital."

"Brad my boy…" came the solemn, hangdog reply, "…any and all…updated diagnosis would be the same, I'm afraid. Twenty-four, maybe forty-eight hours…max."

"You don't *know* that for sure. At least they could, you know, ease your discomfort."

Reaching over, Boone gripped the young man's shoulder and applied a gentle squeeze.

"I do appreciate the concern. Truly."

The older man then retrieved a handful of facial tissues from a mostly empty box sitting atop his side of the dash and began to rub the recent leakage from his facial hair.

"I'm grateful that in a lifetime of making friends and acquaintances, I was fortunate enough to greet you as my last."

Vigorously rubbing both eyes with a thumb and forefinger, Brad was temporarily lost for words.

"Not to get overly maudlin, but I sure could've done so much worse. Before this is over, I…might have to depend on you more than I'd originally anticipated."

Following an approximate thirty-seconds-plus of staring unblinkingly through the rain-streaked driver's side window, the younger man turned to his employer wearing a grim, tight-lipped smile.

"Well then, if I'm going to help you finish whatever it is you need to finish, let's at least get some air outside this tin can. Maybe, if you're up to it, we'll grab something at the snack bar. I could do with a fresh cup of Joe, preferably one of the turbo-caffeinated variety. You game?"

The older man's eyes gleamed with renewed vigor at the mere suggestion.

"Absolutely. Actually, a Twinkie sounds damn good about now. Maybe all that…sugar and starch will provide the necessary fuel I need…to finish that story."

~ * ~

"All right then, where did I leave off?" the older man inquired, elbows propped atop the rickety tabletop as one pasty hand gripped a half-eaten chocolate Ding-Dong, Twinkies having been currently out of stock, and the other a mini bottle of Sprite. The truck-stop diner held only a handful of patrons, the majority displaying similar spent, wear-and-tear expressions as the B & B boys, weary travelers taking a short but much-needed sabbatical. For his part, Brad sipped black coffee and nibbled the edges of a micro-nuked bean burrito. Squinting through rising steam over the edge of the paper cup, he no longer tried to hide his concern for his employer, whose condition was rapidly deteriorating.

"Boss, I'm fine if you'd rather wait 'til we get back on the road."

His employer paused to push both the half-eaten snack and mostly empty Sprite to the side and pull the small recorder from a jacket pocket. Smiling shyly, he balanced it next to the napkin holder as if to hide its presence.

"I would normally, but I really need to expedite getting this on record since, well, I might have an additional favor to ask on the way to Baymont."

Brad cocked a brow but did not reply.

Following a brief scan of their surroundings, the nearest occupied table consisted of a young couple and their infant, whose squealing, food-tossing tantrums trumped an old man's tale from the past by a country mile, Boone levitated an extended forefinger over the recorder's play button.

"Anyway, that's for later. I believe we were, um, nearing the conclusion."

The older man paused, hands folded together as if about to pray, eyelids fluttering as he chewed nervously on his lower lip as if straining mightily to board the correct train of thought.

Feeling pressured to intercede, Brad instantly regretted his choice of words, delivered in a bland, weather-is-fine way that inadvertently diminished the seriousness of the subject matter.

"Things weren't looking good for the home team, boss. Being that we're sitting here jawing about it, I can only speculate the ending could've been worse."

If nothing else, this unintentional diss seemed to wipe the cobwebs from the older man's subconscious and push away, at least temporarily, whatever sideroad he had briefly taken.

"Son, to be blunt," he said, the ever-darkening circles under both his baggy eyes reflective of his tone. "I've found the term *happy ending* to be solely a fictional one, at least in my personal experience. Unfortunately, that day in Shangri-La did little to alter said belief."

~ * ~

"Weird, but as the last decade and a half have passed, I find myself doubting my own memories to some degree. First off, the dialogue I described between the three of us, whispered from the corners of our mouths and between pursed lips to avoid discovery, well, the more I've studied it through the years, the more I doubt its credibility. That is, though there was obviously communication between us, it's almost like it was, and I know this is gonna sound nuts, telepathic or some similar thought-transference phenomenon.

Boone sighed, his hands wringing with increased fervor

"As far as the plan, slap-dash and full of boulder-sized plot-holes it was, logic should've dictated absolute disaster for the three stooges stone-stupid enough to follow its tissue-thin blueprint, right?

A mischievous smile creased his thin, pale lips.

"Let me precipice my failing memory of the rumble by saying this: whatever doubts I'd had before that day of a higher power, those being some grave, *serious* doubts, I sit here today proof-positive that not only such an entity exists, but was hovering over us that day, maybe hidden inside one of the passing storm clouds. Not that anyone got off scot-free, far from it, but I'm here to tell you the good Lord lent us a hand when it counted. The gods might've picked exactly when to intervene, but an intervention it most *definitely* was. Please tell me later if you agree or if my definition of miraculous is a bit of a stretch.

"That in mind, you will find a Bible amongst my book collection back in Turtle Bend. A well-perused edition, especially in the last decade or so...

Pausing for a sip of Sprite, Boone then cleared his throat and spat into a wadded napkin.

"I didn't even see Janet take off but felt her scoot past me just as my own legs churned forward at roughly half her speed, making a beeline toward Huggy just as Toby crisscrossed in my path like a human freight-train. As far as those miracles I spoke of, JD, um, Janet spinning that sprayer like Namath to Maynard at Shea certainly adds credibility, seeing that she tossed it while diving headfirst and it hit my hands chest-level as I was truckin' it full speed.

Boone paused, his head tilted, and smiled.

"Broadway Joe Namath, Don Maynard. Late '60's Jets. My apologies for such a Jurassic-era pigskin reference. So, I snatch that bad-boy without breaking stride, amazing traction considering that rain-slicked concrete, and, swinging it around by the hose, slung it around just as Huggy was jostling the blonde into position as his human shield.

"I felt a vague sting at my lower side left, just below the rib cage, but it didn't at all effect the torque of that roundhouse swing. Swingin' for the fences, baby. Now, just as that hard metal cylinder introduced itself to Huggy Bear's left temple and my forward momentum led me straight down into the wet sand, taking the blonde with me, I became acutely aware of a series of popping sounds.

"Didn't think much of 'em at the time. What with rolling the girl's squirming carcass off my legs and combat rolling over to Huggy, who was down on all fours with a hand pressed to his head, his mouth opening and closing like a beached seabass sucking air. No doubt his noggin was ringing like a school-bell but damned if he wasn't still clutching that pistol in his free hand.

"Now, you'd figure the odds were looking good for an upset of historical proportions, as I'd just about reached 'im and was cranking the sprayer for what I hoped would be a decisive blow. That, Brad, is precisely why oddsmakers are usually poor slobs with three-pack a day smoke habits, bad posture and pot guts. I was just bringing that metal base around to kiss the back of Huggy's skull when its trajectory was knocked seriously off course, as was my entire frame by a fierce hip check delivered by none other than the blonde woman, screeching like a wounded Hawk with both teeth and claws bared.

"As I stumbled off to the left and into a sinkhole between sand dunes, the sprayer's dented base barely missing my own noggin and twisting the shit out of my right ankle in the process, I watched her hop atop Huggy's back like some crazed bronco buster, one set of fingernails digging into his left eye and the other his neck.

"Down on one knee on what I first thought to be a snapped ankle, I was allowed a quick scan in either direction to see how my mates were doing.

"Toby first: standing steel-toed boot to designer Oxford with Magilla Gorilla's badass self, trading titanic blows akin to a pay-per-view heavyweight bout. Definitely the big guy in his natural habitat, though from what little of the skirmish I saw before turning away, the damage inflicted indicated an early draw. The man-ape's firearm lay a few feet to the grappler's left, its blue-steel barrel buried in the wet sand like a tent stake.

"Janet: Her left shin drenched in something darker than the falling rain, the host leg splayed at an unnatural angle from where she sat perched atop the red-haired woman's chest, whose right arm punched and jabbed with little effect, most of the blows striking shoulder or forearm, the left pinned to her side. Now, I saw sweet *Tropical Thunder* pissed before. I mean truly pissed off. This was another level altogether. This was rage. A fugue state of blind, murderous anger. With her free hand, JD was ramming something into the squirming woman's eyes, nose and mouth. Actually, more like forcing it via short, sharp jabs into every available crevice. Before turning away, the blonde's screeching cut off abruptly, not a good sign, I watched JD dig deep into her cargo pants and yank out a handful of tiny, dark pellets, many of which sailed airborne before being shoved forcefully downward toward her target's screaming mug. *Rodenticide.* Good girl, I remember thinking. Smart as hell and equally mean. A mouth, eye or nostril-full of that stuff might not kill her dead, but she'll probably wish it had.

"Turned out I lingered on Janet's exploits just a blink too long. Story of my life in times of great duress, it seems. Huggy not only managed to sling the blonde from his person but was in the process of dotting her chest and stomach with dime-sized holes. Nope. Hold it. Rewind that, as it's not really accurate. Being as I only saw the exit wounds, can't really estimate the entry hole sizes. I understand it can vary depending on caliber. Anyhow, the blonde wobbled back a few steps before collapsing onto her back, her shirt drenched dark crimson and her eyes rolled back into her head. Whatever her sins, that girl obviously drifted off to meet her maker, but not without leaving her mark on the shooter responsible.

"Scrambling to his feet, Huggy stumbled left to right then back and forth like a drunken wino, cupping his leaky left eye, that whole side of his mug as red as his victim's shirt despite some pretty intense rainfall. There were strips of ragged skin hanging down from the right side of his neck where her nails dug several individual trenches, the rawness beneath already swelling like the skin beneath had been poisoned."

Boone's gestures grew increasingly animated; eyes gleaming and flesh gaining a much-needed hue.

"Despite this, he was doing his damnedest to acquire a bead on yours truly, even managing to fire off a few shots in my direction while staggering in the wet sand and falling to one knee. In retrospect, if I'd hesitated even a step, there's a good chance his last attempt might've found something more substantial than the tip of my right earlobe. As it was, I jammed the stainless-steel bottom of the sprayer tank directly into the center of his face, crushing his nose, bursting both lips and even cracking off a few teeth from his upper plate. Took three more similar blows to put 'im down, his eyes pulled wide and resembling egg whites swimming around in a bloody red stew, my last blow apparently imploding the very foundation of what remained of his mug and leaving him damn near unrecognizable.

"I'd just tossed away the sprayer and crawled on all fours between the two bodies to retrieve Huggy's popgun when Janet sounded off like a bullhorn's megaphone at my back. This was about the time I took first conscious notice of that vague stinging at my left side and the sticky warm wetness accompanying same, though at the time I couldn't spare a split-second to seek out the exact source.

"Don't ask me how, she was setting new standards for grit and guts, all rolled into one tight, one-hundred-five-pound package. Janet managed, mangled knee notwithstanding, to reach Toby and the Ape-man and was currently creasing the skull of the latter with one of the Maglites. Having already shattered the light in half from the force of previous blows, she commenced ramming a jagged edge into the side of the hitman's mug just as I zigzagged their way.

"It wasn't 'til I reached 'em, nearly tripping over Red, she was rolling from left to right, covering her face with both hands as if the skies were pouring acid rain, that I fully understood JD's rage. The Ape-man had, he'd…" Boone paused, his moistened eyes gazing blankly over Brad's shoulder, "beaten Toby damn near to death. Fact was," Boone lowered his head, briefly covering his mouth with an open palm, "and I was only allowed a single glance, but I thought…he did exactly that, at least until I noticed Toby's chest rise and fall and heard a wet, rattled gasp. For once, my timing was right on, as Ape-man just backhanded Janet off his back and was rearing back to finish the job on Toby when I shoved the barrel of that revolver against his right temple and…" Boones darting eyes refocused to lock with Brad's own "…yanked the trigger. Hell, I didn't even hesitate. No warnings, no false hopes that the asshole would freeze that wrecking-ball fist in midair. Gotta confess, a part of me was gonna savor the recoil as the ruthless bastard's head flung back and he rolled off my friend like a bloated slug.

"What I got instead was a sickening click. Then another. Finally, a third, before the lunkheaded bastard even took notice of my presence, before I could even lunge back, he belted the hell out of me with, what was either a backhand similar to the one that floored Janet, or maybe even a headbutt. Considering that noggin of stone he toted around on that no-neck torso, I'd have to wager the latter. Either way, it rattled my teeth something fierce. I'm talking I saw no mere stars but a whole damn constellation, coming to on my stomach with a mouthful of wet sand.

Translation: I no longer pondered how anyone could've got the best of Toby in a straight-up street brawl. That ugly pug hit like a freight train. Now, I had no earthly idea how long I'd been out, but rolling over onto my back, what I saw through the blurriness hinted at a short nap of no more than ten-twenty seconds tops. Anything of longer duration made no sense really. I mean, feisty as Janet was, no way she'd maintained that stance for too long."

Boone smiled broadly, tipping his Sprite bottle as if in tribute to a fallen, past ally.

"As I crawled around like a crippled, half-blind roach on all fours, my head spinning like a top, I was being forced down to one knee each time I tried standing. Somehow, divine intervention if you will, I was able to keep an unfocused eye on the unlikely skirmish playing out just a dozen feet ahead, knowing the clock was running out on all present if I didn't manage to intervene in some dramatic way.

"Janet rode the Ape-man like a bronco buster, propped on that V-shaped back with both legs coiled to the front like a boa while jerking, yanking and tugging on the sprayer hose she had curled around what little neck he possessed. I swear," he laughed, lightly slapping the tabletop with a bare palm, "if not for the stakes involved, as in life and death, I might've collapsed into involuntary hysterics.

"It was like some Bizarro-world rodeo event. *Thug-riding* or maybe *Goon-roping*. If nothing else, that little firecracker managed to force Magilla off of Toby, who in turn was actually conscious and hanging onto one of the asshole's ankles."

Boone shook his head, sighing heavily.

"Beat to a bloody, unholy pulp, the big man wasn't about to yell uncle. No how, no damn way. Boy didn't know the word quit, or at least didn't *understand* the common definition. You see, he had always been the same way in the ring. Stubborn as a bull and twice as determined.

"Now, despite these Herculean efforts, they were still hopelessly outmatched. Even through a net of falling rain and my own bleary orbs, I could see JD losing steam while, if anything, no-neck was doing his best *Incredible Hulk* impression. You know, the madder he got, the *stronger* he got. I remember my own sense of desperation damn near paralyzing me, my lower extremities strangely numb even as my head swelled and my ears rang so loudly that even though I could clearly see Janet screeching and shrieking through bared, bloodied teeth, it was all weirdly muted."

Boone paused, his hands folded again as if to pray, his head briefly bowed.

"I spoke earlier of miracles. Well, you decide. There I was, barely coherent and unable to completely stand without twin tsunamis of dizziness and nausea knocking me back down. Frantic ain't the word. If I didn't find a way, and quick, of putting that animal down, we were all dead. Plain and simple. End of the road. Cast off our mortal coils. Insert cliché of choice, but it was the cold, stark truth. Shaking off short bouts of double-vision, I glanced around, scanning the mussed sand for something, anything to use for a weapon since it was damned obvious hand-to-hand wasn't in the cards. Our packs appeared a football field away, considering I was scuttling along with the speed and dexterity of a sedated sloth. Then, as I leaned hard to the left and barely avoided toppling onto my right side, my right hand struck something hard, something sleek.

"No time to praise my grand luck, the unbelievable odds of such a find being real and not just some delirium-fueled hallucination, I cradled that bad boy in my right hand and shook the sand free from its frame before acquiring the firmest grip I could manage. No-neck's Magnum, minus the silencer, no doubt dislodged during the early stages of his brawl with Toby.

"I remember holding it up to my face, damn near pressing it against my nose since closing the distance eased the mirage of seeing twin barrels and wondering just how in the hell I was gonna manage to successfully line up a target when I couldn't yet lean up without wanting to barf up a lung. Well," Boone raised a forefinger into the air and smiled, "here comes that word again. The 'M' word. Just as I'd struggled to sit up and squint in the direction of the continuing melee, using the Magnum's front site as a guide, I watched Janet, slung by the hair over no-neck's shoulder. I'm talking head over heels like a hollow ragdoll, the sprayer hose still wrapped around his chin with that dented tank hanging between his shoulder blades like the giant hand of a grandpappy clock. I shot a quick glance to my fallen comrades, Toby stretched on his stomach and motionless but with a clutching hand still hovering near no-neck's feet and Janet sprawled on her back with that maimed leg curled beneath her. I couldn't make out if either was still breathing and, badly as I wanted to crawl to their immediate aid, there was the little matter of King Kong stomping Tokyo to deal with. Don't have to tell ya who would be playing Kong and who would represent Japan's capital city in such a scenario.

"I saw 'im checking out both Huggy and Red before turning those beady-little eyes my way, accompanied by what was either a Cheshire-cat-grin or severely pissed-off grimace. Regardless, I figured I had about five seconds tops before a fatal beating would commence. He took a second to unwrap the hose and toss the sprayer tank away like so much confetti, then turned back and charged ahead like a mad bull, head down and shoulders back, stubby little legs churning and kicking up brown streamers of sand. Having no time to think can be a positive. Just acting on instinct. Acting to survive.

"This time, there was more than a sharp click. Thank the Big Man upstairs, there was a recoil, so robust it damn near flung the weapon from my grip. I held on for dear life. Fired again. One more time. Lowered it to my side, dropped it in the sand and fell forward into a puddle of my own warm, sticky but somewhat rain-diluted vomit."

Boone paused; his eyes briefly distant, unblinking.

"Looking back, I could have sworn I hit solid paydirt with that first shot, an upper gut or chest shot, since no-neck had hit the brakes like he'd smacked into a brick wall. Nobody was more shocked than yours truly when the forensics report stated he'd only been struck once. One blessed time. That, they deduced, had been my third and *final* attempt, a face shot that blew out the majority of his upper plate and exited out the back of that tree-trunk thick neck. Of course, this all meant I missed 'im not once but twice."

With a nervous laugh, Boone went on.

"Good thing I didn't just nick his shoulder or shave a testicle, right? After that third and last boom, I'd just assumed, *and* well, being that I was later diagnosed with a severe concussion, therein lies the divine intervention I spoke of. No way I successfully dropped that ape in human skin without some outside help, if you get my drift. No-neck was no more than two dozen feet away when he charged, so what the hell slowed 'im? The '*shock*' of the Magnum blast? Not exactly expected behavior from a seasoned hitman. The second shot supposedly missed as well, so at that point he could've…no…*should've* reached me and snapped my fool neck before I ever got off a third.

Leaning back, Boone crossed his arms and arched a brow dramatically.

"You tell me, Brad. The old adage, *it just wasn't my time* doesn't seem at all adequate to explain such an enigma. Regardless, here we sit. Must be a reason. Maybe, just *maybe* I've finally found the answer."

~ * ~

Final Frontiers

"Should we go? I'm feeling a little *too* comfortable. Wait any longer and you might have to fireman-carry my tired old bones outta here."

Roughly three minutes since he concluded the story, or at least an impending epilogue, Boone appeared frighteningly worn. His frequently pasty complexion reaching new levels of ashen, his eyes bloodshot and drooping, his entire deportment that of a man on the cusp of utter collapse. Having powered down the recorder, he tucked it beneath one arm as if it held a priceless treasure.

"Sure, just let me go pay the tab," Brad replied, scooping up the receipt and heading toward the cashier, a white-haired geriatric who'd been eyeballing them curiously since their arrival.

Secured inside the Charger a few minutes later, Brad feared the older man might tumble to the pavement on the way, thus he offered a cupped hand beneath Boone's right elbow, their shared silence was palpable but not at all awkward. The rain returned in the form of a cold, light drizzle, just enough to keep things suitably chilly and damp. Considering the circumstances of their journey and the enigmatic conclusion still to come, a warm, bright sunny day simply didn't match the mood.

As Brad tapped the address Boone provided into his phone's GPS, the older man leaned back with a resounding, bone-weary sigh, his eyes closed and his breath escaping in short, raspy whistles.

"How far again? In minutes I mean?" he asked weakly, swallowing hard in the aftermath.

"With uneventful traffic, I'd say hour and a half tops. Maybe you can take a quick nap. You can always finish the story once we near Baymont. Hey, might be a good idea to find a motel nearby, you know, so you can recharge the old batter…"

Boone reached over and gently tapped the younger man's forearm, nodding feebly.

"No time to waste now. Literally, every minute counts. Afraid I'm…running on fumes but I'll just have to dig deep for some reserve fuel."

Adjusting the car heater, Brad regarded his employer with a cocked brow, his eyes gleaming with mischief beneath the bill of his baseball cap.

"I could, you know, get us there quicker. Add a little extra lead to the heel, you might say."

As pained as it appeared, Boone managed a smile.

"Wouldn't want you ticketed, though if you *do,* I'll surely foot the bill, pun intended."

"Roger that."

Short of peeling out in Hollywood action-flick fashion, Brad nonetheless steered them from the lot at a dramatically brisker pace than they arrived, setting the stage for a similarly speedy trek toward whatever conclusion awaited.

~ * ~

"I wish I could say the memories of leaving that island were as nearly as crisp, but they're as hazy today as the seventeen Springs since."

Staring out the passenger's window as he spoke, Boone's voice cracked and rattled with exhaustion. Perhaps it was dim lighting on a hazy, cloudy day, but Brad could've sworn his employer's hair whitened considerably since leaving the diner.

"What few details I recall are so bleary and dreamlike it's debatable whether they represent fact or fiction. What I do know for sure is that by the time that coast guard cutter picked us up a few miles off the shoreline, I'd somehow managed to not only commandeer the goon's boat but also drag Janet and Toby along for the ride, even providing some half-assed medical aid. All this despite the gunshot wound to my side, two broken ribs and a concussion that would birth random headaches for the next six months. Now, I've heard that high levels of adrenaline allow one to perform mighty feats of strength and endurance. Maybe. In this case, however, I defer to that earlier, spiritual speculation. Hate to keep kickin' a dead horse, but there was more to such improbable actions than meets the eye. Sure, I might see piggy-backing Janet to the pier, but Toby? That was two-hundred-plus pounds of dead weight, brother. Mission improbable, especially considering my aforementioned ills."

Boone hesitated just long enough to glance upward, shrugging playfully in the aftermath.

"So, that sting you felt..." Brad inquired without looking over, instead focusing on navigating them past a trail of slower traffic.

"Huggy's peashooter. A Beretta Nano nine-millimeter as I recall. Passed right through without any major damage. Not that getting plugged is ever a good thing, but as an alternate to his partner's Magnum, well, it was definitely preferable for survival's sake."

With the Charger securely positioned in the fast lane with no immediate competition, Brad took advantage of the older man's hesitation.

"Speaking of, did *all* the good guys survive?"

Boone's haggard visage somehow conveyed sadness and mirth simultaneously.

"Happy to say, yes they did. Not without alterations from the original models, but six foot above ground sure trumps the other option. Toby sustained the most damage, no argument. Broken nose, shattered jaw, broken orbital, and three fingers blown off his right hand, courtesy of no-neck's forty-four. I still maintain this early loss of digits from that sledgehammer right of his is the only reason Ape-man got the best of 'im. Worse yet was the brain damage incurred from the beating. Toby didn't know his own damn name for several weeks. Luckily over time he was able to regain a good portion of his mental faculties. Still, he never seemed quite the same. A little...slow on the uptake, if you can dig that. That bastard hitman beat the razor wit right out of him. We kept him on at the company in name only until we could get him on disability.

"As for Janet, she underwent knee replacement for the cap no-neck had blown off as she dived for the sprayer. Bastard had also broken her left arm and tore some ligaments in the same wounded leg on that last toss. Needless to say, her dancing career was a thing of the past. She later confided that in the long run that was more a positive than a negative. She stayed with the company for a few more years, as fiery and loyal. Eventually remarried and moved to Dallas. Last I heard she was running an on-line business from home. As mentally tough as anyone I've ever met, it never surprised me how quickly she bounced back. Man, I surely missed that lovely firecracker after she left us. Definitely one of a kind."

As the older man paused to cough into a cupped palm, Brad looked over and was relieved to see the hand smear-free upon being retracted, as he purposely slowed their progress upon seeing the Charger's MPH meter sitting at just under eighty-five.

"I assume the bad guys didn't make out as well?" he asked, adjusting the vehicle's cruise control to eighty and locking it in.

"Hard to fathom, but Huggy Bear, real name Pierce, was reportedly still breathing when the medics arrived. Passed on in a coma a few days later from massive trauma. The mystery blonde was Kate Morgan or Morton or something similar, a one-time porn actress turned prostitute. Pierce, danged if I recall his given name, was both her pimp and sometime boyfriend, and it was three bullets from his Beretta that took her out, but not before she half-blinded him and, thank God, created just enough of a handicap to keep me from the same fate.

"Magilla no-neck was otherwise known as Jake '*The Jackal*', only this time the family name escapes me. Anyhow, the evil bastard was paid muscle and a part-time enforcer out of New Jersey. No sorrow to say he was dead as a hammer, as was his employer, Martina Flores, the latter via a gut-full of Rat poison and crushed thorax, courtesy of Janet."

A short coughing fit struck the older man, after which he lightly dabbed his mouth with a hanky, the mucus exposed there a light shade of crimson. Brad, switching lanes to pass a lumbering Ford Van blowing thick plumes of smoke, only spoke once the older man seemed to have phased out, staring blankly out the passenger window at a passing freight just off the highway.

"What about that guy in the cabin?"

Not quite flinching, Boone nonetheless twitched to attention, a small blood dimple visible at the tip of his grayed goatee.

"Oh, I'm sorry. Drifted off there for a sec. That would be the late Sebastian Wilde, one-time tennis coach, fitness guru and occasional gigolo. How we had ended up sharing the same stretch of deserted island was a matter of the worst damn timing possible. In a nutshell, Sebastian and Katie were bumping uglies, much to the chagrin of Miss Flores, a woman of high income but low esteem when it came to male suitors. Once she found out about the affair between her well-paid boytoy and the former porn queen, well, let's just say she let her fingers do the walking through the yellow pages, hitman-for-hire section. As for Pierce, he was similarly displeased with the misbehavior of the most popular call-girl in his growing stable of concubines. Sooooo, once Flores and Pierce crossed paths and swapped tales of adultery, a plot was hatched involving revenge of the grisliest kind.

"With Jake already on the payroll to take out Sebastian, the decision was made to utilize what was thought to be the abandoned cabins of Shangri-La Island, which, when open, had once been visited for a long holiday weekend by none other than Sebastian and Miss Flores. Why, it was none other than the dainty Martina who sketched out her lover's grisly demise, asking Jake to round up a couple of dozen of the meanest, hungriest rats to gnaw their way into Sebastian's black heart. Sorry..." Boone paused, displaying both hands as if to surrender, "...added that last part myself. Shameless I know, but does fit the soap-opera narrative quite well, don't ya think?"

Brad nodded without meeting the man's gaze, though he could practically feel the unrestrained gleam of mischief behind them.

"The SCLED, um, that's South Carolina Law Enforcement Division's timeline estimates that on the day of our appointment to treat the islands, Sebastian had been stowed inside the cabin as vermin-buffet for at least forty-eight hours. It was just plain shitty luck they picked that exact date to drag his lover to the island to not only show off what they surely figured would be a fairly cold corpse, but add her to the pile before burning the cabin to ash to cover up both murders."

A 'who knows?' gesture, accompanied by a wry grin.

"Whoops. Things didn't quite go as planned."

"Messed with the wrong damn exterminators," Brad exclaimed, smiling back. "More like *terminators.*"

"Yeah well," Boone replied, somber and solemn yet again, "when I said just plain shitty luck, it was as much theirs as ours."

"How did the media treat it? You guys find your way into the papers or local TV?"

"Oh yeah, we were hot copy for a few days, at least until some random drive-by gang-shooting killed an eight-year-old in Myrtle Beach. I granted only a single interview on the subject, that being to the Charleston Courier the day I was released from the hospital. I recall one helluva migraine the morning of. Nearly threw up on the reporter. All in all, the media couldn't give two craps about a trio of bug-stompers, or how they survived a pair of professional hitmen, much less put 'em down. Nah, instead they circled the Flores-Wilde angle like ravenous vultures. Toss in the Morton/porn star element along with the merciless pimp driven by jealous rage and we barely rated a mention. Only natural I guess, money and sex. Honestly, I was relieved to be relegated to sideline duty. Pretty sure Janet and Toby felt the same way. We all got quietly together for a meal on the one-year anniversary. Of course, some jackass journalist recognized us and snapped a picture that ended up on the internet in the form of some sleazy, crime of passion titillation piece. Goes without saying we never dared meet in public again, at least not on the Carolina coast. All that said, we all understood just how fortunate we were to be meeting at *all.*"

They rode in silence for several minutes, ample time enough for Boone to power down the recorder. Exiting the freeway onto an even more desolate four-lane state highway, it was Brad who reignited the conversation, no doubt feeling a deadline of sorts in the not-so-distant future.

"Damn, Boone. I can't...just can't *imagine* how you could, well, not only get over something like that but not constantly relive it like some continual nightmare. When I think about what you...what your family has been through, from your great uncle to your dad and now you. *Damn.* I repeat, what are the odds? Astronomical is the word that comes to mind."

Either unable or unwilling to respond, Boone instead stared straight ahead at a deserted highway, chin resting on an upturned fist. Within minutes, both chin and first drooped as the possessor of both appeared to drift into a deep slumber, his head slumping against the passenger window, shimming lightly with the sporadic impact of car tires vs potholes.

"Thirty minutes away, boss," Brad announced a quarter-hour later, purposely louder than usual. "Maybe less if this stretch of blacktop remains this deserted."

The older man's eyelids raised as gradually as a slowly raised curtain, his initial expression the clueless, blank-slate type normally associated with late-stage dementia sufferers. Using a shirt sleeve to wipe away a thin stream of reddish drool, he regarded his driver through a tight squint while coughing wetly into the crook of the same sleeve.

Alternating glances from the roadway back to Boone, Brad instinctively let off the accelerator.

"Hey, you all right, boss?"

As if on cue, Boone tipped severely to the left, eyes rolled back into his head and body ragdoll-limp, the seatbelt preventing him from landing squarely in Brad's lap.

Pulling onto a gravel shoulder just wide enough for the Charger's width, Brad hopped from the driver's seat and sprinted to the other side, nearly sliding atop the loose gravel into a rocky ditch from his own forward momentum.

"Boone. Boss, you with me?" he shrieked, unlatching the seatbelt and pulling the older man's flaccid form upright as a substantial rain spotted his exposed back.

With no apparent response forthcoming, he applied a gentle backhand tap to either side of Boone's ashen cheeks. The slack expression, mouth agape, complexion that of freshly fallen snow, remained frighteningly unchanged.

"Come to, boss, come to. Stay with me."

A gasp, wet and stinking of decay, followed by a glut of crimson vomit spewed forth, Brad lurching back just in time to dodge the sticky mass.

"H-how clo…close are w-we?" Boone muttered, his formerly white goatee now drenched in a reddish/yellow custard of warm bile, his left eye half-open even as his right remained clamped.

Reaching past the older man, Brad retrieved a mini pack of facial tissue from the center console and, after pulling a handful free and exposing them to the falling rain, gently wiped the older man's chin.

"Half an hour give or take. Listen Boone, I *really* think we need to get you to a hospi…"

The older man shook his head vehemently, as if shooing off a pesky fly and began digging into his front pants pocket, from which soon emerged a tiny, metallic blue pill box.

"Wha-what time is it?"

"Almost one-thirty. Boone, list…"

"There's a mo…motel just as you…enter Baymont. The Sack-o…out motel. Book us a…room. Just need a few…hours of downtime. Think the r-ride got me. Terminal butt-sores."

A pained, pathetic attempt at a smile before dry-swallowing a pair of white, octagon-shaped pills.

"Hydrocodone," he muttered weakly, donning a mask of severe discomfort while leaning his head back against the seat-rest, "Got enough in…stock to carry me the rest…of the way."

Brad stepped back and stood, hands on hips as sporadic drops of rain dripped from the bill of his ballcap.

"You sure about this, Boone? Honestly, you look like hammered shit."

"I am, and I'm sure…I do indeed. Let's burn…some rubber. The sooner I'm able to…lay down, the sooner I'll be…able to get back up."

They rode, Brad maintaining a consistent clip of between eighty and eighty-five, only slowing when traffic dictated, which was rare save the occasional mini convoy of lumbering semis.

At two-oh-six, Brad spotted the first road-sign proclaiming *'Baymont-2 mi'* and roughly sixty-seconds and one narrow off-ramp and sharp right turn later, *'Baymont City Limits'*. All the while, his motionless employer napped, or at least appeared to, his narrow chest, Brad would swear the man had lost weight in the double digits since departing Turtle Bend, rising and falling so faintly as to nearly be undetectable to the human eye.

Upon locating the Sack-Out Motel just past an Exxon station, just across the way from what appeared to be a haphazardly boarded-up Food Lion grocery store, he'd gently shaken Boone awake, leading him to their assigned room, a sparsely furnished, thinly carpeted spaces which reeked of stale cigarettes, mold and bargain basement aerosol spray.

"I'm...the dope has...is...has worked it's magic. Go-gonna hit the hay for a few hours," Boone explained, sitting on the edge of one of two twin beds, each cloaked in similarly garish red, white and blue colored blankets that appeared to have been pulled from a Spirit of '76 time machine.

"In case I go...full coma, make sure I don't snooze past ten. We...have much to...discuss before you go."

Wavering a bit as he knelt to remove his boots, he arose with an expression of utter fatigue but, before allowing himself to fully collapse onto the creaking bed, addressed a standing Brad one final time.

"I...do appreciate you...sticking around more than you could ever know, son. I...was going to let you drop me off and call a cab when...needed. Truth is I don't...trust myself. It's vital I wake in time to...meet my appointment."

With that, the older man laid back and, within a matter of minutes, could be heard lightly snoring.

Eyeing the man's briefcase propped near an aged TV stand centering the beds on a far wall, Brad briefly considered taking a peek but feared a surprise detection enough to brush away temptation. Instead, checking his watch with a heavy sigh and seeing it read just past three PM, decided on a quick tour of the town, what little there was to investigate.

He would return at a quarter past five, this after a leisurely ride down the small town's main street and stopping at the local Sonic drive-in, one of only three fast-food joints he'd spotted, the other two being a Burger King and a Jet's Pizza, for a double cheeseburger, fries and a chocolate shake, the majority of which lay on his chest like an anvil as he keyed the motel room entrance.

The television, an ancient thirteen-inch supplied with rabbit ears no less, had been powered up with the sound muted, and Brad breathed a sigh of relief at the regular rise and fall of the older man's chest as he dozed, spread-eagled on the twin bed with his socked feet hanging off opposite sides.

"Sure you don't need some ice? I saw a machine near the office."

It was a quarter past nine and Boone sat on the edge of the bed gripping a small plastic cup of bubbling Sprite, staring blankly at the television showcasing an old rerun of Sanford and Son.

"I'm good, thanks. Not dancing a lively jig anytime soon, but better. Ah, the magic of modern pharmaceuticals."

Standing a bit unsteadily, Boone retrieved his clothes case and walked gingerly to the bathroom, gently shutting the door behind him.

Brad soon heard the shower initiated and reached over to turn up the TV volume while manually switching the channel, no remote in sight, it was true 'retro' viewing, to the local news.

Roughly forty-five minutes later, Brad couldn't help but crack a wide smile birthed from sincere awe as Boone emerged decked out in a light blue checkered plaid shirt, button-up, light brown tweed vest, sky blue silk tie, dark grey khakis and tan penny loafers, the scent of aftershave practically engulfing the relatively cramped space.

"Well now, Slick, looks like you clean up pretty good after all."

"Gotta look better than I feel."

As Boone stood before the dresser mirror and combed through his whitish/gray mane, the younger man circled around and looked the snappily dressed older man up and down as if judging a prize bovine.

"So boss, fess up. You have me drive you all this way for a date?"

Boone halted in mid-comb, his grave reflection suddenly that of a man prepping for his own funeral.

"You might say that."

Gripping the edge of the flimsy dresser for balance, he turned to Brad and gestured toward the edge of the nearest twin bed. It was, according to the ancient radio-alarm on a nearby lamp stand, straight up ten PM.

"Have a seat. I want to cover a few things before you escort me one final time."

Chapter Six

"So, before I sermonize for what I'm sure you're secretly relieved *is* the last time, how about answering a question for me?"

Each man sat on the perspective edges of their beds, facing a static-filled episode of '*Gunsmoke*' from its early black-and-white years, Dennis Weaver's iconic Chester limping through the streets of Dodge in search of Mr. Dillon. Boone Harrison, dressed up like a dog's dinner with hands folded in his lap, glanced sideways at his hired driver with a brow cocked quizzically. When compared to earlier that day, seemingly at death's door if not at least climbing the porch steps, it appeared the older man was soaring from the magical effects of a mythical second wind.

"Fire away," Brad replied with a mild shrug, his tone not quite successful in masking an underlying apprehension.

"What *really* awaits you in the sunshine state?"

Briefly, so rapid an alteration to be nearly undetectable, the younger man's eyes widened, his throat constricting as if from a sudden, complete blockage of the thorax.

"My wi...Gina. Boss, we covered this already."

"Yeah, we did. Not *all* the pertinent details though, am I right?"

Folding his arms, Boone peered straight ahead at the TV, where a still-youthful Marshal Dillon was sharing a beer with an equally spry Miss Kitty.

"I understand if you don't feel the need to confide, it's just that, well, you've endured three-plus days of my never-ending jaw-jacking. Just figured you might need to unload before we part ways. Had a feeling you've been on the cusp a few times along the way. Can't offer much but an older man's advice, but it's there for the taking."

The younger man sighed, inhaled deeply and repeated same, his expression growing increasingly pained until, like a cresting wave, it broke, melting and reforming like heated wax into a weary, hangdog wince

250

usually associated with emotional exhaustion.

"Gina left me three months ago. Three months, five days to be exact. Met a contractor through her work. Smarmy Jackass was only in Turtle Bend for a few days but they…" he paused, head bowed, resuming through gritted teeth, "…obviously hit it off. We'd been having some issues, sure, but talk about not seeing it coming. Runaway freight hit me chest high, man. She ran off with 'im to sunny Florida a few days later. Packed a bag, left a post-it stuck to the fridge. Six and a half years, flushed like so much butt-burger."

Smiling a bit at the 'butt-burger' reference, Boone maintained an appropriately stoic, borderline solemn tone.

"So, the purpose of your…this visit is what? Reconciliation? Revenge?"

"I hoped to see if I could just talk some sense into her. I mean, what she did was…made no damn sense."

Brad wrung his hands fiercely, flashing a wide, toothy smile of pure malevolence.

"Don't think I haven't fantasized about beating that prick to a raw, bloody pulp. Scoop up all the extracted teeth and hand 'em to her as she cried her cheating eyes out."

The evil grin dissipated as quickly as it materialized, replaced by a frown so somber it would've made the unhappiest circus clown appear positively ecstatic.

"It's like…the…such hate is poison in its purest form. When I think about how I've…how I hurt and she's…" he paused, whistling through pursed lips, "…she won't answer my emails or letters. Lord help me, but I still love her so much. I just figured it was worth a shot."

Boone remained conspicuously silent, nodding feebly, as if gauging if the younger man was going to resume. When this did not happen within thirty seconds, both staring deadpan at the fuzzy screen as Doc Adams now shared brews with Chester and Matt at the Long Branch saloon, he stood stiffly and strolled gradually toward the room's lone window, peeking through noticeably dingy blinds.

"If you want advice, I'll gladly offer. If not, I'll respectfully keep my opinion to myself."

Brad, blinking rapidly as to aid in quick drying the moisture collecting in each glistening orb, waved silently as if to give permission.

"You're still a very young man. Move on. She obviously has. A partner that leaves one in such a cruel way is not likely to be swayed back into whatever situation they so hastily bailed on. Besides…" he turned slowly around, arms crossed, head slightly bowed, "…trust and loyalty are forever lost. If they cheat once, they're apt to repeat the act sometime down the line. Believe me, I speak from experience."

"One of your…wives…"

"Barbara Jean. My second. Damnedest thing is, I never completely lost it for her either, no matter how atrocious her acts. Still, I had to let her go and press on. Wasn't easy. Hardest thing I ever did. I guess an addict of drink or drugs might compare it to the unrelenting pull of their respective vice."

With that, Boone walked over and placed an open palm on the younger man's left shoulder, the two briefly locking eyes, wise sage to upstart pupil.

"Spare yourself additional scars and drive right on back to Turtle Bend. From there, map out the freshest of starts. Might sound corny, but the world is yours.

"Personally, I found mobility and freedom are made effortless without dragging a chain of past hurts around like a rusty anchor. You'll be surprised how time and new experiences dull all that pain to a smooth, virgin finish full of possibility."

Sighing deeply and exhaling in huffing increments, Brad simply nodded and excused himself from the room, returning roughly fifteen minutes later, just as the end credits to Gunsmoke rolled up the jagged TV screen.

"Feeling better or about the same?" Boone asked, having reclaimed his previous spot at the bed's edge.

Brad flashed a thumbs up and did the same, the bed's aged springs creaking obvious disapproval.

"Better. Much. Thanks."

Slapping the tops of both knees with bare palms, Boone arose and commenced to pace the cramped space with hands on hips.

"Okay then. My turn then. I'll try to elaborate as concisely as possible, as we'll need to head out no later than eleven-forty-five to make the appointment. Initially, I didn't feel the need to share any details about tonight's mystery meeting, but the...my sudden deterioration deems it necessary. About...why we're here. Needless to say, it isn't business or some corny romantic rendezvous. It's more about rectifying, no, it's not quite a correction. More like meeting an obligation. It's facing up to an issue, a problem that's been put off and ignored for far too long."

In lieu of verbal reply, Brad simply nodded along as Boone slowly paced from one edge of the small room to the other.

"I'm here to meet, well, more like face down, a close relative. A relative I've avoided with great effort. Shames me to the core to say, but blatant cowardice trumped all else through the years, the decades. For whatever it's worth, I always had a fairly justifiable reason to hide from this particular obligation."

"I always told myself I had too much to lose to chance, well, satisfying the commitment. My present condition leaves no more room for excuses. Truth is, I've been alone for years. Just didn't have the guts to face it. To face her."

"This person a close relative?" Brad inquired as Boone had strolled over to peek yet again into the mostly deserted, dimly lit motel parking lot, as if expected an imminent visitor.

"The closest. My daughter. She is very ill. She does...has done bad things. *Very* bad things. Things I can no longer dismiss or ignore out of blatant fear. Especially being so close to, well, meeting my maker."

Brad stood from the creaking bed and strolled over, placing a hand atop the older man's left shoulder.

"So, I know it's not my business, this being a family matter and all, but Boone, you're in no shape to help anybody."

Just a hint of a hoarse, sarcastic giggle escaped the older man's lips as he turned, locking eyes with the other man and flashing a sad, shaky smile.

"It's not about *helping*, son. Things are way beyond that stage. It's more about consummation."

"You mean saying goodbye?"

"In a sense, yes. A closing. Give me a few minutes and we'll be on our way."

Stepping away, the older man checked his wristwatch before leaning down to scoop up and tote the briefcase into the bathroom, closing the door gently behind him.

It was more like five, Brad checking his phone to see the time was eleven-thirty-six as Boone reentered the room.

"Got an address for your GPS, though I ponder its usability out here in the boonies."

"You'd be surprised. Shoot," Brad replied, finger at the ready.

Moments later, Boone stood half-in, half out of the room, hands hidden in pants-pockets as Brad retrieved his car keys and flipped off the lamplight centering the two beds.

"You going empty-handed, boss?"

Boone shrugged, holding out and exposing bare palms.

"Just me and my shadow."

For some reason, Brad found said remark nothing short of chilling; a foreboding sense of things not being what they seemed poking his subconscious like a hot, probing syringe.

The two assumed their respective positions inside the Charger, Brad pausing before keying the ignition.

"You sure about this, boss? I just don't feel at all right just dropping you off at some desolate farmhouse in the middle of blessed nowhere, and at the midnight hour to boot."

"But I won't be alone," Boone replied flatly, "I'll be with family."

Inexplicably, and for the second time in less than five minutes, Brad felt a cold chill race his spine.

~ * ~

Beneath a cloudy, moonless sky, the Charger cut through the darkness of a winding, deserted two-lane highway just outside the city limits, the GPS having pointed them eastward past any detectable form of civilization.

Riding in silence, they were instructed to detour onto an unmarked, unnamed, one-lane dirt road centering a gathering of tall pines, red maples and Fall dogwoods, their bases cloaked in big bluestem and switchgrass. The deeper they drove, the more it at least appeared that the foliage was closing in, narrowing the trail while simultaneously deepening the level of darkness from just past dusk to pitch-black.

"This road gets any skinnier we'll be forced to walk 'er sideways," Brad quipped nervously, leaning over the wheel to better scan the dirt surface for jagged rocks or potentially damaging ruts.

"Looks like maybe a quarter of a mile up ahead on the right," Boone replied, leaning over and forward until his forehead nearly grazed the dash while scanning the GPS's glowing screen.

"Listen Boone, even if there is some form of livable domicile out here, I don't think I should just dump you off and make tracks. What if there's no phone? Least I could do is hang out 'til we know you're not being stranded."

Boones squinting eyes never departed the screen.

"I do appreciate the offer. It's not necessary. Surely my daughter has transportation and access to outside communication. What you *can* do, and I only ask you wait 'til sunrise, is carefully peruse the contents of my briefcase and in the next few days mail the addressed package I left. Makes no difference if the postmark reads Florida, North Dakota, or anywhere in-between," he concluded with playful wink directed Brad's way.

"Consider it done."

The older man sighed wearily, momentarily breaking from the GPS monitor to gaze steely eyed over the dash.

"I know there has been an air of mystery surrounding the whole shebang and I deeply appreciate your patience. Trust me, the contents of the briefcase will fill in so many of the blanks, a few of 'em you probably didn't even realize were empty.

"Just so you know, full payment is enclosed, as well as the necessary forms to legally assign you as power of attorney over my vast belongings." The older man giggled in concluding this last portion, just as the Charger lurched hard right to avoid a thick, pointy limb sticking into the road like a colossal spear. Brad, swallowing hard, only replied after steering them out of the thicket-infested shoulder and back onto the path.

"Power of at…but shouldn't your daughter or the grandson in Arizona be in charge of the…your assets?"

"I trust you and you alone to honor the instructions I've left," the older man said matter-of-factly, darting gaze alternating between the GPS screen and the curved road ahead.

"Home base appears to be one-hundred yards and closing, captain," he quipped in a horrid Scottish accent, coughing harshly in the aftermath and garnering a comical double-take from his driver, who secretly wondered if the older man's pain meds were doing a lot of the talking.

Approximately two and a half minutes, two wheel-deep ruts and several whispered profanities, courtesy of Brad through gritted teeth, later, a wide clearing swam dimly into view on their right, soon accompanied by an equally murky light source.

"Must be the place. Jesus, talk about living off the grid."

"That's my Ginger-bear. Always preferred to remain hidden, even in plain sight."

Brad started to inquire of the cutesy nickname but figured anything that saccharin-sweet had to have originated from the daughter's childhood.

"Dig it," Boone whispered so softly Brad pondered if he'd even meant to speak aloud, the older man's arms outstretched with clenching hands gripping the dash as if prepping for impact, "…a haunted farmhouse. How very appropriate."

At Boone's insistence, Brad killed the lights, cut the engine and steered the Charger to a rolling stop a few feet from a stone-posted mailbox on the opposite side of the residential driveway, parking roughly twenty-five yards from the homestead itself.

A faint porch light, seemingly the lone source of illumination, did little but frame the entrance, leaving the twin structures of house and barn bathed in shadow, as was the pickup truck positioned between them.

"No lights on inside."

"She's in there. Up, awake and aware."

"It is after midnight, boss. Maybe we should try this at first light. Don't wanna wind up with a backside full of buckshot."

"It's perfectly fine," Boone said firmly.

Turning toward Brad, his face only half-lit, the older man appeared positively fossilized.

"My Gwen is waiting. This time, I can't...I *won't* disappoint."

"Boone, I really don't mind wait..."

His latest plea interrupted by an outstretched hand, he reached, reluctantly, to clasp it and was briefly distracted by a faint reflection that led his gaze to a bulge beneath the older man's swede vest. A metallic glint, black handled, silver monogram. Brad felt the pulse throb at his neck and temples, an abrupt sensory overload, though somehow, he managed a firm enough handshake, miraculously free of the shakes.

"Thank you for all you've done, son. I'll take 'er from here."

"I...you're welcome, sir, and thank you."

He watched the older man fumble for the inner handle.

"Sir, are you gonna be all right?" he inquired, voice quivering despite a Herculean effort.

Without turning, his employer did not answer until a foot was firmly planted onto the Northern Mississippi terrain.

"I think we both know the answer. Godspeed, Bradley."

~ * ~

Boone strolled casually down the gravel/dirt drive, stopping halfway while alternating glances at the barn to his left, stereotypically dark shaded, probably red though it was impossible to gauge in the darkness, and the homestead to his right, a rustic, single-level cottage, log-cabin styled complete with front porch and twin picture windows facing the roadway.

When the older man didn't budge for two full minutes, Brad deduced he wasn't merely undecided on which structure to check first, but most likely waiting for the sound of crunching gravel as the Charger pulled away and out of sight.

Brad did just that, first pulling forward and backing into the drive before easing down the path previously trekked. Peeking through the rearview, he saw that his departure had indeed coincided with Boone trudging slowly toward the homestead's front porch.

257

A few hundred yards of dodging now semi-familiar ruts and fallen limbs, Brad braked, shifted to park and killed the lights. The driver's window slid down, the hum of a cricket concerto filling his ears. An alien sound that under other circumstances the city-born northerner might've found soothing but, on this night, this time, birthed something more akin to a creeping dread.

A man, a very sick man, was reuniting with a long-lost daughter after who knew how many years, perhaps decades the way he spoke, and brought nothing substantial to the meet save a purposely cloaked handgun?

A man who had entrusted him, a perfect stranger a mere three day's past, with everything he would leave behind. A man he had come to know through fantastic, mostly tragic tales from his family's history. A man he grown remarkably fond of in a very short time. A father-figure. A friend.

A man he wasn't about to desert or discard, regardless of the former's insistence that he do so. It didn't take a genius to deduce that something was tragically amiss. Inhaling deeply and exhaling uneasily, he struggled mightily to push down the stark fear attempting to first dominate and then extract what instinct begged him to do.

Backing the Charger until he found a suitable spot from which to turn, Brad steered by sheer chance and the dimmest of moonlights.

Whatever it was his new friend was facing down this night, he would not face it down alone.

~ * ~

Returning to the southern edge of the property, he was careful to park the Charger an even wider distance away than the spot from which he'd first delivered Boone. Approaching the house from the east, he was able to follow a line of knee-high Dwarf Burford shrubbery all the way to the edge of the porch, a lone blub throwing off a faint, murky glow due to a veritable swarm of moths fluttering within its aged dome cover.

Since exiting the Charger, he half expected the shrill bark of a dog, be it single pet or unsecured pack, as most isolated farmhouses were apt to populate. It was with no small amount of relief that, having covered the lengthy distance from car to homestead, nary a single bark, yelp or muffled growl emerged.

Stepping lightly onto the planked deck, his fear of a resounding creak was soon eased at the wobble-free firmness of the cedar boards, possibly the target of a recent renovation. Sliding past a set of wooden rocking chairs right out of a Rockwell painting, the curtained windows gave no hint of interior illumination, he stood before the mesh screen door fronting the entrance and, hearing nothing over the incessant hum of the crickets, tried the screen handle to find the door secured.

Side-stepping over and leaning in, he scanned the second picture window for an opening but found none. Sighing, he tiptoed carefully from the porch in order to slink around to the back of the house when a flash of light struck the peripheral of his left eye. The rear of the barn.

Pulling up the collar of his jacket, Brad paused only briefly to ogle the pickup, from its oxidized hood and scattered splotches of rust a vehicle nearing classic status, only to brake to a complete stop at a stack of chopped wood and, feeling foolish but not nearly enough to prevent the action, scooped up a splitting axe protruding from a nearby block.

Moving forward in a slight crouch, the light taking a wide triangular shape, a voice briefly froze him mid-step. At first barely audible, an additional two steps toward the source brought clarity. A female voice. Gwen. A choice to be made. Eavesdrop like some spooked, sneaky kid or step forward like a man.

Back tucked tightly against the open barn door, Brad clutched the axe's slick hickory handle to his heaving chest like a protective talisman, temporarily satisfied in his decision to reincarnate a long childlike tendency.

~ * ~

"Hey, don't be mean-muggin' me, old man. I told you, he slipped his bonds. I was just defendin' myself. Pure instinct."

"You promised, Gwen. Seventy-two hours, remember? Well, by my watch we made intros at just past hour sixty-seven."

"I tell ya, it was him or me. Old geezer was pit-bull aggressive and stouter than he looks. Danged if he wasn't still swingin', clawin' and bitin' even after I gutted 'im. Didn't cease brawlin' til most of his innards had wrapped his ankles like coiled snakes. Never saw anything like it."

"That inhuman rage no doubt fueled at seeing his beloved in…that state."

"Collateral damage. It happens, as you well know."

"Oh yes, most definitely, though the difference is I never went out of my way to collect said damage."

Head cocked in the direction of the conversation, Brad could only guesstimate the pair's position within the massive structure as being close enough to easily hear but far enough away so their respective shadows remained out of sight. The female's voice was booming, boisterous and bordering on uncouth, the accent unmistakably southern in origin, practically dripping sorghum.

Boone, meanwhile, came off as restrained enough but definitely annoyed, as if struggling to control a building anger at whatever disagreement had arisen.

Not exactly the heartwarming father and daughter reunion one would expect, though Brad found he was neither shocked nor surprised at such a development considering the lone personal item brandished by the sire had been a carelessly cloaked firearm.

"Ah c'mon now, let's not get into comparin' scars, be they mental or otherwise. We *are* what we are, no matter how the track record was compiled."

"Oh, but the difference *is* night and day, Ginger-bear. The only thing we have in common is our penchant for blatant cowardice when it comes to our own demise."

"*Horseshit.* You got yours and I got mine. No matter how you tally 'em it totals up the same. If you came here lookin' for some kinda sanctification, I ain't qualified to hear *nor* forgive sins, nor am I willin' to even try. Don't work that way for us *forced* to wear the black hat.

"Make no mistake, yours might be lily white on the outside, but the interior is as dark as a mineshaft and soulless as a jackal."

A short pause, during which time Brad thought he detected the faraway howl of a distant canine. Tugging at his drooping collar from the effects of a cool, consistent breeze had him wishing he'd unpacked a thicker coat.

Once Boone did reply, it was a voice cracking with emotion.

"I never considered…would *never* do what you've done to…family."

"Well, there's family and then there's *family,* right? Our kin ain't exactly The Walton's."

"No proof. Just another damn excuse to eradicate without the same level of guilt."

"No proof? No proof, you say. You tellin' me cousin Brett wore angel's wings? How 'bout great nephew Jonathon? Oh yeah, real choirboy there. Even *this* one confessed to a weird satisfaction in guttin' hogs and throttlin' yard-bird. Sweet little country farmer my dimpled ass."

"NOT the same thing, Gwen, and you damn well know it. You had no proof Ronnie ever harmed anyone…EVER."

"No proof he hadn't neither, but odds are he'd stopped more than a few heartbeats prematurely. Killin' is killin', it's just a matter of a slow progression up the food chain. Hell, even *I* started with mashin' frogs and skinnin' cats."

Boone coughed, a harsh wet hacking that lasted a full half-minute, before responding in a raspy, strained tone that Brad knew all too well. The old man was fading fast and, considering the less-than-cordial dialogue being traded, wasn't apt to bounce back as in days past.

"You had no right. You…*never* had the right. Just the easiest way to sate your bloodlust."

"Your opinion, Father, but hey, true or not, you were never willin' to put a stop to it."

Another pause, cough-free but no less foreboding, had Brad pondering if the old man were stroking-out.

"I came tonight as asked. You…lied. Misled. Dishonesty not nearly the worst of your traits, sad to say. Least you could, could have done is bury 'em proper. The flies are having a picnic beneath that tarp."

"I was thinkin' more along the lines of cremation."

A short pause, during which the source of an elongated sigh and hearty clearing-of-the throat was easily identified as Gwen, each precluding a statement practically dunked and subsequently drenched in obviousness.

"You know, Father, you really look like hammered cow-pie. So, what's the diagnosis this time?"

"The big C. Both lungs. Spread to the right kidney and beyond."

"Terminal?"

"Yes."

"Of course, it is. What's this, number three on the fatal 'til it *ain't* fatal list?"

"N-not this time, Ginger-bear. No amount of…stubbornness or undivine intervention is gonna derail this train."

"Uh-huh. Color me skeptical. Anyhow, enough with the diversions already. Back to my earlier question on just how you arrived here on this fine, crisp but not yet cold Fall Mississippi evening."

"Told you. I hitched."

"Well, there's one thing that's never changed, no matter the years in-between. You are one sorry liar. How dare you rail *me* about dishonesty? Daddy please. Fine. Knowin' you, I have to figure certain details were kept to a minimum."

"You'd…figure r-right," came the delayed, bone-weary reply, bookended by equally forceful coughing jags.

"Danged if you haven't sprung a substantial leak at that. Hear, let me get that for ya…"

A short pause, additional coughing though strangely muffled, as if Boone were hacking into a thick blanket.

"Gotta say, that ain't good. How long you been like this?"

"O-on and…off ma-maybe six…or seven m-months. Progressively…worse."

"So, all those damn hand-rolled smokes finally come to roost. Well, looks like ya finally found your personal Waterloo after numerous college-tries. I recall the oceans-of-booze phase. The eat-yourself-into-a-diabetic stupor phase and of course my personal favorite…" Gwen laughed as if suddenly recalling a particularly hilarious, long-forgotten knee-slapper, "…the *suicide jobs* phase. Never could figure out if those were actually preplanned or if an overabundance boredom or time had made ya one stone-stupid SOB. If I was a bettin' woman, I'd go with the former."

"G-give me…the…pistol, Gwen. This…has to end…can end, for…both of us."

"Not a chance, old man. That wasn't the deal. This was never about surrender on my part. Don't be blamin' me for your fragile state or walkin' in here so carelessly and pitifully unprepared. 'Sides, I still got unfinished business, as you well know."

For the scant few seconds his rant lasted, Boone briefly regained the gruff, authoritative tone of enraged father scolding unruly child.

"NO! He's got…a family now, Gwen. Don't even…*think* about it."

Her braying laugher was nothing less than a sarcastic smirk made vocal.

"A regular Ward Cleaver, huh? *Sure,* he is, at least on the surface. The art of deception runs through our veins almost as prominently as that…*other* common trait, right? Bet he has hobbies. Hobbies the wife and kiddo have no clue of. For whatever you think, old man, I don't rush into these things half-cocked. The exact opposite, in fact. The fact is, I've uncovered our boy's been leading a bit of the ever-popular double-life. Haven't quite nailed down the sordid details yet, but I will. Face it, he's just another mad dog off his leash and mad dogs have to be put down."

"Damn you. Clearly, the maddest of them *all.*"

"Straight from your loins just as he's straight from my own. I mean, I get the whole protective grandpappy angle, but we ain't exactly talkin' your typical lovin' clan here."

Brad leaned his head back against the barn door, his expression a twisted scowl, unable to comprehend just exactly what he was listening to. It sounded as if they were rehearsing a stage play rife with tragedy.

"Leave him…leave *them* alone, Gwen. For god's sake, e-end this."

Once Brad heard the old man's voice break and deteriorate, first into a series of whispered, incomprehensible whimpers and finally wrenching sobs, any chance of what he was witnessing being fictional melted away like a sliver of ice tossed into a pan of boiling water.

Perhaps more shocking was the daughter's cold, emotionless

response, a monotone, mechanical speech straight from a computer app.

"Too late for that, old man. How many times did I request your assistance? How many times did I beg and grovel? Remember the first time? Everyone remembers their *first* time, right? Chandler, Arizona, late summer, distant cousin Marcus."

"Of course. H-how the hell could I forget? Added child-killer to your resume that night, as I recall."

There was a short pause, a calm before the storm moment, the woman's eventual, blaring retort more nitro high-explosive than M-80 small-ammo fire.

"*YOU THINK I WAS AMUSING MYSELF? PLAYIN' GAMES, OLD MAN?*

Continuing this latest rant, albeit at a much lower volume, the woman sounded positively drained.

"This night, all these years later, never…should…have…came…to…be. I'm…I have never and *will* never be strong enough to end it on my own, you know this. You've always known this. Thing is, I can't honestly say I ever *want* it to end. It's second nature. Guess I'll find out once I officially run outta quarry."

"Dennis…somehow…found the courage."

"De…really, old man? Dennis was lookin' at life plus twenty, remember? Talk about incentive! He might've went down as the only slob in history to actually *serve* 'em. So please don't be comparin' me with little brother."

"H-half-brother."

"I stand corrected. Half-bro in biological terms but still equal parts a natural-born killer."

"He…was defending himself against…thugs who meant to take his wife and children's lives. There's a difference between…killing and…*enjoying* the process."

"Maybe, but even money says he reveled in it once the process had 'im in its grip."

"You…don't…*know that!*" Boone shouted, the fervent screech petering out to a loud, choking cry.

As the man's sobs gradually faded to a series of choked gasps,

Brad stood on increasingly wobbly legs and at a definite crossroads. Should he simply charge in, wide-eyed and axe raised like some unhinged psychopath or stand his ground for further developments? Just as he had slid a few inches further toward the door's outer edge, a slim, elongated shadow emerged into the escaping light, initiating an involuntary flinch in which he fumbled clumsily, nearly dropping the cumbersome axe.

"J-just do it then," he heard Boone croak, prompting the shadow to descend until its eventual evaporation, "Do wh-what you do…best. Why…draw this o-out? N-nothing I say will…detour you. I see…that now. God help me, I see it…all too clearly."

The reply was as icy as the request had been defeatist.

"God ain't listenin', Father. Not to the likes of us."

"Point t-taken. So, are w-we just gonna stand here and…gab 'til I keel from…boredom or you gonna sh-show some…mercy to your o-old man?"

Another short pause, during which time Brad noticed even the chilled, midnight-hour breeze seemed to halt, the quiet so deafening for a full thirty seconds that he feared the thumping of his heart might give him away.

"How long before you peter out on your own? Best guess…"

"How…should I know? I've very little…experience in the art of…dying. Why?"

"Just pondering."

"Don't tell m-me the…queen of callousness is going soft?"

"Well, you are my father, after all."

"So? You've been…stopping hearts and chopping off damn near every limb…of the family tree. Why the…sudden attack of conscience now? I've b-been parent in…name only for…too long for *even* me…to recall."

"This is true. Still…"

"Chicken s-shit."

"Oh, you're gonna *goad* me into it now? What's next, callin' me poopy-pants or maybe butt-hole?"

His scalp tingling as if lit ablaze, Brad couldn't believe that they seemed to be bickering, actually bickering, about the quickest way to end

Boone's life. Surreal as it all seemed, he no longer held any rational hopes of the whole thing being some inexplicable, elaborate hoax or fictional play reading. Regardless, he was thoroughly mesmerized.

"Like you...said, I'm your...father. I could...*insist*."

Despite her wisecracking dialogue, the daughter's tone relayed nothing resembling humor, instead a biting, building frustration and even an undertone of sincere compassion.

"Gonna ground me if I don't? Maybe yank off your belt and give me a good wackin'?"

"Now, Ginger-bear..." Boone whispered, cooing as if speaking to a small child, "...you called for...this reunion, remember? Demanded it...for...so, so long. Well, I'm...here."

The daughter's stuttering reply was a shrill, fire-alarm screech, those specific words emphasized for dramatic effect echoing from the interior of the vast confines of the barn like delayed explosions.

"Like *HELL* you are. Oh yeah, there is a wasted husk of what you *used* to be standin' here pleadin' like a dyin' dog for mercy, but that wasn't the deal. It's a gyp, damn you. Tell me, old man, you really think *THIS* is what...I wanted? *DO YOU?*"

"Poor triggered Gwen. So very twentieth century, a-aren't we? Well, what you see is...what you get. Now, either shit or...get off the...pot," came the whispered reply, so faint in comparison to be almost incomprehensible.

"Sure, why not? Better than sittin' here watch you hack, wheeze and bleed out from rotted innards. Just...give me a sec to choose the proper tool. Believe I have just the thing."

A frantic shuffling was soon followed by rapid footsteps heading away from the rear door and deeper into the barn, the sudden silence tempting Brad to rush inside to his friend's aide. A creaking door that he figured must the barn's front entrance added an extra layer of bravery to his rapidly thickening hide. Another creak, quieter but drawn out as if perhaps guided by the midnight winds.

Resting the axe end of the handle atop his right shoulder, Brad sucked the night air greedily and held it, inner thighs and calves trembling in anticipation of a sudden spring.

"Got it," a not-too-distant voice exclaimed excitedly, the continuation growing closer and thus freezing Brad in place yet again, "It ain't easy keepin' up with inventory when one is constantly on the go, 'specially those items wastin' away from neglect. Ya see though, I knew there was a reason I've hauled this antique piece of weaponry from state to state and coast to coast."

A labored sigh, as from the conclusion of a marathon run, followed by a mischievous, immature giggle like those associated with an excitable teenage girl.

"Ain't it still a beauty though? Not bad shape considerin' it was more than likely manufactured with Truman warmin' the White House throne."

"Is t-this...it c-can't be..." Boone mumbled weakly, obviously taken aback.

"Oh, but it is. This here smoke-wagon sent many a storm-troopin' goose-stepper straight to hell, I'll bet. War ain't exactly hell for folks like us though, is it? More like a paid vacation with all the frills: crackin' skulls, perforatin' guts and blowin' assorted holes in the enemy, all in the name of patriotism? Yowsa. Talk about a kid in a candy store! Anyhow, it sure beats that pipsqueak peashooter you strolled in here packin', right?"

"B-but how...did you? It was...my going away relic from the TDCJ b-back in the d-day...l-lost this somewhere in between...Texas and...Florida, I...think."

Yet another pre-pubescent chuckle.

"You never were much for lockin' doors. Grandad was like that too, if I recall the stories. Anyway, I stood right over your bed. Wife number...four, was it? Pretty thing. Reminded me of that chick from *Bewitched*. Gotta hand it to ya. You could always charm 'em. Not a single albatross among that vast stable of wives."

"M-my god. You...s-stalked...us all?"

Suddenly void all good humor, the reply was as chilled as a Dakota dusk in January.

"Don't flatter yourself, old man. Rarely did our paths cross, at least physically. Anyhow, you just relax while I free that shootin' hand. You a born southpaw, like me?"

"Wh-why you...handing it...I don't wa..." Boone protested, though so timidly it was clear the old man was officially running on fumes.

"Hold still now. Don't wanna carve into a rich vein by mistake."

Silence reigned, save a series of weak, barely audible whimpers, for another half-minute to forty-five seconds, during which time Brad realized either one or both of his booted feet had gone numb. Retrieving his cell, he wasn't the least bit surprised there was no signal but silently cursed the gods regardless.

"There ya go. Locked and loaded. Now, you got a choice, don'cha? You can turn that antique barrel on yourself or the one you came here to plug."

"I...came here to talk, to reason, to convince, not...to..."

"Enough jaw-jackin', old man. You've got to the count of five to fish or cut bait."

"Gwen, I'm...not going to justify...your miserable existence by...shooting you down and thus...becoming a similarly lost soul."

"Five," the daughter said flatly, in stark contrast to her father's heartfelt pronouncement, "Question is, does the pathetic old coward have the nards to end his own misery?"

Moments passed, Brad unaware he was holding his breath yet again, the brief sabbatical broken by a loud huff and subsequent curse.

"Yeah, I thought so. Just give me the damn th..."

A series of sharp clicks, three in all, timed roughly one second apart.

A howling guffaw that soon transformed into a wrenching sob then back again; the verbal equivalent of the two-faced mask representing both happiness and sadness, alternating in a schizophrenic outpour of contrasting emotions. Brad decided no better time might arise to make an appearance, before the woman could regain all of her faculty's, bracing his aching knees and tingling feet for a prospective lunge.

"Well, color me equal parts tickled *and* perturbed!" the woman proclaimed, clapping enthusiastically, the old man's response not nearly as cheery, "Your sickness...apparently knows no bounds."

Brad circled around the edge of the door, axe held high, just as Boone had thrown the pistol at his daughter, a surprisingly forceful end-over-end toss that she nevertheless easily dodged with a graceful sidestep, taking notice of the new arrival only after retrieving the discarded firearm.

"Who in blue blaze…oh. Well, hello there, Ace. Woodpile's out back, if that's what you're gropin' for."

Chapter Seven

"Boy, I can't say much for your overall judgement, but I've got to give props for possessin' a spine forged of the stoutest alloy."

Brad stood paralyzed of both body and mind in a wide stance, the axe held at chest level and gripped at both the narrowest and thickest areas of its aged hickory handle, eyes darting spastically from father and daughter and the almost surreal extremes of their current state. The majority of the barn's massive interior remained cloaked in darkness other than the lantern-lit portions revealing several planked stalls and a hay-filled loft.

"Oh g-god *no*, Brad. W-why? D-damn it," Boone moaned, his freed left hand clenched in a ball and shaking with either uncontrollable rage or frustration. Perhaps a hybrid of both, his right held snugly by what looked like a cable-tie. Strapped with braided rope at the ankles and across the upper chest to what appeared to be an antique high-back Carolean-style chair, the old man bled from both nostrils and a half-dollar-sized gash at the center of his forehead.

As for the woman he knew only as Gwen, her appearance wasn't at all what he'd pictured from the associated voice. Slim in build but obviously well-toned in a sleeveless black tee, blue jeans and worn hiker boots, the forty-something woman appeared at least as tall as her captive shire, her hair a butch-styled shave once referred to as a *high and tight*. Thin but tightly muscled arms crossed definitely, she regarded their uninvited visitor through the same piercing, brown-eyed gaze as her father, their respective noses, chins and overall bone structures strikingly similar.

"So, what to do now? *What...to...do*," she exclaimed while gnawing her lower lip, her left hand clenching the archaic firearm while the right was filled what appeared to be a sharp-tipped, ivory cutting instrument forged from animal bone.

"Wh-what…is *this*? Is she really…your daughter?" Brad asked, a nodding gesture directed at Gwen even as he locked eyes with her father.

The old man used the bare inner elbow of his left arm to wipe the sticky streams of half-dried, reddish mucus from beneath both nostrils. On the whole, he looked as though he'd been a recent participant, and verified loser, in a nasty street brawl. His plaid shirt and tweed vest equally blood-spattered, the left knee of his khaki's missing a large chunk of fabric, his left foot loafer-free, a brown-sock hanging half-off a ghostly-pale foot.

"Gwen, yes. Current last name…I can't be sure. Watkins was…the last I recall."

"Watkins?" his offspring howled, "Ditched that cheap bastard a decade back. If I was forced to choose at gunpoint, I guess I'd claim the ol' birthname, just for nostalgia's sake. That confessed…" she paused long enough to cock a brow while studying the young man from boots to crown, "…just how much did my old man tell you?"

Brad's eyes darted wildly from Boone to his daughter and back again several times, finally matching her raised brow with a similarly befuddled lift of his own.

"Ma'am?"

"Did I stutter, *mon ami*?" she replied in a shockingly natural French accent, "*ne comprends-tu pas*?"

Though the younger man could manage only a mild shrug in reply, Boone's surprisingly heated intervention provided the former a much-needed respite.

"He *only* knows…you're my daughter. I…didn't dare…divulge any of the…dirty little family secrets you so gleefully revel in and…use as an excuse for a lifetime…of depravity. Could…couldn't risk him…thinking I was as…hopelessly demented as…some. Please by all th-that's holy…refrain from exposing us…to all your worldly…tongues. I…get the point already."

"Really? You get it, do ya? Well, let us compare then how many foreign shores you were forced to land upon and…blend in to, dear father. Perhaps should I say…*puedes contestarme eso, padre*? How 'bout…*Oshiete kure, chichi*? C'mon now, Father, surely one of 'em rings a be…"

"Anata no imaimashi bijinesu no dore mo," Boone countered without hesitation, "Enough…self-righteous self-pity, girl. I did my…some time across other borders. Surely not as much as…yourself but …y-you see…I wasn't forced into…hiding by my own…immoral deeds."

"Yeah, yeah, *whatever*. The white-knight boy scout act don't cut it with me, old man. I know different. Now, back to your protégé here, in plain old English this time."

"Please," Brad shot back with a hint of levity that fell pancake flat. "While I took a little Spanish, you lost me with the Mandarin musings."

"*Japanese*, genius. Now, let's say my old man is speaking gospel on just how much you know. Ain't gonna blow smoke onto your privates, it really makes no difference in the big picture. Still, I am curious."

"Ma'am, *Gwen*, I'm lost on more levels than you can imag…"

Lowering the axe to waist level, Brad addressed his patron while failing miserably to halt the nervous shakes that threatened to transform his entire frame to a bowl of quivering Jell-O, a semi-disabling condition only escalated by what his peripheral caught just to his left. What appeared to be a pair of prone bodies parked in the far-left corner, haphazardly cloaked by a blood-soaked blanket.

"Boone, are those…are they…" he babbled, head tilted dramatically toward the presumed corpses while speaking directly to his demoralized patron, "Boone, what is this all about? I thought you came here to…reunite before, well, you know…"

Both men openly flinched at the woman's screeching, comically wide-eyed response.

"*BOONE?* Really, father, *Boone*? So, you voluntarily took that name for what purpose exactly? Thought it might change your luck to claim grand-dad's soiled, stained, disgraced given moniker? Old man, that is truly demented if ya dwell on it. Kinda like if Dahmer sired a son who later changed his name from, I dunno, Peter or Paul to Jeffrey. It ain't like I ever had the gall to mimic Ma's given."

"Don't have to…justify anything to…you," Boone snapped while struggling mightily to maintain full focus on the younger man, "Brad, forget wh-what you've seen or h-heard here. Sounds…impossible I know, but there is…no other option. G-get away…from here and…forget you…ever m-met me."

Before Brad could articulate a reply, Gwen slid over to stand directly between the two men, the aged revolver tucked snugly within her jean's waistband as she tossed the bone knife playfully from hand to hand. Brad, meanwhile, spent the moment's respite by checking his cell, still predictably signal-free.

"Fat chance, daddy-oh. He's waist-deep in the soup now. Won't ever know for sure how much you told 'im, but even a little is a damn sight too much."

"Gwen, y-you don't have to….do this. J-just let the boy…go."

"What? You would dash my rapidly fadin' hopes? Negative," she spat without turning as her father's head dipped until his bloody goatee rested atop his narrow chest. "You just sit there quietly and root for the combatant of your choice."

As the slender stalker took a half step in his direction, Brad's flinched as if physically goosed.

"You want…to *fight* me?"

Gwen Harrison's lustful, toothy smile, revealing at least one gold-plated chopper, was nothing short of predatory.

"No entirely accurate, young sir. What I want, is to *kill* you."

"G-Gwen, I…beg y-you. D-don't do this. It's so…lopsided as to be…a farce."

The woman's teeth audibly chattered as they clamped, her lips curling to non-existence, her nostrils flaring wildly.

"Put a cork in it, *Dad*. At least this one has a fighting chance, unlike the scrawny, dried-up husk I'd counted on for a good scrap."

Taking a half-step back, Brad gazed past the woman to Boone, who's head alternated between rising and falling, a low, incomprehensible murmur escaping from between drool-coated lips.

"Lady, I'm not…I'm only here to help my friend. I'm not gonna fi…"

"That axe speaks otherwise," Gwen grinned, tossing both the bone knife and pistol aside and out of reasonable reach, "Now be a gentleman and lay it aside. If I'm going, it's gonna be as squared a match as possible. You're a big enough boy, probably got me by forty or fifty pounds. Just remember, the only rule is there ain't any."

Following a slight hesitation, Brad flipped the axe blade over handle to land a few feet to Boone's left and inadvertently showering the old man with a spattering of uprooted soil.

"Boone?" he pleaded; arms upraised with the palms out.

"I'm so…sorry, my boy. So…very…sorry," came the solemn reply, stuttered between wrenching sobs, "I'd…stop her if…I could."

As Gwen shuffled a step closer in a slight crouch, arms hanging loosely at her sides, Brad twisted slightly to the left and planted his right boot atop the hard clay while briefly eyeing the grassy field beyond the barn's back entrance.

"Run and I'll catch you. *Bank* on it. Don't know Jack about you, *Brad*, but I doubt you wanna cash in from a shot in the back."

"Lady, you're crazy."

Gwen Harrison practically beamed.

"Oh, I'm *waaaay* beyond that, Ace."

She lunged, he retreated; a clumsy lurch that saw him first bounce off the barn door before regaining a semblance of balance. Hands on lips, Gwen flashed a warped grin fueled by unabashed arrogance.

"Maybe my father had a point. If you're just gonna breakdance and back pedal 'til we reach the back-forty, this ain't nothin' but a farce. Either way, you ain't leavin' this property upright, understand?"

Tucking her arms behind her back in mock defiance, she scooted forward and closed the gap until the two stood barely a reach away.

"Tell ya what. I'll even grant ya one free shot. Pick, spot and whack away."

"Jesus…Gwen," Boone could be heard moaning in the background.

Straightening his bowed back and locking his knees, Brad stood flat-footed with the palms of each hand full exposed.

"Lady, I don't know you or what this is about, but the constant death-threats I can do without. Now, how about we sit down and talk this out like adul…"

"Awww, fuck a duck," she growled, sailing forward with such quickness that Brad had time only for a comical, wide-eyed, jaw-dropping gawk and semi-juke before being jolted at the breastbone by a work-boot's hardened heel, sailing back with arms windmilling to land with a resounding thump, his lungs instantly voided of the majority of their precious cargo.

Rolling slowly onto his left side while gasping for breath, he'd managed to rise to one knee before being battered from the rear by a fierce flurry of kicks and punches, the former concentrating on his kidneys while the latter reddened both ears while opening an inch-wide gash at the tip of his chin.

A final, vicious kick between the shoulder blades resulted in a face-first landing atop a clay terrain so polished and slick to mimic recently lain tarmac, peeling back the flesh of his upper forehead in raw, tattered strips.

Before he could attempt to push himself upward, a boot was planted firmly at his lower back and clutching fingers hooked underneath his chin, tugging gradually upward.

"Boy, you're about as challengin' as a crippled girl-scout," Gwen spouted, barely out of breath, "This here dance is gonna end before the band strikes up the first no…"

A volatile mix of elements both physical and mental, the main ingredients being stark fear, unbridled rage and a tsunami-like rush of adrenalin, converged in a single volcanic moment, the results of which surprised even the source, who found himself standing upright, albeit wobbly, having miraculously freed himself from the woman's proposed death grip.

"Weeeeeelll now, that's better," Gwen said from the shadows, grinning devilishly and poised on all fours, having been thrown like a bronco rider and, upon impact, combat-rolling a dozen feet to Brad's right.

"I've always found it fascinatin' how those about to die can dig deep for that one extra gear."

"B-back off, lady. Just…stay away. I'm just…I just want to help Bo…your father."

"Oh, and you're welcome to do so," she chided, hopping up and shaking her head vigorously from side-to-side as if clearing a buildup of cobwebs, "That is, once you remove the lone obstacle blockin' your way."

Swallowing hard, Brad only then noticed the two had scuffled their way to the left of the light escaping the open barn door, thus leaving the structure's interior and the captive Boone temporarily out of sight.

"L-Listen, I'm telling you for…the last time," he huffed, eyes still adjusting to the lack of light while scanning the immediate area for a possible weapon, "…I'm not…go-gonna fight you. I just…want to help my fri…Boone."

The woman's casual shrug and equally nonchalant reply did little to ease tensions.

"Duly noted, and I'm tellin' you for the last time, Sport, that for you to accomplish said goal, this here girl is gonna have to be flat on her back and toes up."

As he stood a good dozen feet or nearer to the barn entrance and thus the discarded axe, Brad took off in a wild sprint, arms and legs pumping with surprising precision despite a palpable stiffness plaguing each.

Twisting past the open door's squared edge and a mere step away from the threshold, he felt a sharp stinging at both shins as his legs folded inward, instinctively raising both forearms face-level to prep for impact with the hard clay floor.

He could hear the woman's guttural growls while tumbling forward, rolling at least semi-gracefully onto his haunches and twisting around just as she dived at him with arms outstretched.

They impacted in midair, Brad leading with his head and shoulders like a human battering ram with Gwen catching the full impact as her arms provided little in the way of defense, a resounding crunch and muffled groan proceeding the two bodies sailing away in opposite directions.

In the aftermath, Brad lay on his left side with the palms of both hands cradling the multitude of wounds at his forehead and scalp, each splayed finger receiving a fresh coating of draining life source.

Peering over through a squinty, bleary gaze, he could make out Gwen's gradual belly-crawl over the entrance threshold and didn't have to guess her immediate intention was frighteningly similar to his earlier plan.

She was going for either the bone knife or axe. Either way, he figured he had roughly ten seconds or less to interrupt said mission or die.

Never in his relatively short lifespan had he felt a stronger motivation, battered skull and rubbery limbs be damned.

Once upright and following an initial stumble back into a creaking barn wall, it took less than three full strides before he fell to his knees, somehow managing to acquire the steeliest grip he could muster while dragging the squirming, kicking, screeching opposition along by her ankles.

Using both his substantial weight advantage and what remained of a rapidly dwindling energy supply, Brad dragged Gwen a dozen feet outside the entrance and, with a final thrust in the opposite direction, darted forward in a wobbly gait.

The hand that grasped his left ankle clutched and constricted like five separate vices, his forward momentum sending him toppling onto his chest to bang his bloodied forehead onto the dusty terrain. Desperate not to find himself pinned to the ground in a similar fashion as minutes earlier, realizing there was little chance of escaping a second time, Brad first rolled to his right before rising clumsily to his feet and staggering a dozen feet or more in the same direction, where a knee-high stack of chopped wood served as both blockade and brace.

He paused only long enough to scoop the smallest log possible off the top row and, gripping it by its narrow base, cocked the two-foot by six-inch chunk of oak over his right shoulder while simultaneously turning in expectation of impending attack.

The woman was gone. Boots wide apart and dug in, Brad's head thrust about as if on a swivel, first left then right and, crouching slightly, scanning the vast, grassy field at his back for any hint of a moving shadow.

No sign nor sound. Sighing heavily and thankful for the brief respite, he could only deduce Gwen scrambled back into the barn as he'd completed his frantic roll toward the wood pile.

"Shit...*Boone*," he whispered, taking off in a limping sprint for the entrance while taking delayed notice of a litany of updated aches and pains, to include a throbbing left knee and rapidly stiffening left shoulder.

The probability that he was rushing, battered, bruised and bleeding directly into a trap wasn't at all lost. In fact, as he departed the darkness for light, booted feet thumping like an approaching pachyderm toward the wide opening, Brad's recently extracted inner warrior openly relished the possibility.

Boone lay on his side, facing the barn's murky interior, still attached to the overturned chair and weakly struggling with his binds. His free hand rested on an object mostly hidden by his bulk. An object Brad wasn't able to properly identify though something about it appeared strangely familiar.

Crouching low with the log still cocked, he drew to within a dozen or so feet from his friend when a sudden, sharp pain pierced his opposite shoulder. Dropping to his left knee, already barking from previous spills, he continued to scoot toward Boone, who was visibly fighting the cable tie binding his right hand.

"Boone, j-just hang on, I'm…I'll…what t-the hell?" Brad whispered harshly, halting in mid-lunge upon spotting the jagged handle and, fortunately, the *majority* of the bone knife's blade still protruding from his upper left shoulder.

He never heard Gwen approaching cat-like from his left, tiptoeing in her bare feet from the gloomy confines of the nearest stable.

First extracting the log from his grasp with a perfectly placed front kick, she then spun airborne and pulled the knife from his shoulder, landing with ballerina grace on his opposite side as he was swatting at nothing at air from the opposite side.

"Gotta say, I am impressed," she exclaimed breathlessly, having retrieved the jagged log and flipped it over a shoulder into the darkness beyond, the bone knife being flipped casually from hand to hand yet again, "You had ample chance to shag ass to potential freedom. With any luck at all, you'd be toolin' down the road in that sweet ride with only a few unsightly bruises and cuts to speak of. Though it's a trait I've never been known to possess, I do admire those who can show such unyielding loyalty."

As he staggered up to pose flatfooted with but one useful arm remaining in a woefully limited arsenal, Brad felt a warm stickiness trail his left side, the puncture wound itself taking point as most painful in a myriad of contenders.

"Unlike most, as you sail tranquilly down the River Styx, you can honestly boast to the boatman that you went down honorably," she concluded. Using a bare heel to kick up trails of dust and dirt like an enraged bull readying a charge, the bone knife held low at her left side.

Brad could hear Boone's desperate groans grow increasingly fervent but wasn't allowed even a passing glance his way as the man's hopelessly psychotic offspring flung herself forward, a vicious leg-sweep sending him flailing onto his back with teeth-gnashing force.

Sucking for air with no tangible success, Brad discovered his energy meter woefully pegged. He blinked madly to remove the assorted floaters from each tearing eye, a narrow tunnel of vision clearing just in time to see Gwen straddling overhead, the bone knife posed to strike.

Strangely, and so unlike the gloating, goading dialogue she'd spouted since intros, her stoic, haunted expression bore no such cockiness, no satisfaction in impending victory. If anything, she appeared weary, *disillusioned.*

"Credit where credit is due, kid. You were a helluva scrapper," she uttered despondently, lowering herself until both knees propped gently atop his heaving chest, "Wish I could say you were dyin' for a good cause, but lyin' to ya now just don't seem ri…"

His entire frame abruptly jarred as if from a powerful impact, Brad's funneled gaze was temporarily lost to an onslaught of abrupt blackness as warm liquid of unknown origin rained down in a virtual Falls to spatter his eyes, face, neck and scalp.

Bootheels pushing frantically into the hard clay surface, Brad scrambled from underneath a great weight that fell away as if hoisted airborne from his squirming frame. At the time of the drenching, a coppery stench all-engulfing in the aftermath, he'd heard three distinct sounds. A muffled thump, akin to a sack of potatoes striking a hard surface followed by a deep, drawn-out sigh and finally a single, gut-wrenching sob.

Though mysteries abounded, he was hapless to their origins until, upon wiping his eyes with a jacket sleeve and blinking madly until his vision cleared at least somewhat, Brad's bloodshot, squinty stare locked on all the required clues.

Father and daughter lay huddled together, the latter cradled in the arms of the former, an axe handle protruding from the left side of her neck and shoulder like some recently hatched extra appendage. Blood gushed from the massive wound to soak Boone's shirt and vest. One side of the double-edged blade completely submerged through Gwen's shoulder into her upper chest.

"You...can finally rest...easy, Ginger-bear," he cooed, his face dotted with nickel and dime-sized spatters, the handle-end of the axe resting just past his left ear.

The fatally wounded woman peered up, glassy-eyed, her lips wriggling. Her mouth opening and closing sporadically. Brad felt a surge of hot bile rise to the back of his throat and forced himself to look away, where his eyes locked on the overturned chair. He blinked several times, widening his still-bleary eyes in case what he was seeing was indeed real. Satisfied it wasn't just some trauma-related hallucination, he shifted focus back to Boone, who was leaning in to apply a gentle kiss to his offspring's sweat and blood-coated forehead.

"B-Boone, your...h-hand," Brad sputtered, pointing with a shaking index finger toward the older man's right arm, currently tucked behind his dying daughter's back to hook beneath her armpit. The jagged stump, though openly seeping, wasn't extracting nearly the volcanic output one would expect, especially when compared to the woman's massive amount of leakage.

The older man's severed hand remained cable-tied to the chair's arm, chopped neatly just above the wrist. Brad suddenly realized the object Boone had been blocking while struggling to escape his final bond. The same proposed weapon he had so neatly tossed away when directed to do so. The same implement now buried to the hilt upon carving a V-shaped chasm into the shoulder and torso of their erstwhile assassin.

Removing his jacket, Brad tossed it aside, the signal-less cell going along for the ride, and, locating the bone knife lying a few feet to his right, began sawing the seam of his right shirt sleeve, his left saturated to the elbow in his own leakage, to use for strips, his thoughts already turning to finding a workable splint to complete a tourniquet for the older man's mutilated arm.

"Boone, we have...we need to tie...get some pressure on that..." he rambled, ripping frantically at the shirt. "You're losing too much...for god's sake, Boone, we...I gotta wrap that forearm."

The old man smiled morosely, his tear-filled eyes never leaving those of his daughter, whose subtle convulsions grew fiercer, the torrent from her neck and shoulder subsiding to that of a steady ooze, much like the jagged stump which caressed her.

"Bradley...please...s-stop.

"Admirable...and...a-appreciated...b-but far...from...realistic."

Even as the pair grew equally pale, Brad felt the anxiety that threatened to overpower him melt away to a reluctant acceptance, falling to one knee as if to participate in group prayer.

Gwen managed to reach up and, with groping fingers, gently caress her dying shire's cheek.

"It's...all...right now, sweet g-girl. N-not your...f-fault. A-any of it. Finally, t-time to...r-rest. Time to...sleep," Boone stammered in-between quiet sobs.

The same hand, which so softly touched his ghostly pale flesh, shot upwards with renewed vigor to snatch a handful of hair and jerk viciously downward, it's possessor's expression a scowling mask of rage. A wounded, expiring animal striking out for final vengeance.

"Y-y-you...c-c-come...bu-burn in...he-hell w-where...you...belong..." she snarled, a wet gasp accompanied by either the occasional spray or waded glut of crimson leakage, "...r-right there with...g-g-granddaddy...and m-me. W-We all...d-de-deserve to...b-boil in...the sa-same...st-steamin' p-p-pot."

Her father, perhaps instinctively and understandably unable to verbally console, hugged his only born ever tighter to his blood-soaked bosom, an act that inadvertently served to pry the axe blade from its semi-sealed state and initiate a final, fatal arterial spray from the pulsating wound.

Gwen Harrison passed with a feeble, warbling sob, having donned a permanent mask of insanity. Wide-eyed, though the left's lid would gradually lower over the whitish orb, and teeth bared in a fit of loathsome, predatory madness.

"Oh m-my poor...Ginger-b-bear," Boone whimpered, gently kissing her exposed forehead and leaving a bloody lip-print in the aftermath, "G-god s-surely…understands and will…surely grant…mercy on your c-cursed soul."

Head spinning with a toxic mix of confusion and shock, Brad fell to one knee while maintaining an arm's length distance between father and daughter, one dead and the other on the very cusp of following suit. As if a weak, tattered mind equaled easier accessibility for telepathic trappings, Boone turned to him and answered a query he'd formulated mentally but had yet to ask.

"M-my briefcase…b-back at the…hotel w-will answer y-your…many questions. I…left a…folded note with the combo in my…jacket pocket. There is…a…ca-cassette tape…I recorded ju-just y-yesterday f-for you…your ears o-only. Everything…you'll need to…make sense of…this t-tragic mess you…witnessed this…n-night."

In shocked awe at the amount of blood pooling at the pair's splayed legs, Brad thought of asking if the farmhouse possessed a working landline but quickly dismissed such folly and instead reluctantly switched gears to an infinitely grislier subject than rescue. As much as he loathed himself in the moment, he also realized the subject had to be broached before it was too late.

"Boone, if…you don't make it, w-what…do you want me to do? The police are gonna…I mean, those…the bodies," he paused, gesturing with a protracted nod towards the motionless shapes sheltered beneath a blood-drenched tarp.

The old man's demoralized expression gave little in the way of clues.

"Honestly, it's like…walking in on a movie in the last ten minutes of runtime. I…just please…tell me what to say. Should I…give them your…the tapes?"

Boone shook his head so vehemently it threw a light, reddish mist from his matted coif, laid flat by his daughter's blood-drenched death-grip just moments earlier.

"No, no god…*no*. Brad, I know…I've asked so…much of you already. I have…but one last…request, and p-please, by all that's holy, understand that….as insane as it…sounds, it is truly the…only l-logical…option."

Though Brad's initial disapproval and adamant, flat-out refusal to participate in the older man's plan was as passionate as it was decisive, deep-down he realized almost immediately the fruitlessness of his argument.

How could one deny a dying man's last request? A dying man holding the daughter he had been forced to kill in order to save the life of man he'd known less than four full days. More-over and perhaps more importantly, how was Brad to explain his participation in an inexplicable bloodbath, the origins of which he couldn't even begin to contemplate? As cruel and inhuman as Boone's suggestion appeared on the surface, the way he'd explained it, with such banality and aplomb, it wasn't a huge leap from loony to logical.

Before attempting a virtual scavenger hunt of the farm grounds for the required item needed to implement the plan, he spent several minutes designing a makeshift tourniquet and securing it to Boone's stump. Oddly, the older man no longer seemed able to register pain, as even as Brad applied enough torque to cut off all circulation to the open wound, Boone showed no signs of discomfort, instead using his remaining hand to gently stroke his deceased daughter's forehead.

As it turned out, a five-gallon gas can, perhaps three-quarters full, was located at the rear of the barn near a vintage Massey-Ferguson tractor, the equally retro oil lantern providing Brad the required light pegged for double-duty as the night would conclude.

"M-make sure you...saturate...some of the h-hay...bales so...it goes up...but g-good," Boone suggested for at least the third time, the older man's eyes growing increasingly glassier, his movements all-but-ceased save a trembling lower lip and the occasional leg spasm, his once-grayish facial hair now soaked a reddish/black hue.

"It's...it's done, Boone," Brad replied, feeling the need to shout his responses as if addressing the deaf, "I soaked the perimeter but still have enough left..." he paused, looking away as his chest hitched and forced to swallow hard and cough several times into a bare palm before proceeding, "...to finish the job."

As so many times since their initial intro four days previous, the older man seemed to read his thoughts.

"Ronnie was...a distant k-kin. His poor wife just...ca-caught in...t-the crossfire. Th-they w-were...chi-childless...thank g-god. G-good people...as far as I...knew.

"You...you'll understand more...once you h-hear the tape. W-wish I had th-the...time left to... 'plain it...face to f-face, but I don't wanna...p-pass halfway...t-through with y-you ...thinking m-me...cr-crazy as a be-bedbug."

With that, the older man reached out with a trembling hand, groping for and, with aid, finding the young man's, squeezing gently as the two briefly locked eyes, the former somehow reading the desperation in the latter's pained expression.

"Be...a-at peace, son. You're...not kill-killing...a-anyone. You're just...cremating...four spent...h-husks."

The man Brad knew as Boone Harrison expired soon after, his eyelids descending in minute segments and fingers going limp as a final gasp pushed through pursed, blood-smeared lips. The time of his passing, according to Brad's Omega watch, was one-sixteen AM.

By a quarter of two, the hardest of the prepping had been completed. This included the grisly task of removing the axe from Gwen's stiffening corpse, the rapidity of which was not nearly as baffling as that of her father's rapid hardening, as if each had passed days and not merely hours earlier.

Having retrieved and scattered several unfurled bales of hay around and atop not only their bodies but the dead homesteaders as well, Brad used the last of the fuel to saturate their respective husks. Though he pondered the faint possibility of enough DNA surviving to not only properly ID the bodies but his presence as well, he recalled Boone's adamant assurance that neither he nor Gwen would leave behind a match, from teeth or otherwise, for authorities to do so. How this could possibly be, considering some of the wilder allegations he'd overheard, would have to remain a mystery until he was able to listen to the mystery tape Boone had left behind. A tape that was never far from his mind, even as he stood on the outskirts of the property and watched the barn glimmer a bright yellow and eventually implode onto itself. As desolate the location, PS EarthLink had previously shown the homestead as the lone such structure for four-plus miles in either direction, he'd felt little apprehension while standing calmly by to witness the archaic barn's near-complete annihilation.

He drove from the property at precisely two-seventeen AM, the faint glow reflected in his rearview mirror shrinking to a firefly's glow as he'd steered the Charger onto the state highway leading back to Baymont. Minutes later, while reaching over to power on the stereo, an instinctive, almost mechanical act of habit, he discovered one of Boone's hand-picked CDs had been left inserted to override the XM station, the current selection so ironically fitting he actually laughed out loud. That is, until the laugh gradually disintegrated into a wrenching sob that forced him onto the nearest shoulder, least he steered the weaving vehicle into the nearest ravine or grill-first into one of the many oaks or elms lining the roadway. Hunched over in the driver's seat, warm tears trailing both cheeks and unable to control the steady convulsing of his upper body, hands clenched tightly in his lap, his thoughts grew as black as the night. Thoughts of his wrecked marriage and the pathetic road-trip into self-loathing that brought him to the very spot in the road to nowhere he currently cruised. Thoughts of the older man he so naturally befriended in a few short days and whose life he'd witnessed come to such a tragic end. Thoughts of the man's psychotic offspring and the many unexplained mysteries leading up to her equally appalling demise by such shocking means. All circling back to thoughts of the loveless dead-end he was so willing to follow to its inevitably painful conclusion.

All this as Boston's classic '*Don't Look Back*' filled his ears with a message of hope, of renewal, of a happier existence if only one had the guts to execute the needed about-face. As well-worn cliches went, that old nugget about being handed a second chance couldn't have been more apt.

It wasn't until approximately midway through the CD's next offering, Sammy Hagar's rib-throbbing rocker '*Heavy Metal*' that the spell abated to the point where, regaining a measure of composure, he could at least successfully steer consistently between the road's badly faded lines.

In the thirty-plus minutes to reach the motel, minus a quick stop at Baymont's lone all-night pharmacy for bandages, hydrogen peroxide and band-aids for the raw wound across his forehead and still-seeping gash at his left shoulder, Bradley Kane did some serious mulling, covering assorted subjects praying on his tattered mind, but one in particular that demanded an immediate decision.

At just past three AM, and upon retrieving both he and Boone's meager belongings, he dropped the key in the palm of an understandably drowsy desk clerk, his haphazardly bandaged forehead barely raising a brow, and pulled from a mostly empty lot. Deserted two-lane gave way to equally desolate four-lane highway at just past three-thirty, which gave way to an only sporadically populated interstate at just past four.

Eyes swollen, bloodshot and feeling as if coated in grit, Brad booked a room at a Holiday Inn Express just outside of Memphis as dawn broke over the East Tennessee horizon. With any luck, he figured to be crossing the border of the southernmost Dakota in less than thirty-six hours. In the meantime, there was the little matter of a mysterious briefcase and an equally cryptic tape contained within.

~ * ~

Sleep-deprived and bombarded with assorted body aches, and despite his third coffee in the past hour, Brad desired nothing more than an all-day coma but was simply not going to be able to nod off. In the forty-five minutes since checking in, the young hotel clerk's darting eyes sporadically landing on the bloody head bandage, Brad's similarly drenched left shirtsleeve wisely cloaked by his jacket, he'd showered, brushed his teeth and pretended he could delay the inevitable, even briefly debating making an anonymous call to the authorities, but to say what exactly? With DNA technology being what it is, such a knee-jerk, reckless decision might possibly lead to incriminating himself in not only the murders of the farm couple, but the deaths of Boone and Gwen as well. If so, how could he possibly explain what he knew? How can one fill in blanks to questions they have no conceivable answer for?

In the end, wounds duly washed, medicated and neatly rebandaged and while leaning gingerly against the headboard of a single Queen bed with the provided flatscreen powered up but muted in the foreground, Brad balanced the briefcase onto his bare abdomen and, locating the tiny rolling lock, entered the three-digit combination Boone provided.

Removing the recorder and mini cassettes, he then extracted a yellow file jacket and finally what appeared to be a leather photo album with Navy-blue covering and a ringed spine, lining up the trio of objects so all were within easy reaching distance. Within the file jacket would later be found a gold key ring housing presumably Boone's apartment key and that of his beloved Jeep Cherokee.

Checking the recorder, he found the tape pre-rewound and ready to play. Having briefly removed the tape, he'd noted the message *'BK's ears only'* scribbled along one of its narrow white strips. Adjusting the pillows at his back and neck, his assorted ills temporarily forgotten, Brad felt an electric tingling at his still-damp scalp. Extracting a nervous sigh, he pressed play.

~ * ~

"I'm taping this as you've gone out for food and a sight-seeing venture of all that the township of Baymont has to offer. Hoping you take your time at least long enough for me to finish this up, otherwise there are likely to be some fairly sizable plot holes that may never be filled. Also hoping these damnable meds keep me upright and energetic enough to do the deed.

First off…"

Clears throat, coughs.

"…my name isn't really Boone Harrison, but one intimately more familiar to you. Boone was my father's given name. I am…would've been Dalton Caleb Harrison. More later on why I chose and have chosen on several occasions throughout the years to confiscate an alternate identity. As for the Boone moniker, I decided years back that my final alias would include the family monarch. More on that as we proceed."

Clears throat.

"Secondly, and this is most vital, Bradley. I want…need you to take my word that I am not delusional, crazy, cracked, touched, disturbed nor insane."

Laughs.

"I can, unfortunately, just about guarantee the following claims will surely make it sound as if I am all of the above. This leads to point number three, though truth-be-told, it's more of a request. Thirdly, you'll be apt to ponder how my recollection of past events sounded so…clear and detailed. I can only chalk it up to possessing what has been described as a photographic memory, only one of several family traits and, well, by far the *least* problematic.

"I would ask that as you listen to this recording, please follow along with whatever verbal instructions I provide in displaying certain items from both the jacket file and photo album. Both will hopefully assist you in comprehending whatever subject I'm covering at any given moment.

"That said, please reach into the file jacket and stack the contents for easy access. The first article of papers will be tainted yellow from age and measure approximately five by seven."

Brad did as instructed, retrieving a thin stack of papers, all but the page Boone has alluded to as standard-sized

"Now, please study the article I just spoke of. Careful it doesn't crumble into yellow-tinted ash between your fingers."

Laughs.

"Notice if you will the full name, date-of-birth listed, as well as the sections listing both father and mother of child. Take a few moments, please. I can imagine it's a lot to take in.

Dalton, of course, represents myself, Boone and Carolyn Harrison the parents. They homesteaded just as Duluth was starting to incorporate. Take note of the Territory of Minnesota heading on the form, as it was still four years short of being officially added as the thirty-second US state. The daughter I spoke of and that I came to reunite with this night is Gwen. She was the product of my second marriage, that to the former Barbara-Jean Wilkes."

Pauses.

"God, but I loved Barb like no other, rest in peace all their lovely souls. Perhaps she was that mythical being scholars used to refer to as a soulmate. If only she could've…stayed faithful."

Sighs.

"S-sorry, train of thought got severely derailed there for a tick. I know, understand it would be unnatural not to be skeptical, Brad. You didn't know me near long enough to take any of this at face value. To buy what I'm selling without serious doubt would be as foolhardy as it is woefully naïve. I now ask that you now retrieve the photo album and flip to its opening sheet. If needed, take a few deep breaths. Search out a libation of your choice."

Laughs.

"Smoke 'em if you got 'em. Believe me, the ride is only gonna get further and further out there as we proceed forth.

"Now, that first grainy black and white shot is, as far as I know, the only such captured image of us as a family, taken while we were attending a traveling carny show just outside St Cloud. I seem to recall Ma insisted Pa invest, his mild protests about the cost to no avail. You'll find a date scribbled on the back. I just ask that you be extra careful if you do remove any of the snapshots from their sleeves, as they are apt to be extremely brittle.

"The next paper in the stack is a signed and duly stamped employee agreement between myself and a company that might ring a bell. Attached to the agreement is a folded piece of newspaper. Above the article is a photo. You can make your own connection without my spelling it out. I'll give you a minute before I proceed further."

Pauses.

"Brad, I do so apologize for not coming clean, as they say, from the beginning, but surely you can understand my predicament. Honestly, if I divulged the truth at any point during our trip, would you not have deserted me at the first opportunity? Maybe even kick me to the side of the road, briefcase in hand? Whatever happened at that farmhouse with Gwen…"

Pauses.

"…if I…passed without telling you the truth, it's more likely due to my fading health or perhaps how…quickly I perished. This is why I feigned, at least to a point, severe fatigue once we arrived here. I ha…needed to record this to prevent leaving you permanently perplexed as to what just the hell this has all been about. Now back to the newspaper article you are likely eye-balling this very moment..."

~ * ~

Approximately halfway to Kansas City, a light snow began to fall, melting harmlessly upon impacting the Charger's well-heated windshield. Navigating mostly light traffic, save the usual brigade of scattered semi's, Brad steered and accelerated on autopilot, both mentally and figuratively. His mind focused solely on the previous night's discoveries, the Charger's engine minding the directives of its cruise-control setting.

A short ten hours earlier there had still existed doubts, despite a mountain of tangible evidentiary proof to the contrary, as if the whole fantastic thing was somehow fraudulent, a meticulously plotted, well-staged practical joke or the cruelest of scams. These doubts, however, grew increasingly fainter once he rewound the tape, and, having restacked and stored the accompanying documents, photos and newspaper articles, reassigned himself to another round. Upon waking earlier than anticipated, he had not slept until dawn and only fitfully thereafter, despite ingesting a threesome of extra-stout Motrin, he'd sipped his mid-morning coffee while giving them a third go-round. He then departed for KC at just past one PM amid dark, foreboding clouds and temperatures just above freezing.

Without a doubt, the bruised, tattered, droopy-eyed but weirdly rejuvenated man was a starkly different individual who traversed the same roadway from the other direction a mere two days previous. A new man, a true *believer*, no longer weighed down by the blackness of yesterdays. A man with a fresh perspective who now, more than ever before, understood the value of time and the importance of making the most of just how little one is allowed in this lifetime.

Three and a half days later, a mini-U-Haul fully packed and secured to the rear of the Charger, he made a final stop at a Turtle Bend post office. The medium-sized package was bound for Chandler, Arizona with no return address provided. Though he briefly trifled with the idea of delivering the package in person, he eventually decided the receiver might find such personalized service infinitely more suspicious than a random mailing.

Though he kept the majority of his promises as far as inheriting Boone's possessions, the classic book, sports-cards and music collections packed safely and snugly into the U-Haul, the keys to the Jeep he'd tossed into the package, along with the secret pin and password to a safe-deposit box containing just over fifty-thousand dollars in cash, sans the twenty thousand he'd kept for the promised transportation fee.

His own possessions duly garnered and the apartment lease legally axed upon paying a small fine, he departed Turtle Bend with a palpable sense of relief. Though he could only imagine what disbelief, fear and despair the anonymous mailing might birth, he also understood his late patron's reasoning. From the senior Harrison's perspective, it wasn't meant as a warning to invoke fright or panic, but an audio manual of survival to what *might* come.

With no definite plan, Bradley Kane would drive east, northeast to be exact, avoiding the Mason-Dixon line at all costs, to start anew, for as his most recent employer advised through vast experience, it was never too late for a new beginning.

Epilogue

By the light of the Arizona moon, with assistance from a nearby campfire, he read the hand-scribbled note yet again. Delivered the day before to his PO box, he had figured it the latest client request, albeit tucked within a thicker package than usual. It wasn't as if the PO box, opened and maintained with strict confidentiality, received unsolicited mail or the like.

The tiny recorder tucked within one of his hunting vest's many pockets, he'd listened while laying back on his sleeping bag and staring into a cloudless sky, a crisp breeze aligning the fire's yellowish flames perfectly to properly the illuminate the pages on display.

Lending an ear to the recording for a second time, he found himself paying closer attention to minute detail and, more specifically, the timeline given. Every few minutes he would peer over at whatever photo or article he'd been perusing to study the dark tree line to the north of his chosen campsite. Not that he expected any unannounced guests of the human variety, the desired residence a good mile and a half further down the sloped valley, but as a decade-plus of experience had born out, it never paid to grow too comfortable.

At just past one AM, he removed the tiny buds from each ear and, rising for a quick stretch, kneeled next to the fire and stoked same with a thick branch, the popping and sizzling noises strangely calming. Never considering himself the outdoorsy type, he nonetheless appreciated the rare opportunities that did arise to reacquaint with nature.

Back atop the sleeping bag, he laid back with gloved hands tucked behind his head, the splayed fingers all but obliterated by a thick brown mane that flowed onto hunched shoulders.

Could all or *any* part possibly be true? He mused, a thin smile painted across his deceptively youthful, clean-shaven mug, a mug flawless save a single, pencil-thin scar running a straight swath up his left cheekbone to just under a gray-shaded eye.

After all, wasn't it true he was often confused as being high school or college age? Wasn't he often carded at bars and liquor stores? With birthday number thirty-six just months away and already on marriage number two, you would think the natural aging process would be accelerated and not the opposite, especially considering the stress associated with his chosen profession. On the upside, his youthful look had many times helped him gain the advantage, though the nickname utilized by his peers, '*Babyface*'. did serve to rile at times.

Back to the contents of the mystery folder, he had less difficulty buying the timeline, the photos, licenses and assorted newspaper articles appeared genuine enough and a few simple google searches would serve to verify the latter, than the whole family curse angle. Sounded a little too X-file-ish and in his business, there was no room for anything outside the realm of reality. What you saw was what you got. There was no magic, *black* or otherwise, that could alter real world events; past, present or future. That officially dismissed, there was no denying the bizarre implications. By any measure, logical or otherwise, it *was* damn strange.

Being the analytical type by nature, he was a numbers guy. A stats guy, a facts guy. Black and white with nary a shade of gray to muss up the works.

In this case, facts appeared to be just that. Fact *one*: The more recent photos, digital in origin, he surmised by their slick, textured appearance, without a doubt matched those of the individual featured in the newspaper articles. Of course, there were variations; hair styles, facial hair, etc., but it was without a doubt the same man. Body shape, size, right down to the squareness of the shoulders and the slumping of same. Not a brother, not a grandfather or great grandfather. The *same* person. Identical within each and every physical characteristic. He knew this without conjecture, as facial recognition was, after all, vital in his line of work. How to explain? A train massacre in 1896; a hippie-cult radio-station bombing in 1969? An East coast island bloodbath in 2004? Last but definitely not least, to meet one's demise mere days ago at the hands of his own child? A child, now also deceased, but first birthed, by rough estimation, around the turn of the twentieth century. A child that would've been what? A...great *aunt*? It was enough to raise the hackles of even the most jaded of critics.

Additionally, there were the assorted forms of identification, from employer/employee agreements to driver's licenses to state ID's, the Texas Department of Corrections, to the military variety, an Army buck private, according to the heavily laminated card in one and a Senior Airman, USAF in still another, and of course, the holy grail of alleged evidence, a barely readable birth certificate from the state of Minnesota. Though names varied wildly from each document. Jason Markum, Barton Stevens, Peter Willingham, Dalton Harris and of course the Dalton Caleb Harrison moniker claimed on the holy grail document, all shared one undisputable trait. The style of handwriting of whatever signature was provided.

Logically speaking, other than the mythical time-machine, there was but one explanation. The claimant was straight up telling the truth. Stating facts as he knew them, regardless of the implausibility.

As for dear old granddad, he couldn't help but secretly scoff at the mere notion of said elder being born the year that spawned the beginning of the American civil war, the shirtless pics, front and back poses, several zoomed-in and others including facial recognition and dated a mere two weeks previous, were obviously meant to seal the deal as far as authenticity of the claims went.

As for family resemblance, he had to admit 'Grandpa' and his own father did share more than a few similarities, the most glaring being the same pointy nose and prominent, when sporting a haircut that allowed full visibility, ears. This would, of course, require further inspection, as comparable pics were few and far-between when it came to the late, less-than-great old man. As to this latest, supposed elder's weird, wild claims, there was the here and now.

Thus, flipping back through the newspaper articles and various wounds mentioned, it all seemed kosher to the many scars the pictures so clearly and meticulously displayed:

Natrona County Times, dated Feb 11th, the year of our lord 1896
Headline: '*Big Horn Train Massacre yields but a single survivor*'
Wounds mentioned: Upper right shoulder/back (bullet wound)

Miami Herald, dated 18 May, the year of our lord 1969

Headline: '*West Coast Drug Cult tied to fatal radio station bombing*'

Wounds mentioned: Numerous back burns/scarring in undisclosed area

Charleston Courier, dated April 21st, the year of our lord 2004

Headline: '*Island Murders tied to New Jersey Syndicate*'

Wounds mentioned: Left-side rib cage (bullet wound)

The photos provided, ten all told, in bright, crystal-clear color, verified all listed wounds, the burn marks especially telling, as was the upper-back exit wound. Of course, photoshop in the right hands? Who's to say they weren't just masterful frauds? This would beg the *sixty-four-thousand-dollar* query, that being why the hell bother with such an elaborate ruse? Additionally, what the hell was up with the obviously aged Jeep key and hand-written address containing both the vehicle's whereabouts and an undisclosed stack of cash?

Tucking both the photos and articles back into the provided folder, he lay motionless for a full half-hour, peering blankly upward into the starlit sky before giving the recording one more listen, specifically the last few minutes, which served as a personal warning of sorts. Fast-forwarding to this segment, he thought there was something inherently sincere in the older man's voice, an honesty that, unless originating from a master thespian, was virtually impossible to dismiss as anything but heartfelt:

"...*asking you to accept all this on face value alone. I suppose this is why I maintained the articles, identification papers and so on for all those decades. I know what you're probably thinking. No judging here. I'd be of the same skepticism if I were in your position. Since I've apologized numerous times for being an absentee elder, I hope you can understand why I didn't dare get too close. Talk about crazy ol' grandpa, I would've surely played the part to perfection. Needless to say, I kept up with you as best I could through the deca...years. Anyway, long story shortened, I only ask for the benefit of the doubt.*

"*The so-called bane of the Harrison's, I flat refuse to use the 'c' word...*"

Laughs.

"...has, at least to this point, provided a hard argument in favor of tangibility, of legitimacy. I balked for decades, but there is no denying the...some truth to Gwen...your aunt's claims. There is the obvious, almost supernatural longevity of the bloodline and, as much as I despise admitting it, the unnatural bloodlust seemingly engrained within us all. My daughter, my son..."

Clears throat.

"... that is, your father. As for myself, there is a history as well, just, executed in a more...legal fashion, brought on by circumstance alone. I had not one but two wars to sate my urge, as well as those well-documented tragedies that somehow befall me every fifth decade or so. Bad luck or fate? You can't know how I've contemplated. No clear answers, I'm afraid.

"As for Gwen and Dennis, they...well, succumbed to the urges under less...civilized circumstances, openly searching out the darkness and finding, well, I can only guess an uneasy solace in its evil, ebony embrace. Sounds dramatic I know, but I truly can't say what drove them to be...what they became.

"I can say, or at least repeat what is supposedly behind our family situation. That isn't to say I necessarily believe a single word of it or the speculative mythology behind it. Take it or leave it. Label it impure shlock or pure, shimmering gold. I'll leave that to you, but here she is:

"The story goes that my grandfather, I guess that would be your great grandpappy, if you're bothering to keep score, Thomas Dale Harrison by name, was struggling mightily to make ends meet as a blacksmith in the Dakota territory of the mid-eighteen hundreds. Along with a ragtag gang of similarly strapped farmers and assorted malcontents, he decided to make a drastic move toward financial stability, via a highly chancy, damn dangerous, totally illegal venture.

"They called themselves Barrett's Raiders, named after Chauncy Barrett, their unofficial leader, former cattle-thief, rapist, and gun-for-hire. To hold down a slot within the Raider's ranks didn't take an overabundance of brains, just a ruthless streak of meanness and the willingness to put aside all existing morals in the name of financial gain at any cost. Allegedly it took some doing, but Thomas D. Harrison found

he could fake it well enough on both counts, what with a dispirited wife and two hungry ankle-biters in tow.

"As for what the Raider's specialized in, well, their name says it all. With a good portion of the southeast left in disarray from past battles, it wasn't difficult to seek out townships ripe for raiding, considering the many remote villages below the Mason-Dixon, many of which were left either totally unguarded and without proper law enforcement or abandoned, save the women folk and their kids. The War Between the States hadn't been kind to such places, thus it was easy enough for Barrett's bandits to sweep in to pick the exposed bones clean."

Sighs.

"In a few short months they'd covered a good portion of Kentucky and Tennessee with a head count of nearly forty men. Story goes that along that long, winding path, they'd robbed, raped, burned and pilfered their way into a sizable fortune in gold and silver jewels, all the while killing anyone who even put up the mildest argument, be it town elders, women or sprites.

"Story also goes that Chauncy Barrett commenced to savor the killing part over all else, even going as far as burning down a Tennessee plantation house with an entire family barricaded inside. Three generations burnt to a cinder as he circled the mansion on his demon-steed, firing random shots into the smoke-filled night like some power-mad demigod. Word has it many within his rank grew to fancy it as well, to the point where they were no longer as taken with thieving as they were terminating with extreme prejudice and relish.

"Now, question is, as far as our family linage is concerned, was Thomas Harrison counted among 'em and if so, had he too succumbed to such brutal, uncivilized madness? No clear answer on that second query, I'm afraid, though he was still among their ranks when they crossed over into Alabama, the spring of '64. By that time, many others, about half the original number, abandoned the concept, departing for greener climes once the raping and thrill-killing established priority.

"So, it's told just as they'd prepared to camp for the night on the outskirts of Huntsville that one of their advanced scouts had run upon plantation land complete with a three-story antebellum and surrounding

slave-quarters. At first thought abandoned, Barrett and the boys soon discovered otherwise in the form of a family of three housed inside one of the many available bedrooms. Seems a rather large clan owned and resided on the property. All but one remaining couple having fled since the surrounding area became a battle hotspot between warring Reb's and Yank's. Well, it goes without saying that their decision to babysit the homestead was one the couple wouldn't live very long to regret.

"The husband, all of twenty-one and armed with nothing but a measly Kentucky musket rifle, was beaten to a bloody pulp before being strung up from an oak limb on the rear of the property. His young wife wasn't treated nearly as charitable. She was raped by at least a half-dozen Raiders before a head shot put her out of what must've been considerable misery. Worst of all, it's reputed Barrett himself cut the throat of the couple's six-year-old son, though only after making the child watch his ma being put down like a crippled filly. Now, all that brutality allegedly had its fervent opposers, one of 'em being your great grandpa, who not only refused to engage in any way but even pled for the young woman's life, receiving a fairly substantial beating for his efforts. As the tale goes, Chauncy Barrett had to be talked out of adding Thomas Harrison to that night's casualty list. If so, a narrow escape for both yours truly and yourself.

"All right..."

Sighs, clears throat.

"...here's where the Harrison family tree supposedly had its future roots permanently soiled. As with all within our bloodline privy to the following speculation, it's up to the individual as to its legitimacy. As dawn birthed on that ill-fated Alabama plantation, the mansion duly ravaged of its valuables and set ablaze, one of Barrett's cutthroats discovered an additional resident hid away in one of the slave quarters. Though the mystery man's official moniker was never revealed as far as anyone knows, it was speculated his origins began in the West African country of Nigeria, supposedly a devout worshipper of the Yoruba religion. Rumor also had it he was a master practitioner of vodou. As such, it's said when found, he'd been smack-dab in the middle of a ceremony of some type, chanting, gyrating and pumping his hips to some Haitian beat

only audible to his own ears. I've heard variations of exactly what type of black magic paraphernalia he had on hand. Everything from headless chickens to sautéed bat wings to human-bone necklaces, though nothing verifiable.

"Anyhow, it's said that Chauncy found the former slave's act so humorous he insisted it be continued to its conclusion, wherein the man, described in legend as black as coal, save eyes that spewed flames of the brightest yellow, cut his own throat with a sharp edge whittled from a warthog's tusk, a real showstopper that ignited a rowdy ovation from those who bore witness.

"So, fast-forward a few months, when one-by-one, those once associated with Barrett's Raiders and present at the plantation slaughter, the gang long disbanded and spread out over several southern states, commenced to meet their respective ends in the most bizarre and unexplained ways, to include, believe it or not...death by wild Mustang stampede, leading to assorted broken bones, including the spine, both legs, arms, and a crushed skull via multiple hooves.

"Death by wild boar or boars, resulting in partially consumed torso and genitalia, the complete devouring of the fingers on both hands, removal of the nose and the extraction and ingestion of both the left eyeball and earlobe.

"Death by runaway stagecoach, resulting in a broken pelvis, shattered ribs and a crushed chest cavity. Possibly a contender for death by suicide, subject as yet to be discussed but is forthcoming.

"Death by choking, in one case, via chicken bone, in still another, asphyxiation via pigs' feet.

"Death by suicide, numerous cases, methods to include throat slashings, hangings, and the ever-popular bullet to brainpan. Most unusual by far, if such rumors are to be believed, suicide by over-consumption of pinto beans, a reputed five-plus pounds spiced with red peppers, the result of which was a lower-colon rupture.

"As for the passing of Chauncy Barrett, his was supposedly the worst of the lot, as if the alleged vodou curse reserved a special brand of retribution just for him.

"Now, I cannot and will not speak to the validity of said curse, but

there isn't any doubting the hellishness of the man's passing and unlike many of the others, it is documented in the newspaper print of the day.

"Occurring approximately one year following the plantation murders and subsequent breakup of Barrett's Raiders, the faded obituary described the circumstances of Chauncy's death as a tragic equestrian accident. More like gruesome, grisly, ghastly and probably closer to repulsive as in hard to stomach for those present. You make the call.

"Anyhow, just as a precursor before the epilogue, Chauncy did quite well for himself in the aftermath of the many raids he'd overseen, procuring a two-hundred acre spread in southern Texas, where he'd raised cattle for income and broke wild horses for hobby. Even proclaiming himself the Mustang Master of The West and claiming there was no stallion he couldn't properly break, for a steep price of course.

"It was a late October day when the so-called Master met his match in the form of a tri-colored Spanish variety steed whose affluent owner previously employed a half-dozen renowned bronc busters to tame with nothing to show but shattered egos, not to mention bones, and a building frustration. Well, Chauncy had all but guaranteed a different result, at twice his usual breaking fee.

"As reported, it was a cloudy, overcast morning when Chauncy hopped aboard that snorting, wild-eyed Mustang, having allegedly waved to his adoring fiancé like some conquering King on the eve of his empire's greatest victory. A thin, wiry man with shoulder-length hair and a handlebar mustache that swallowed the majority his thin face, Barrett's demeanor changed little since his Raider days, at least according to those in his employ who would later comment on his horrific demise.

"In other words, the mad bastard was still as mean as a stepped-on rattler and utterly without conscience. It was said his loving fiancé, a Latin lovely hand-picked from a stable of assorted concubines, was the constant target of his many drunken tantrums, enduring numerous beatings in trade for serving as his unofficial second-in-command and official heir. Unbeknownst to the ranch tyrant, fickle fate was about to reward his loving lady with an unexpectedly swift payout.

"Just as Barrett blasted from that chute like a flaming slug from a Colt forty-five, two additional riders rode in from opposite sides of the pen

and began to cautiously circle the bucking, jerking Mustang. It was said the two riders were on scene for security, to pull Barrett away if the Mustang decided slinging the cocky bastard off its back wasn't apt to sate its fury.

"As it happened, allegedly, no such brazen assault would be necessary, as it would be Chauncy Barrett's unfortunate wardrobe choice that would do more damage than any half-ton steed could ever manage. It was later debated why Barret hadn't chosen to do a pre-ride to test the width and length of the chosen stirrups vs the oversized raps spurs he'd strapped on his slick, cowhide ropers, but hey, such recklessness is often the rule and not the exception. Technically, it probably shouldn't ever have happened. Couldn't happen again in a thousand such scenarios, some would whisper, many of those veteran ranchers and bronc riders. Then again, toss in some random, expertly cast vodou curse and such odds aren't quite as far-reaching. Allegedly.

"The gist was this..."

Sighs.

"...and I gotta say, if true, it couldn't have happened to a nicer guy.

Four or five seconds into the attempted break, that snorting, highly pissed off steed had yet to reach full rage mode and Barrett, credit given where due, was hanging tough. That is, until the Mustang did, and he no longer could. Jerked hard to the left, halfway back in the other direction and finally straight back, the Mustang's head and torso ascended fully as it balanced solely on its back legs. As for its equally off-balance rider, Barrett tilted severely first in one direction then another before beginning an inevitable dive off the steed's back to presumably land flat and hard on his own.

Only, he never landed. Instead, he was slung forward and straight up, courtesy of the overly bulky spur strapped to his right boot locking firmly into the comparatively undersized stirrup.

"Many present would later claim they heard Barrett scream like a prepubescent schoolgirl, but only once, before the sharp echo of snapped bone drowned out a chorus of gasps from an otherwise silenced crowd.

"From there, it only got worse, substantially, as one of his *supposed rescuers rode up next to the sprinting Mustang with intentions of roping it and thus basically using leverage from his own horse to get it under control.*

"What he managed instead was to ram his own panicked filly into the hard-charging mare, muzzle to shoulder, flipping head over boots out of the saddle and breaking his eager but damn fool neck in the process.

"Rider-less, the filly naturally and, no doubt wisely, chose flight over fight and lurched into the opposite direction of the still-fuming Mustang. Now, that rider-less, spotted appaloosa was said to be a much larger animal in size, though it definitely paled in both tenacity and fierceness. Severely spooked, she sprinted toward the same open gate she'd originally entered through.

"Problem was, and it was a dilly, in ramming the other horse, the filly accidentally picked up a hitchhiker, or at least a portion of one.

"Like I said, a thousand-to-one. Call it bad luck. In the case of a murdering, merciless jackass of Chauncy Barrett's ilk, call it karma. Either way, I'd wager no human person has died in such a manner before nor after. Whether a vodou curse had beans to do with it is up to interpretation, but I will say this; no so-called spell or manufactured jinx could've done it better.

"As that hulking appaloosa rode east, nostrils flarin' and seeking a way out to safer, calmer climes, the still-bucking, still highly perturbed wild Mustang headed west, the former with an alien boot not that of his original rider planted firmly into the stirrup hanging from its left side, tied together with the latter animal, who had yet to relinquish the opposite boot of its possessor. Now, you might be thinking, as I know I myself contemplated upon first hearing this rather dark interpretation, at some point in the proceedings, why didn't the damn boots just pull off the bastard's feet?

"Dark forces at work? That whole karma thing again? Or maybe Barrett was one of those fancy dandy's who needed the assistance of a pit-crew to remove his custom-made Ropers. I'd heard such boots existed for those inclined. Regardless, they didn't budge, nor did they tear. Damn fine boots for sure. A testament to their maker. Cheaper pair might've peeled apart like parchment paper under such sudden, intense pressure.

Thousands upon thousands of pounds per square inch-type pressure.

"*Nope, as it was told, the only thing that peeled apart that day was Barrett himself, halved from groin to left shoulder, the heavier appaloosa dragging the right half out the same gate she'd earlier entered, trailing what was said to be several dozen feet of viscera, while the Mustang claimed the shredded half containing Barrett's head and the majority of the ribcage, the mare's continued tantrum tossing vital organs around like party favors.*

"*It was said the expression frozen on Chauncy Barrett's face was a bizarre hybrid of shocked surprise and unrelatable terror. The kind usually viewed on cartoon characters at the moment of their eminent demise, like Wile E. Coyote just before the dynamite explodes in his face. Unlike Wile E...*"

Laughs.

"*Barrett was not gonna miraculously reappear in the next scene. Rumor was it took three of the territories best undertakers to sew 'im back into one tangible, solid piece for the burial.*

"*In the end, it was claimed that all those in attendance at that Huntsville plantation met their makers within a calendar year. Unlike almost everything else connected to the tale, this has been officially documented through various historical documentation. Well, all except one, who had refused to participate. Thomas Dale Harrison had since moved his family to Oklahoma territory and lived out a mostly uneventful existence, as if his non-participation in the plantation killings had let 'im off the hook. Or so he thought once five or six seasons had come to pass and nothing of consequence had occurred.*"

Clears throat.

"*Your great granddad passed away in April of nineteen-ninety-three. At the time he was going by the name David James Pierson. Dave Pierson was listed as sixty-two when he died from complications from lung cancer. Being that my father, your grandpappy, was birthed in March of eighteen-thirty-one, that made Thomas' age at death, his official age, one-hundred and sixty-one. Now, considering that he allegedly sucked down mostly home-rolled smokes for over twelve decades, it was, well, just a matter of time. Even a curse of immense power can't stave off the effects of tar and nicotine for just so long. Honestly, lighting up was one of the few vices I didn't possess over the years. Guess I'd heard how drawn-out and downright miserable that expiring from cancer sticks could be.*

"By now you've surely looked over my own birth certificate and what it claims. I...understand this isn't exactly the proper way to say goodbye to one's grandson but believe me when I tell you I was...I just couldn't face the truth if that other part of our supposed curse affected you as it did my Gwen. I watched her deteriorate through the decades, buying full into the hearsay and acting on it in the most maniacal manner. Or what I at least perceived to be hearsay. I speak of course of the rumored effect not tied to our family's bizarre penchant for longevity. That being the supposed...bloodlust inherent within the Harrison clan.

"To be honest, anything else is pure speculation, I can only speak for myself. That is, if I ever felt a pull, an urge, to take human life. Without conscience. Without regret. For the base thrill of it. That answer is a definite no. Now, the argument can be made, justifiably so I'll admit, that my own so-called urges might've found various outlets through the ye...decades via those previously mentioned scenarios. If you've found time to give the other cassettes a listen, just know that I'm one-hundred percent guilty of a form of criminal impersonation. While I did have a great Uncle Dalton Jeremiah Harrison, he was never employed as a telegrapher in Wyoming territory, nor did my father open his own security firm. Through an entire century and parts of two others, I held upwards of seventeen different jobs, earning retirement checks as a correctional officer, security freelancer and exterminator, under separate monikers of course. Earned 'em all, every damn one, especially the assorted prison guard gigs."

Laughs nervously.

"There are stories there I didn't dare share in the tapes, even to kin, 'least whatever doubts remain concerning my sanity be all but confirmed as certifiably looney-tunes. Moving on, and with sincere apologies to Uncle Dalton, my father, and even all the oblivious folks whose names I utilized through the years, there was simply no way to maintain the same identity without raising some serious eyebrows. Hell, if you check the enclosed ID's, you'll see I fought in two World Wars and

damn near another in Vietnam, but nothing struck fear in this boy's heart like the possibility of ending up in some government lab playing guinea pig. Can you just imagine? Poked, prodded, dissected and brain-jabbed, all for the secret of a longer life, a sip from that mythological fountain-of-youth. Talk about a curse. All that aside, yes, I have killed, both in the name of war and my own survival, but there was never a rush of jubilation or any type of tingling, euphoric sensation in the aftermath. Just a hollow numbness. So, whatever the cause behind our family's freakishly long lifespans, a vodou curse cast to turns us to monsters just doesn't compute as reality.

"Now, my dear Gwen will argue the counterpoint ad nauseam, going as far as making it her life's work, her words, to track down and, lord help her, terminate our kinfolk. God how that hurts to confess, mainly because I...I never did anything to stop her, even when she openly begged me to do so."

Faint clicking, static. Faint clicking, taping resumes.

"Fair warning, as of the time of this taping, there is still an outside chance she, meaning Gwen, might someday...track you and yours. Just...be prepared. Report any suspicious activity to your local authorities. She's damn good at what she does. I will be engaging in a long-delayed face-to-face with my dear daughter very soon that might very well detour her...such future endeavors. In fact, by the time you're listening to this, said meeting is long since passed. I hope and pray I was successful, not merely for you and yours, but all others currently claiming limbs on the Harrison family tree.

"I close with this. Take it as a teaspoon of positivity in an ocean of negative waves. Not everything about being allowed triple of what's considered a normal lifespan falls under the label of negative. I've known triple the sorrow yes, triple the sickness, thrice the tragedies, probably triple the vices. I've also known three times the happiness. I was married numerous times and for the most part, enjoyed wonderful companionship. At one time or another, I lived in almost every corner of the US, as well as military-related treks overseas. The things I saw, the people I met, and oh lord, the changes I saw.

"Boy Howdy, from cultural to agricultural, from the main form of

travel being the covered wagon to a gradual switch to motorization. From a time when our womenfolk were no better than second-hand citizens, to their gaining voting rights and eventually a mostly level playing field. Sure, I didn't approve of a crap-ton of the cultural stuff, 'least not 'til I properly adjusted and, gritted teeth and all, adapted. You see, I always had ample time to adjust. Some changes were subtle. Some not so much. I had no choice but to roll with the changes. For the most part, I think I did pretty damn well. What they called the roaring twenties was a hoot for the most part, while the nineteen-sixties were the hardest by far, followed by all the political upheaval and PC horseshit of the last two decades. Let's just say that, in my opinion, technology was, is, both a curse and a blessing, though I do lean heavily toward the former. I'm of the belief that the world was a much better place when the opinions of every Tom, Dick and Hazel weren't spewed forth for all to hear or read about on that two-headed monster known as social media. Honestly, I never gave two steaming shits how my hometown mechanic voted or the current romantic status of his teenage daughter."

Pauses.

"Sorry. Always seem to blow a gasket on that specific subject. Brings out the curmudgeon in me for certain. Now, where was I? Oh yeah, well anyway, from the great depression to the space age, dig it, I was there. The war stuff, well, I could fill up a half-dozen of these cassettes. Rather not relieve the majority, truth be told.

"Anyhow, as years progress you just might find yourself in a similar struggle. If so, just know you were not the first and if you have sired offspring, you quite possibly won't be the last.

"Hate to end on a sour note, but I'd be remiss if I didn't speak of my own grandfatherly failures. Obviously late in the game to make proper amends, and perhaps that's how it should be. A life spent constantly on the run, changing identities and personas, being dragged from one universe to the next, is hardly the place for a young, impressionable mind.

"If, however, you are able or do decide to address your own offspring in the coming years, just know hiding them from danger is akin to a form of neglect. They need...deserve to know. They are owed the knowledge. I only wish I'd had the courage to reach out to your father or

yourself so much sooner. Who knows, perhaps the...this affliction skips a generation, kind of like balding."

Laughs.

"If it doesn't, you'll know when you've passed that transparent line of demarcation from normal to abnormal.

"Whether or not you live long or overlong, Brent, just live. Live, love and cherish the good times, tolerate the rest as best you can.

Salutations, grandson. Dalton Caleb Harrison signing off."

Tape clicks.

A burst of static.

Tape shuts off.

~ * ~

Brent Harrison slept uneasily, a common affliction on the eve of any early-morning assignment. As dawn arose from the east, early-morning cloud cover stubbornly blocking the sun's best attempts to officially initiate proceedings, he sipped coffee from a steaming mug, the heat from a recently stoked fire warming his normally pale cheeks rose-red.

He'd contemplated much during the night and early morning, coming to a single, set decision in the aftermath. To take a much-needed, well-earned sabbatical, perhaps as long as a month if needed, and delve further into the origins of the mysterious package.

As he knew people who specialized in tracking even the most enigmatic mailings, learning both the shipping address and shipper would not likely prove to be anything more than a delayed annoyance. From there, he would seek additional answers. *Demand* them in fact, and in no uncertain terms, to determine if retaliation was in order for wasting Brent Harrison's time.

In the meantime, there was the job at hand. Dowsing the campfire with the remainder of his Java and a few well-placed, dirt-shoveling kicks from his Wolverine boots, he went about the task of disassembling the tiny, one-man tent and repacking the four-wheel drive Toyota 4-Runner parked just outside the nearby tree line.

According to his client's notes, the mark normally left his cabin at just before seven AM, like clockwork, give or take three to five minutes.

Steering the 4-runner over mostly rocky terrain, he wound and weaved between sporadic blockades of blue spruces, Douglas firs and Rocky Mountain Junipers, departing a grassy, slope-strewn valley for that of the bare, flat and hard-clay surfaced variety.

At precisely six-fifty-one AM, just as the sun's rays pierced the thinning cumulous to slash a razor-like swath into the surrounding hills, he exited the vehicle and fell to one knee, left eye tightly squinted and right focused with cool, predatory intensity through the inch-and-a-half lens of a Monarch scope. A two-story cabin loomed approximately one-hundred fifty yards to the east, fronted by a maroon Nissan Rogue.

At precisely six-fifty-seven AM, laying prone, he adjusted the Barrett MRAD rifle atop its bipod stand and instinctively began to regulate his breathing while simultaneously shutting down all external and internal bodily functions, save that of his right eye and right trigger finger.

At precisely seven-oh-three AM, a single, muffled shot was launched.

At precisely seven-oh-nine AM, the 4-runner backtracked.

At precisely seven-seventeen AM, the 4-runner pulled onto a deserted two-lane state highway, a scant eight to ten minutes from the nearest interstate.

In that brief stanza, Brent 'Babyface' Harrison pondered, perhaps for the first time in a clandestine career now spanning nearly a dozen years, whether or not his chosen profession had been chosen by chance, natural skill, or just perhaps, a wholly *unnatural* urge.

Regardless, he mused, and as the mysterious man claiming to be his grandfather might say, only *time* would tell.

Also by the Author
at
Rogue Phoenix Press

Blue Falcon

During the patriotic heyday of the cold war era, Deron Barrow gained a measure of fame portraying tough-as-nails war movie host *Sergeant Ace Claymore*, his fledging television career soon derailed amid lurid details of a checkered, real-life military history. Decades later and living in relative reclusion in a small Mississippi town, Barrow is approached by a pair of young documentary filmmakers and offered the opportunity to separate fact from fiction regarding a pair of infamous tragedies; one at a remote Air Force base and the other an infamous hotel massacre at an iced-in Arkansas lodge, the question of Barrow's status as either hero or villain left to interpretation. As filming draws to a close, the many vengeful ghosts of Barrow's bygone days fire a final, potentially fatal salvo, pressing the fictional Sergeant Claymore to the forefront once more, the actor behind the makeup forced to revisit life-or-death survival skills once reserved for a television soundstage.

Prologue
No Rest for the Weary

14 February 2004
2339 hours

The Droopy Eye Inn, six-point-three miles west of Pine Bluff, Arkansas on Interstate 530

She leans in until he smells a sickening, nauseating mix of recently leaked blood and evacuated vomit. Lips atremble, she peeks through the narrow slit of her left eye, swollen roughly half as grotesquely as her right, which resembles a ripe melon split partially in half.

"Wh-what's he waiting on? Why don't he j-just finish i-it...us a-already?" she stutters in a hoarse whisper and he feels a faint mist of warm spittle coat his exposed neck. Looking at her, he thinks it's a miracle she can speak at all, considering her lips have burst like stomped grapes and several teeth have been violently extracted.

"How the hell would *I* know? Afraid the ol' telepathy radar is currently on the fritz," he barks harshly, his anger and frustration fueled not by the foolhardiness of the query but the constricting binds of fear currently squeezing his midsection like a fleshy vice. In a pathetic attempt to make amends, he reaches back with a free hand, groping momentarily before eventually discovering her own sweat, blood and puke-coated mitt.

"Listen, just concentrate on shielding the kid. Once that door's breached, cover her with your body, look for an open space to dart through and take off. I'll do my best to play human barricade."

In lieu of a verbal response, she gives his hand as tight a squeeze as she can muster.

"Wish I at least knew her name," she finally manages in the almost deafening silence, the last word more a choked garble than actual word.

"Plenty of time for proper intros later," he replies with a matching squeeze, two sets of intertwined fingers fusing as one.

The trio squat together in a bathtub that strains to hold their combined bulk, the man on one knee, the woman on all fours, the child sitting with her back to a badly discolored tile wall: the six-by-eight bathroom and its flimsy, faux-mahogany door the lone source of blockade between themselves and the room within.

"He's probably just reloading," she decrees with a resounding sigh, the limited confines of the tiny space reeking equally with spilt fluids and desperation. "Piece of shit coward."

"Right," the man nods, the constant throbbing at his bloody scalp fighting for pain domination with the open, slowly seeping wound at his left shoulder. At the moment, it is a dead heat he chooses not to rate as victor, lest his weakening sanity pass them both in a wild sprint to the finish line. The mini-Louisville Slugger curled into his free hand sits propped atop the opposite shoulder, the handle slick with sweat.

"M-maybe he's out of ammunition," she continues with nary a trace of sincerity, wincing painfully as if to affirm the idiocy of such awkwardly out of place hopefulness.

Turning towards and shooting the crouching child—her face as pale, slack and emotionless as when the attack had commenced—a quick, steely-eyed glance, the man's expression and tone are dismissive without undue arrogance.

"Not likely. Dude appears supremely confident, like he's been plotting this or some other similar raid for a lengthy spell. Skidded into that parking lot doing at least forty but the heavy chains on the tires prevented even the slightest damn skid. Armed lunatics of a similarly warped mindset are notoriously meticulous planners."

"H-how about your friend? You think he's...he made it? Maybe he's hiding out like us in one of the last few rooms down the line."

"Yeah, well, maybe," the man replies unenthusiastically, recalling the mercifully brief but graphic image of Terrance reeling back with a grunt, eyes-wide with shock as a softball-sized hole appeared at his ample midsection. "Seemed like a tough old bird, for sure. We can hope, anyway."

After a half-minute's silence, during which time the only discernable sounds are that of their own ragged breathing and that of falling sleet pecking the motel's tiled rooftop, the woman responds in a dull, robotic monotone as if speaking to herself while applying increased pressure until he feels jagged nails dig a groove into the back of his hand.

"H-he's was just shooting blind into the windows and doors of every room. Just pointing and s-shooting. But then, no witness left b-behind, right?" She grins, a sad, horrible parody of a smile that the man doesn't have to actually visualize to know exists.

"Why n-no sirens? It's been what, ten minutes since that nine-one-one call?"

"County badges are probably a half-hour drive away in *good* weather," he counters calmly as to lower the rapidly rising frustration of her tone. "Interstate's like a hockey rink out there. Side-roads are twice as slick. They're probably slidin', slippin' and stumblin' all over and around each other trying to get here."

"Never th-there when you need 'em, r-right?" she huffs, thumping the side of her head lightly against the shower tile. "Small-town cops more...used to busting stills or chasing down...chicken thieves. Jesus wept."

Figuring diversion to be the best course to deflect a building tsunami of hysteria, the man largely ignores the comment and instead dons a mask of bravery, albeit one forged from the thinnest of iron wills. Chest pumped, clinched jaw set tight and chin jutted with a wholly false bravado that nonetheless appears genuine, he finds falling back into a character he'd long since abandoned remarkably easy considering the real-world circumstances at hand. He twists around and peers into tear-filled eyes, their foreheads mere inches apart.

"Hey, we *got* this. Trust me. I'm no stranger to what appears to be unsurmountable odds. Just follow my lead, all right?"

She nods in silent anguish, her damaged lower lip trembling uncontrollably even as her death grip eases. The man couldn't help but think there was a rather attractive young lass beneath all the swollen, bloated bruises and open wounds presently on display.

"Okay, I'm thinking he'll blast the windows and outer door open for drama's sake, just like all the others, like something from the eighties B-movie the crazy bastard *thinks* he's starring in.

"After a quick scan, he'll more than likely plant a boot against the john door as to conserve ammo. First appendage that floats into range..." he pauses with a wink towards the upraised bat, "...and I'm swinging for the fences. I'll either pull his ass in here to commence the pounding or shove 'im back out. Either way, you snatch the kid and dash the hell past wherever we're not. My Jeep is better on mud than ice, but it'll take you to safer climes as long as you don't gun 'er too severe or lead-foot the brake. Road's flat enough going west to get you into Pine Bluff without grille-planting a ditch. You got the keys, right?"

The woman nodded, her breathing visibly calmer than when his spiel has initiated.

"Shouldn't we wait, I mean, on you?"

"Negative, sister. If I score the knockout, I'll wait around for the county boys. If not," he shrugs casually, forcing a shaky grin, "well, you sure as hell don't need to be in range in case he exits this room looking to thumb a ride."

Yet again resembling a pain-induced grimace than actual smile, the woman strains mightily to match his level of optimism, however faux.

The child, eyes wide and unblinking, thin lips pursed to a purple tint, shifts just slightly in the woman's grip before releasing a weak gasp as if to acknowledge an understanding of the conversation. The man gauges her age at between perhaps five and seven, a rail-thin waif with marble-round, gleaming brown eyes and a shoulder-length, tar-black coif whose fleeting existence was now hopelessly distorted for whatever timespan remained.

"The name's Fowler, by the way," the woman whispers, gently tonguing a deep, raw chasm at her ravaged lower lip in the aftermath. "Dana Fowler. Not exactly the Valentine's Day celebration I h-had in mind."

"Barrow," he replies with the wink of a badly bloodshot right eye, his thick mustache moistened from melting snow. "Deron Barrow. Same here. Not a damn thing sweet to see here, right? Still, pleased to make your acquaintance, ma'am, though I sure as hell wish it was under better circumsta—"

The initial blast echoes like a detonated bomb, the man instantly leaping from the tub and planting his back flat against the wall in the limited space between the shower and bathroom door, the woman's shrieking wails lost in a follow-up explosion that opens a fist-sized hole at the center of their flimsy barricade.

"Showtime, soldier," the man groans between gritted lips, inhaling deeply and holding it with the mini-slugger poised at shoulder-level, his free hand reaching back, palm out, like a fleshy red light for his charges to obey.

Terse, tension-packed seconds pass as if sporadically freeze-framed to move forward in fragmented puzzle-pieces, the man's squinty gaze frozen on the smoking ruin of their shattered blockade.

So, this is it: reality warfare revisited, all these years later, he ponders as the pulse at his temples pounds a frenzied solo. *The life-and-death real deal, up close and personalized, only this time with a different twist. Not just my ass on the line this time around.*

The broken door sails inward with a vicious jerk at the insistence of a square-toed cowboy boot with a snake design running its smooth, suede length from tip to heel.

Wouldn't you just know it? Shit-kicker heaven, the man muses, lunging forth with a booming roar as the bat uncoils in a blackened blur.

One
Into the Think Tank

(From the Private Journal of Deron Joseph Barrow)
August 2019 Entry
Boone's Crossing (four miles east of Holly Springs), Mississippi

That mid-morning in late April—might as well have been mid-July as far as my sweat glands were concerned—as I sat slumped over my trusty old Selectric II, pecking away at a snail's pace, started out like most. The day's second cup of coffee sat cooling to my right, parked just inches from the piled pages of the initial draft of what was fast becoming a manuscript of doorstop-size proportions; a half-eaten bagel with cream cheese took up the opposite end of the scar-infested oak typing stand, the latter purchased for a cool three bucks at a Corinth flea market a few years previous. Last but not least: a half-emptied tube of Ben Gay propped on a nearby window seal, its pungent scent radiating from an exposed left knee that still, despite three early-morning coatings, throbbed and pulsed like a rotted molar.

It wasn't until I detected the faint sound of tires rolling over the gravel drive to the north side of the property that normalcy and routine were fated to take a permanent powder, though I was as yet ignorant of that fact. Looking back, it wasn't as if a sudden surge of telepathy would've changed what was to come. Some things are just meant to be, no matter the timespan between that first domino falling and the last following suit. What one sows, he or she shall eventually reap. Cliché city, I know, but truer than a dozen of the most prophetic fortune cookies. As one learns when youth becomes middle-age and beyond, twenty-one years is but a flash on that ever-spinning wheel of time.

I spotted the mystery vehicle, not nearly as covert once its humming engine grew closer, as it glided slowly between the aged elms at the east end. The roaring engine cut off even as it continued its final roll, leaving the unmistakable guitar chords of AC/DC's "Back in Black" thumping from the stereo to pick up the slack.

Rising from the rickety high-back that had served as my writing throne since the manuscript's inception, the sharp cracking of my knees—one in particular—managed to temporarily drown out both a stiff mid-morning breeze and the glorious bellowing of Brian Johnson.

Radio silenced, a vehicle door soon slammed. Heavy boots or similar foot apparel crunched atop loose gravel.

"Greetings and salutations from civilized society!" shouted a familiar, gravelly voice, "Where ya at, partner?"

My own voice, having gone several days in mute mode from a welcome lack of human contact, croaked and cracked like a pubescent teen.

"Coming at you, Tank. Long time, brother."

He stepped around the Ram thirty-five hundred's sleek, massive hood just as I hopped down from the shack's lower step.

"I'd say. Three, four months, right?"

"At least."

Matching grins: the sincere, comfortable kind shared only by those whose bond is forged not just merely by time but circumstance. It'd been two, maybe three months since our last jawing session. I found I welcomed this particular intrusion. Lance "Tank" Garrett was without a doubt one of very few I could say that about.

We shook hands firmly and strolled silently towards the main house, where a matching set of recently refurbished rocking chairs awaited atop the front porch.

"How's the knee?" he asked, head titled to study my gait as we ambled along.

"Nuts and bolts still holding firm but I won't be entering a marathon anytime soon. Hey, I've got a semi-fresh pot of java brewed up," I offered as our destination was reached and we soon began rocking away in almost perfect unison.

"Had plenty. More than a cup these days and I might as well tote a porta-potty on my back for easy access."

The shared nod executed was also with almost supernatural sameness.

"So what ya been up to out here in the middle of blessed nowhere, Deron Joseph?"

Two sentences and I was already dead-letter certain this wasn't just a social visit.

"Stopped by the station on the way. Locked up tight. What gives?"

Without breaking stride, Tank pulled a pack of smokes from a front shirt pocket and proceeded to light up. Five years my senior—meaning he'd tipped just over six decades of earthy existence—the man's weathered face appeared carved from granite. His slim features served as a clever disguise for the rock-hard muscle worn as an outer shell.

"Lost my slot, at least 'til they figure out how to retool to something more hip. In other words, probably tap city as far as my future employment goes. No sweat, really. More time to tap the keys."

Tank grunted, and we rocked in brief silence as, in the distance, a semi's horn echoed like the foghorn of a lost schooner. Being that the main highway was a four-plus mile ride from the homestead, the wind on rare occasions would serve proof of the four-lane's existence.

"You still that certain someone's favorite charity, I take it."

"By the tenth of every month, like clockwork."

"So no pressure to bring home the weekly bacon then. At least there's that."

I'd often pondered how a man's perspective is altered if his reasoning to maintain gainful employment is tied only to the time it fills and not the necessity of the salary earned. In the almost fifteen years since my last bona fide "to eat or not eat" job, I wondered how many life decisions, especially the bad ones, might've gone the other way if that certain financial buffer hadn't existed. Luckily, I also realized that obsessing did little nothing to solve anything so utterly hypothetical.

"So," I switched gears quickly, the previous subject birthing a tidal wave of unease and mild shame, "how goes the security biz?"

The earlier breeze having evaporated, Tank's face was temporarily cloaked in a stagnant cloud of fag smoke, the pungent stench of which served as a flagship of memories both haunting and treasured.

"Honestly dude, didn't Lucky Stripes stop production in the late eighties?" I jabbed, frantically waving both hands to clear to air between us.

"Hilarious as ever," he retorted, just the hint of a smile denting that granite visage. "Though I recall last time you told that joke it was

Chesterfields.

"As for the aforementioned query, there is definitely no shortage of crime on the mean streets of the Rock, partner. Gangs are basically runnin' three-fourths of our fair city."

"I foresee no issue with job security for, say, the next century or thereabouts."

"Correct me if I'm wrong, but weren't you thinking of hanging it up around this time last year?"

"Yeah, well, it's kinda embarrassin' to confess, but I'm not exactly humpin' it from dawn to dust these days. More like a series of weekly cameo appearances to make sure things are copasetic at the home office. Not an easy thing givin' up a slice of cake that rich. 'Sides, I get the feelin' that a permanent reassignment to the homestead might just cause some serious dents in my own marital status."

I reached over and tapped a heavily tattooed forearm with a tip of an elbow.

"You hinting that Wendy might prefer you keep busy and out from under foot?"

"Hinting, *hell*. Nail on the head, brother. Anybody ever ask me about the secret to a thirty-plus year marriage and I'll tell 'em it's keepin' your distance for the majority of said span. Give each other ample space. Wendy and I have found a Grand Canyon-type area agreeable."

"Nice. Wish you'd have shared such invaluable wisdom around two wives back," I ribbed, tossing up both arms in faux exasperation.

With that, Tank scanned the surrounding grounds as if expecting the sudden teleportation of a familiar face.

"Speaking of which, where's Jenny? I was hopin' for some of those special eggrolls of hers."

"Lumpia?" I inquired indifferently, understanding the tap-dance he'd initiated.

"Yeah boy. Mouth-waterin'."

"Afraid you'll have to hop a bird to Cebu, dude."

"Oh, she visitin' the homeland, is she?"

"You might say that."

Tank's rocker hit the brakes, obviously breaking our paranormal rhythm. I didn't have to glance over to imagine the dramatically tilted head; the squinted eyes; the characteristic sneer of befuddlement.

"Aw, crap. Don't tell me. Trouble in paradise, partner?"

"A fool's paradise if it ever qualified to begin with," I replied, noticing with no small amount of embarrassment the disorder of the front yard. Knee-high grass infested with crabgrass and dandelions that hadn't seen a mower blade in what appeared like a solid month. On either side of the mailbox—a good thirty-yard walk down the dirt/gravel (mostly dirt) drive—leaned a pair of rust-ravaged garbage cans overflowing with tattered bags that somehow, miraculously, had been spared the local raccoon population's curiosity. Lucky thing the nearest neighbor was old man Pruitt a half-mile up the road or I might've found myself victim of a surprise midnight garbage bonfire.

"Is it any wonder? Jeez Louise, the place is a sty *unfit* for pigs. Can't remember the last time I hauled the trash away. For that matter, the last time I dragged a bag from the kitchen."

"So she left your lazy ass for not takin' out the garbage?" Tank snorted while rejoining the rocking party and, within seconds, falling right back into a steady cadence.

"Tip of the separation iceberg."

"'Zat so?"

"Let's just say Jen didn't consider Holly Springs the American dream she'd envisioned, much less Boone's Crossing. Can't say I blame her. Not exactly a thrill a minute."

"Well, it ain't like you didn't do some travelin' in, the what? Five or six years since she flew over?"

"Almost seven. Yeah, if you consider Jackson, Biloxi and Orleans a proper representation of the country as a whole. Kind of pathetic, in retrospect."

"Didn't you trek over to Gulf Shores a few winters back?"

I nodded casually, though in truth the very fact I'd completely forgotten that specific trip underlined my indifference to the subject as a whole. Bottom line, I hadn't cared enough to resolve the problem of my latest, soon-to-be ex-wife's boredom and overall dissatisfaction with small-town life.

"Biloxi, Mobile, Orleans; same thing really. A natural beach lover that one, for obvious reasons. Me? I couldn't give a rat's hairy hind end if

I ever saw another spec of sand."

Never a big fan of secondhand cancer-stick smoke, even in my heaviest bar-hopping days, I nevertheless found myself appreciative of its company when compared with the drifting stench of neglected trash.

"So, pray tell old buddy, what *does* Deron Joseph Barrow give a rodent's ass about?"

"Same as the last time we chewed the fat, I reckon."

"That book thing, ya mean? Holy cats, man, you've been hammerin' away at that for what, three years now?"

"Four, but who's counting?"

"Well, right off the bat I'd say your better half."

We traded sly grins, tendril-thin smoke billowing from each of his dramatically flaring nostrils.

"Touché, partner."

"So, she purchase a one-way ticket?"

"For now, yeah. We'll see. We've been face-timing on Skype every other day or so. Maybe she just needs some time. Maybe we both do."

The casual jawing session having apparently run its course, we rocked quietly for a full minute. Knowing Tank like I did, and thus figuring waiting on him to get the actual purpose of his visit might mean rocking on that front porch until the passing of summer into fall, I quickly caved.

"So what's up? I can't imagine you made that multi-hour drive just to swap tales of marital woe."

"Tell ya what, I might just have a cup of joe after all," he replied with surprising sternness while staring straight ahead into nothing. "You might want to pour yourself something a tad stouter."

With that, we relocated indoors to the living room, which was, sad to say, not much of an upgrade in terms of neatness from the disaster of the front yard.

"Maid's year off?" he cracked while clearing a space from the couch as I searched the kitchen cabinets for two clean cups.

"Hey, feel free to commit a neatness if the urge arises," I managed to volley despite a building trepidation.

"Brother, I'd have to rent a backhoe."

The old hacienda, built in the mid-seventies, far past its prime and bought on the cheap by yours truly nearly a decade past, was most definitely missing its mama. Jenny was, if not quite your basic OCD neat freak, not one to tolerate the overt slob tendencies I'd acquired in her absence. During our Skype sessions, I'd at least possessed the common sense—and survival skills—to strategically clean up whatever area might pan into camera range.

Moments later, with steaming mug of Death Wish in hand, Tank sighed heavily, looking as blatantly ill-at-ease as I'd witnessed in our almost three-decade friendship.

He sipped noisily, eyeing me with a pained scowl as I took a seat in the recliner directly across from the couch.

"Dang good joe. What ya got there, a White Russian?"

I raised my cup—a large black mug with a faded Mississippi State Bulldog gracing its bulk—and executed a semi-toast.

"You know I cut out the booze years ago. Well, all but the occasional brew. Now, what's this dreadful news that you seem to think will shove me, arms flailing, right back *off* the souse wagon?"

As Tank paused for an additional sip and accompanying grimace, I felt my heart skip a beat. I hadn't felt such a rush of dread since a certain military court proceeding that concluded quite negatively for yours truly.

"Well, maybe I am bein' a bit of a drama king in that respect. You be the judge."

Maybe it was living relatively stress free for such a lengthy spell, but as my old friend sat his cup aside, folded his arms, leaned back and commenced with his tale, I was only able to quell the shaking of my own hands by squeezing that MSU mug to the point of implosion.

"A few weeks back, I had a potential client request a meetin', a client that had requested me by name as their first contact. Not exactly a regular occurrence these days—I'm more of the on-site consultant type after the sale—but not altogether bizarre either.

"So meet 'em I did, for brew and nachos down at Carlito's downtown. Straight-laced and very professional, as clean-cut, stone-cold serious and to-the-point as any I've met. No beatin' around the bush with those two. A man and woman, the former tall, slim and bespectacled, a walkin', talkin' CPA if I ever saw one, the latter sweet-talkin', strikingly attractive and upper-class elegance personified. Turns out their interest in me had beans to do with security, and everything to do with the fact that I might steer 'em to *you*."

And there it was. In the aftermath, every ounce of pre-explanation stress and concern were vanquished, snuffed out like a candle flame in a monsoon. Two quick sips of brew—unlike Tank I preferred a little coffee with my sugar and cream—and a quiet belch later, I regarded my old friend with a deep frown birthed from utter disbelief.

"And this was supposed to trigger a mental meltdown? Damn, Tank. You really consider me that unstable? Don't tell me, media types digging for that exclusive front-page story? Better yet, internet bloggers with far too many slow news days of late that caught wind of a potentially hot take? You *do* understand that this is far from a new phenomenon in the last decade-and-a-half or so? Hell, If I had a ten-spot for every jackass junior-grade TV producer or B-grade novelist that proposed to give my story the 'fair, unbiased' angle it deserved, you and I wouldn't be parked in this shithole but some Pacific island mansion with a staff of buxom, scantily-clad servants providing refills along with unlimited eye-candy."

My rant had little or no effect, as Tank's expression remained as hard and stoic post-rant as it had pre.

"You ought to at least listen to 'em, Deron."

"And why the hell should I? What separates them from all the others just looking for a quick cash-grab at my...at the expense of those who lived it?"

Tank leaned forward, eyes squinting as if he were staring directly into the midday sun.

"You consider me a pretty decent judge of character?"

I nodded, albeit stubbornly hesitant. Lance Garrett was, in truth, probably the best judge of people I'd ever known, but I wasn't about to lose the argument, even in the face of such cold, hard fact.

"Well, I can't really explain it but they were just...different. As you recall, I was present at more than a few of those previous, um, offers, through the years. These two were, well, sincerely passionate, for want of a better term. Besides, I think you need to consider at least a courtesy listen for other reasons."

Here it came, right on cue. Even if I wasn't in the mood to hear it.

The truth is known, very often, to hurt. This was no exception. Still, logic and good sense be damned, I didn't have to like it.

"Look around ya, buddy," he continued, in the tough-love, tried and true 'schooled-by-Tank' mode that I'd witnessed countless times as a casual observer but rarely been the target of. "It ain't squalor, sure, but it does bring to the forefront that you could, and should, be doing better for yourself, and to Jen for that matter. Not-so-mystery monthly allotment aside, you don't *have* to just scrape by. Plus which, twenty-plus years is a long spell to be fightin' a battle when you're both the one throwin' the haymakers and catchin' 'em on the chin.

"Besides, if the story is told the factual and correct way, why shouldn't you cash in? From my corner, I don't see a damn thing to be ashamed of. Truth to told, I never have."

Sure, I wanted to get mad, go berserk and start throwing shit while screaming at my oldest—and perhaps only *true*—friend to take his advice and opinions and shove 'em. Instead, I calmly sat back and sipped quietly as he did the same. We traded slurping noises—dueling smacks, if you will—for several surprisingly mellow moments, the ticking sound of a nearby wall clock the lone distraction other than our own swigging.

"So, tell me what impressed you so much about this pair," I finally said, potential berserker mode having quickly passed.

Perhaps relieved at my relatively easygoing response and openness to the prospects, Tank retrieved yet another smoke and parked it between bared teeth. To this day, it amazes me no end those possessing the almost supernatural skill to belt out lengthy speeches with a cigarette bouncing wildly atop a lower lip as if stapled into place. I swear Tank could negotiate hurricane winds without misplacing a single spec of tobacco.

"Well, if I was to put my finger on it, it was the fact that they weren't pushy in the least. Cool, calm and professional with nary a single hard sell tactic. Then again, it could be they're savin' all those peculiar techniques for you. Bottom line, the lady in charge simply stated they had an idea for a project that wasn't about demonizing the bad guys or sanctifying the good. Fair and balanced story-tellin', I think she put it, written to cover all the dramatic bases with one-hundred-percent honesty and without the usual Hollywood sweetener or punch-ups. They weren't promising the moon, just asking for a fair shot to tell a story that deserved tellin'. I tell ya, Deron, my inner BS monitor was as quiet as a church mouse for the duration of the interview. No easy feat, advancin' years and fadin' superpowers not withstandin'."

"Agreed," I replied, pausing for a trio of sips of rapidly-cooling java. "But like you said, they might be saving up the PR push for yours truly, complete with the requisite promises of fame, fortune and infamy. Remember those assclowns from Full Moon? Their suits spouted the same crap and the final script draft read like some soft-corn porn serial killer space opera."

Tank nodded knowingly while finally touching his smoke. Pretty subtle, hardly noticeable at all, but that was the first time I took note of a slight tremor of his left hand.

"Or that independent crew out of Santa Carla that offered to fly me to Amsterdam for a month of unlimited booze, dope and carnal sins, all for the right to change my character into some kinda Bizarro-World hybrid of Dick Clark DJ by day and transvestite vigilante by night. Of course, the fine print of their contract also stated this would constitute full payment for my permission to thoroughly butcher reality."

"Yep, seems I do recall you tellin' me about *that* particular offer," he cackled softly, tendrils of smoke spewing from both nostrils. "From what I gather about these two, they're strictly documentary flick-makers dedicated to their craft. That was one thing that struck me as original about 'em. They confessed right off that any budget would be of the shoe-string variety and whatever money was paid out in the aftermath of the project would come from profits made on home video and streamin' services. Apparently, they do have some seriously tanked-up PR folks in the company bullpen that have the capability to take such a project and slowly turn it into a hit on the home market."

Lying to myself was pointless. There was a twinge of excitement at the possibility. A faint tingling at the scalp, a spattering of butterfly wings tickling the inner gut. Conversely, a palpable sense of distrust remained firmly intact. Not nearly a virgin to such conflicting emotions since the late nineties, there was but one way to declare a clear winner: tally up the pros and cons of either taking a dive or retreating back to square one.

"I dunno. Trust is a hard thing to come by, especially considering that most days I'd rather not be reminded about the subject matter at hand. Time hasn't altered that mindset. I may not be the hothead of yesteryear, but the level of stubbornness has increased ten-fold. I get what you're saying about the money and closure and the need to stop beating myself up over the whole deal but allowing a group of strangers to have the final say is, to me anyhow, comparable to tip-toeing barefoot and blindfolded through a field littered with claymores."

"I got'cha, boss. I'd be similarly cautious, if not more so," he said between huffs before pausing to paw through his wallet, though not before donning a pair of reading glasses to aid in the search. I couldn't help but smile at the sight, tempted to bombard my old friend with assorted geezer jokes. That is, 'til I recalled my own rapidly deteriorating state.

Pocketing the bifocals, he leaned up and over with hand (complete with barely detectable shake) extended, a black and gold business card pinched between thumb and forefinger.

"Still, here ya go. They said take your time, but not too long, whatever the hell that means."

Solid in stock—no Vistaprint dot com special here—with bright, vibrant blue lettering inside a dark crimson border, it read simply "Dragon Lady Productions, LLC" and provided phone and fax numbers along with an email address and website URL.

Tank pushed himself from the couch, having tossed what remained of his smoke into the coffee mug, which briefly shook so vigorously I thought he might accidentally toss it across the room.

"How long?" I asked, gesturing towards the clutched cup, now clasped in a double-fisted death-grip.

He briefly regarded his own grasping mitts as if they belonged to someone else, obviously having grown accustomed to playing dumb, before remembering to whom he spoke and coming clean with a resounding sigh.

"Funny. The right started shakin' first but now the left has passed it by in both consistency and frequency of tremors. Didn't cave to see a sawbones 'til 'bout six months ago, and not even then until Wendy threatened to slip a mickey into my mornin' java and haul me there herself. Parkinson's runs in the genes from way back from my ma's side. Guess I was hopin' it would skip more than a single generation. No such luck,

Chuck."

"Prognosis?"

"Not good, señor. I'll fight the bastard all the way though. This you know. I worry more for Eric and hope like hell it does at least skip the next one."

Eric, currently a junior at Memphis State and the couple's only child.

I nodded, smiling as broadly as possible despite feeling as if I'd been gut-punched.

"For now, worry about yourself. Goes without saying you can count on me for anything you or Wendy need."

"Good for now, but the offer is duly noted and appreciated."

No doubt desperate to switch channels, he tip-toed over and around the assorted piles of organized mess littering our path towards the front door.

"Say, since I drove all this way, how's about an early lunch?"

"Sounds like a winner. Take your pick: the Sonic drive-through or Maggie's Munchables."

"Maggie's still servin' chicken 'n dumplin's with cabbage and pinto beans?" he grinned mischievously. Same old Tank. Never one to forget a plate of top-notch grub, despite, if I recall correctly, only visiting the source of said spread a single time in his lifespan.

"Best in the state, maybe this part of the country."

With that, Lance "Tank" Garret, former security police specialist, non-commissioned officer and participant in many an armed conflict and all-around tough guy, smacked his lips like a drooling toddler at the mere prospect.

"Well by all means, soldier, lock up this here hooch and let us make tracks. Promise to get ya back to your precious typewriter before dark."

As had been the case for the duration of our friendship, said promise was kept, as was the continued oath we'd unofficially reestablished while shaking hands upon his departure.

From there, I had some serious decision-making to undertake. No better place than behind the keys of my trusty Selectric with a fresh cup of steaming joe parked nearby.

Blacktop

Blacktop is a terror-filled road-trip atop the dark, isolated back-roads of West Texas. Equal parts action/thriller and sci-fi/horror whodunit, it guides readers through a shock-filled maze, beginning with the hijacking of a commercial bus and concluding with a furious battle royale pitting the ultimate in extraterrestrial evil versus the few survivors of that initial abduction.

In Sheep's Clothing

1880's, Utah territory: an entire unit of U.S. Calvary soldiers has vanished from between the walls of Fort Drake, a remote site surrounded on all sides by warring Indian tribes and whose lone mission had been to protect the local gold-miners of nearby South Pass City. A trio of snow-crested mountain ranges away at Fort Lagrange, Wyoming, golden-boy Lieutenant Drew Barron and three hand-picked subordinates are tasked with solving the mysterious disappearances, their laborious quest littered with assorted dangers; roaming marauders, bloodthirsty wolves and a blizzard of epic proportions. At trek's end, Fort Drake is found to be deserted until a trio of unlikely allies crawl forth from hiding just as the frigid grounds fall under attack yet again, the survivors forced to barricade themselves within the cramped confines of the post armory. Faced with dwindling supplies, bone-chilling temperatures and a relentless enemy poised just outside their rickety safe-haven, Lieutenant Barron and those within his care will soon discover they have yet to confront the worst that the newly dubbed 'Fort Dread' has to offer.

About the Author

Born and raised in northern Alabama, Terry has been writing short stories since he was a pre-teen and began penning full-length novels in his early twenties. He is an Air Force veteran and former corrections officer who has resided in five US states and overseas, and currently homesteads in Hendersonville, Tennessee with his wife Liza and a killer canine (Maltipoo) predator named Dexter.

VISIT OUR WEBSITE

FOR THE FULL INVENTORY

OF QUALITY BOOKS

http://www.roguephoenixpress.com

Rogue Phoenix Press

Representing Excellence in Publishing

Quality trade paperbacks and downloads

in multiple formats,

in genres ranging from historical to contemporary romance, mystery and science fiction.

Visit the website then bookmark it.

We add new titles each month!

www.ingramcontent.com/pod-product-compliance
Lightning Source LLC
Chambersburg PA
CBHW061932170626
46813CB00006B/2369